China Miéville

THREE MOMENTS OF AN EXPLOSION: STORIES

MACMILLAN

First published 2015 by Macmillan
an imprint of Pan Macmillan
20 New Wharf Road, London N1 9RR
Associated companies throughout the world
www.panmacmillan.com

ISBN 978-0-230-77017-1

Earlier versions of the stories within were originally published as follows: 'The Rope is
the World', *Icon Magazine* (print and online), December 2009; 'Covehithe', the *Guardian*
(online), April 2011; 'Estate', the *White Review*, issue 8, July 2013; 'The 9th Technique', self-
published in *The Apology Chapbook*, October 2013; 'The Design', *McSweeney's Quarterly Concern*,
issue 45, December 2013; 'Säcken', *Subtropics*, issue 17, Winter/Spring 2014; 'The Condition of
New Death', 'Syllabus', 'Rules', and 'A Second Slice Manifesto' as handouts by the Foundation
for Art and Creative Technology, Liverpool, for their exhibition *New Death*, March 2014; 'Four
Final Orpheuses', 'Three Moments of an Explosion', and 'The Crawl' at chinamieville.net in
April 2012, September 2012, and June 2014; 'Polynia' on tor.co.uk, June 2014; 'The Buzzard's
Egg', *Granta*, issue 131, April 2015; and 'Listen the Birds', *Conjunctions*, issue 64, June 2015.

1 3 5 7 9 8 6 4 2

A CIP catalogue record for this book is available from the British Library.

Printed and bound by CPI Group (UK) Ltd, Croydon, CR0 4YY

Visit **www.panmacmillan.com** to read more about all our books
and to buy them. You will also find features, author interviews and
news of any author events, and you can sign up for e-newsletters
so that you're always first to hear about our new releases.

This book may be returned to any Wiltshire
library. To renew this book phone your library
or visit the website: www.wiltshire.gov.uk

Wiltshire Council
Where everybody matters

THREE MOMENTS OF
AN EXPLOSION:
STORIES

To Maria

I'm indebted to all who helped me with these stories, especially Jamie Allinson, Mark Bould, Nadia Bouzidi, Mic Cheetham, Meehan Crist, Rupa DasGupta, Andrea Gibbons, RL Goldberg, Maria Dahvana Headley, Chris John, Simon Kavanagh, John McDonald, Jemima Miéville, Karen Mirza, Susie Nicklin, Helen Oyeyemi, Anne Perry, Sue Powell, Maggie Powers, Max Schafer, Richard Seymour, Jared Shurin, Julien Thuan, and Rosie Warren.

My sincere thanks to the editors who worked on various of these pieces: Ben Eastham and Jacques Testard; Justin McGuirk; Richard Lea; Jordan Bass; David Leavitt; Yuka Igarashi; Omar Kholeif; Micaela Morisette and Brad Morrow; and all at F.A.C.T. Liverpool. I'm deeply grateful to Nicholas Blake, Rob Cox, Julie Crisp, Jessica Cuthbert-Smith, Sam Eades, and all at Pan Macmillan; and Keith Clayton, Penelope Haynes, David Moench, Tricia Narwal, Scott Shannon, Annette Szlachta-McGinn, Mark Tavani, Betsy Wilson, and all at Random House Del Rey.

Several of the stories in this collection were written during a fellowship at the MacDowell Colony, then as a residency fellow of the Lannan Foundation. I am profoundly grateful to both organisations for their generous support.

'The horses dreamed on their feet and the wild animals, crouching to leap even in their sleep, seemed to be collecting gloom under their skins which would break out later.'

Ilse Aichinger, 'The Bound Man'

Contents

THREE MOMENTS OF
AN EXPLOSION:
STORIES

Three Moments of an Explosion

1. The demolition is sponsored by a burger company. Everyone is used, now, to rotvertising, the spelling of brand names and the reproduction of hip product logos in the mottle and decay of subtly gene-tweaked decomposition – Apple paying for the breakdown of apples, the bitten-fruit sigil becoming visible on mouldy cores. Explosion marketing is new. Stuff the right nanos into squibs and missiles so the blasts of war machines inscribe BAE and Raytheon's names in fire on the sky above the cities those companies ignite. Today we're talking about nothing so bleak. It's an old warehouse, too unsafe to let stand. The usual crowd gathers at the prescribed distance. The mayor hands the plunger to the kid who, courtesy of the Make-A-Wish Foundation, will at least get to do this. She beams at the cameras and presses, and up goes the bang, and down slides the old ruin to the crowd's cheer, and above them all the dust clouds billow out *Your Way* in soft scudding font.

2. It's a fuck of a fine art, getting that pill into you so the ridiculous tachyon-buggered MDMA kicks in at just the right instant and takes you out of time. This is extreme squatting. The boisterous, love-filled crew jog through their overlapping stillness together and hustle toward the building. Three make it inside before they slip back into chronology. Theirs are big doses and they have hours – subjectively speaking – to explore the innards

of the collapsing edifice as it hangs, slumping, its floors now pitched and interrupted mid-eradication, its corridors clogged with the dust of the hesitating explosion. The three explorers have brought climbing gear, and they haul themselves up the new random slopes inside the soon-to-be-rubble, racing to out-race their own metabolisms, to reach the top floor of the shrugging building before they come down and back into time. They make it. Two of them even make it down and out again. They console themselves over the loss of their companion by insisting to each other that it was deliberate, her last stumble, that she had been slowing on purpose, so the ecstasy would come out through her pores, allowing the explosion to rise up like applause and swallow her. It would hardly be an unprecedented choice for urban melancholics such as these.

3. You can't say, you can't tell yourself that it's the intruder's spirit doing any of this, that there's a lesson here. It's neither her nor any of the other people who've died in its rooms, in any of the one hundred and twenty-six years of the big hall's existence. It's not even the memories, wistful or otherwise, of the building. The city's pretty used to those by now. The gusts, the thick and choking wafts that fill the streets of the estate that's built in the space the warehouse once occupied, are the ghost of the explo-sion itself. It *wants* something. It's *sad* – you can tell in its angles, its slow coiling and unfolding. A vicar is called: book, candle, bell. The explosion, at last, lies down. As if, though – the two drug enthusiasts who got in and out of its last moment insist – out of pity, rather than because it must.

Polynia

When cold masses first started to congeal above London, they did not show up on radar. By the time they started to, perhaps two hours later, hundreds of thousands of people were already out in the streets and gaping skyward. They shielded their eyes – it was cloudy but very bright. They looked up at glowing things the size of cathedrals, looming above the skyline.

They'd started as wisps, anomalies noticed only by dedicated weather-watchers. Slowly they'd grown, started to glint in the early-winter afternoon. They solidified, their sides becoming more faceted, more opaquely white. They started to shed shadows.

Social media went mad with theories. The things were dismissed as mirages, hoaxes, advertising gimmicks for a TV show. They were heralded as angels, abominated as an alien attack or a new superweapon.

The first appeared over City Hall. This was plausibly a strategic target, which increased the sense of panic, though Parliament was only a few miles away and would have seemed a more obvious choice. Others quickly thickened into visibility over Lewisham and Elephant and Castle and up my way.

Some stayed still. Others began to drift slowly, seemingly randomly, according to their own currents, not the winds.

All but military flights over the city were banned. The army and specialist police units came onto the streets. Jets went low overhead, and bristling helicopters rose suspiciously and seemed to sniff at the sides and undersides of the eddying things.

I was eleven – this was almost fifteen years ago. There was me, Robbie, Sal – she was big for her age and bossed the rest of us around a bit – and Ian, a nervous kid to whom I wasn't nice.

We were under Mass 2, as it was later dubbed. It rocked sedately from side to side over the skies of Neasden as I and my friends ran in urgent delight around the gawping north Londoners. We ran to keep up with it, following it toward Harlesden. It seemed to be the most excitable of the visitations, heading east and south like an unstable ship.

From every one of the masses sank microclimates. We were all wearing our thickest clothes in the air that poured off them. It was like a bitterly cold wind flowing straight down, gusting with wispy snow.

It was all frenetic; it's hard to say just what happened when. I remember running really fast past the clock on Station Road, where it meets Wendover Road and Avenue Road, barrelling by a woman in a black jilbaab and knocking her shopping over so she shouted at me furiously and I yelled something like 'Shut up you old cow!' to make my friends laugh even though I knew I was in the wrong. It seems strange to me now that I remember that, that I took a moment to answer her, that she was so angry with me, that she even noticed me, in the shadow of what was overhead.

'Look at that thing, man!' Robbie said. Army vehicles went past the Portuguese cafes and the Islamic bookshop.

We ran full pelt all the way to the West London Crematorium. As if they'd have let a gang of raucous kids like us in to the grounds, normally, but they didn't care: everyone was pushing through the gates because the mass was right overhead. It rose above the gardens of remembrance. There must have been funerals going on that day, with hundreds of strangers in the garden, and that thing above.

People were trawling for information, watching the news on their phones, but by the time the government scientists announced the results of their tests (whatever they were and however they'd taken them) their conclusions were obvious to everyone. We all knew that what hung above London were icebergs.

Military pilots made heroic manoeuvres through the cold vortexes around the masses. Their undersides and flanks were frost- and snow-furred ice. On top, invisible from London until we saw the footage from the planes, jutting toward the lowest cloud, they were almost snowless. They were like white glass, hills and hillocks of blocky facets.

The city heat met their cold. On day two a frozen stalactite like a giant icicle broke off Mass 4 and plummeted to the ground, destroying a car in Dagenham and starting a whole new panic. I texted with my crew. We agreed to meet right below Mass 2 again. It was as if we were goading it. We were eleven and death couldn't touch us.

The berg had stopped above the common of Wormwood Scrubs. A line of police officers surrounded the grass. 'You ain't coming in,' one said to us. The dirty parkland stretched behind him, overlooking London. Above it was the ice. We shivered in its shadow. I could hear the screams of London's feral parakeets freaking out in the trees.

We were debating how to slip past the cops but before an hour passed they took some instruction over their radios and did not so much usher us in as simply give up being guards. Mass 2 was on the move again. We went whooping after it.

After the fall of that first pillar people got nervous. There were instructions to stay indoors, as though it would be better to be crushed by a ruined house than by the ice itself. In fact the bergs were very solid. In the first week of their existence, only three slabs of any size came down, causing damage but no fatalities.

They weren't the only chunks to break off: they were the only ones to fall.

I was at Brent Cross Shopping Centre with my mum and dad and my sister the first time I saw one of the icebergs break. It was a few days after their appearance and we were shopping for football kit I needed. We were in the car park and I was looking at Mass 4, I think it was, hovering miles away above Ealing. My dad told me to hurry up, and as he turned we heard a cracking. A chunk of ice the size of a building broke off the northern edge of the berg.

I gasped and my dad let out a horrified noise as the block toppled sideways, spinning – and then stopped. It didn't fall – it drifted away horizontally. It bobbed, spinning, leaving a little wake of suspended ice. We looked at each other.

The breakaway drifted back, and coagulated again with the main mass, a day and a half later.

It was two days post-manifestation that the first official government survey team made icefall. Scientists, professional explorers, a few international observers, an escort of Royal Marine commandos. In the press release, they all wore cutting-edge Arctic gear and determined expressions.

They went for Mass 3. It had a horizontal plateau breaking

up the slopes of its topside, onto which a helicopter could lower them. By now, all the icebergs had been given their own names, usually based on their silhouettes. The *London Evening Standard* declared this the 'ascent of the Saucepan'. They live-streamed the delivery online, soldiers in thermal clothes lowered on swaying cables onto the pristine blowing surface of the ice, to make base camp almost a mile over Battersea.

Over the next five days we all followed the team's terse dispatches, their tweets and photographs, footage from their cameras, as Mass 3 itself described a wobbling circuit above the city. People leaned shivering out of their offices to look as it overflew. 'The Saucepan' was escorted by military helicopters. If you were at a high point in the city, looking out at the icebergs, you could see Mass 3 was surrounded with the specks of aircraft.

We read the reports of the team struggling up sides of ice, stared at the images they beamed down. Of course we were all caught up in the drama, and no one would deny how brave they were. Now, though, a few years on, so it's not like pissing in church any more to pass comment, it's fair to say that it was mostly the sort of thing you'd expect from any Arctic adventure. Freezing winds, terrible ice, and so on.

I suppose I'm saying that Mass 3, like all of them, is exactly what it looks like: an iceberg. No more, no less. Cold, austere, barren. Awesome, of course, because since when were icebergs not? But, and bear with me with this, except for the fact that it's levitating above London, it seems no more nor less awesome than its cousins in the sea.

There were, though, two exceptional images from that expedition. The first is the iconic shot of the team crossing an ice bridge between two forbidding white crags, with the slates and aerials of Wandsworth far below. The second is the selfie of Dr Joanna Lund, taken close to the iceberg's summit.

Dr Lund looks unhappily at the camera. She's slight, with squinting eyes circled in dark, her hat pulled down hard over her ears. Behind her is the pinnacle. You can just see the rest of the team at its base, looking up at the white blocks. There's the usual hard beauty of such landscapes. The city is not visible. The ice could be any ice. But there's a flat quality to the light and something in Lund's expression that makes the picture profoundly unsettling.

In the debriefing after the team's extraction, the government was keen to stress that they had, of course, considered the possibility that the icebergs might collide. If that was true, any protocols they had in place utterly failed.

On the morning of 17 June, the very day that last photo of Lund was released – while, we were told, the team were attempting an ascent of that troublesome ice – Mass 6, nicknamed Big Bear, began rolling with unusual speed across the skies, north away from Croydon.

At first this caused no particular alarm. But as the hours passed and Mass 6 accelerated, and as Mass 3's own sedate trajectory altered, it became obvious that the two were on a collision course.

The helmetcam of Lund captures the catastrophe. The crew are bracing behind frozen slabs. Swinging into view below them with the yawing of Mass 3 are the towerblocks of Peckham. And looming abruptly out of the south comes a cliff of ice. Mass 6 moves fast.

Everyone in London heard the impact.

Considering the scale of the things, it wasn't much more than a glancing blow. The two ground together horribly, breaking off great chunks that spun into the sky. Mass 6 lurched to the east. Mass 3 pitched.

Lund staggered as her nook tilted. Her brace held, the steel cord did not snap, but the ice in which it was tethered crumbled. In seconds she slid down angles it had taken her hours to ascend. We saw the footage from her point of view. She careered down a chasm that now sloped hard and became a funnel.

I watched the file many times, though my parents told me not to. I'd slow it down, feeling sick and adrenalised as Lund descended. She'd been issued no parachute. I'd loop back to the start again and again, every time the ice released her into the air.

Mercifully, the camera gave out before she hit the ground.

We played games of London Iceberg. Robbie's great-aunt was in sheltered housing up towards Wembley, and we'd meet him there because at the back of the complex was a slope of rubbishy grass down towards the railway lines, that we could access by climbing a low fence near a neighbouring garden.

Robbie's great-aunt would give us biscuits and ask us what we were all up to. Her house was untidy and full of papers and books. She was small and smiley and, I now think, shrewd and amused by us, though her attention always seemed elsewhere, as if she was listening for something. Robbie was kind to her. It was strange to see him so gentle, Robbie with his boxer's face and megaphone voice. He'd been in a bodycast as a small child, and had been making up for it since. He called his great-aunt Nantie and we never knew her real name.

'Those things,' she said once, interrupting our awkward chat while we sat politely in her living room, standing up suddenly apropos of nothing and opening her front door so we could see that one of the bergs was indeed approaching. When she sat back down she said, 'Life in a polynia, eh?' She smiled, watching our reaction to the word.

'That's a lake with ice all round it,' Ian said. I blinked at him, angry that he knew that. He wouldn't look at me. Nantie laughed.

I looked it up myself when I got home. He was right. I scrolled through images of ice-holes and belugas.

We'd do our best to talk politely with Nantie as long as we could. When we ran out of anything to say we would go outside and wait until Robbie could get away too and then we would all run, slip through the barrier and slide down a scree of trash to a wire fence, only a few feet above the train lines themselves.

Sal was usually the first down. She would wait for us by the wire, finger-snarling her long hair into knots, and whistling impatiently through her teeth.

'You're like a fat bear!' she might shout at Ian as he picked his careful way behind me. He was not fat at all but she called everyone fat. She would make lumbering motions at him and Robbie and I would laugh and I would try to speed up, to come down and stand with her while Ian descended without looking at us.

It was the steepest slope we could find in our area, one that took real effort to get up and down. We felt like we were mimicking, honouring, what the explorers above us were doing. We would watch the trains that rushed below. I know I wasn't the only one, looking down, who imagined looking down from a lip of ice, at London.

Ian and I were most into the bergs, so he wanted to hang out with me. That was complicated. I wanted the company of someone who read all the magazines and knew as much as I did, or almost, but I was also infuriated by his owl-eyed camaraderie. Sal used to look at me scornfully when he and I talked. There was always a wet spot on his cuff where he chewed.

Sometimes I'd go to his house. If I had some cool cards in my pack of Iceberg Updates, we'd compare collections, maybe swap a few.

Lund came down in the forecourt of a supermarket. The police got there as fast as they could, but of course locals uploaded their pictures of her body and of course we found them, and showed them to each other with a complex of emotions I cannot put into words.

I still have the image somewhere. The hollow feeling in my stomach was never mere ghoulishness. I got to know the faces of all the onlookers in that picture as well as I did the strange configuration of Lund's body. I think I was horrified; I think I did care.

I wanted to have saved her, and if none of my friends were watching, I would reach through the wire fence when trains went past, stretch out my hand into their gust and imagine that I did.

There were days of rain and we wondered if the water would erode the icebergs, bring them down in a cascade of slush. But the second wave of survey teams trudging on their surfaces reported that even the worst downpour only melted them for a centimetre or so. They would quickly freeze back into their pre-rain shapes. While the scientists investigated, a small, powerful cross-party group of MPs demanded that the government blow up the icebergs with incendiaries.

It was during these wet days that some commentators first suggested a connection between the appearance of the icebergs and the growth of coral across the facades of Brussels. It had been three years since the brain coral, pillar coral and prongs of staghorn coral had first started to appear. Every week contractors removed the thick outcroppings and worm-waving extrusions on the European Parliament and its surrounds. They still do, cracking and scraping the bony stuff off and scrubbing down the surfaces. Every week it returns, leaving the buildings a fishless reef.

While that link was mooted, survey teams clambered the slopes of Masses 1 and 4. They ascended the geometric pinnacles carefully, planting anchors and trudging up with spiked boots. They found nothing but more wind, and they came down again.

Flights resumed in the rest of the country. Heathrow and Gatwick and City stayed out of action but Stansted reopened. The BBC announced that it had commissioned a drama series set among investigators on Mass 2.

Sometimes when I met up with Ian, just the two of us, we'd shadow one or other of the masses. My favourite was 5. I called it the Ice Skull, claiming it looked like one. He liked 2, the smallest and lowest and most stalactite-bearded, which circulated mostly around our neck of the woods. We liked it when the bergs went over brownfield sites and wasteland: we would walk underneath them and kick old brick bits and garbage out of the way, looking for secrets in the ice's shadows.

We collected images, information, stories. It was these days that opened up the city to me, sent me down to New Cross, over to Silvertown, south and east and areas I'd never been before, wherever the icebergs went.

In Stepney a newsagent was taking every other publication out of his shop window and filling it with, of all things, copies of *New Scientist*. 'I tell them,' he kept shouting to someone inside. 'I keep tell them.' He waved a magazine at me jovially. 'Look,' he said.

On the cover were photographs from a southern mission years before I was born, icebergs rising from the water. Next to each of those images was one of a mass over London. The frozen slopes and slices and cracks were the same. The crags overhead were close to identical to those that had once floated in the Antarctic.

'Look, they melt!' he said. 'First they melt and now look they come back.'

Sometimes the gusts of cold below the ice were particularly bad, became brutal mini-winters, freezing the air into little storms. It had been a while since London had had proper cold, even in December and January. The local fashion for berg-coats started then, a vogue for the lightweight, all-year warm clothes most of us still carry, that you can slip on and off if ice crosses your path above.

I had never seen real snow before, proper deep snow. One afternoon outside a shopping centre by Dollis Hill, near a patch of dead trees, Ian and I found a pile of it bigger than either of us. It looked a bit wrong to me. Afterwards, I realised that it had been too angular to be a drift. It was a rare instance when a sizeable chunk of iceberg matter had fallen straight down.

We messed around with it a bit but I was late and I left Ian there. When I got home he'd messaged me with a picture of a dirty, melting mound of slush. He'd kicked his way right into it. In the middle was a battered padded tube, a bit bigger than the core of a toilet roll. It was sealed and wrapped in black plastic.

THERE WAS STUFF IN THE MIDDLE OF IT FROM UP THERE, he had written.

SNOW LANDED ON RUBBISH FOOL, I wrote back.

Meanwhile, an unauthorised expedition uploaded footage onto the internet.

The man staring into the camera wears a woolly hat and a bandana over his mouth. Behind and way below him is a vista of night lights, of London in the dark. A microphone is clipped to his collar and his voice is clear despite the rushing wind.

'Right,' he says. 'So, this is, like, the fourth fucking time we've been up the Shard.' Links to videos of the three previous expeditions on that huge building briefly appear. 'But, you know, kudos on the "increased security", Mayor.' There are sarcastic cheers out of shot.

The camera turns to show other figures clustered by the aerial tower of London's tallest building. The climbers wear a cobbled-together variety of colours and styles. They hoot and wave. The shot zooms down on the south London streets where you can just see pedestrians.

'Anyway,' the first man says. 'You've seen me before. I'm Infiltrex. Or –' He pulls the bandana from his mouth to show a surprisingly soft face. He looks like a cool older brother, the kind who might buy beer for you. 'Ok, so I'm Ryan,' he says. 'I think this time man's going to go uncovered. It's time for the big one.'

The camera pans up. Filling the night sky overhead, astonishingly close, is a jagged field of ice. It looms, and it's approaching. It's so low that the longest extrusions dangling from its underside reach down below the level of the Shard's tower point. On which, the camera briefly shows, two explorers wait.

'Come on, quick,' says Ryan, out of shot, 'we ain't got much time.' An icicled ceiling closes over them, invoking ecstatic claustrophobia.

'We've been watching and waiting. This is the lowest of the lot. This is the one that's going to fuck up your architects' plans. And it's lower now than it's ever been and if we've got this right . . .'

It's never been quite clear what equipment the crew used: the camera doesn't show it, though there's been speculation about 'grapple guns'. What we know is that there's a sound of percussion, and shouting, and the footage cuts to that from a helmetcam, and for less than two seconds you can see someone dangling from high-tensile cable. With that literal cliffhanger, the video pauses for several seconds, entirely dark. To open again on Ryan's face, filling the frame.

'Here we are,' he says. He's holding the camera himself. It's daylight. He lets us see that behind him is an edge of ice, then air and cloud, then, almost a mile below, that London crawls.

The fashion for urban exploration had been declining. There had been a glut of handsomely photographed excursions into deserted hospitals and neglected storm drains. The ascent of Mass 5 was a new scale of feat for these infiltrators, and it re-kindled the fascination. 'Yeah, we know what they're doing,' said some pixellated informant to the BBC, in a disguised voice, 'but no clue how they got up there.'

'Look, Battersea,' says Ryan breathlessly, waving down at the roofless chimneys, bracing himself to climb a crevice below a companion's kicking boots. 'London Eye. Is that Fuckingham Palace?'

There's a long climbing montage, as deliberate as anything in *Rocky*. When Ryan reappears, he has more stubble. He is not so boisterous. Breathing gear bobs around his neck.

'Ok then,' he says. You can see the ice blocks that distinguish the mass's peak. 'You getting me? We have a bit of a theory, so to say. You seen the soldiers marching up and marching down again, right? But there's more than one way to climb things. Ok so Jo's quicker'n the rest of us, she's gone on ahead, and . . .'

Two hundred metres above him, a figure in a red jacket hauls herself up. She's just below the top of the steep ice pile.

'Keep on her, man,' Ryan says. 'We're up in a minute. Right behind you, Jo!'

The woman looks both too close to and too far from us. She swings an axe. The footage is unstable. She climbs another few steps, around a cold crag, the camera veers for an instant, returns, and she is gone. She is nowhere.

'Jo? Jo? Jo?'

Ryan's eyes are wide.

'She's fucking *up*, man! I told you.'

I stared at the screen.

'You got to take the right direction,' Ryan says to the camera-person. 'Shall we? After you, bruv.'

I texted Ian, again and again. WHAT YOU DO WITH THAT THING YOU FOUND? I said. IN THE SNOW. I texted him this because dangling from Ryan's rucksack was a distinctive tubular pack exactly like the one that Ian had kicked out of the ice.

Ryan climbs the ice blocks. You can hear him wheezing. You can see the undersides of his companion's boots. Then he looks up and he's alone, surrounded by clouds. Then the footage ends.

I got hold of Ian eventually. 'I left it there,' he said. 'It was disgusting! It was all covered in dirt and it was in the rubbish!'

I made him come back to Dollis Hill and show me exactly where he'd found it. He made a lot of noises about how I was being stupid but he was scared of me so he came.

There was no ice overhead. Every pile of rubbish we passed he paused and ostentatiously investigated.

I was looking at the signs on a newsagent's noticeboard, as if they might help. A young woman was saying to her baby, 'Oh please stop, just *please* stop.' In the distance, from the east, came a big thundering sound. It was ice shifting, one of the bergs changing. We knew how to tell that from the noise of a storm now.

'You're so stupid,' I said.

'You *said*,' he said. 'You said it was nothing.'

'Shut up. Leaving it, you're so stupid.'

He said nothing. Pigeons wheeled. I looked slowly down and caught Ian's eye. We stared at each other for a minute and I saw something in his expression and I stepped toward him and he ran abruptly in the direction of the Tube station. I didn't even feel surprised. I went after him, shouting almost dutifully, but he was way ahead of me and he got into the Underground before I got near.

Ian stayed off school for days. He shut down his social media accounts. When I went to his house his mum opened the door and stared at me with new dislike. 'He isn't coming out,' she said, before I could speak. She closed the door and said through it, 'Don't come back or I'll tell your dad.'

Who did I have to talk to about what was happening?

Someone found another padded tube and sold it to the *Daily Mirror*. A young woman handed one to Channel 4 News. 'We should stress that there's no way to confirm this is indeed what the contents claim,' the newsreader said.

It was reinforced cardboard, water-sealed in black plastic, wrapped in dense bubble-pack.

'It was sitting there in the middle of a pile of snow,' said the woman on the TV. 'Something about it didn't look right.'

They showed the note it contained. It was handwritten in big script. *Message 4*, it read.

This is Ryan. Were climbing by the brow. We had to leave John or Duro we call him.

He found old spikes and rope. Like there was another camp before. He said there was something in the ice shaft like something dark like an old animal froze in there bare years ago but we never saw it there was all cracking and stuff falling and when we reached him we couldnt see it. He stayed there just whispering.

If we look down we see you but refracted. Hope these don't hit no one. Well pack them in snow to be safe. There are birds or 'birds' up here.

We have pictures in our cameras we cant drop. Ice here looks different.

Hello from here.

It used to say 'Hello from the redoubt.' Someone had crossed out the word 'redoubt' and, in a different hand, tried 'ghostberg'. Someone had crossed that out too.

In the underneaths you couldn't tell whether London was cold because of the icebergs, or if it was just cold again, really cold for the first time in a long time. On the 25 December, Mass 6 went low over the Serpentine Lido, while the Swimming Club were doing their traditional Christmas Day plunge. The downdraft flash-froze the water and a sixty-two-year-old man died. 'He was doing what he loved,' the club secretary told the news.

Gunships buzzed the berg. People massed on Parliament Hill again, to watch soldiers drop onto the lower slopes. It was like an invasion.

My dad took me to watch from the viewing platform at the top of Centre Point. It was nice of him – he wasn't that interested himself. Honestly, I'd rather have been outside, in the streets, right underneath, but I was touched. The building authorities had set up some high-powered telescope so you could take it in turns to stare through the glass at tiny figures crawling up the mountain's side.

We heard they found the remains of Ryan's camp, but that the explorers themselves were gone. The soldiers went deep into cracks and caves – they released some beautiful shots from inside – but they found nothing.

Robbie's great-aunt died.

'That's why he ain't been around,' Sal said. I hadn't noticed. 'His family went away after. You know what happened?'

One night Mass 7 had sat for several hours above north London with the sheltered complex squarely below it, so the residents had turned up their heat and huddled in bed early. The next morning, when the iceberg had moved on and the sun had started to melt the frost on the grass, they found Nantie sitting on a bench in the shared gardens under a glaze of ice.

'She had like a scream of agony on her face,' Sal said.

I told my mother Sal had said that and she was furious.

'That's absolute rubbish,' she said. 'You know I know Robbie's mum. Her aunt was very very peaceful. She must have just had a little snooze in the garden and just not woken up. I hope when it's my time I get something like that.'

The front door had been open, she told me. I remembered how Nantie had got up suddenly to open it, that time, as if she had known an iceberg was coming.

*

Ian still wasn't at school. His parents must have got in trouble for that. I went back to his house. I texted, ITS ME O COME ON IM OUTSIDE MAN. After a minute he opened the door. When I entered, his mother looked at me suspiciously but did not kick me out.

'Come on then,' he said.

We sat in his room and from behind some books on his shelf he pulled out the thick and battered cardboard tube.

He watched me stare at it. 'No one's seen this,' he said. 'My mum ain't even seen this.' He took the lid off its end and removed a letter. We unrolled it on the bed.

Message 1. Dear London. I recognised the script from the news. *Whats the first thing we learn about icebergs? That we only see the tip. 9/10ths of every one is out of sight.*

You have to know how to climb right. Then you can get up and look down. We can see you.

From here we can see all of all these bergs, too.

Whats the point seeing up here if no one knows?

Were going to keep climbing. Wish us luck. Heres a present we scraped up.

'What present?' I said. 'What's scraped?'

'Wait,' Ian said, and went down the stairs. He returned with a small plastic tub. It was full of ice.

'There was like a thermos in there,' he said. His eyes were wide behind his glasses. 'Like for tea? It was stuck in the tube. It was a bit cracked but when I opened it, it had this in it. And it was starting to melt but I scooped it out and put it in this and put it in the freezer.'

The ice was a single mass of angles and shapes. I could see it had partially melted and refrozen from smaller pieces.

'What if your mum or dad finds it?' I said.

'I've shown them already. I said it was an experiment. They don't care.' We eyed each other.

In the kitchen Ian filled a bowl with hot water and took the lid off the Tupperware and put it inside. The box floated, bumping against the sides.

I tried not to show anything. I'm sure Ian felt the same breathless edginess I did. The ice started to melt immediately. It cracked and pinged.

There was another noise, a hiss as if someone had half-opened the top of a fizzy drink. It was air, frozen into the ice for however many years – thousands? millions? – being released. Now I know that's called the seltzer effect: you can hear it on Arctic survey ships, from the few shards of ice that still bob about, when they hit warmer currents. We listened to the hiss of old air from some bit of sky.

I put my arms around that bowl and pulled it close, stuck my head over it like I was sick and inhaling menthol fumes. I breathed in.

I could smell nothingness. I felt light-headed, but that might have been because I was breathing so deep. I imagined that I could feel little boluses of cold air go down into my lungs.

'Give it to me,' Ian said. I felt a spasm of that instinct for cruelty that sometimes made me a little bit giddy around him. I kept breathing and pushed him away as he tried to get closer.

The ice melted quickly. It didn't take long. I held him back, inhaling as hard and fast as I could while he muttered and whined and pleaded, until the bubbling sound stopped.

I raised my head from above cold clear water. I looked straight at Ian and willed myself not to show guilt.

He stared at me with an awful wounded look. He took the

bowl from under me and I let him. Still watching me, he put the box's curved plastic corner awkwardly to his lips and drank the water down.

We stared at each other. 'You should hand in that letter,' I said at last. 'It isn't yours. They wrote it to everyone in London.'

He just kept staring. I got up and left.

Soldiers kept going up the icebergs, and coming down again, and if any of them worked out how to get to the other bit of up, we never heard about it. If that's even a thing. If that's real. None of the unauthorised explorers ever came back. I stopped hanging out with Sal, and when Robbie returned he stopped hanging out with me.

By the time Ian came back to school, it was pretty easy for me to avoid him. Sometimes I might catch him staring at me across a classroom or the lunch hall. When that happened I'd some-times say to myself in my own head something like, 'I saw it first,' thinking of the snow in which the tube had been packed. If he did take that letter to the authorities they never released it.

I used to expect to bump into him. I still live in the same area, and so did he for a long time, but London kept us apart. My mum did tell me once that he'd visited Nantie's old gardens, which she said was nice, to pay respects. I think he's been deployed now.

I thought I'd end up working at something to do with the icebergs, but my job's in import–export. I have to spend a fair bit of time in Europe. I've been through the Great Brussels Reef plenty of times. I have a little bottle-opener of the Belgian flag cut from a bit of its coral.

Even a dull business like mine has what you could call its own myths. When anything messes with supply chains all kinds of weird stories start coming out. The funny thing is how many end up turning out to have something to them. Quite often I see on the news some banalised version of a rumour I heard months before.

Right now, there's a slowdown on some electronic components from Japan. The whispers are that the workers are locked out because the factories are unusable, and that the factories are unusable because they've filled up with undergrowth from the rainforest.

I love the London bergs. They still circle, and they don't get in the way of business.

I have to assume the government did make it all the way up those troublesome blocks. I don't even exactly know why I wish I didn't think this, but I think there must be British soldiers watching me from the circling ice in that other bit of sky, from those slabby shapes. They're not blowing them up and they must have their reasons.

Ian joined the army, the new specialist iceberg unit. He might be one of those looking down now. He drank the water, I breathed the air.

Whatever the season, the masses kick out as much cold as they ever did. They shed ice dust constantly, and they make faint, feathery snow out of the air below them. You wake up sometimes and if they've gone low during the night they leave a snail-trail of thin ice and snow across London in the shape of their route. It might be warm summer, but you'll open the curtains onto iced windows. You'll come out of your house and there'll be a line of frost bisecting your street.

The Condition of New Death

The first reported case of New Death occurred on 23 August 2017, in Georgetown, Guyana. At approximately 2:45pm, Jake Morris, a fifty-three-year-old librarian, entered his living room and found his wife, pharmacist Marie-Therese Morris, fifty-one, motionless and supine on the floor. 'I opened the door onto the soles of her feet,' he has said.

Mr Morris testifies that he checked his wife's pulse and found her cold. His claim to have *gone to her side* to do so has been the source of much controversy in neothanatology, this action of course being impossible in the case of the New Dead. Mainstream opinion is that this is the inaccurate memory of a distraught man. A substantial minority insist that there are no grounds to assume such error, and that Ms Morris must therefore be assumed to have been Old Dead at this point, and that her status changed seconds after discovery.

Mr Morris went to the telephone in the north-eastern corner of the room and summoned an ambulance. When he turned back to his wife's body, New Death had unmistakeably taken hold.

'I turn around,' he has said, 'and her feet are right in front of me again. Pointing directly at me. Again.'

During his call, Ms Morris's corpse appeared to have silently rotated on a horizontal axis approximately 160 degrees, around a point somewhere close to her waist.

With great alarm, Mr Morris began to walk around the body, but he stopped when, in his words, 'those feet wouldn't stop pointing at me'. Ms Morris's body appeared to him to be swivelling like a needle on a compass, her feet always facing him.

He remained frozen, his wife's feet a few inches from his own shoes. He was unwilling to move and thereby provoke that smooth and perfectly silent motion. That was how the paramedics found him, by his dead wife.

At one point in the highly confused moments that followed, a medic demanded that Mr Morris be careful not to tread on his wife's hair. Which was, however, from Mr Morris's perspective, on the other side of her body from him.

Thus the specificity of New Death began to emerge.

After the Morris case was that of the Bucharest aneurysm, then the Toronto crosswalk, then the Hong Kong twins. New Death spread at accelerating rates. News coverage, which had started as sporadic, amused and sceptical, grew rapidly more serious. Two weeks after Ms Morris New Died, the sinking of the overloaded ferry *Carnivale* sailing between the Eritrean coast and the Italian port of Lampedusa gave the world its first harrowing scene of *mass* New Death.

Now, with the last verified Old Death having occurred six years ago, and the upgrading of all human death seemingly complete, we are inured enough to the scenes of countless New Dead left by drone strike, terrorist attack, landslide and pandemic that it can be hard to recall the shock occasioned by that first spectacle.

The shots of almost a hundred drowned migrants, dead despite their life belts, their bodies oddly stiff, their legs not slanting, their feet not sinking but visible at the surface of the water, are still iconic. It might be thought that, occurring on water, the apparent rotations of the New Dead would not appear quite so unnatural (old-natural, to use the now-preferred term) as the same phenomenon on land. This, however, was not the case.

The quickly leaked footage showed the instant and exact swivels by which every drowned migrant's feet always precisely faced every camera. These remained in perfect synchrony. All feet always faced all cameras no matter what abrupt and contingent motions the boats or helicopters made, or where they were when they made them. These movements were obviously not the results of currents, winds or hidden engines.

The feeds from the headcams of rescue divers were even more shocking. In it, the drowned dead without flotation devices all sink slowly, and every one of the bodies, at every level, is stiffly oriented perfectly horizontally, with its feet pointing toward every rising, panicking diver. This of course is the case even in the footage shot simultaneously from quite different directions, in which the same corpses can be identified.

In the weeks that followed, more and more scenes of the smooth, precisely flat and silent rotation of the dead were released, the bodies horizontal on slopes of varying inclines, in a Baghdad plaza or on a Mexican hillside or the site of a Danish school shooting. It was, however, the *Carnivale* disaster that inaugurated the era of New Death.

There is variation among New cadavers. Arms and legs may be splayed to various degrees, though the range is attenuated relative to that possible in Old Death. The bodies of victims of dismemberment or explosive force do not reconstitute, though their components, even if scattered, lie according to the condition of New Death – they are, in other words, New Dead in pieces.

Stated most simply, New Death is the condition whereby human corpses now lie always on a horizontal vector – no matter the angle of the surface or the substance of the matter below them – and now orient so that their feet are facing all observers, all the time.

Two facts about this epochal thanatological shift were quickly established:

i) New Death is *subjective*.

   All observers in the presence of New Dead, in person or via imaging technology, will perceive that body or those bodies as oriented with feet toward them. This remains the case when those observers are directly opposite each other. *Perception* and *observation* are constitutive of New Death.

ii) New Death is *objective*.

   Physical interventions have verified that these subjective impressions are *not illusory*. The New Dead have mass. They can be interacted with. The basic positional predicates of New Death, however, cannot be overcome. As the notorious Bannif-Murchau experiment showed, multiple observers of a single New Dead, all perceiving the body's feet to be toward them, all instructed to take hold of the cadaver at the same instant, all coming from different directions, *will all grasp the feet at the same time*. This sometimes shocking and occasionally dangerous vectoral/locational slippage would of course have been impossible in the pre-ND era. It is not just biology, but also physics, that has changed.

New Death has had no impact on death rates or causes. Nor has the agential status of the dead vis-à-vis the living changed – they remain as quiet as their Old Dead precursors. New Death is a phenomenon not of *dying*, nor of *death*, but of the *quiddity of deadness*.

Philosophies of its causes, effects, and meanings (if any) are, of course, in their infancy. But they have, very recently, taken an exciting turn.

At the 2024 Mumbai Conference *The New Dead and Their Critics*, PJ Mukhopadhyay, a graduate student of digital design, gave a paper on 'New Death as a Game'. In the course of her presentation she pointed out, almost in passing, that a *locus classicus* of a foot-to-viewpoint orientation of the dead was the earliest generation of First-Person Shooters.

In such games, no matter where 'you' stood, your defeated enemies would lie with their feet towards you, shifting as you shifted. This would be the case until, finally, after a programmed time, their bodies winked out of play.

With this insight, we have entered a new era of New Death Studies. In the words of the most recent issue of the *Cambridge Journal of Philosophy*, 'no one is yet clear on why Mukhopadhyay's observation is important. That it is important – that it changes everything – no doubt remains.'

Understanding remains evasive, but culture is pragmatic and quick. Those for whom showing the soles of feet has been an insult adapt no less than do those who delight in insulting them. A plethora of ceremonies are emerging around the interment and veneration of New Dead. Theologies of all traditions are, mostly, smoothly accommodating them, with new interpretations of old texts and ways. The New Dead are already completely banalised representationally in movies, television dramas and other commodities – including, of course, video games. The point is not that rotating sugar-skeletons with wind-up handles are sold by Mexican vendors: the point is that they sell in similar numbers to any other *Dia de los Muertos* items.

This insouciance is admirable. But it is also somehow inadequate. We have tweaked our various bells and smells, but we still die as we always died, and live as we did before we died.

We are not ready. What would being ready constitute? What might the endgame of New Death be?

This is not a manifesto. It is not even a prequel to such. We don't know what to call for, to live up to the potentiality of New Death. This is a call for a manifesto to be written. An exhortation for an exhortation, a plea to have it demanded of us to live as we must and New Die well.

We must proceed according to a presumption that we might have something up to which to live, that there might be a telos to all our upgraded dead, that we might eventually *succeed* in something, that we might unlock achievements, if we die correctly. And, conversely, that if we do not, we will continue to fail.

What the stakes of that success and that failure might be, none of us yet know.

We will all learn.

The Dowager of Bees

I was inducted twenty-two years ago in the windowless basement room of a chic Montreal hotel. The door was small and said JANITOR outside. Inside, the room was gorgeous, full of lush gaming-related paintings and shelves of hardbound rule books. Four of us were sitting at a card table while two defeated young wallflowers watched, big-eyed and silent.

'What's a Willesden?' said Gil 'Sugarface' Sugar. He was elderly and, everyone said, paunchy but still punchy.

'Willesden,' I said. 'It's in London.'

He said, 'I'm not calling you the Willesden Kid.'

'It's an honour to play with you.'

'Get on with it,' said Denno Kane, a baby-faced dark-skinned polyglot renowned for Vingt-et-un but eager to put down money wherever there were cards.

Sugarface and Denno went way back, and they went there with the dour Welsh woman twice my age sitting opposite me. I'd met her in Detroit. She'd been taking a break after bankrupting a small city with a pair of sevens. She'd watched me clean up small-fry stockbrokers.

'Nice fingers,' she'd sneered: I did tricks when I dealt. 'I'm Joy. No surname.'

I pretty much shouted like a fanboy that I knew who she was. 'Let me play with you,' I said.

She'd laughed full of scorn but she liked my front. Now here I was, one of three designated hors-d'oeuvres and the only one left at the table still playing.

We'd nearly died of happiness when they told us to bring the packs. The other two spent a lot of money on theirs. I bought mine from a gas station around the corner. Sugarface didn't pass comment on the logo on their backs.

My co-rookies went out as fast as expected but, with luck I deserved not at all, I was keeping up. The big three didn't mind. I wasn't disrespectful. I wore my most expensive suit. Sugarface had on a tux without a tie, Joy a churchy dress. Denno wore a green t-shirt with sauce stains.

He won a big hand. 'How you doing?' he said.

'An honour to play with you,' I said.

The two Collateral Damage got up and very politely thanked everyone for their time as if anyone even gave a shit they were talking. They left.

'*O tempora, o mores,*' Joy said.

Denno swore in Russian, then Greek.

More rounds. I had a straight. Didn't raise too high. Joy to show. She was as good as they said: her face was flint.

'Well,' she said at last. Peered over the back of her cards and laid them slowly down.

Denno whistled. Sugarface gasped and sat back.

Two of Spades; Seven and Jack of Clubs; Eight of Diamonds; and a card I'd never seen before.

An image of an elderly woman done in black and bright yellow. She wore a fur coat, held a clutch, and a cigarette in a long holder. There were insects on her stole and by her face.

'Hell,' Sugarface said. 'God damn.'

'Full Hive,' said Joy. 'The Dowager of Bees.'

She took out a notebook and wrote something and handed it to Sugarface, who signed the page with a rueful nod and passed it to Denno. The shiny yellow card sat on the table with the reds and blacks. The woman was as stylised as all face cards, bordered and reversed beneath herself.

Denno passed me the paper. 'On the dotted,' he said.

'I don't get it,' I said.

There was a moment.

'Oh ho,' said Sugarface keenly.

'What is this?' I said.

'Well, *mazel tov*,' said Denno.

'The others had to be gone, sure, right,' Sugarface said.

'Ok, haze the newbie,' I said. 'That's cool.'

'Show some respect,' Denno said.

He went to the shelf and came back with a leather-bound edition of *Robert's Rules of Poker*. He flicked through pages and held it open in front of me, pointing to the relevant section.

It was in a chapter entitled 'Hands that Include Hidden Suits'.

'Full Hive,' I read. 'Dowager of Bees + one black Jack + three number cards values totalling a prime number.' There was a lot more but he slammed it closed before I could read on.

'I've got that book,' I said, 'and I don't remember . . .'

'Trust me, it's going to beat whatever you've got,' he said as he put the volume back. I showed him my straight hesitantly. 'Please,' he said. 'You're physically hurting me.'

'Sign,' Sugarface said. 'You owe Joy a favour you don't want to do.'

'What favour?'

'You listening?' Denno said. 'One you don't want to do. Sign. You have a year and a day. Don't make her come asking.'

It didn't seem ridiculous. Everything felt very important. My ears were ringing. I looked at the card, the big stingered insects. Everyone watched me.

Joy's page said '1) D.o.B. Favour', and then the signatures. I signed.

Sugarface clapped. Joy nodded and took her notebook back. Denno poured me an expensive wine.

'Long time since I saw an induction,' Sugarface said.

He collected the cards. I watched the yellow lady with the gas station logo on her back fold in with the rest of them. He shuffled.

'Mine was in Moscow,' he said. ''66.'

'Your induction?' Denno said. 'Kinshasa, me. Eleven years ago.'

Joy said, 'Swansea Bridge Club.'

I said nothing. I got dealt three of a kind. I won a little money. I wasn't focusing any more. No one said anything else about the favour owed.

'Having a good time?' Sugarface said.

The card didn't show up again. I rubbed the deck between my fingers and it felt standard and cheap.

When we were done and packing up, I walked as nonchalantly as I could to the bookshelf and picked up those rules. I checked the contents page and the index, for Dowager, Bees, Hidden Suits, Suits (Hidden). Nothing.

I realised that the others had stopped talking and were staring at me indulgently.

'Bless him,' Denno said.

'The round's finished,' Sugarface told me. 'You won't find anything now.'

He threw all three decks into the trash. I was still reading, looking through the lists of hands. There was nothing about a Full Hive.

'You're only inducted once,' Joy said. 'Buy yourself something nice.'

She waited in the doorway without complaining while I went to the bin and rummaged around in the cigarette ash and fished out every card and separated out the deck I'd bought.

It contained no Dowager of Bees. I did find extra cards: there were fifty-five, but two were Jokers, and one was instructions for Solitaire.

I made sure I had her address, and three hundred and forty-seven days later, I found Joy and did her a favour I didn't want to.

The second time I saw a hidden suit was in Manchester.

It was six years later. I wasn't a Poker top-ranker but I could hold my own, and besides, I'd diversified, could play you at Baccarat, Whist, Rummy, Bridge, Faro, Spoil Five Euchre, Chemin-de-Fer, Canasta, Uruguay Canasta, Panguingue, Snap. Pretty much anything. I'd find ways to bet on any of them too. I won my first car at Tarabish. It made me want to win more.

There was a GameFest (they called it) at the Corn Exchange. Mostly families checking out kids' stuff. The few professionals there were goofing around or accompanying friends. There were five of us in a little roomlet made with temporary walls in the corner of the hall. We were drunk and playing unlikely games for petty cash and giggles.

We were on Old Maid. That's the one where you start by removing one Queen, then deal the fifty-one and pass cards one hand to the next and get rid of pairs until everyone's out except some poor schmuck who's left holding just that last mismatched Queen, the Old Maid. They lose.

A civilian would say it was pure luck. No such thing.

We thought up a way to bet. Antes into a pot, which got distributed as people came out. Whoever had the Old Maid would end up losing double. It was a burning hot day and I remember a blaze of light came right down through a high window and made our table shine.

I was out, sitting back safe, having made my cash. People took cards from each other and discarded pairs triumphantly. Three people left. More passing. Pairs down. Two. A woman in her twenties with a strawberry-blonde bob and a leather jacket too battered not to be second-hand, facing down a plump, blinky, middle-aged guy in a corduroy jacket. We watched them swap and throw down cards, their faces set, and then someone gave a little cry and I frowned because the two of them were sitting back staring at each other, and each still held a single card.

'Did we mess up?' someone said. 'Did we miscount?'

The man turned his: the Queen of Spades. He was the Old Maid.

We all looked at the young woman. Her eyes were wide. She looked at me. The back of her card looked the same as all the others. I didn't feel drunk any more.

'Show,' I said.

She lowered it face up. Its background was dark flat grey. The design was of two rows of four links of metal picked out in white.

She swallowed. She said, 'Eight of Chains.'

*

Someone went to bar the door.

'What now?' her opponent said. He was terrified. 'I don't know what happens.'

'None of us do,' I said.

'Gin's my usual game, I don't . . . What's the *rule*?'

A tall guy to the young woman's right was leafing through a tatty paperback of *Hoyle's*. The fat man looked up a gaming site on his phone.

'I don't understand,' said a boy of about seventeen. 'What is that?'

By that time I knew that, definitionally, if he didn't, everyone else present did understand what was happening. If there's any, there's only ever one.

'You've been inducted,' I told him. 'Just watch and listen. Who else had it?' I said. 'At any point?'

The guy looking with the rulebook raised her hand. 'I got dealt it,' he said. 'She took it from me. Here we are.' He started to read. '"Old Maid: Rules for Hidden Suits." It's the *what* of Chains?'

I said, 'The Eight,' but the man with the Queen interrupted.

'Got it,' he said, squinting at his phone. He sagged with relief. 'I'm still the loser,' he said. 'I still lost.'

I could see the boy was about to complain that he didn't understand again and I showed him a warning finger.

The young woman licked her lips. 'There must be a forfeit, though,' she said. 'Even so.'

The big guy hesitated and nodded and passed her his phone. She read. The rest of us were too polite to ask but I caught the eye of the man with the rulebook and he gave me a tiny reassuring nod.

'Ok,' the young woman said. She was tense but controlled. 'Ok, that's not so bad.'

'Right?' her opponent said. 'It could be worse, right?'

'That's not so bad.'

We all breathed out. I picked up the cards and folded them back into the deck and shuffled. We all got silly as the tension eased. I made the cards spring from one hand to the other and dance about. People cheered.

'I don't understand,' the boy said. 'Can I see?' He held out his hand for the deck and I made the cards jump through the air to land right in front of him and everyone laughed, even the woman who'd ended up with the Chains.

'You can try,' I said. 'I wouldn't hold your breath, though.' He went through the deck and, of course, did not find the card. Without asking, he picked up the phone too, but the round was over and there was nothing about the hidden suits on the site, or on any site.

The young woman took a while to clear up her stuff and she kept looking at me. She wanted me to wait for her.

'You're really good at that stuff,' the big man said, making flickering fingers.

'Many hours,' I said. 'Sleight and magic.'

He glanced behind him. The woman was putting on her jacket. He lowered his voice.

'I almost didn't give her the phone,' he whispered. 'The Eight's not so bad. Which is good, because . . .'

I shook my head so he wouldn't tell me more.

'But if she'd seen what it said about the Nine,' he said, and shook his head. 'Or the Six. Or if she'd ended up with the Two of Scissors . . . !'

'She didn't,' I said. It was crass of him to talk this way. 'There's no percentage thinking about the might'ves.'

He left as the young woman approached. He gave me a friendly wave. As if I wasn't a hypocrite. As if all of us, all players, don't live in a dense forest of might'ves.

The kind of event for which I'd hoped when I was young and endlessly practising passes, turning cards around my fingers, didn't come. I couldn't have said what it was exactly anyway – some chimera, something epochal, valuable, ostentatious and secret.

I didn't cheat often or big enough to attract notice, my big wins I won straight, but occasionally, depending on the stakes, the game, my opponents, my finances, and whim, I'd twist my fingers according to muscle memory and take a trick that would otherwise have escaped me, withhold from my opponent some card I knew they needed.

If I was very drunk I might show Belinda a trick or two. She loved seeing them and I loved to see her look when I showed her. Sometimes I called her Chains. Sometimes she called me Bees.

She had more luck than me, and she bet higher, and she knew hands and odds and combinations better, but she lost more, too. We once worked out that our earnings were almost identical.

We went to Paris for the art. We went to Brazil and took pictures of the Jesus. We played Go Fish in Bucharest. We loved watching each other at the tables but didn't play against each other often because we knew we wouldn't hold back.

We'd swapped numbers that day in Manchester, but it was a few weeks later that she called, and her mood was good when she did, so I figured she'd got through the forfeit.

She didn't ask me if I ever cheated and I didn't volunteer any information and I never did it against her but she was too good a player not to suspect.

For the first year or so we didn't talk overmuch about the hidden suits, though we said enough to start to use those pet names, shyly. Every once in a long while she'd disappear for a day or two and come back tired and thoughtful. I knew it was the terms of the forfeit and I didn't say anything.

Once in Vegas a Canadian oncologist blithely told us there were hidden suits in the Baraja deck too. I was appalled by the conversation and we made our excuses.

I understand the interest in the Baraja, the Italian deck, the German with its other colours, the Ganjifa, and so on, but I was always a devotee of the standard modern Rouennais fifty-two. I loved the history that led to what we play with, the misprisions, the errors of copying that got us suicide Kings and one-eyed Jacks. I loved the innovation of the rotational symmetry that isn't a reflection. I loved the black and the red, against which the colours of the hidden suits are so stark – blue, grey, green, the white of Chains, the yellow of the Bees.

'I only saw one other,' Belinda told me once, carefully. 'The Nine of Teeth. But just for an instant.'

The difficulty is that it's bad form to talk about them brazenly, but once you're inducted it's also a good idea to learn as many rules for as many hands featuring as many cards in as many suits in as many games as you might ever play, just in case. And you can't exactly look them up most of the time.

No matter how proper you are, there are questions you'll end up hearing asked, or asking. What bird is it flying above the Detective of Scissors? Where's the missing link on the Nine of Chains? Why does the Ace of Ivy grow on bones?

You might feel you know these cards, whether you've seen them or not. 'We all end up getting to know certain cards pretty well, I guess,' Belinda said to me once. 'One way or another.' You might have a favourite.

The third time was Lublin.

We were playing Bourré in a deconsecrated church. I'd faced two of my opponents before, and had had a fist-fight with one. Belinda and I were taking turns: she stood behind me with her hand on my shoulder. She could see my cards but no one else's.

I picked up my hand. Five cards. One of them I'd never seen before.

One two three four blue smokestacks, protruding into blue sky, gushing stylised clouds of blue smoke.

I showed nothing. Belinda's hand twitched. I wasn't afraid anyone noticed but to me it was as if she screamed, '*Oh my God!*'

I went into my memory for whatever I had about the Four of Chimneys. What it would do in combination with my other cards. I weighed up possibilities.

There was a lot of betting. I got tenser and tenser. When I eventually laid down my hand I cannot tell you how much I loved the sound of everyone's amazement. They were calculating the extra losses my win would mean for them, they were gasping with envy, they were stunned at the sight of the card.

No one asked what it was. Everyone present was a previous inductee. The only time that ever happened to me.

People passed me their chips and their extra chips. They wrote down their secrets for me. I wondered what I'd do with the horses and keys that were now mine. I hadn't only been dealt a hidden card; I'd played it well.

I've told myself repeatedly that it was an instant's insanity to do what I did, something I can't explain. But then, I had been perfecting finger-tricks for a long time.

As everyone relaxed and a heavy-faced ex-soldier picked up the deck and collected our hands, I laughed at some witticism and nodded and barely looked at him as I folded my cards and passed them. I don't know if Belinda's hand tightened again. I didn't fear that the dealer, or anyone else, would notice the fleeting fingertip motion by which I extracted the Four of Chimneys from my hand and slipped it into my cuff.

I didn't know if it would still be there when I got home. But I sat in my bathroom and rolled up my sleeve and there it was, waiting to be folded back into the deck so it could leave as it arrived.

'You're going to have a long wait,' I whispered.

Four chimneys, two by two, two facing up, two down, blowing smoke in strong dark blue and black lines.

I felt shy. I put it away.

'What a game,' was all Belinda or I ever said about that night. We carried on. We won more than we lost.

I kept the card in stiff clear plastic in my wallet. I didn't want to scuff it. Sometimes I'd take it out and glance at those block-print chimneys for a couple of seconds, until I got all anxious, as I did, and turned it over and looked for a lot longer at the back.

I've played with super-expensive decks as well as with the gas-station plastic. Pros aren't that precious; mostly we use the workhorse deck produced by Bicycle, as close as you can get to a default. It's had the same meaningless filigree on the back for years. You want choice? It comes in red or blue.

We'd been playing a red-backed Bicycle deck when I got dealt the Four of Chimneys.

I kept up my finger exercises. I listened for stories about the hidden cards. I maybe listened extra hard for stories about hands with Chimneys. I was never superstitious but I did develop one tick. I liked to hold the card against my skin. I liked to feel it pressed against me.

Before a big-pot game, I'd take my Four of Chimneys out of its little case – always with a thrill of excitement, surprise, regret and relief that it was still there – and slip it under a band on the inside of my right forearm behind my wrist, under my shirt, a kind of simple cuff holdout. It made me feel lucky, is how I thought about it.

Some freight shipping companies put aside a few cabins for paying customers. You can cross the Atlantic that way. We got word that one of them had set up a floating big-money game. Of course we booked passage. It was expensive, even though it wasn't as if we were tripping over pleasure-seekers or looking down from our deck onto a sculpted pool. It was a merchant ship: our view was a deck full of containers.

For two days we kept to ourselves. On the third day, before play, I was out under the sky and someone tapped me on the back.

'Kid.'

'Sugarface!'

I was astonished he was still alive. He looked almost exactly the same.

'Should have guessed I'd find you here,' he said. 'Been following your career.'

Belinda liked him a lot. He flirted with her and stayed on the right side of sleazy. He told her exaggerated stories of our first meeting. He showed her the face he said I'd worn when I saw the

Dowager of Bees, not even hesitating to find out whether she'd been inducted before he told the story.

In the evening I tucked my card face down into its little band on my right wrist as usual and flicked it before covering it with my shirt and jacket. We gathered in the makeshift state room and sipped mojitos while the sun went down.

Seven players. I'd sat across from all but one before: it's not that big a world. Besides me and Belinda and Sugarface, there was a Maronite computer programmer I'd once beaten at Pig; a French publisher who'd partnered me during a devastating hand at Bridge; a South African judge known as the Cribbage Assassin; and the captain. He was a puffed-up little prick in a blue brocade shirt. He was new to all of us. We realised this whole gig was his brainchild, just so he could play big.

He named the game, of course. Texas Hold-'Em, of course. I rolled my eyes.

The Lebanese guy was weaker than I'd remembered. The judge was cautious but smart and hard to read. The publisher built up slowly with sneaky bets. Sugarface played exactly like I recalled.

Belinda was my main competition. We tore into each other.

The captain could barely play at all but he didn't even realise. He preened. He barked at people that it was their deal, their bet, told them what they needed to win. We all pretty much hated him. His ship, his trip, his table were the only reasons we didn't tell him to go fuck himself.

I was playing well but Belinda was playing better. She beat me with two pairs. Furious, I made one of my cards spin over my knuckles. The programmer toasted me and the judge applauded. Belinda smiled kindly and took several thousand dollars off me with an offhand bluff.

Deep night and the sky was like a massive sheet of lead. We changed the cards. The captain took a new pack from a drawer and tossed them to Sugarface.

Bicycle cards. Red-backed. Sugarface opened the packet and dealt us our two hole cards.

Usually most serious players just keep them face down in front of them but that night I wanted to hold mine up like in a cowboy film. Pair of Threes. Good start.

We bet – we bet big – everyone stays in. Sugarface deals the flop: three community cards, face up. A Six, a Ten, Jack of Clubs. I have a good feeling, then a bad feeling, then a good feeling. Sugarface winks. This round of betting we lose Mr IT. I can read him easily and I'm not surprised.

Fourth shared card, the turn. Hi there, Charlemagne: the King of Hearts has been shy till now but there he is. There's some muttering and murmuring. Belinda is rock-still while she calculates, even stiller than usual, so she's either in good shape or bad shape and I'm guessing good. The judge goes out. Publisher blows me a kiss and follows.

Sugarface makes us wait a long time, puffing out his cheeks. In the end he joins them.

It's me to bet, and as I consider and see the red backs of my opponents' hands, floating like unmanned boats into my head comes the name of a hand I've heard about over the years.

They call it a Boiler-Room: a Ten; a Jack; a King; a Three; and the Four of Chimneys.

I start to consider what that would win me. What would be the takings from this table, not just in money. And I realise that I'm thinking with a sort of calm wonder, almost wryly, *Oh, this is what I've been waiting for.*

And as I'm thinking that, with my hands stock-still to anyone watching, my fingers are snatching my no-longer-helpful spare

Three and sending it to Hell via my sleeve, and coaxing my stolen card out from under its band, toward my cuff and finger-tips, a clean sleight, bringing it back up and slipping it into position, all in a fraction of a second, all unseen.

Belinda's in, and the captain's in, of course, which I was banking on, and I don't care what piece of shit he's holding, he's not going to beat my hand – my winning hand – now. I'm ready.

The betting's done and Sugarface deals the river, the fifth shared card. It skitters down. The lights flicker and everyone's gasping and everything goes slow, because the last card out of the deck, the last card face up on the table, is a new colour.

It's the Four of Chimneys.

'Oh hell yes,' I hear Sugarface say. '*Mon Dieu,*' I hear, and 'Oh my God.'

That's Belinda.

I stare at the blue in the red and black. A shared hidden card. Everyone can have a hidden card in their hand.

The boat pitches, and for a fraction of an instant I see the night beyond the windows and it's as if I hear a drone, as if some-one's walking on the deck, someone tall and stiff and dignified in a deep coat, smoking, looking in at us with austere curiosity, with satisfaction.

I can hear the captain saying, 'What is this? What does this mean?' and Sugarface saying, 'Just keep quiet and watch, and show some respect; this is your induction,' and Belinda is staring right at me, her mouth open, her eyes wide.

My frantic little fingers are fumbling deeper in my sleeve than you'd think possible but I dropped that Three to nestle I don't know where against my skin, there's no retrieving it, and I can't swap it back in or its replacement back out again, and everyone can see I have two hole cards in my hand, just as I should.

And one of them's my Four of Chimneys, like the one on the table, and there's only ever one Four of Chimneys, if there's ever a Four of Chimneys at all.

Sugarface is looking at me and saying, 'What's the matter, Kid?' and he looks at Belinda and down at the table and at the back of my cards and up at me and his face falls and he says, 'Oh no, Kid, oh no, no, oh Kid, oh no,' and there's more sorrow and fear in his voice than I've ever heard.

'What is this?' the captain blathers. 'What is this card?'

I go to fold but Sugarface takes hold of my wrist.

'Kid, I don't want to see what I think I'm going to see,' he says gently. 'Judge,' he says. 'Get the rulebook.' He starts to pull my hand down. 'I need you to look up "Hidden Suits",' he says.

Everyone is watching my descending cards but Belinda. She's staring at her own hand.

'I need you to look up "Cheating",' Sugarface says. 'I need you to look up "Sanctions".'

Belinda's cards twitch with a tiny instant motion of her fingers as with her free hand she grabs my wrist too. She's stronger than Sugarface. Pushes my cards back up.

'I call,' she says.

'We're mid-play,' he says.

She says, 'Look up a "Link Evens", Judge.'

Even the captain's silent while the judge turns pages. 'Two Four Six Eight Ten including a Chain,' she reads out. 'She can pre-emptive call with that. Nothing can beat it. Wins . . . any single object in the room she chooses.' She looks up.

'And everyone keep your paws off that prize,' Belinda says. She's staring at the hand in my hand. 'No looking, no touching, no turning. Just slide it to me face down.'

The judge looks at the cards on the table. 'If she has a Two and an Eight,' she says, 'she wins. But there's a winner's forfeit ...'

'I have the Two of Hearts,' Belinda says. She sounds exhausted but she smiles at me. 'And I'm holding the Eight of Chains.'

Everyone sits up.

'Wait,' I manage to whisper. 'What's the forfeit?'

No one hears me. Belinda is lowering her cards to show them.

'I win,' Belinda says.

'What is it?' I try to say.

'I win, and I choose a card as my pot,' Belinda announces.

She looks at what I'm holding as her own cards go down, picking a prize to remove from all scrutiny. She meets my eye and smiles. She could always read me. I know she'll choose the right one.

In the Slopes

McCulloch brewed a glass of tea and took it into the front room of his shop, where he found a young woman and a young man browsing. The bell had not sounded when they entered. It was fritzy.

They wore grey cargo pants with bulging pockets, rucksacks over their shoulders. McCulloch nodded at them and sat behind the counter on his high stool. He aimed the remote control at the TV on the wall and lowered the volume.

The girl smiled. 'Not on our account,' she said. She was taller than her companion, dark-skinned and muscular, with long blonde hair up in an artful tangle. She gave McCulloch a look of friendly, frank assessment.

'Where you from?' McCulloch said.

'Swansea.' He could hear the accent in her loud voice. 'You don't sound local yourself.'

'I am now.'

McCulloch's shop was the converted front room of his house. Shelves covered three walls, and there were display units in the middle of the floor. The whitewash was peeling. He could see the whole interior by a mounted, curved mirror that had been there when he bought the place.

Like most of the shopkeepers, in summer he hung bright plastic balls and towels and buckets outside. He had packed them up and stacked them back in his storeroom a week before.

The young man sifted with slow attention through baskets of trinkets, toys and bars of soap in the shapes of collaborators. McCulloch could see that his black hair was already thinning at the crown. The woman skimmed through the books for sale.

'How come you're here?' McCulloch said.

'A dig,' she said.

'I think I heard,' McCulloch said. 'In Free Bay.'

The visitors glanced at each other. 'No,' the woman said. 'We're in a place called Banto.'

'I heard wrong. What's in Banto?'

'You tell us,' she said. 'Mr Local.'

'Fair enough,' he said. 'Not much. Farms. About an hour away. You not been yet?'

'We only just got here,' the boy said, quietly enough that McCulloch strained to hear. 'We got in late last night. We're stocking up and heading there now.'

He brought a keyring to the counter, a twisted figurine in shoddily moulded plastic.

'Four quid,' McCulloch said. The young man raised an eyebrow.

'Nothing's made here,' the woman said. 'It's imported. You'd get it cheaper at home.'

'Yeah but that's not the point,' he said. He counted out coins. 'Jesus, Soph, you're going to break the bank with that lot.'

'I'm not going without crisps.' She set her basket down and McCulloch rang up the goods and stacked them in paper bags.

'How long you here?' he said.

'Three weeks, me,' she said. 'A month, Will. Our prof till February. Nicola Gilroy?' She looked at him for any recognition, and indicated the books he sold. There were photographs of the collaborators, cheap and outdated guides to their sites. There were speculative and absurd New-Age ruminations.

'I don't keep up,' McCulloch said.

When the young woman opened the door the buzzer stayed silent again. 'Thanks,' she said. 'Maybe see you.'

'Elam's the only town, so maybe. There's a club, ChatUp, up on Tolton.' He pointed the direction. He knew they were wondering what an unkempt man in his fifties who ran a store like this could have to tell them about clubs. 'The best bar's Coney Island. Two minutes from here. I'll get a round in. Make up for the groceries.'

When they were gone he checked the books himself. Only two contained indices, and neither listed any Gilroy.

McCulloch stood at his entrance and looked south down the slope to the main square. The sky was still light but the dim neon of the old town was coming on. The municipality had just switched over to the winter schedule and, for a few weeks, the streetlights would start to glow pointlessly early. The streets of Elam were filling with fishermen coming up from the harbour, office workers ascending toward the parks to catch the late strong-smelling flowers.

Beyond his shop's friendly competitors, beyond the amusement arcade which had started its early evening *whoomp*ing as it filled with kids taking off their school ties, beyond the edge of the town, was a fringe of dark vegetation where the ground grew steeper, on the slopes of the volcano.

The signs in the bar that read CONEY ISLAND were in a different font from NUTS! BEER! VODKA! and those that pointed out toilets. McCulloch pushed his way between loud groups and found Cheevers just as Cheevers saw him and waved McCulloch over to the corner where he drank.

As he did most days, Cheevers wore a dark suit more expensive than most on the island. He was only a little older than McCulloch, and similarly greying and heavy. They enjoyed their disparity – the shrewd, well-dressed lawyer and the shabby store-keeper, alcohol buddies alike and unalike enough to bring to mind two versions of the same man from alternative timelines.

Cheevers sat with a trim, pale man. He was forty-something, and his lumberjack shirt was too young for him. 'So?' he was saying to Cheevers as he blinked over a whiskey. 'Is the landlord some displaced New Yorker or what?' He moved to let McCulloch sit.

'I'll let this old lag explain,' Cheevers said. 'John McCulloch, Daniel Paddick. John knows this place pretty well. For an outsider.' An old riff. *Island-born, some of us. Not like Johnny-McCulloch-come-lately.*

'Used to be a strip joint,' McCulloch said. 'Signs used to say *Cunny* Island.' He looked to see if Paddick understood. 'When Jay took over and cleaned it up he only changed the letters he had to.'

'That's classy,' said Paddick. 'How often are people disappointed? Here for cunny?'

'You'd have to have a pretty old guidebook,' said McCulloch. 'Why? Were you . . . ?'

Paddick smiled, took the tease and bought a round.

'You're from London?' he said to McCulloch.

'That obvious?'

'Your mate busted you. Although yes. You've hung on to the accent impressively.'

'I swear it's got stronger,' Cheevers said.

'Stepney,' McCulloch said. 'Long time ago. Wanted out but I'm too thick to learn a new language and too lazy to change money.' The island was technically independent, an imperial throwback.

'When was this?'

'Since way before the new digs. Wondering if that's what brought me?' McCulloch shook his head. 'That your business?'

Paddick nodded. 'I'm an archaeologist. You must get sick of us all.'

McCulloch shrugged. 'Pays my rent. I met your students. Banto, is it?'

'No,' Paddick said. He glanced away. 'That's another lot. I'm in Free Bay.'

'Right. I heard about that. I didn't know about them others.'

'Totally different. Different institution. Different dig, methods, aims. Everything. Last minute. I don't think either of us was expecting to overlap.'

There were always teams at work, mostly around Free Bay and the temple at Miller, where a permanent encampment of excited scholars dug out pillars in a field surrounded by ill-tempered commuters on a ring road. That hadn't been the case when McCulloch moved to the island almost three decades before. Few Britons – or anyone – had heard of it then, which of course had been much of the draw for him. When the second wave of investigations began, the new attention had troubled him.

The island had filled with visitors. Its permanent population had increased. The capital had spread out.

But as it turned out, not by much. For a tiny not-rich place, its local authorities had always been restrained about monetising the remains, and the new times had not substantially altered that caution. Digs, development and tourism were all controlled: the chamber of commerce constantly complained. Elam was only a little larger than it had been when McCulloch immigrated.

Paddick was gazing into his drink. 'Who was it told you about Banto?'

McCulloch and Cheevers glanced at each other. 'Tall girl. Short quiet lad. Came into my shop. I suppose you all know each other—'

'Well,' Paddick said. He finished his drink. 'It's a big enough island.'

When he went to piss, Cheevers clicked Paddick's glass in his absence, then McCulloch's. He raised an eyebrow.

'What was that about?' he said. 'A nerve has been touched.'

'Academics,' McCulloch said. 'Hate each other worse than lawyers.'

'How dare you, sir? I'm curious. Oh, for a sprinkling of the old sodium pentothol.' Cheevers mimed opening a compartment on his signet ring and pouring something into Paddick's glass.

'Curtain-twitcher,' McCulloch said. Cheevers raised an eyebrow.

'Leave it out,' Cheevers said in a dreadful London accent. 'You're the nosiest chap I know.'

'Objection,' said McCulloch. They sometimes played each other's caricature like this, barrow-boy and silk.

A petrol-station-cum-store marked the centre of Banto. There was no town, only a scattered stretch of squalid little farms over acres of dry land and dusty growth.

'I heard there was a dig somewhere,' McCulloch said to the cashier and she showed him on a map. He drove another five miles toward the volcano. It was a bright day and the long-cold cone was languid, framed by clouds and scattered with late blooms. Rooks went back and forth above the slope, intrigued by something. Under a red plastic arrow a sign read DIG.

There was a track between trees, and where it ended there were three big tents pitched by two cars. Some distance away was the kind of flat-bottomed pit with which McCulloch, an islander even if not by birth, was familiar.

A security guard with the broken nose of a fighter approached.

'I was looking for Sophie,' McCulloch said.

'Sophia.' She emerged from a tent and corrected him. She frowned to see him and for the first time McCulloch considered how it might seem to her, for him to have overheard her name, and to have come looking. He was embarrassed.

The young man Will came into view behind her. McCulloch was relieved. 'Good,' he said as the guard wandered away. 'I was hoping I'd find you two.'

Behind them a second young woman came out. Her clothes were muddy and her hair was tied up in a headscarf. It looked like Rosie the Riveter's.

'Why're you here?' Sophia said.

'Just curious,' McCulloch said. 'I couldn't find anything out about this place. And I was up this way and I saw the sign and I thought I'd give it a punt.' He saw Sophia hesitate. 'I can go. It's just I'm here now, and I know you have to do education outreach and that. I could be like a check box for you. And I'll knock something off on future groceries.'

Sophia smiled. It's a small place, he imagined her thinking. We need to get on with the locals. 'Give me a minute,' she said. She headed for the pit.

'You working here too?' McCulloch asked the other woman.

'I'm Charlotte. I'm with the opposition.'

'Paddick?'

She nodded. 'But I've known Soph since we were at York, so I drove over to say hi. Easier than her coming to me.' She grinned, all freckles and dust.

Sophia came jogging back. 'Prof's up to her elbows,' she said.

'But I can show you something.' She led him toward the tents. 'You know about the preservation process?'

As if he could live here and not.

Brickwork, pillars, channels had always protruded from the island's undergrowth and dirt, but it was only in the nineteenth century that the amateur excavations of a local platoon's commander uncovered a mosaic floor that intrigued specialists and scholars. They came, elbowing aside the disgruntled descendants of British soldiers, shipwreck survivors and convicts who eked out a living on the slopes.

The only known antique reference to the catastrophe was an aside by Tacitus – 'The island caught fire. The gods neither loved nor despised those farmers.' Volcanologists said the mountain had been silent for many lifetimes before the eruption, and for the almost two millennia since. There were no eyewitness accounts, no survivors' testimonies – what escape had there been, from this tiny remote place? It was from the Younger Pliny's descriptions of Vesuvius that writers borrowed images of burning darkness, a tree of smoke, of locals in their agoras choking in gases from under ground, of the pyroclastic flow.

A slurry of burning ash and rock had gushed through the townships and temples and boiled the sea. It had left buildings standing, random artefacts carbonised and whole.

When they dug, the archaeologists found holes. Burrows without entrances. For years they simply cracked them open and picked out bones and bits within until, in 1863, they got word that Giuseppe Fiorelli had poured gesso into a similar air pocket of Pompeii, and let it set.

There was a first time that the earth was scooped away from plaster, when the ground gave birth to someone dead.

Bodies had rotted leaving charnel foundations, spaces in the shapes of anguish. Hunkering deaths, the pugilist poses where cooking sinews had clenched. Anti-corpses made by plaster into figures like bones. Even the shapes of their cries were preserved.

After Pompeii, the island.

The hollows left by the preserved dead underfoot were filled, their plaster forms uncovered. Women, men, children, dogs and cats, domesticated bears in the ruins of dwellings. Now they lay in the island's museums, in the visitors' centre at the largest dig.

Sometimes casts were lifted gently onto planes for overseas exhibitions with titles like 'The Other Pompeii'. The most famous figures were named for their dead poses: the Lovers; Defiant Boy; the Runner.

In 1985 McCulloch had seen them in the British Museum. That had nothing to do, he always insisted, with the choice he made later, to live in Elam.

'We're still using pretty much the same techniques as always,' Sophia said. Even guarded at his presence, McCulloch could see she was excited. 'Sort of. But the prof— Well.'

She unzipped the door to the larger tent, and McCulloch went in and blinked in the red brightness of the sun through the canvas. It smelled of sweat. In each of the four sides was a clear plastic window covered by curtains.

Something shone and glinted on the canvas floor.

McCulloch was looking at a half-man. A cast, like those he had seen many times, a person with his arms outstretched, his mouth open below the holes of his eyes. His body ended at his waist, abruptly, but that was not what made McCulloch gasp.

The shape was not dirty pitted plaster. It was transparent as crystal or glass.

The surface of the cast looked polished, but it was studded

with pebbles. There were smears of dirt within its substance. Matter swept up and embedded, muck in suspension.

McCulloch got to his knees. To look closer. Light refracted through the body.

'We're trying a new process,' Sophia said. 'It's a kind of resin instead of plaster. When we find a hole we pour in two chemicals and when they mix they react and get harder and harder. Then two, three days later, you've got this. Don't touch it.'

'Wasn't going to,' McCulloch said.

'Eventually you should be able to, that's part of the point. It's tougher than plaster, and it isn't porous. But we're still getting it right. Different mixes, different set times.'

He wanted to run his hands over the shiny clear face. He wanted to put his eyes right up to the clear hole eyes and look through them.

'We don't know what happened to his legs,' Sophia said.

The figure glowed. Perhaps he had died incomplete like this. Or perhaps long after he was gone, crumbling earth had filled the leg holes and eradicated half of him. Matter absenting him.

'Hello.'

McCulloch stood and turned at the new voice.

There was a woman in tall and straight-backed silhouette in the tent entrance, brushing dust from her hands. Her hair was tied back but it escaped in wisps of black and grey. She stepped into the red light of the tent so McCulloch could see her face.

Nicola Gilroy was a few years younger than he. She regarded him with sullen and mournful courtesy. Her eyebrows were raised, her head tilted back, emphasising craggy features, a Roman nose. She was covered in dirt.

'Prof,' said Sophia. 'I hope it's ok, I just—'

'It's fine.' She made an effort to smile. Her voice was thin enough to be a surprise. 'I gather one has you to thank for the crisps.'

'I'm McCulloch,' he said. 'Hope you don't mind me stopping. I've lived here donkey's years and I didn't know there was a dig.'

'Yes, well. This is recent,' Gilroy said. 'Trowels on the ground cross-referenced with satellite images.'

'When'd you find it?' McCulloch said.

'I didn't. They brought me in. New methods for a new find.'

McCulloch wanted to turn and stare at what she'd brought out of the earth.

'Was this a temple or what?'

'We don't know yet.'

'It's beautiful. The statue.'

'It isn't quite a statue,' she said.

'Fair play. You looking for something specific?' he said.

Gilroy did not answer. As if he didn't know.

Cheevers met McCulloch at the cheaper of Elam's two cinemas. The programme had changed from the one advertised, and neither wanted to see the detective movie now showing. They went instead for tapas across the way.

McCulloch told Cheevers what he had seen.

'Did some googling,' he said. 'Turns out she's not the first to try resin. There's a Lady of Oplontis in Pompeii. You can make out bones and whatnot in her, clumped at the bottom. But she's like wax or dirty amber or something. This one was completely clear.'

'So why's Paddick still using plaster?' Cheevers said. 'Assuming he is. Why's anyone?'

'He is. Everyone is. That's what that kid Charlotte told me.

Gilroy's stuff's experimental.' He rubbed thumb and forefinger together. 'Plus plaster's cheaper.'

'*Terra incognita*,' Cheevers said. 'Although, the *terra's* always *cognita* enough, I suppose. What isn't is the lost body. The *perdidi corpus*? It's the hole that's unknown. *Cavus incognita*?'

McCulloch snorted.

For the first few years of his island life he had not known Cheevers. Given Elam's size, and that Cheevers was hardly unobtrusive, this later came to seem surprising to him. Their association began when McCulloch tried to buy property, a small lockup in the town's outskirts, and discovered that local laws meant he might have to disclose his criminal record.

His crimes had been those of a rough London youth, not shocking, though they had not been trivial. There was a possibility that his application might be declined. This was what troubled him, more than shame. He did not believe he wanted secrets for their own sakes, but he did not want to lose the opaque past he'd granted himself.

He'd found Cheevers in the phone book. McCulloch never cared what loopholes Cheevers had manoeuvred, but he had been able to buy his property in the end. Even now, only those to whom he'd chosen to disclose it knew his record.

Two weeks after the conclusion of their business, he'd met Cheevers again by chance, in a bar. McCulloch bought him a drink and told Cheevers that his non-judgemental, cheerful glee in the information he'd disclosed had initially horrified and now interested him.

'This isle is full of secrets as well as noises,' Cheevers said. McCulloch responded with, 'Sweet airs.' It was obvious that Cheevers didn't expect him to get the reference, that he'd made it only for his own pleasure, but he was delighted when McCulloch surprised him.

What they later came to agree was that the isle was full of noisy secrets. They bantered and played at gossip. A complicated game.

There was no one to whom McCulloch was closer, he supposed, but he didn't inform Cheevers, for example, when he was engaged in one of his infrequent and brief sexual relationships. The men barely discussed their own lives.

McCulloch wasn't invited to the funeral of Cheevers' wife, and he was neither surprised nor offended.

They were eating dessert when the film ended. McCulloch looked up to see Sophia and Will come out of the cinema with Charlotte and two young men he did not recognise. He waved them over.

'My friend Cheevers,' he introduced them. 'Best lawyer on the island.'

'A low bar,' said Cheevers. '*Bar*. Boom-boom. How was the film?' He leaned too close and Charlotte shifted away.

'Rubbish,' said Will.

'We suspected it,' Cheevers said. 'Hence our repast. Get drunk with us.' He poured bad wine.

'We're going to go dancing,' Sophia said. She looked at McCulloch. 'We're going to ChatUp.'

'You lot allowed to fraternise?' McCulloch said.

'Oh, don't you start,' said a young man. 'We're doing charity, letting Soph and Will hang out with us.'

'We're cutting-edge, mate,' Will said. 'You stick to your stone-age ways.'

'Seriously, though, isn't she a bit of a nightmare?' Charlotte said.

'No,' Sophia said. 'She's ace. It's just there's only three of us so it's a ton of work. She's sure there's more stuff down there.'

'She's been wrong before.'

'Not that it's even her dig,' someone said.

'Don't *you* start,' said Sophia.

'What's with her and Paddick?' McCulloch said. The students looked at each other.

'Why are you so interested?' Will said quietly.

'He just doesn't like her,' said Sophia. '*She* barely knows *he* exists.'

'This sounds like the first act of a terrific romantic comedy,' said Cheevers. '"Dig In." Or "Collaborators". Bit melancholy, that, perhaps.'

'I don't think they're going to be snogging in Act Three,' Charlotte said. 'Paddick reckons Gilroy's going nowhere. Not just because he's not a fan of the magic goo. The whole project. He said she's even more of a flake in private.'

'They worked together back in the day?' someone said. Another bottle of red wine arrived.

'Yeah, that's how he knows.'

'Everyone worked with everyone once,' Will said. 'And they all compete too.'

'And she wins,' said Charlotte. 'Sharp elbows.'

'Come on, hardly, look how many of you there are.'

'Yeah, but she got his spot.'

They were not raucous but the wine made them louder and they attracted attention. The phone of one of Paddick's students sounded and he stood and took the call, a few steps away. McCulloch glanced up: it was expensive to get coverage on the island.

There was a strong moon. Insects bothered the restaurant's coloured lights. The dead volcano sat sulking, hunch-shouldered.

'I only saw the one thing,' McCulloch said. 'Looked good to me.'

'Yeah but,' Charlotte said. 'Just because her stuff's going to get turned into more postcards . . .'

'Oh, come on,' Sophia said. 'You know it's not just about making it pretty. You can't see through plaster. We're supposed to be looking *for* things.'

'For what?'

The boy came back. He rapped on the table so everyone looked at him. His eyes were very wide.

'We have to go,' he said. His voice was strained.

'What is it?' said Charlotte. Then: 'Oh my God.'

'They found one.'

'Oh my *God*.'

The students put their hands to their mouths.

'No!' Sophia said. 'Congratulations!'

'We have to go,' the young man said. He blinked at Cheevers and slapped his pocket. 'Can we . . . ?'

'Absolutely not,' said Cheevers. 'May we ask what's been found?'

But all of Paddick's group were already shouting, 'Thank you!' and running into the dark street.

'Are they alright to drive, do you think?' Cheevers said.

'Prof's going to hear,' Sophia said to Will. 'She probably already has. Shit.' She looked excited and angry.

'We better go too,' Will said.

'I'm glad I'm a bit pissed, to be honest,' Sophia said. 'Thanks for the booze. Come on, boy: let's go face it.'

Cheevers and McCulloch sat alone and in silence.

'Well now,' Cheevers said eventually. 'I doubt there's much question as to what was just unearthed.'

'That's a big deal,' said McCulloch. 'Been a fair old while.' He pursed his lips. 'Be nice to see. Take tomorrow morning off? Be at mine at six?'

'Six? *Leave it out*. Why would I do such a thing?'

'Don't you want to see? How long's it been? They're going to be up all night dealing with it. Perfect: they'll be in no state to turn us away.'

Free Bay was a tiny working harbour. Yards out from the field where Paddick's team worked, little boats coughed soot. People had heard rumours: when McCulloch and Cheevers arrived at the dig the next morning there was already a small group of townspeople by the site.

This dig's security comprised a much larger operation of freelancers and island police than Gilroy's. They were not trying to get rid of the crowds, just to keep them behind temporary barriers.

'Stay back, ladies and gents,' one officer called.

'You're loving this, aren't you, Bob?' someone shouted. There was laughter, including from the policeman. He flicked his cap and came to speak to Cheevers.

McCulloch looked down a slope of crabgrass to where the archaeologists milled around a makeshift screen in the pit. He saw Charlotte and raised his hand and she waved back. He could see she was exhausted.

'Look.' Cheevers pointed. Will and Sophia stood on the side of the hole, near Paddick's team. 'Apparently Gilroy was here last night. Academic courtesy. Paddick showing her what they'd found.'

'Bet he enjoyed that,' said McCulloch.

The students began to fold back the screens. The crowd pushed forward to see. McCulloch stood on tiptoe.

Within the wider pit was a deep hole where muck and dirt had been carefully dug out from around a plaster figure. With the tenderness of parents, the archaeologists looped slings around it to haul it from the ground.

The thing rose wobbling into view.

It was perfect. Unbroken. Splayed in a pose familiar to Mc-Culloch, from images, from the island museum. A typical death shape.

Seeing such things in glass cases, reading the captions that described them, McCulloch had been awed enough. Now he saw one delivered. He had to hold his breath.

Its wings were coiled. Its heavy head lolled. The scoops of its great eyes were intricately moulded. There was the spiralling body, like something winkled from a shell; there its many limbs, outfolded. Its little hand-things looked as if they were beseeching.

The archaeologists laid a blanket on the plaster echo of the epochs-dead thing, as if to warm it. They carried it away.

It was almost two decades since the first such shape had been raised and dusted clean.

Almost immediately after that first, archaeologists had uncovered two more, and the curlicues on the temples of the volcano's lower slopes ceased to be decorative filigrees and were suddenly recognisable as images of these other locals. The peculiar dimensions of ruined doorways in the old town made new sense. The mosaics were no longer depictions of mythic visitations: they were simple realism.

All the island waters were sounded and explored. No one found vessels. Where the things came from, and how, no one could know. It was only ever on the island that evidence – conclusive evidence – of such coexistence had ever been found.

The creatures lay with the humans, dead islanders alongside

them. They'd worked with them. Worshipped with them, the scientists said, looking anew at the shards of illustration still visible, the extraterrestrial and the human at prayer together, coronaed, altar-top boxes glowing.

Another cavity. You never knew what, if anything, any such would surrender. The fourth swallowed a lot of gesso. They left it to dry a long time.

They'd peeled the ground slowly away from the definitive image of the Collaborator Culture. One of the creatures, hunkered against the volcano's murderous flow, the wing-like limbs with which it could not have flown but which everyone called wings, curled protectively around two human youths, one girl one boy.

They clung to it. They died together.

In Gilroy's resin, the light would have gone back and forward through the millennia-dead alien's shape in the most complicated ways. McCulloch could have rubbed his hand on its face and felt it smooth under his fingers.

Paddick was laughing by a cement mixer full of sloshing plaster, staring at his find with joy.

'This is quite the coup for him,' Cheevers said. 'What everyone wants but few are granted. He's been doing recon all over the place, applying for digs hither and yon.'

'Bet I know where else,' McCulloch said.

'Some chap in the ministry likes the cut of Gilroy's gib, I gather, hence bumping her up the queue. But look at Paddick. Revenge is a dish best served in plaster. Something particularly choice for him about finding it using the old untrendy techniques, wouldn't you say? And not in Banto, but in this most untrendy old place.'

'Gilroy must be spitting.'

'Those who saw her visit report she was a model of professionalism. Congratulated the team. Asked to be shown over the whole site. Examined the specimen with appropriate fascination. And with grace.'

Cheevers was engaged in what he called 'a dull swine of a case'. McCulloch did not see him for several days.

McCulloch was a man who thought himself content in his own company. He was always startled on the rare occasions he realised that he was lonely. This time, he did not have it in him to pursue conversation or sex.

There was a small cave system halfway up the cold volcano. He had visited it when he came to the island, and once since, years ago. A path had been cut within, with a rope to hold onto. A sign by the entrance explained what rocks and types of formations were inside, what species of bats. McCulloch realised he wanted to go back into the mountain. But he didn't do it. He did not trust that it was not some lugubrious performance for himself, some nostalgia for his first days here, or for a childhood trip to Chislehurst Caves in London. He would not risk it.

A few visitors came into the shop. He hoped one would engage him in conversation. None did, but after a few days someone phoned him.

'Can you come?' A young man's agitated voice.

'Who is this?'

'I got your number from the book. Can you come?'

'Will?' McCulloch remembered decrepit call boxes outside the Banto petrol station. 'Where are you?'

'I'm at the dig. You have to bring someone. Paddick's here. Him and Gilroy are going to kill each other.'

'What? Call the police.'

'I can't, they'll take her away, and— Do you know any cops? Can you send them? But talk to them first, you have to tell them, they *can't* take her, not now—'

The call ended. McCulloch swore.

McCulloch parked skew-whiff across the Banto path and shivered as he emerged into a cold, very bright day.

Paddick was by the dig site, one of his colleagues restraining him. He was screaming at Gilroy. She stood in unlikely smart clothes, her fists clenched. The terrified security guard stood between them.

Sophia and Will watched. She had been crying, it looked as if with rage.

Will ran to McCulloch. He hesitated as a thickset policeman hauled out of McCulloch's car and straightened his cap.

'Hensher's alright,' McCulloch said quietly. 'I've had a word. What the hell's going on?'

'Thanks,' Will said. 'They can't take her away now.' He looked back at her. 'I can tell she's got some plan . . .'

Gilroy saw McCulloch. He blinked at the sight of her fury. Her face looked bleached in the sun, and dust and dirt swirled about her business suit.

'What's going on?' Hensher said. He jogged heavily toward the confrontation.

'She's a fucking thief is what's going on!' Paddick shouted.

'Calm down. What's she stolen?'

'Yes,' said Gilroy. 'What have I stolen?'

*

In the red tent, by the half-man, was a new cast of clear set resin.

It was an alien limb.

It was small and intricate. The width of a thin human arm, its three joints extending from each other in contradictory directions. At its end, blurry with the slow motion of years of earth, was a mitt, a claw in scissoring intersection. It glowed like illuminated lucite.

Within the crystalline limb were facets, flecks of light. There were stones and the husks of insects embedded in it, too, and shards of metal, swept up, not fallen to what had been the bottom of the body's hole, or fallen once but risen again, suspended alongside those glinting colours.

Everyone stared at it. Hensher kept them back.

'She stole it!' Paddick shouted. 'Then fucked off in her gladrags to report a *find* to the ministry.'

Gilroy made a disgusted noise and walked out. 'Hey!' Hensher went after her. The silence within the canvas was strained. Everyone listened to Hensher remonstrating with Gilroy, and that she did not respond.

'Show them,' Paddick said to his colleague.

'Fuck you,' Sophia said.

'Show them!'

The other man looked pleading. He thumbed through files on his phone and held it up for McCulloch to see a picture.

'This morning we dug *that* up,' Paddick said.

Another cast, another of the extraterrestrial immigrants. It lay on its side, smashed against the wall of a ruined plaza. It stared toward the camera, a sad alien death in plaster.

The thing was missing one of its top two limbs. McCulloch looked at the jewel-like arm at his feet.

'See?' Paddick said. 'You see? She *stole* it.'

'You found that this morning,' Sophia said. 'She found this *two days ago.*'

'Yes,' Paddick said. '*After* we invited her to our dig. Where we'd already started pouring plaster into the hole. It's not enough that she snakes Banto away, now this . . .'

'Wait,' McCulloch said. 'I don't get it. What are you saying? That she stole a bit of hole? She stole a bit of your hole and replaced it with earth?'

Paddick looked at him in uneasy fury. 'Well I don't *know,*' he shouted. 'But look at it, look at the joins. This is *clearly* the arm from our body.'

'We found this,' Sophia said. 'Days ago. By the pottery dump.'

'Look at all that shit in it,' Paddick said. 'What's she put in it, bits of crystal?' he said. 'She's not a scientist, she's a fucking jeweller . . .'

Will said, 'This way we can see what's inside.'

'It's a *hole,*' Paddick said. 'That was once an arm. If there's anything inside it it's bugs and bones. It's not like we don't do X-rays, you know . . .'

'So crack it open,' Gilroy said, walking back in, Hensher behind her. 'Crack open your cast. To show there's nothing inside.'

If you broke it and ground it up there would be no specimen, only dust. Take a second cast of it before you did, to make another model, and all you'd end up with was an echo of a hole. Anything there ever had been within would be gone.

Hensher kept Paddick and Gilroy apart. 'You're leaving,' he said to Paddick. 'Do I make myself clear? Take me to your dig. It's that or I'm arresting you.'

McCulloch sat in his car. Will leaned close to the window to whisper to him.

'She's talking to the earth,' he said. 'She's talking to herself when she doesn't think we're listening.'

'What d'you want me to do about it?' McCulloch said.

'You want to help, don't you?' Will said. 'I don't know.' His desolation startled McCulloch. 'She wants me to do light analysis on those glimmers,' Will whispered. 'As if that's my field. Thing is . . .' He hesitated. 'I think she *did* steal it.'

McCulloch stared at him. Will nodded. Before McCulloch could ask him to explain, he backed away and shook his head.

Hensher got into Paddick's car and McCulloch started his own and followed them down the uneven path, watching the dig recede, seeing Gilroy jump into the pit in her unsuitable clothes.

Sophia watched her professor, her arms tightly folded. Will watched McCulloch.

He followed Paddick and Hensher back toward town but soon let them pull out of sight. After a few minutes he pulled over onto the hard shoulder.

The land to either side looked as if it had been cultivated once but long left fallow. He could see ditches and the overgrown remains of hedges and he could smell a farm. In the distance a large hoarding stood at an angle to the road. Whatever it had advertised had long been illegible. Sections of its panelling had fallen away and through the holes McCulloch could see the volcano. It was raining some way up the slopes.

It would be light for a while yet. He turned his car around and drove north, back past the turnoff. Into the foothills. Past isolated businesses: stonemasons; a cafe for truck drivers; an unlikely garden centre. It was some years since he had been in these uplands. The abrupt change in altitude meant that even

the plants here were different from those in Elam and its surrounds. It was not hot but there was something to the light that
put him in mind of a sticky high summer. He watched a cardinal
fly.

When the sun at last grew low, he wound a way back south
by a dawdling route. He timed his journey well: it was just dark
when he parked by the entrance to the dig. He took a pocket
flashlight from the glove compartment.

McCulloch walked the mile or so of path, his hands in his
pockets. There were two new guards but they were young and
bored and spent their time chatting and smoking by the roped-off
entrance. McCulloch stood against a tree and watched them,
barely even hiding.

The lights were on in the living-quarters tent. McCulloch
walked the site's perimeter.

He could hear Sophia and Will though he couldn't make out
what they were saying. He heard a can open and realised he was
very thirsty.

As he approached the red tent, McCulloch heard whispering.

The window was covered, the plastic curtain drawn. The spot
of a flashlight beam moved over the canvas, from inside. Mc-
Culloch moved as silently as he could, making sure his shadow
would not fall over the cloth.

He heard Gilroy within.

She spoke quickly, a long low monologue. McCulloch put
his ear close. Gilroy's voice went up and down with a controlled
urgency.

'I try every night,' she said. She paused as if at an answer. 'It
couldn't be any different now, it couldn't be other than it is. You
know that. Things are different than they were but still, they're
close enough to the same. So. Come on. Please. Come.'

The surface of the tent vibrated minutely from her words.

Her voice got quieter, and came from lower and lower down. She was crouching, or kneeling. 'Come on,' she said. 'What'll it take?' She whispered. She must have been whispering right down by the ground. Into the earth. 'What are you waiting for? I'll do what I can. Come on.'

Her voice grew fainter and fainter until McCulloch could not hear her words any more, only a beseeching murmur. Her light moved and, abruptly, coloured glimmers shone across the canvas like a constellation. She was shining a light into the resin limb or into the half-body, McCulloch thought, to make a starburst.

He heard her hiss with effort. She'd picked something up, he thought, something heavy. He imagined her cradling something.

All the lights went out. There were long, silent, dark moments.

At last McCulloch heard her stand and brush away dirt. The tent vibrated with the zip and swish of the door as she left.

Her departure shifted the curtain closest to him, twitched it a fraction aside. McCulloch could peer into the dark interior.

When he was sure she was not returning, that no one was nearby, he turned on his own tiny flashlight and shone the beam into the gap, right into the crystal remains.

A burst of light filled the tent. It scattered and amplified, brighter still than when Gilroy had turned her own torch on, so bright that McCulloch gasped and fumbled with his torch and turned it quickly off.

He waited, in agonies. But no one had noticed the glow. No one came. McCulloch sat on the cold ground and waited for his heart to slow.

*

On the island everyone was walking on the emptiness of death, the alien dead. Animals tunnelled without intent from one corpse-hole to another, linking the gaps with evidence of life.

When the resin became the default material by which the casts were made – as it surely must – McCulloch would stock up on new trinkets. His keyrings and dolls would not be white but brittle clear plastic. The factories of China would set up new supply chains.

Specimens would go missing. The plaster dead were whole or nothing: set them in an alcove to guard a room, but break them and all you would have is a stub like a knuckle, nothing into which you could stare. McCulloch told himself there was nothing appealing to a thief in such remains, and that he knew this because he'd been a thief once. The resin remains, though – cut one apart, shape its pieces and polish them, and the collaborators' parts would be jewels on chains.

McCulloch did not know who'd taken him to Chislehurst's tunnels when he was a boy. He remembered standing there, though, a cave. He knew he hadn't thought it at the time, but when he considered the visit now, he imagined himself standing in the space left where dead giants had rotted into nothing, there beneath what would become London.

Cheevers called him early the next morning. 'Meet me at the cop shop,' he said. 'Not the old town one – you know the one in Vanderhoof?'

'Course I don't.'

'Budley Road, by the covered market. Hurry up. Gilroy's been arrested.'

When McCulloch arrived, Cheevers was in the vestibule,

talking urgently into a payphone under the poster for a drugs helpline. He nodded a greeting.

'Just liaising with Hensher,' he said when he hung up.

'Fuck it,' said McCulloch. 'He promised he wouldn't take her in. And for what? She didn't even touch Paddick . . .'

'It isn't that.'

'What then? How d'you know?'

'I'm representing her is how.'

McCulloch blinked.

'What's your excuse?' Cheevers said. 'Why are *you* helping? That lad Will told me he'd called you yesterday, why Hensher softly-softlied.'

They met each other's eyes. There was a ghost of amusement in their urgency, a wry recognition of each other.

'Why you lawing her?' McCulloch said.

'Oh, because of what kills cats,' said Cheevers. 'As if you don't know. It was you got me intrigued, and it was the charming Sophia called me and got me over here today. She said the police turned up at dawn. She's still there, keeping an eye on the officers keeping an eye on the site.'

'Sensible girl.'

'Very. She'll go far. When they arrived they arrested Gilroy. For what, you ask?' Cheevers paused for effect. 'For *illegal dumping*.'

'What? What does that mean?'

'Well, it turns out that concoction of hers hasn't technically been ok'd by the Environment Agency. Paddick must've made some calls. Lord knows what strings he's pulled but he's managed to get her arrested under pollution legislation drafted after *Bhopal*.'

'That's fucking absurd,' McCulloch said. 'She ain't even leaving it in the ground.'

'Indeed.'

'Will she get out?'

'Oh, certainly. The question is when. They can only hold her forty-eight hours, but at this rate they might well.' Cheevers raised his eyebrows. 'For a departmental turf war this has turned unco' nasty. Look, I need to speak to my client, she's crawling the walls.'

'They're not going to let *me* in . . .'

'The chaps here aren't taking this very seriously,' Cheevers said. 'I know several of the officers, and they know they're being used. They've already let one of Mother Hen's little chicks in there with her, they're certainly not going to mind you being my assistant. Consider yourself deputised.'

Gilroy stood staring up at a window too high to look out of, going up and down on her toes. When Cheevers entered she turned and came straight to him.

'How are we looking?' she said. 'What's the situation?' She showed no surprise at McCulloch's presence. Will stood in the corner and tried to catch McCulloch's eye.

'You've put them in touch with your university?' Cheevers said.

'Of course. With my department and with Chemistry.'

'Well, excellent. I'm afraid they'll probably hold you a while. They can, technically, and someone seems to want to.'

Gilroy closed her eyes. She leaned against the wall and McCulloch looked at the profile of her face, her high forehead, the arch of her nose, as if they were rock forms. She startled him by speaking. 'I need Will and Sophia to get on with things. While we're waiting.'

'We can't, Prof,' Will said. 'Soph's there but she's alone and the cops have taken the mixes away and they won't let her do anything.'

Gilroy set her lips and nodded at some decision and opened her eyes.

'Listen,' she said to Cheevers and McCulloch. 'We found some holes yesterday. We'd already filled them before all this happened. It's hardening right now. I think this might be major. Can you help?' She looked at McCulloch. 'Will told me what you did yesterday. If that policeman hadn't been there I don't know what the stupid man would have done.

'Will, I need you to talk to the Ministry of Antiquities. My contact is Simeon Budd.' She said the name carefully. 'Sophia has the car?'

Will nodded.

'Cheevers, can you please take him?' she said. She did not seem to consider that he would refuse, and he did not. 'And you might put in a word to get him inside, if there's any difficulty? There shouldn't be, though. Will, tell Budd we cannot leave whatever we've found under there. Whatever they decide about all this bloody silliness, they have to let you dig it up.

'It'll be hard in a day. If I'm not there by then, Sophia's to take charge. Will I be there, Cheevers?' He shrugged and shook his head. McCulloch watched Gilroy make another decision. 'Don't wait if I'm not,' she said to Will. 'Got that? Take it out of the earth as soon as it's ready.

'Do not wait.'

McCulloch drove a long way back from the police station, via the seawall. He parked as close as he could get. He did not often come here. He stood in the low spray. It was not a vigorous sea. He could hear it slopping fitfully through runoff tunnels under his feet.

He'd returned to London once, for eight days, in 1993.

McCulloch would not quite have said he missed the streets of Elam, but on that visit he knew, certainly, that they were where he wanted to be.

McCulloch had taken a sour, troubling pleasure in telling no one he was there. None of the few family or erstwhile acquaintances who'd made strained efforts to stay in touch with him. He didn't like the satisfaction he felt as he walked, provoking something by going to his old places, marking as many changes as he could. *I won't come back*, he had thought, and he had not.

He'd felt as though, if he only kicked a piece of rubbish the right way, he might dislodge something great from beneath him. Remembering made him grow self-conscious. He returned to the shop at last, where Cheevers eventually called him.

'Our boy's not the most honey-tongued,' he said down the line. 'But he did his best and with a little help from myself I think we were convincing enough. It's obvious that Gilroy's already been very persuasive, and I most certainly want to see what's down there. I didn't pretend otherwise.'

His excitement was grating. McCulloch rang off. He tried to remember what flavour of crisps Sophia had bought. In the end he put one of every pack he had in a canvas tote bag printed with the spreadeagled outline of the collaborator protecting two human youths. Below the image were the words 'Can you take the heat?? In ELAM!' He put two flapjacks and some nuts and a drink in with the crisps.

McCulloch drove unusually fast into the falling night, up unkempt roads out of the town. When the weak old Datsun rocked along the runnels toward the dig, by the tents he saw police cars.

At the end of the lane Sophia was shouting, remonstrating furiously with the police, who blocked her passage to the dig and the red tent. McCulloch pulled up quickly and ran out to where five or six officers gathered before her, making calming gestures that were not placating her.

'McCulloch!' she shouted when she saw him. 'Will you tell them? I have to go. Gilroy's escaped.'

'What?' McCulloch said.

He struggled to reach her, shouted at her to repeat what she'd said. A sergeant took him aside.

'Do you know her? Can you calm her down? We can't let her go. To be honest no one knows what the hell's going on.'

'What's happened?' McCulloch said. 'What's she talking about?'

'Look, I don't know any more than you. Gilroy's gone. She's not in the interview room. We just heard. Don't look at me like that. I don't know anything else. No one's supposed to have said anything: for all we know this girl might be aiding and abetting. She has to stay put. Can you calm her down?'

Sophia let McCulloch lead her away. She was quiet – abruptly and coldly calm.

'He's been asking me if I've seen her,' she said. 'If I've *helped* her. What's he on about?' She pushed her hair out of her eyes.

She led him onto a spit of rock over which they could watch and be watched by the police.

'Cheevers is pretty hopeful,' McCulloch said. 'About letting you do it.'

'It'll be ready in a bit,' Sophia said. 'I told her she should call the resin process Gilroyfication. She laughed but like she didn't get it. You've seen it. The pieces. The light.'

Her face changed and McCulloch looked where she was looking. Led by a police car, two official-looking black cars picked slowly along the track. Two men and two women in suits got out of the front one. From the car behind came three students McCulloch half-recognised, and then Paddick.

He was in overalls – dig clothes. Sophia ran toward him and he glanced at her and away again. He spoke to his government minders and walked quickly toward the dig. The police got in Sophia's way.

'What the fuck's he doing here?' she shouted.

McCulloch grabbed one of the civil servants. 'What is this?'

'Who are you?' the man said.

'A mate of Gilroy's. What's Paddick doing? You need to hold him off, mate. You know Alan Cheevers? He's Gilroy's law. He's talking to Budd. This girl's going to get permission to dig this up as soon as it's good to go.'

'Is that so? Well, I've just come from Budd's office and that's why we're here. With Gilroy a fugitive there's a certain urgency, everyone agrees. Including Cheevers.'

'So what you doing? Let her in.'

'Oh it's coming up, but we're hardly going to let one of Gilroy's do it, are we?' the man said. 'That's why Paddick's here.'

Sophia hollered curses. 'Stop him! Fucking intruder! It's him you should be arresting!'

Deep in the dirt, illuminated by floodlights, Paddick and three of his students dug around a clotted-looking, muddy shape.

'That's ours! That's the prof's! She found it.'

The rough outline of a human body. It was not in the boxer's pose typical of those who died in heat: it lay fully extended like a diver. Its arms and legs were still hidden in the earth, hands shoved into a piled-up mound where something was yet to be uncovered.

'I'm begging you,' Sophia said. 'I know this stuff better than anyone except the prof. Way better than *him*. It's not *ready*. Don't you understand? It hasn't been long enough. You have to wait.'

Paddick cranked the lights up. He dug faster, scooping out ground from around the body quickly enough that his students looked alarmed. He started to brush the shape clean.

'That's way too hard,' Sophia shouted.

One of the ministry women remonstrated with him but Paddick paid no attention. He picked clots of earth from the body, he wiped it with a cloth, showing the clear resin.

What he was uncovering was a woman.

Paddick rubbed her midriff so hard one of his own students shouted at him. The arc light shone into the uncovered Perspex and the whole area around the dig shone. Paddick wrestled with the body, sending scintilla everywhere.

There was too much light. The gemlike flaws, the shards of colour in the body-shape glowed. It was thick with them. They were scattered through the figure, with the dead bodies of beetles and mice, little stones, the tips of roots.

Paddick wiped the clear face clean, and gave a scream and stepped back in shock.

'Jesus,' Sophia gasped.

Paddick's students gazed.

McCulloch's mouth went dry.

The cast glinted. The moment stretched. The vectors of the find like glass on glass, it was hard to parse the gasping face as a face, let alone a specific one. But still everyone stared at the harsh transparent features between Paddick's hands. The lined and angled contours, the aquiline jut of a nose.

Light poured from it. The thing shone.

'She's not *ready*,' Sophia said. Not loud, but McCulloch could hear her.

Paddick gripped the figure. One of the women from the

Ministry of Antiquities jumped into the hole and shouted for help, tried to wrestle him away, but he kept yanking hard on what was uncovered.

And the resin was not yet set, and the woman-shape started to bend at the waist as if in pain.

Paddick pressed furiously on the face as if to make sense of it. Those features, so precise, so familiar moments before, began to sink as if at a vacuum within. They distorted into an ugly and incomprehensible mask. Unrecognisable as anyone, and barely as a human.

The figure twisted. Light still shone, the glimmers glowed, but they diminished as the body-shape twisted and contracted like a toy on the fire. Its hands and feet stayed in the earth as if tethered. McCulloch could barely watch.

The glow of colours went out. The thing was not a crystal person any more: it was a horrible nothing full of dead bugs like currants in a bun.

The police went in at last and pulled Paddick away. He was staring, looking as if he had changed his mind. The hole filled with people struggling to rescue the find as it sagged.

McCulloch turned away and came out from under the tarpaulin and did not look back. He stood by his old car and looked up at a night with no moon.

'You fucking *bastard*,' he heard Sophia shout.

He breathed deep and tried to slow his heart and watched the constellations and remembered recognising Orion's Belt for the first time, in the sky over a London cemetery, where he, a wistful teenager, had gone to smoke.

For two days after the excavation McCulloch did not answer or make any phone calls.

The police announced an island-wide search. Gilroy was not found. Then or ever.

He spoke to no one. There would be stories of the professor's disappearance. They would become more and more embellished. McCulloch did not want to hear.

On the second night he went back to the edge of the sea. The quietest and darkest part of the shore he could find. He sat on pebbles with his toes in the waves.

Surely the flow must have pushed the dead into the surf, and cooked them. Set in the cold water while they mouldered into ooze. Surely the shallows around the island must be punctuated with hidden hollows, he thought, body-holes full of seawater and ragworms.

McCulloch did not have caller ID, so he picked up his phone at last. It had been three days. It was Cheevers.

'Where've you been, man?' Cheevers said. 'Have you heard from Will or Sophia?'

'No.'

'I can't believe we got there after all the confusion. The thing was more or less just a blob by the time Will and I turned up! But you, you saw it. I saw you didn't have to make a statement, lucky you. I think everyone involved has agreed to draw a line under this particular shitshow. What did it look like?'

'. . . I can't. I can't describe it.'

'They poured some solvent on it which melted it right down to get out whatever was inside. Right now they're arguing about whether or not Paddick's fit to stand trial. I don't think there's any way he'll be found not sane.'

'What'll he get?'

'Destruction of Antiquities . . . Maybe six months? We know he's got someone on his side – he won't go down very long.'

'Yeah, he has. Got people on his side. Just how curious were you to see that thing?'

'Care to expand?' Cheevers said after a moment.

'Ministry bloke said you agreed he should dig the thing out.' McCulloch could hear Cheevers' breath. 'That true?'

'No. All I said was it was urgent it come out.'

'*After* they decided he should do it.'

'That was a *fait accompli*. You should have seen them when they got word Gilroy had disappeared out of her cell—'

McCulloch rang off.

The phone rang every couple of days. If it was Cheevers Mc-Culloch did not know. He did not answer or check his messages, or go to Coney Island or do anything but sit behind his counter half the day and drive in the lowest uplands into the evenings.

Three weeks after the woman was uncovered and ruined, Sophia came into the shop.

She was dressed more formally than he had ever seen. Almost prim. McCulloch felt a wash of care that disarmed him. He controlled his smile, made it cautious. She smiled back.

'Wasn't expecting to see you,' he said.

'Come to say goodbye,' she said. 'I'm going to London tomorrow. Will's gone already. He went on Friday. Some of the others . . . Well, Charlotte went a couple of weeks ago.'

'Right,' McCulloch said. 'Good luck.' They were both silent, and after a while he grimaced theatrically. 'I'm sorry that it's all been a bit . . .'

'Yeah. You know they kept the half-bloke and that arm. You should go to the museum. They're there. I was talking to the curator, and she said they're going to shine spotlights through them. That could look pretty great if they do. You heard what they decided about the resin in the end—?'

'I heard.'

There was nothing toxic in it. The government had ruled that it could be used again.

'Remember?' she said, and looked at him closely. 'I remember what it looked like all the time. Don't you?'

'Course.' They were silent a while.

'You didn't see it after,' she said. 'I got up close. You were gone.' She shook her head. 'People are going to get used to seeing them cast like that. They won't look like jewels any more.'

'I sort of thought the opposite: that they always would.'

Sophia considered. 'That would be nice.' She hesitated. 'Thanks. It was nice of you to help. After the first time we came in, anyway.' She even grinned. 'If you count extortion as less than nice, then you weren't that nice that first time.'

'Who is?' he said. 'Sorry about Gilroy. I know you liked her. Both of you, I mean.'

Sophia met his eyes and her own eyes narrowed. She looked quizzical, almost amused.

'Really?' Sophia said. 'Oh, I think she did ok.

'And "liked" her?' She shrugged. 'Will was in a bit of a state afterwards, I suppose that's true. Me?' She shrugged again. 'I respected her. Learnt a lot. I don't know what you'd say I felt about her.'

She bought a keyring, like Will had done. A plastic figure of a dead alien cast in plaster. McCulloch tried to give it to her but she said no and gave him money. Sophia had the door open when he called her back.

'Hey,' he said. 'What was the other thing you found? Next to – the woman?' She said nothing, and showed nothing on her face. 'Come on, I was right there. That cast Paddick messed up was pointing towards a big mound of mud. Something you hadn't uncovered yet. Did you?'

'Yes. We hadn't filled that hole yet.'

'Were they not connected?'

'Good question. That's not a hundred per cent clear. When we did fill it we weren't allowed to use the resin, obviously, so we did it with plaster. Old school. We dug it out and, yeah, it was right up by where she'd been. The woman you saw. You remember her hands?' She held hers out as if straining to reach something. 'In the earth? It was like she wanted to touch what we found. If it was anything.'

'If?'

'Yeah. You can't always tell. That happens sometimes. The ground moves about, hollows appear just naturally. There are a million weird holes everywhere. You pour stuff in, you never know what shape it's going to make. What's going to come up. What we got was big and sprawly and opened out, like with chambers, and a bunch of what might've been wings and arms and legs, or might've been rat tunnels, or might've been nothing. Might've been just holes.'

'Did you keep it?' McCulloch said at last.

'Someone did, maybe.'

Fiorelli and his workers must have erred on the side of caution. After their first uncovering, they must have filled all manner of random chasms, made cast after cast of the shapes left between slabs of straining earth. They were doubtless all destroyed, those statues of impossibilities, spindly crevace-spiders, Giacometti burrow-people in plaster.

'Whatever it was, if it was anything, it looked like she was holding onto it, or trying to,' Sophia said. 'Holding its hand.'

She walked to the front of the shop. She could be wearing

any necklace or bracelet beneath her high-necked long-sleeved clothes. McCulloch looked up and watched her go in the rounded security mirror, her body distorted into something wide and shining.

'Even if it didn't have one,' he said. Even if there was nothing there.

Sophia turned in the doorway. She said, 'Just like she was holding its hand.'

The Crawl

A Trailer

0:00–0:04

Blackness. Slow, laboured breathing builds into a death rattle.

Voiceover, elderly female (A): 'We lost the world.'

0:05–0:09

Series of fixed-camera shots of cities destroyed, deserted but for wind. The urban images become interspersed with close-ups of wounds and dead flesh.

Voiceover, A: 'To the dead.'

0:10–0:13

An overgrown yard crowded with rotting corpses. They shamble.

At the furthest corner of the lot, something hidden in the weeds snatches a zombie and pulls it down and out of sight.

0:14–0:16

Young man (Y) runs through charred remains of an art gallery. A mob of bloody dead run after him.

0:17

Blackness. Sound of wet explosion.

0:18

Y has turned, is staring at a swamp of decaying blood, all that is left of his pursuers.

Voiceover, A: 'We're all prey to something.'

0:19–0:21
Interior, a broken-down shack. Unkempt men and women surround Y. He says, 'They were taken!'

A young woman says, 'By what?'

0:22–0:28
Montage of zombies. Some shuffle, some run. Every one of them is taken, yanked into the shadows by something unseen.

Voiceover, A: 'First they walked. Then they ran. Now it's a new phase.'

0:29–0:33
Close-up, a dead man's face. Camera pulls back. He is one of many zombies in a city square. They crawl toward the camera.

They do not crawl on their knees but on their toes and their knuckles or fingertips or the palms of their hands. They move at odds with their own bodies, like humans raised by spiders.

0:34–0:35
Director card.

0:36
A dead hand slowly lowers a gavel.

0:37–0:39
A schoolroom. We see the elderly woman, A, for the first time. She speaks to survivors.

She says, 'Life adapts.'

0:40–0:44
Voiceover, A: 'So does death.'

A lone zombie on the flat roof of a tower. Looks down at humans on the street. Grabs its own solar plexus with both hands.

Cut to humans below. Drop of blood hits one man's shoulder. He looks up.

The zombie flies overhead, descending, dripping, its arms outstretched, tugging its own ribcage apart and its bones and skin taut, making them wings.

0:45

A bat crawls across cement on the points of its folded wings and its stubby feet.

Voiceover, A: 'There are new ways to be.'

0:46–0:49

A man staggers in a book-lined library. A zombie clings to him with all its limbs, biting his chest. It stares at him. It is sutured to him. The stitches go through both their flesh and clothes.

0:50–0:52

A cellar packed with fresh corpses, knee-deep in oil. A fat nozzle descends the stairs and gushes, slowly filling the room and covering the motionless dead.

0:53–0:54

The hand continues to lower the hammer.

Voiceover, unknown man (B)'s voice: 'A different collective.'

0:55–1:00

A montage of crawling zombies, alone and in groups, in many different locations. Some chase living humans, some chase standing zombies. The crawlers tear their quarries apart.

Voiceover, A: 'The dead who walk and us, we're both a problem.'

1:01–1:04

A zombie crawls vertically, gripping the wall of an elevator shaft in ruined hands. The shot pans: human survivors stand, oblivious, by the open door one floor above.

Voiceover, A: 'Something's taking care of it.'

1:05–1:08

The dead hand touches the hammer to the wood at last. It makes a tiny click.

1:09–1:14

Survivors in an aircraft hangar, by a broken drone. There is growling. Dark smoke pours from the drone's engine.

Cut to a control room. A dead drone pilot watches them on monitors, blasts the jet with one hand. Pull back: he has been stitched spreadeagled throughout the room, a flesh web.

1:15–1:18

Y hefts heavy hydraulic spreaders. There are fragments of the dead around him. He whispers, '*They* didn't come *back* . . .'

1:19–1:23

Night. A factory. Its windows are lit from within and we glimpse grotesque silhouettes.

Voiceover, B: '*We* haven't got *there*, yet.'

1:24–1:27

Close-up of the face of the young woman who spoke at 0:20. She is newly dead.

Voiceover, A: 'What wouldn't rage? We're eggs that don't want to hatch.'

The corpse opens her eyes.

1:28

Blackness.

Voiceover, A: 'We knew it was war . . .'

1:29–1:33

A bridge over a river. Two zombies kiss so hard their faces distort as they shove into each other. Behind them, a violent battle between crawling and standing dead.

1:34–1:37

A ruined office. The clicking of a keyboard.

A young female voice off-camera: 'Someone's at work.'

1:38–1:41

A dark room. A group of long-dead corpses sit, quite still, around a table.

At one seat is a living man, shivering with cold. He pushes a sheaf of papers forward, as if for consideration.

1:42–1:45

A rocky hillside. Hundreds of zombies crawl into the entrance of an old mine.

Voiceover, A: '. . . Not that it was *civil* war.'

1:46–1:49

Night. Zombies stand motionless by a wire fence. Beyond it are rough edgelands that are rapidly becoming invisible.

Voiceover, A: 'Between the second dead . . .'

1:50–1:55

Close-up of swaying flesh. Pan back to show a zombie on the back of another, as if it were a horse. The shot reveals hundreds of the crawling dead. A few are mounts for other zombie riders.

The crawlers labour on hands and feet through scrub and trash, towards the town. We can see the wire, the standing zombies waiting.

1:56–1:58

Blackness. Title card.

1:59–2:04

Close-up, wooden floor. A decaying hand slaps down in the centre of shot. It lifts away and a foot replaces it, on collapsing toes, then hauls out of shot.

They leave a wet stain and crumbs of flesh behind.

Voiceover, new voice, guttural whisper: '. . . And the Crawl.'

Watching God

Nailed to the top of the tower over our town hall entrance is an iron sign that reads 'Every man's wish'. Below it the high stone step looks down a long cut of rock over the edge of the cliff into the bay and the sea beyond it, and consequently at the ships when they come.

Our town hall has two floors and the tower extends to the height of a third; it is by some way our biggest and tallest building. Every three days in the main hall we hold the market where we exchange clothes we have made or into which we no longer fit, vegetables we have grown and animals we have caught, any small fish we might have netted and the shellfish we have prised off rocks in the rockpools at low tide. In its other rooms the hall is also our hospital and our library. It is our school and our gallery.

Though most of the frames on the walls of the gallery room contain images, a few have quotations within them – some attributed, some not. They are handwritten in fading ink, or typewritten with a blocky typeface that does not match that of any of the machines on the isthmus, or torn, it looks like, from books, with half-finished phrases at either end where the page continued. Many of the older books in the library room have torn pages within them, of course, no matter how vigilant Howie the librarian is, but these have not been taken from any of them.

Like most of us, I had a period in my youth when I became deeply interested in the quotations, you might say obsessed. I read them all many times and considered which were my favourites. I liked 'I must deliver a small car to a rich Baghdadi'. I liked 'choosing the fauna of his next life'. One day I found, as do we all, a small gilt frame below a window onto the woodpile in which in small smudged print I read, 'Ships at a distance have every man's wish on board', and below it in smaller slanted letters, *'Their Eyes Were Watching God'*.

Adults do not mention this artefact to children but let them find it according to their own investigations. As is presumably intended by that restraint, I recognised within it the words of my town's battered metal flag with the tremendous excitement of discovery. For a short breathless time, I believed I was the only person who had made this connection.

I came to understand that it is from the assertion in that frame that stems our traditional attitude to the vessels that visit our waters. Certainly it is a metaphor, but we have tended none-theless to regard the ships as arriving at just the right moment to load up on those hopes and aspirations we have been accreting and nurturing over the days of their absence, with which we have just (we allow ourselves to think) reached a surfeit when the ships reappear, though many of which we'd find it hard to state. When the ships come into sight beyond the bay we feel our inner loads lighten and become aware how freighted we had become with jostling thoughts.

The vessels usually sit motionless in the waters beyond the edge of the bay for two or three days, lit up from within, their portholes glowing. When – it has seemed to us – their holds are full, they move again, up anchors and sail with our wishes out over the horizon.

To the disappointment of my mother and my friend Gam,

both intellectuals, I am not much of a reader. But though the library room was never one of my secret monarchdoms (what I liked most was to climb the bleached trees at the edge of the forest and take birds' eggs and empty them carefully and paint the shells, or to build hides with fallen branches and old nails), when I found that framed clause I did spend hours over many days hunting the spines in the library room. In vain: there is nothing by anyone called *Their Eyes Were Watching God*, not among the ur-texts in their hard covers, nor in the books of new literature written by townspeople in living memory and bound in thin wood and rabbit- or rat-skin.

The ships that visit us are of many designs. Some are powered by sails (the wind on the seawall and the cliffs has been known to pick people up and throw them all the way down into the water or onto the rocks, you must be careful). Most move by engines, venting exhaust as they approach the unfinished sentence. There are trunked, single-piped, raked, complex-stacked, split-trunked and combined outlines and vents. A few of these have chimneys higher than the masts of the tall ships, so they look like they will topple. Some are small and squat with flared smokestacks like those that front steam trains, of which we know from books.

Some of my friends like to watch the ships when they first appear, the only presences in otherwise empty water. I like to watch them as they get closer to the sentence.

Most of the oil paintings in the gallery room are of flowers and hills but there are some of ships, very bright things with skirts of foam, yawing jauntily. Those, it is easy to see, carry wishes. We have no cameras (Gam tried to make one from a diagram in a book but only made a box) but we do have some photographs also on display, most black and white and a few in a speckled and unsaturated colour. There are pictures of animals that we don't have on the spit but that we know from books, of huge cities taken from up high that look like ink-smeared blocks put together badly, and of ships.

You have to look closely at those photographed ships to make much of their shapes. Some are just dashes at the edge of water only a bit less grey than they are, some are black tangles, some look almost like cracks or mistakes on the lens. Some are like shadows come up out of the water. The greater the distance at which they sit, the harder it is to imagine them carrying any wishes with them.

I think *Their Eyes Were Watching God* was looking at a painting, not a photograph, to write those words. I don't know why every woman's wish is not listed as on board the ships too.

There is sea to the north, the south and the west. A few miles to the east you get to the forest and the ravine and no one can get past that. The ships always come into view from the same quadrant, following the coastline a mile or more out. When we were children we would wave at them but no one ever waved back that we saw. We have no telescopes though we know what they are.

Tyruss and Gam worked for a long time and made something that looked like a telescope, even with an almost-round bit of glass at each end, but when you looked through it it didn't make things any bigger. Some people like to try to make things from the books. Gam gave the telescope to me.

Mostly no one pays much attention to the ships. If you are walking past a neighbour on the cliff-walk when a new vessel has just arrived you might, when you say good morning, that it's a fine day, also mutter that this one has a particularly tall mast, or that it's a long one, or that it's flat in the water, but you would be as likely to say something about a nice tree or a flower bush, or as likely to say nothing.

My mother always seemed embarrassed when I talked about the ships – children do talk about them – and when I got a bit older I asked her why and asking her made her uncomfortable.

No one minds those few adults who do want to discuss them doing so with each other so long as they don't involve the majority who would rather not. Chomburg used to light big smoking fires on the stones of the beach when the ships appeared, burning bits of plastic and rubbish and wood and inedible fish, trying to make signals in smoke, so you would see horrible big globs of stink going up into the air and if the wind changed it made the town smell bad, so everyone asked him to stop doing it and, though with his usual bad grace, he did.

There are those who think that there are no people on the ships at all. We know what sailors are, but there may be none on any of these vessels.

Two ships have sunk in my lifetime.

The first went down when I was with my mother in the woods, picking mushrooms and checking traps for rabbits. I carried the bag while she carried me – I was little – and we came out of the trees and saw pretty much the whole town gathered in front of Misha's workshop, arguing excitedly. People started shouting at my mother as soon as they saw her, telling her what had happened and what they had seen. As soon as she understood she took me quickly down the path to the shore and we looked out at the sentence but by then the ship had gone completely under so there was nothing new to see, though I told myself there was more chop between the wrecks than there had been.

It must have been laying deep grammar, my mother said.

Then one cold morning when I was fifteen I was braced halfway down the cliff, trying to steal from a kittiwake nest. With a certain luxurious terror I was listening to my rope creak. I don't know what alerted me that there was something to see but I looked over my shoulder as best I could, out over the water. A battered steamer was coming towards us at a good pace. It was low in the water, and still far enough away that it looked like a misprinted image.

I braced my feet on the lichen and sheer chalk. The ship did not slow. When it abruptly upended I discovered I was not surprised. I imagine some unseen squib puncturing a hole just so, timed so that as the ship passed between the weatherbeaten promontories of other scuttled vessels, its bow shoved down as if under a big hand and the steamer burped black smoke and plunged under at an angle to come to a hard rest against some sunken reef or obstacle. Perhaps against the ship I and my mother did not see sink. There was a grinding across the water and with a resonant cracking the steamer's stern broke off and fell into the waves.

Over the next half a day the ship fussed and fiddled and sank more while people watched. It settled finally in a last configuration, jutting like an overhang over the scattered bits of its own broken tail that stuck up from the underwater rise on which they had landed. The wreck took its position in the graveyard place, among the other remnants: rusting humps of chimneys, the stumps of masts breaking the water like reaching fingers, flanks, decks, the keel of an upturned cargo ship.

These shallow acres where rocks wait below sight are the waters of the sentence. The dead vessels obtrude from the surf and discolour it in their new broken shipwreck shapes. Each is a word, assiduously placed, set to self-ruin precisely.

I spoke to Gam, who was one of those intent on decoding the sentence. You could often find Gam drawing on rough paper, marking the positions and shapes of the sunk ships from one or other point on the cliff or the shore, connecting them variously with scribbled lines, measuring the spaces between them and applying various keys. Gam was sure that, seen from the right place in the right way, the sentence would make sense. Once I saw Gam sketching from the town hall roof. No one was supposed to go up there. I promised not to tell.

Look, I said, they keep adding words. You can't decode it or translate it yet; it's not finished.

No ships have come for a long time.

Before this, the longest I remember without visitations was a little over a week, and it has been much longer than that.

For several days no one said anything. You might have started to detect a little anxious crinkle around their eyes when you said hello to people. You might have thought the wind felt a bit colder. More people seemed to me to be at Gam's station, standing out under the grey sky at the cliff's edge, staring at the sentence with more concentration than I'd ever seen before.

A certain panic has entered our days. You may not know you notice them, but all of us have had ships creeping almost silently – except perhaps for a very faint sound of engines or the crack of a sail – in and out of our vision our whole lives, and their absence is frightening. Though their presence has been a fearful thing, too. It is not good form to admit that.

Now that there are no ships people have started to talk – like children – about what they might be and where from, what they do. Theological questions normally avoided.

If they've been observing us, some are asking, have they

stopped? Have they got what information they wanted? Why have they never come ashore?

They can't, of course, is what others say. They have to be at a distance, to stay there, to have every man's wish on board.

There will be a meeting in the town hall to discuss what to do. Caffey, by a long way the oldest person in the town, says everyone is making a fuss over nothing, that we shouldn't worry, that she remembers a time (before anyone else was born) when a fortnight passed and no ships came. But Caffey has licence to say all kinds of unlikely things (she lives near our graveyard and likes to scandalise everyone by saying that we'll thank her soon enough, less effort to get her there). Even she admits that this shipless period seems longer than that other in her faint memory.

I will not go to the meeting because I know there is nothing we can do to bring the ships, if we want to, and all the talk of calling them that has started, of getting their attention, of invoking them, is foolish. I hope it is foolish because if it is not it is sinister or will soon be. Another two or three shipless weeks and the worst people in town will start eyeing the weakest. I will not go to the town meeting because I know it will be an argument between those with sense and panickers whose eagerness for sacrifice is unseemly. There will be one of the regular upsurges of rumours.

Instead of that pointless meeting I am going into the woods and asking Gam to come with me, to help me with a project.

I decided to make a start on a raft when I found the big clearing full of dead and fallen young trees. I did so always listening and ready to hide at the sound of anyone approaching, but I was undisturbed. To the dry wood I strapped big plastic containers that had once held water and were now floats full of air. I think lightning must have struck there, I don't know, but I had been working to strip and shape the blackened wood with tools I borrowed from Misha's workshop, and then strap and nail them together, and I had made a reasonable start but I had got bored and without either patience or expertise had stopped. I showed Gam what I had done and said I wanted help to start again. Gam made unconvincing cautious noises but got started immediately.

Of course I'm not the first person to build a raft, or a canoe, or a coracle. It is not allowed but people do it sometimes. Mostly they get found before they put out to sea. Sometimes townspeople disappear and the story goes that they rowed out and their craft held and that now they are somewhere else; or if, as is often the case, they disappear when a ship is visible on the horizon line, stories inevitably start that our lost neighbours are on that ship. Broken boats do wash ashore.

Gam worked out how best to tie the thin trunks together. I said the raft didn't have to be strong, or to last long, only strong enough to go out a way and back again. Gam asked where we were going and I looked in a way that said don't be stupid. I said that maybe what we needed was to see the sentence up close, that maybe that was how you crack it.

We finished some time after dark but I had a hand-crank torch and I was certain the meeting would continue into the small hours (it did). Gam and I lifted our raft, and each with a crude oar over our shoulders we hauled it through the fringe of woods and down a long route, away from the town (though its low lights still illuminated us through the bushes where it was closest), past fat pillars of rock and to the sea.

Every few minutes Gam would say that this was a bad idea and that we should not do this, not, to be fair, because it was not allowed, but because it was dangerous. Neither of us could swim more than a bit. I did not argue because I knew curiosity would win by the time we were by the water.

It was cold but not too cold at first and the wind was low. The spray slapped us like angry hands and made us gasp but that was all. We pushed the raft out into the low surf.

We were rowing for longer than I had expected. Even a few yards from the shore we were both quickly sodden and vastly colder. There was an almost-full moon but the diffuse grey light was impossible to do much with. It made the foam glow and it rose and fell and confused us. The currents were insistent and we were lucky that they seemed to want only to pull us straight back to the pebbled beach rather than across our route, so though we had to strain we did not have to triangulate or do anything except row as hard as we could through our shivers, directly out, until our hands were terrible messes. It was a very stupid thing to do and I am fortunate I did not die. Gam tried to keep our spirits up by talking incessantly about the ships of the sentence and the ships that visited. About the anxiety they brought. That surprised me: the sea was eliciting confessions. Gam admitted to hating the ships, which made me raise an eyebrow.

What are we going out there for? Gam said and I did not have much of an answer.

Bits of ship architecture began to emerge from the shadows ahead into the light of the torch. We bobbed between extrusions thick with shellfish and guano as I considered the slanting floors, decks, dissolving doorways blocked by weed in the black water below. We had not aimed for any word in particular, we could not have done with our crude raft and in the dark like this, and when we felt the nasty scraping of our underside against corroding metal we both started. We lowered ourselves carefully over the sides, gasping at the cold, and our feet touched down on the roof of some old ship, a roof that rose, a steep metal meadow of growth and decay on which I shone our light, out of the chop of the channel.

We pulled our raft out of the water and sat heavily on the metal rise as the surf sounded. Across what now looked like a mile of low water we could see the lights of our town and the ghost outlines of the cliffs.

When I had my strength back, I stood and shone my light around. We were near the apex of a pyramidal mount of rust broken by what had been windows. From the water a little way off jutted a bow like a whale's head. Beyond that was the side of what I think was a tugboat. We were in an archipelago of ruin, and between each corroded specimen, each word, the waters swirled in complicated microcurrents.

I wondered aloud if we should go on to another, maybe the tower of girders near the farthest rocks. Gam did not answer, was too busy staring into dim vistas of wreckage and gasping that we had done it, that we were here.

Colonies of birds shuffled a bit and a few of them took off but mostly they were untroubled by our arrival, and I imagined that they were used to things hauling themselves up from the waters to sun or moon a while.

Does the sentence make any more sense from here? I said. Gam did not answer but startled me by taking hold of me from behind and turning me around and trying to kiss me. I suppose I had known this might happen. I tutted and pushed and we wrestled for a while on the slope of the old metal. I shoved and Gam stumbled and trod on a decaying anemone abandoned by the sea and skidded violently and fell. Gam's head cracked on the corner of the metal. I stepped forward but I was not quick enough and Gam pitched into the sea and was caught up by the gnarly undertows threading between the wrecks and yanked under as if by ropes much faster than you would think natural. Quickly I pointed the light but I could see only swirls and spray and the black water, and a bit of blood mottling the last of the ship's paintwork, discolouring the remnants of a painted logo, of which we know from the books.

I probed with my oar. Water tugged it and I wondered if it had sucked Gam down into the body of this word, to go up and down its stairwells for a long time. I put my hand into the cold but I had no way to know what shards and sharp edges were below.

Gam did not reappear. I waited a long time. When I saw the lights of the town hall go out I pushed the raft back into the waves of the bay and rowed for the land.

I was only one person, with one oar. On the other hand this was the way the currents wanted to take me. I think it was about the same amount of effort and time to reach the stones of the shore where I kicked and pulled the raft apart to set its pieces adrift, before sneaking, exhausted, back to my house where I knew my mother would be sleeping.

People said Gam must have gone to sea, which I suppose was not untrue. Some wondered if, rather than by water, Gam had picked through the trees and down the sheer channels of the gorge, impossible and impassable as we all know they are, and had got to the mainland that way.

That would be enough to have Gam spoken of in approving disapproving awe forever, but on top of that some people are saying that it's Gam we have to thank for the return of the ships.

In the late afternoon of the third day after we paddled out to the sentence and Gam didn't come back, there was a sudden immense rumbling in the bay. I was not there but I heard about it from Tyruss, who was, who was looking sadly out to sea. There were a series of percussions and booms and the biggest wrecks of the sentence all lurched ponderously, suddenly, at once, in many directions. They came down shattering themselves and each other. Every word fell apart in water that was, Tyruss said, quivering.

When the submerged upheaval was done almost all the ruins were under the waves. Only a few protruding feet of a very few of the biggest wrecks were still visible. The sentence was all but effaced.

Some people thought it was an earthquake, some that it was a submarine, torpedoing the remains. There was a vessel there the whole time, they said. That explains it. Watching by periscope.

In any case, a new ship arrived that evening.

Most of the town were already gathered, as I was, gazing at where the sentence had been. There was a huge cheer and a gasp of astonished delight at the sight of the massive riveted ironclad that appeared, that looked almost crenellated with all its decks and radar dishes and such. It approached the hidden sandbanks and reefs closer to our shoreline than we were used to. We could make out more details of its topside. We could see no people.

Despite this new proximity there was a quality to the ship that is hard to describe, whereby it seemed even less in focus, even more like an imperfect reproduction, even more as if it were copied from a photograph, than the ships to which we were used.

Taking up a huge area on its flank was a symbol, stark and black and white and blue. It was the sign of a company. It looked like many letters superimposed, like several words, or a whole alphabet, printed on top of each other.

People did not take long to simmer down. It was twilight and the vessel's unfamiliar outlines picked out against a vivid red sky made us uneasy. Still, almost all of us stayed, many for hours, right into the night, watching the new ship, almost all of us almost always in silence.

Once again ships are visiting our waters. It is rare again for many days to go by without a new vessel powering into view.

They are still of countless different designs, but they are almost all now larger, newer, more studded with equipment we do not understand, than those ships we grew up watching. And every one is painted with that same big dense logo as was, and is, the first.

The second ship appeared two days after that first and no one knew what to do. Once again we gathered. Of all the novelties of our recent situation this one we all found the most troubling: that the new ship was churning straight for our waters, as ships have done for as many years as we have records, but that its predecessor had not yet gone.

Nor has it still, nor will it, is my opinion.

No one had ever seen two ships afloat at once before. In pictures in the books in the library room, in pictures in the gallery room, yes, of course, there are images of several ships together, there are seascapes and harbours quite crowded with them, with ships jostling all the way to the edge of sight, seeming to shove each other aside to get a better view. In the waters of the real world, though, we had only ever been visited by one ship at a time, unless you count those sunk for us, those surrendered.

The first of the logo-ed ships was at anchor very close to the last visible vestiges of the sentence and it was toward it that the new ship sailed, coming so close and fast that many people started to scream that they would collide, that there would be another explosion, but there was not. The new arrival, a long lean cargo carrier, slowed and stopped, its bow half-blocking the first vessel from our view, settling into the waters still unsteady from the remains of the old sentence.

Since then two more have come. A paddle steamer slapped slowly and inefficiently into place behind and at a right-angle to the previous two newcomers. A low stubby vessel followed it less than a day later, poking skew-whiff into the bay between two last sticking-up crane-tops from the earlier generation of arrivals.

None of them leave. They just pile up where the wrecks are.

I have a premonition that time will move quickly for these new ships. That they will not sink but that it will not take long before the first of them is a floating ruin, a skeleton, a series of shored-up iron ribs in a crumbling corpse buoyed up by its fellows. They are writing a new sentence, if the wrecks ever were, or are, a sentence, more quickly than before, in bigger, louder words, words all of the same brand, the brand of the new company, the company that has won control of this route in a hostile takeover.

This new carrier cannot speak whatever it is saying truly into silence, of course: whatever it is building to with the bodies of its ships it does on older wreckage.

I have tried to descend the ravine but I can find no way through the trees or down the rock face. I was not the first to decide to take a raft to sea and I will not be the only one who decides to go to sea again, now, in this new situation, to walk on the beginnings of a new sentence. I am, though, unless someone in the town is visiting at night and returning before the morning, which – looking at these new ships – seems to me unlikely, does not seem to me something these vessels would allow, the first to have decided to do so.

You might not have thought it to watch me, but I paid close attention when Gam fixed up the first raft and I have made another all alone. It is too cold tonight, I do not want to row with cold deep in me, but as soon as the cloud covers us a little and insulates us from the freezing sky I will go back out to the sand-bank, no matter how dark it is.

Last night Caffey and Misha and my mother said surely we all felt lighter now. Said no, we don't know exactly what's happening, but we know that there are ships at a distance again.

I think Gam was right. This is a drop-off, not a pickup. Ships at a distance come not to collect, but carrying freight. They come carrying fear. And it is our fear but it is not our cargo. It has been ordered and is being delivered on behalf of someone else. They bring it to be rendered. It is on their behalf that it will be rendered here.

The 9th Technique

The Precise Diner was on the outskirts of Rhode Island, near the interstate, at the end of a strip mall that had seen both worse and better days. The diner's name and its better-than-necessary food, its posters for vampire films from Turkey and Vietnam, the worn toys that filled its wall nooks, combined to ensure that a good proportion of its customers were students. They would come in and haul chairs from un- or underoccupied tables and crowd them around their own in large boisterous groups.

Alongside that young clientele, and the quieter locals who indulged them, were a few muscular men and women, all sitting alone. They were not many, but there were enough of them, and they were distinctive enough, to be noticeable. Each sat and ate and waited for something.

There was one woman who was clearly no soldier, as it took little in their bearing for her to gather the other solitary diners were. Her name was Koning. She was not old, though she wore her hair in a way that one generally only saw on the old, and rarely even on them these days. She wore drab clothes, not quite convincingly. She was heavy and heavy browed and well made-up. She had been sitting alone for a long time, watching everyone who came in while slowly she ate first a bowl of oatmeal, then at last a lunch of salad and pasta as small and as late as she could get away with without infuriating the staff. She was unique in the room in being a buyer waiting for a seller, a civilian hanging on for a soldier.

Every hour or so, a customer would come in and tentatively approach one or other of the soldiers' tables. He or she might glance at a picture on a phone, or a scribbled description, to make sure this was the right contact. The newcomer would sit opposite the waiting diner and whisper. The students never let up speaking and laughing loudly, insufferably, a useful braying camouflage.

At the quieter tables, the new arrivals would pass envelopes into which, with varying degrees of insouciance, the off-duty soldiers would peer. In exchange they might hand something over when they passed the salt (if their companions ordered food for appearance's sake), or nod at gym bags stashed ready by their visitors' chairs, or reach across the table and put objects gently in top pockets. The buyers would always exit quickly after such handovers.

Some of the shouting young must have been paying a bit of attention, but most were genuinely oblivious, Koning thought, watching them and the exchanges they missed. The symbiosis between those students and the sellers of illicit wares they thought of, if at all, as local colour, was, on the former's part, mostly sincerely blind.

The soldiers did not acknowledge each other. They would arrive, be ushered to a table at the room's edge and wait and eat while those who had contacted them worked up the courage to come in. Few of their buyers were local, and *caveat emptor*, they would think, as they hedged and hemmed and hawed outside and made their dealers wait, as they fussed about the wards and protections they suspected surrounded the venue, the investigators watching. Which there were. The Precise was a locus for attention, but attention quite unconcerned by such as them.

Koning watched many exchanges. Even caught one or two eyes, and dropped them again. At last, mid-afternoon, and the most patient of her servers growing curt with each offer of more coffee, each refill of iced water, a tall massive man in his early thirties came in, looked around, ran a hand over his stubbled scalp and nodded at her. He sat and ordered the special without asking what it was.

'You're very late,' she said.

'Go fuck yourself,' he said. Both spoke mildly. He ate whatever it was that came, enthusiastically. She did not look at it either. They eyed each other.

Koning pushed a book across the table at him. He picked it up, raised an eyebrow and nodded. It was an old leather-bound edition. *Gotto*, the cover read. *Lafcadio Hearn*.

'Classy,' he said.

'Instead of an envelope,' she said.

'Yes, I get it,' he said. He opened it and flicked through the first pages.

'He went to Japan,' Koning said. 'It's about Japanese ghosts.'

'I know who he is,' the man said, and added, 'Not just ghosts.' He looked closely at the book. You might think him a dealer. He thumbed more pages, until halfway through the volume he reached the point where they were painstakingly glued together, solidified, hollowed and made into a box. In which, though he did not open it to look, was money.

'It's all there,' the woman said.

'What if I want to read it?' he said. He sounded mournful. 'What if I get halfway through this book and want to know what happens next?'

There was more silence. 'Then you can take the money out and buy yourself another copy,' Koning said.

He grinned like a boy. 'Yeah,' he said. 'Philistine.' He closed the book without ever checking its hidden compartment or its contents. He put it in his bag, and brought out a small stoppered bottle. The woman glanced around and back at him.

'Should you be . . . ?' she said quietly, indicating the surrounds. He made a disdainful noise.

'Come on,' he said. He waggled the bottle and something tiny rattled within. The woman winced and took it from him. She held it up to the light.

In the glass was a clot like dark earth, finger-sized and studded, gnarled with tiny things impossible to identify, that did not look as if they belonged in the ground. She breathed out in reverence. Her heart was going fast and she wanted to keep staring, but she put the bottle away. The man continued to eat. Koning had expected him to leave.

'So it was you who got it?' she said finally.

'Me. I pulled it out. Right out of the box. I took it out.'

'How long have you . . . ?' She spoke carefully. She stopped, struggled and went on. 'How long were you stationed at Guantanamo?'

The man looked at her with some kind of inscrutability. Chewed slowly. After a long time he shrugged and swallowed and wiped his mouth with his napkin.

'Long enough,' he said, 'to go get that. It was a long time ago.'

Koning had mined the bulletin boards, hacking secrets, sniffing sources. She'd spent years on her investigations. She knew how to track things down. In this particular economy to be a shopper took effort and arcana. She could have made an informed attempt at identifying several specific transactions occurring at the Precise while she was there: these commodities were not anonymous.

Across the globe, in dark places of the earth, secret lairs were rarely caves of monsters or marvels but markets. Shops. The worst-kept secret in circulation was that certain activities invested items in their proximity with certain affects, effects and powers, and made them hugely valuable. And that thus it was imperative that they be sold. That, certainly, had been the case for as long as there had been people and things, but there were always fluc-tuations. The occult economies of charged items were always jostling. War had flooded the market.

Helmets that remembered the last sounds heard by those who died. Melted iPods pried from burnt-out tanks – if you could make them play again, they would infuriate djinn. What you wanted, the level and the type of item, would dictate where you went to buy. If you were doing business with a soldier in the eastern third of the US, the Precise was one of few possible venues. An illicit economy, of course, but equally of course one tacitly permitted. Like looting, like rape, so long as it was con-ducted within limits of plausible deniability, a degree of witchery, theft and fencing was a perk of service, and it relied on the black market in artefacts.

You have asked for this office's views on whether certain pro-posed conduct would violate the prohibition against torture found at section 2340A of title 18 of the United States code. Koning could recite the passages. She had recited them. Why would you not? That was what they were for.

There were ten techniques to run. Attention grasp. Walling. Facial hold and slap. A brilliant document. Yoo and Bybee, prophets without honour, martyrs and Crowleys of the State Department. Lists make magic, the rhythm of itemised words: you do not list ten techniques, numbered and chantable, in aus-tere prose appropriate for some early-millennium rebooted *Book of Thoth*, and not know that you have written an incantation.

Actions of unpersoning, and positions, deprivations, and the waterboard. Quite stuffed with fret, that last one. That was the locus of attention, in and beyond the mainstream. Abomination from one perspective, it was advertising copy from another. Koning could never have afforded that cloth, that first soaked cloth. It was, she understood, still wet all these years on from that first questioning. It could now do all manner of things towels wet or not had no business being able to.

But hidden, like Bybee behind Yoo, was a less celebrated spell. Behind number ten, the crescendo, that water, was the ninth technique.

9. Insects placed in a confinement box. You would like— Again these were the words of the lawyer-magi. Koning was never without the memo on her person. Quietly she read again the words she knew and emitted a bad guttural sound to speak the black redactions. She wrapped the bottle in the printout. You would like to place Zubaydah in a cramped confinement box with an insect. You have informed us—those plurals and the consummate second person, talking across time, addressing all the later scandalised readers of those pieces declassified in a brilliant act of exonerative amplification, making everyone complicit. All purveyors of the demand post facto, all part of the collective. This you have informed us, they whispered. You have informed us that Zubaydah appears to have a fear of insects. In particular, you would like to tell Zubaydah that you intend to place a stinging insect into the box with Zubaydah. You would, however, place a harmless insect into the box.

'He was crammed in there,' the man soldier told Koning. You have orally informed us that you would in fact place a harmless insect such as a caterpillar in the box with Zubaydah.

'That's what it was.'

A small room, a soiled and wet-legged man hauled away

without care. The confines of the chamber seeming still to vibrate with his recent screams. Koning imagined the man who was now gathering his money-stuffed and reconfigured book, then reaching into the box past piss-pools, reaching for the bewildered, peristalsising, miraculously uncrushed little government weapon in the war against terror.

'The little motherfucker cocooned up a couple of days after I got it out,' the man said. He was standing, pulling on his jacket. He made no effort to lower his voice. A couple of the other customers glanced at him. Koning waited for her magic pusher to continue. When he did not, she said, 'It isn't dead.' She looked closely at what she had bought.

'I know,' he said. 'No.' He held up a finger. 'I don't care what you want it for. I can see it about to come out of your mouth.' He smiled. He winked in friendly fashion and walked out, leaving Koning gazing at the chrysalis, to leave when she was sure he had gone.

Koning was a self-made expert. She snuggled what she'd bought in the nest she had made of shredded grimoire and scrunched-up rules of engagement. She watched it. It did nothing.

She tended it insofar as anyone could tend a carapace, hard outlines, inert edges. It did not have the look of something spun: it seemed accreted. From bits of things organic and not, a scab of metal and soil leavings. She strove for patience during the thing's slow becoming.

Metamorphosis is death. Inside a pupa larval flesh breaks down utterly, as if in chemical spill. Eyes do not become other eyes nor mouthparts mouths. All parts are lost in a reconfiguring slop, as absolutely formless as a salted slug, that *ex* liquid *nihilo* self-organises into a quite other animal. A cocoon is not a transformation pod but an execution chamber, one that doubles as a birthplace, and is parsimonious with matter.

Saturated with the specifics of Zubaydah's moment the caterpillar, or whatever it was now, was bloated with more than physical calories. Nurse that right, how could it not on its intricate and extruded emergence unfold not only new limbs, not only many-hinged jaws and paper wings burring with stiff motion, but time too. It shared its matter backward. Insects are echoes: that's always the secret. They are translations of screaming hinges into bug-body form, sound for chitin-point manifestation. Push a big door right, it opens in all its iterations.

The flea, the ghost of which Blake celebrated and traduced. The killer of Alexander. The jiggers that infected the *Santa Maria's* crew, exiling them on their ruinously invaded feet. How to reach through history to such as them, to all the insect bodies like holes drilled in time? How to yank at them and make changes?

Koning had a plan. Who doesn't have a plan? As if the power of insect time-tinkering in general was not enough of a draw. For her there was a scheme of lunatic and grandiose scale. It had for years had her spending family money on sideshow nonsense and impossibilities. A mention of the para-economy of war-wrought artefacts and a long chain of connections later, and here at last she sat, in her room, watching the chrysalis of Zubaydah's tormenting unstinging insect, waiting for it to hatch, to open into the insect road.

It barely matters what she wanted, though it mattered vastly to her. Something had gone wrong: something had got us here. Something had been – this was her wager – truncated. Insectfouled, interrupted, deflected to this insect telos. That she had bought, a first step to a fix. She wanted to reach down the opening it would hatch. She had a vampire to swat. A complicated long-gone politics to finesse. How, but down the insect road, could she tussle with the mosquito hungry for Lord-Protector blood, the parasites of which had spittle-ridden into the body of Cromwell, at last in his sweats to kill him? A complex ambition to reshape history, to tweak the development of the Mother of Parliaments, by nudging the date of a regicide's malarial death.

Koning stared for many hours at what she had. She would bend over the bottle, stroke its glass with her nail, lift it up occasionally, shake it very gently. She tried to resist the urge, to let it be.

She slept in her study where she would wake abruptly and repeatedly throughout the night and go to where she had left the specimen, beside the powered-down monitors and unused equipment to which she had originally intended to attach it. When she sat up in the small hours of the third or fourth morning of her ownership, she felt something very faint move across her face. When she turned on the light it was swaying as if something had pulled it back on its flex, and just released it. She stood underneath and though she could see nothing that might cause them, with every swing of the shade she felt more threadlike touches. She picked up the bottle, and pens, paper, bits and pieces that had been scattered around it on the table slid a few inches closer together underneath her hand, as if the glass dragged them a moment, as if they had been attached to it.

Was the nub within grown larger? She stared until she wondered if it was twitching. She held the bottle in her left hand, rubbing imagined fibres from it with her thumb.

She scanned her books of history and wrote in the margins of her many notes – equations, intentions, toxic algorithms. She went over all the mechanisms she had prepared. She had, over many years, carefully worked out the Byzantine ramifications, a cascade of causes and effects intended to extend the life of one long dead.

When she stood in the morning and walked she tugged her feet through resistance and small things rattled on the shelves as if everything was knotted together, as if silk spread out, right through the bottle, its glass made porous, and tangled everything. The chrysalis was bigger. It almost filled the container.

It was impossible for her not to become excited, not to feel her heart speed up and her breath come faster, but she strove to keep control. When she returned to the room later in the day and saw after a moment of scanning that things were no longer where they had been, that the stuff that had surrounded the chrysalis was now not moved but gone, she held her breath completely, to let it out in a slow gasp when she saw the bottle itself.

Its glass seemed to bulge, it was pressed so hard from within by the expanding matter of the insect's case. It was hard to tell, the pupa that stuffed the bottle was so compacted and matt and dark, but what flecked it might include the plastic of a pen now gone from the table, brittle chewed-up wads of lost paper. Koning bent over it again, for a long time, and when she sat back she gave a little cry and clapped her hand to her scalp. She lifted the bottle – it was much heavier than it had been – and looked for and thought she saw a knot of hair in it, in the stuff, a new knot, the colour of her own.

Can you do it? she thought. *What I want?*

Things kept going missing. The bottle grew heavier. The glass did not break and it did not bow or bend or inflate grotesquely as if heated and made soft but it was harder and harder to lift, denser and denser with shadow. It filled and then was more full, more and more full and with that repletion came more invisible fibres on Koning's face every time she looked.

She prepared. *Is it? It's now. It's happening.* She made her

118

tools ready. She sat trembling at her desk, watching the glass, strangely formal, into the night, pulling closer, watching, breathing shallowly and ready for the insect. Carefully she considered what she wanted, and what she wanted to do with it.

She reeled. Far-reaching as her aspirations were, Koning's skills were adequate, her calculations plausible enough, that the plans were hubristic but not quite mad.

But the bottle remained. The chrysalis would not crack. The caterpillar would not hatch, would not become whatever it was supposed to.

Days passed, remained unholed, her plan undone. The pupa was a thousand pounds, coiled in glass that should give. Koning stared and shook, her eyes failing to focus.

She must have eaten and drunk sometimes. Time. Weeks. The light in the room changed: the tree outside the window was gone but that could have been autumn shedding its leaves, a windstorm tipping it over and workers in a truck hauling it away. She blinked. The bottle showed her its dark.

There were no gauges to check. Her books and machines were gone, and all that was left was the room, the bottle and Koning herself. Once when it was very cold Koning turned, slowly, to look out of the window. Her eyes were burning. It was winter, and everything outside had disappeared.

Maybe that was snow. All the pupa would do, endlessly, was grow.

The Rope is the World

What do you want to see?

What is the nature of your enterprise?

When did you become aware of what the rope is? Well.

The Earth is a thin-spoked wheel. Its spokes are irregularly spaced: we must look like the plucked remnants of some bicycle ridden by a ragged girl or boy, if only to God.

For a long time in pre-pre-history these elevator shafts, these guy-ropes, spacewires, these towers, were impossible. They were a joke, an academic wheeze. A recherché thought-experiment. But one day, and abruptly – whether it was due to the explosive advance of carbon nanotube science, the augmented energies of the slippage engine, the de- and revaluation of American industry and the rise of the parabuck economy, or whatever – they looked possible. They were possible.

During the years of it's-all-in-fun what had been stressed were the savings the economics of lift would, theoretically, if-we-really-meant-it, allow. Initial outlays were clearly gigavast, but lifting one ton of cargo out beyond everyday gravity to orbit by elevator was this or that many times cheaper – some absurd margin – than doing so by rocket, by shuttle, by alien indulgence. Now that the space elevators, the skyhooks, the geostationary tethered-dock haulage columns, were shockingly feasible, research projects were all human-spirit this and because-it's-there that. As if, faced with them, the mere savings were as vulgar as they in fact were.

Equatorial nations, with real estate on that precise vector where geosynchronicity could occur were bullied, cajoled, annexed and wooed. The economies of Gabon, Indonesia, the several Congos, Brazil, Ecuador and Nuganda went behemoth with parabucks and renminbis toxic with intricate conditionalities and obligations. Twenty-seven years of UN-backed Ecuadorian martial law after preparing the first orbital platform with all kinds of fanfare (years which in retrospect really flew by), Freedom Tower, the first space elevator humanity ever started, that had descended splendidly and slowly over years, to Isabela Island in the Galapagos, opened.

It was redundant, of course. The technology at its centre of gravity, its furthest end and first part built, the base station in the Clarke Belt, was antique compared to that at the Earth, the last, when the extruded tower finally reached it. The shaft ascended in skyhook archaeology.

In any case, this, Freedom or Isabela Tower, the Rope, was the first to be started, but the third to open. It had been overtaken during its growth by towers built by a Chinese and US consortium respectively. Freedom Tower was born a freight museum.

It tried to scratch an income by reconfiguring itself, adding elements of a holiday block and folly. It was favoured by perpetrators of spectacular suicides. Depending on the level chosen a person could jump *to* and burn up *in* their death, simultaneously. Launching from over twenty-three thousand kilometres, the most flamboyant suicides could aim their bodies in eccentric orbit. Theoretically, they would continue their lifeless circumnavigation for ever, though much of the corpse-litter was cleaned out of orbit.

There were three, then seven, then eleven space elevators. Terrestrial bases, counterweights in space, moonlets or junk masses quickly known as conkers. And stretched between them, more than thirty-six thousand kilometres of columnar carbon and neosteel, to where geostationary orbit occurred, so the towers jutted straight up. From their conker bases little voidcraft pootled back and forth to the colonies, carrying payloads brought up on the huge elevators like vertical trains.

Ranging from the size of city blocks to the silkiest skyscraper thin, the tracks and reinforced columns, the unspeakable tons of matter, studded with windows, extrusions of opaque purpose, satellite dishes, cables and airlocks, rose and kept going. Up through the measly few kilometres of breathable air; past where planes flew; through the strato- and mesospheres; past the Kármán line where space is; past the space stations orbiting at their paltry three, four hundred kilometres; into the permanent night, adding the glimmers from their speck-windows to the light pollution.

Defences kept them safe from meteorites, radiation, the ripples from earthfarts. The Earth itself sat, sits, a fat wheel-hub with its spokes.

It's unclear what the watching extraterran emissaries made of all this. The Sab, the Posin, the Hush had arrived with various norms of etiquette in Earth's cosmic neighbourhood over the preceding decades, and proposed interaction of varyingly comprehensible kinds. Earth's trade representatives would point out the features of our space elevators, and by all accounts the visitors uttered alien equivalents of polite, uninterested *Hmmms*, like a queen visiting a biscuit factory. It's completely unknown how or if their own vessels exited their own planets' pulls.

The towers were – and are – named, sometimes, for their most notorious sponsors: The Real Thing; iTower; I Can't Believe it's a Space Elevator. Mostly though, what stuck was more generic. One was called the Beanstalk, one the Skyhook, one the Skytower, and so on. One was the Rope.

Between one and one and a half million storeys each, and

each with a workforce the size of a huge city. Thousands of kilometres of vertical track in those pressurised tubes; viewing stations; zones for education and recreation; guard and/or police stations; waste disposal engines and rubbish chutes longer than Russia; workers' hostels; engineering labs; tool sheds; little gardens. The overarching purpose was always to haul things up and haul them down.

The towers were freight elevators, and they had crews. Crews, very far from home, further from home than anyone had ever worked before, had their families join them. Their families demanded amenities, and so on.

That first, remember, Freedom Tower – Isabela Tower, the Rope – had been going bad since before it was born.

As useless as an Olympic village the day after. Crews kept the impossible white elephant up. A few romantics, sightseers, death-wishers and lost ascended. What freight travelled up it was that of owners who could not afford more salubrious towers, or who wished to avoid their more stringent security.

Isabela Tower became a grey operation, complicit with vertical criminality, pirate payloads, tax evasion, theft. Stretches of shaft broke down, so cargo had to be unloaded and shifted from one lift to another, at celestial junctions, throwing up an economy of stevedores and porters in the corridors and staircases, and the brigands who preyed on them.

Power failed on certain floors way above the troposphere, killing those within and marooning workers to either side between many rooms full of void. It was those advanced ends, at ground level, and on the orbital station, that needed each other. And section by section, over years, the intervening tower was – not decommissioned, but left to its own devices.

It is always startling how fast a generation passes, then another, and so on. And when more and more of the spacebound storeys failed, and went out, the lights, the heat, the oxygen? So long as the pressurised elevators could still travel through them, no matter how dark, or cold, or mummy-littered they were, those floors did not so much matter.

It was hard to relate to the fourth-generation welder, or cook, or whatever on level one and a bit million as a citizen of whatever state the tubes below her feet eventually tethered to, and on which she had never set foot. She was many times further from that country's capital than was the furthest spot from it on Earth. It's sad when anyone dies, of course, but to whom they belong is not always an urgent question. And there has to be security in place to protect the base at one end and satellite at the other from attack or invasion – or exvasion, too. The elevators must be armed, when they pass through those needy layered lands.

Other towers failed. Some moulder, deserted, more energetically emptied than was the Rope. One fell. Two were decoupled from their base-stations in audacious terrorist acts, a little carefully placed thermite that saw the vertical thread-cities suddenly and awfully yanked centripetally up from the Earth, trailing cables and spilling elevators and people, receding spaceward into dreadful orbit at speeds vastly too great for things so big.

Some continued in some capacity. The Earth is still an irregularly spoked wheel.

You do not know how they live, those on the levels where people still live, those of the 1.2 million floors of the Rope. These were isolated communities before you or your parents were born. We have only travellers' stories. You don't know what languages they speak, what they make or learn, to what they pray, what stories they tell their children as they look out of the portholes or call up external camfeeds and stare up at space, or down the perspective line of their shaft towards Earth as lifts full of foreign cargo rise and fall through their territories; how they mark it when those they love die; or if they are there at all, those people for whom the Rope is the world.

The Rope is the world.

The Buzzard's Egg

Good morning.

No? Are you still sulking?

Fine. Be sullen. It makes very little odds to me. I get my food either way.

Speaking of which. See how I light this? See how I put the right wood on it? How delicious is that smoke? I could turn my back and throw the embers over my shoulder at you and some people might say you deserve it, but I don't, do I?

You can see the day. I can feel your golden stare.

You don't intimidate me, looking at me like that. Keep looking over my shoulder, too, through the windows. Don't you think our hills are beautiful?

I know they aren't your hills. But look how the sunlight hits the orchard. You can see the paths where Sirath's been walking. I think that's his name. I'm not sure. The man as old as I, with hair as grey as my eyes. There aren't many people around us here. Sometimes I hear a shout, though, and he looks up. I think it's *Sirath* people call.

Go ahead, eat. I won't look. But do you see the rocks? By the overhang? Those gouges?

Priests and priestesses and soldiers and slaves came from the city – I told you, it's on the other side of the tower. A few months ago. They came with picks and took a whole slice out of the hill.

126

The captain told me a new power was going to be born in the city, out of the mountain.

I don't remember his name. The captain's or the idol's, or if the idol was a he.

Those are eagles. And those, there? Buzzards.

A buzzard and an eagle loved each other. They hated each other but they loved each other too, and the eagle mounted the buzzard, and the buzzard laid an egg. And the buzzard didn't sit on the egg because she was proud. And a dove came and said, 'I'm such a fool, I must have lost this, my child.' She sat on the egg. 'How much bigger my children are than I remember!' she said. 'I can see the sea from up here.'

Have you eaten? Will you eat?

Please. Isn't the smoke delicious? You mustn't get sick.

The sea's forty miles east. I've never seen it. A trader came up the tower once – I don't know why the soldiers let him – and he told me what the sea was. His daughter was riding on his back. She was a tiny thing, and I stared at her until she cried, and he bent up and down and said to her that he was a boat.

So. The egg broke under the dove. What was inside was a bird feathered with things like mountains and iron. It beat its wings and snow came down. It called and a rainbow came out of its mouth, I think.

Maybe you were there. Why won't you speak? Have I been disrespectful?

Will you not do anything? Everything's just sitting there outside. That's just the wind in the trees, in and out, up and down, that's nothing. Sirath won't pick his fruit today.

It's a long way down to the courtyard. Do you see the well? That fountain used to run. Water came out of the mouth of that animal. I could hear it, even up here. It was nice. But then one of the soldiers got drunk – oh some years ago – and he knocked into it and it didn't look like anything had changed but he must have bent its innards, because it never worked again.

He wasn't punished. There was no whipping. Perhaps his comrades covered for him. For a while mosquitoes bred in the last of the water. Now it's just stones down there.

I don't mean 'just' stones, I beg your pardon. Stones must be yours, back in your home, I think?

You have nothing to say? I know those shifts are the light of the sun behind the clouds.

You're like a child. I don't care if you're finished or not. Look at your bitter face. I'm taking your smoke away. I have things to do. You aren't the only thing in my day.

Be alone, then. Go on. Watch the day go then.

Don't look at me like that, it's just a cloth. It's dusty up here when the winds come – are they visiting you? Did you call them?

Not my business. I just think your face should be clean.

My hand's steady even though you're my enemy. Most people are afraid to do this, you know. They wouldn't touch you.

It's nothing. Look at you: you should shine.

I'm sorry about this morning. I'm not saying you didn't provoke me but I shouldn't have shouted. That's all, we don't need to make a whole story of it.

You're hardly my first prisoner of your kind. The soldiers of our city – it takes a lot to stop them. Your little place didn't have a chance, and your people must know that.

Because – I mean no disrespect, but hear me out – your realm's small.

You've clean water, yes? Freshwater and full trees? Woods full of game? The streets of your city, yes?

There are five rooms in this old tower. Spiral stairs for the height of a tree, then the mess, then there's the armoury, then three rooms like this, one on top of the other, swaying in the wind as you go up. All with heavy wooden doors that shake the walls when you slam them.

This is the middle room. Both of the others are empty. The one below I sleep in. The one upstairs only has a bit of rubbish left in it.

There've been times when none of them have had prisoners in them, and times when all three have been full. You can see the niches in the walls. Years ago – before those soldiers down there were even born – the city was rushing in all directions and eating up everything it came to, and taking hostages from everywhere. Our troops would sweep through a city, kill its defenders, take its tributes, lay down new laws, and then to make sure the citizens behaved, they'd take the likes of you.

So downstairs there might've been the she-god or he-god of a city known for its woodwork, or a god of all babies. There was a lizard-headed fury upstairs, once, a god of war. No disrespect but he was better made than you. His wings were lapis and black on the gold. He had a mace in his right hand. He was crushing birds and bones with his left. Very fine, heavy work, lots of inlaid stones.

I looked after him, too. Without favour or malice. I deserve to have that noted, that I do my job well. Don't I light your fires every morning and every evening?

Never mind what happened to him. His people – how could they fight when we had him? When their god of war was gone? So that city's ours now.

Can you feel your people? Can you feel them worshipping? Are they sad? Are they frantic? Are they afraid for you? Does the worship reach you?

Look, down goes the sun again – someone else has that in

hand, you see. Don't tell any priests I said a word about any of this. Though no one should be angry with an old man for speculating. Down goes the sun again and it's all shadows left, like giant blocks.

How are you? Are you lonely? Or do you like to be alone?

You don't have to tell me anything.

The thing is – don't think me cruel, I'm just too old not to tell the truth – I look at you and I know what I see.

You aren't embarrassing. Your work isn't good, though, either.

Some of those we've had here, there's no way I could even carry alone, and I was strong once. They were as tall as I, and the metal on them was thick, with too many gems to count.

Now I'm not going to say we've had none cruder than you. Our forces took a village – the people who lived there called it a city but I'm sorry – some huts in the marsh by the dead forest. And the soldiers brought back their god here, to keep them quiet.

I felt sorry for it. It was wood and clay about the size of my arm, and I could barely tell what it was, it was so worn. There may have been bronze on it once but that was gone. It looked at me with two little stub eyes of some green stone. I mean pebbles, polished pebbles. It could break your heart.

They loved it, their poor swamp god. They loved it and I can tell you, I could tell, I knew, that they didn't know what to do. Whether they should surrender and beg for their little god back, or whether they should keep on warring for it – because they were still fighting us from the dead trees, even with it gone; they had camps in that forest of useless ghosts.

I fed it smoke as carefully as I do you. They surrendered, of course.

Our priests handed it back. They weren't disrespectful to it. Ugly thing. I hope it's ruling its soggy patch, bringing its people fish.

So I'm not going to tell you you're the weakest I've guarded. I've tapped you with my nails. There's thick-enough metal over your wood, a decent mix of gold. Those agates in your face are small but well cut. That ivory's elegant.

But you're little, from a little place. I mean no disrespect. Are your people worshipping you? They can't free you. It must be you're supposed to do things like keep the canals clean. They must be very dirty now. I'm sorry. That worship must be snagging you.

I'm telling you this so that you can tell the people lamenting in your temple.

Send them dreams. Are those dreams you're sending them, over there, going westward, or are they bats? Tell your people to surrender, to behave, to give tribute. It won't be so bad. They can come and take you back.

I know you're kind. I'm grateful and you can't stop me being so. I've been here a long time and I see you. I'm sure you're austere and jealous too but I see you being kind to me. You don't have to say a word. You're a good god.

The soldiers talk to me sometimes, they aren't bad. Sometimes we sit up together and they ask me about who was here before, and tell me what's happening in the city. I cook their food and pour their wine, and sometimes they let me have a bit, diluted with milk or water.

I think if I left the tower and my feet touched the ground – which they know is forbidden – some of them would be unhappy to have to follow their instructions. I don't say they'd cry but I think they might say something like, 'Old slave! Why would you do that? Now look!' or, 'Old man! I regret this!' And then if they put piles of rocks over me after, or tipped me into a gully, they might say something rueful. Maybe they'd be upset, I don't know.

Maybe they'd say, 'Was he unhappy?' I talk about old sadnesses sometimes – no matter how often you say to yourself, 'No, this is yours, keep this, they needn't know, no one cares about your miseries,' it's hard to say nothing. So some of them might say, 'He had a child once and the child's gone.' They might say, 'He carried something with him, poor slave.'

They'll talk about how a man was taken when he was very young and had a tiny baby and a wife, when everything was starting. Taken from a place that called itself a city so it could have a god, and that its little god was taken with him, it as a hostage, he as a slave.

They'd have to report to the city that the jailer was dead – I don't like that word any more than you, but it's what they call me, when they don't call me slave. They'd have to wait here and perform my duties until a replacement was sent.

Oh, you should hope that doesn't happen! I can't help thinking of those rough young men polishing you, or burning your incense. Oh, woeful! I can't help laughing.

You don't need to look at me like that. I've no intention of walking out into the dirt, no matter that I'm tired.

You are kind. I see it in the cast of your eye. I see how wistful you are when you watch the sky. Is that a weapon you hold, or a crook to snag animals? Is it a pole to feel the depth of a stream?

There's lemon-peel wrapped around the wood. It may spit, but I hope you like it.

Goodnight, god.

*

I could take weapons from the armoury, but what would I do? There's no getting past the soldiers. And they're my countrymen now, I suppose.

Officers come sometimes, from the city. And priests and oracles. Not very often, but when they have new hostages to jail, or sometimes to mark a ceremony or anniversary. They all sing, they go, *luh lah, cayya luh lah*, and so on. I could have learnt the tune a long time ago, it's almost always the same song. I choose not to learn it. I'm not called on to sing. It amuses me to watch the soldiers rumbling away.

Once a high priestess and priest came and sang a different song. It was hot, for all the clouds and the storms. I was nearly as wet as them, even stuck under this roof, I was gushing with sweat as I followed them. They were old, older then than I am now, and he was bruised and had scabs on his arms and legs and she breathed hard, but they came quickly up the stone stairs to the captain.

They talked in the armoury. I brought them wine and moved slowly so I could listen. The holies were thoughtful and grim. The priestess kept her eyes on the storm.

'We'll get them,' she said.

'They took all of them?' the captain said. She said nothing so the priest hesitated and nodded.

'They fight well,' he said.

We were at war again. A small war against a fading port. Our battalions had stormed down the river and along the coast. But our enemies had sent their own men, in disguise, into our city. They killed the guards and godnapped our gods.

'Is that why all this shit?' the captain said, pointing out of the window at the hot rain. The old priest rubbed his eyes and hit the table with his fist. The priestess bared her teeth.

Was I alarmed? I don't think any more than a little. Our gods

are well-guarded, though, our soldiers well-trained, our city forti-
fied. I was surprised anyone had been able to take them.

Mostly I was curious. What would happen? All of them? The
Queen of the Gods, the Great Farmer, the Clearer of Filth, the
Soldier with the Whip, the Moon? They were *all* gone? That had
to be bad. The Spirit of the City was gone? Without them, how
could our soldiers fight? But they must fight, I thought. Would
they be able to get our gods free? Would they negotiate? Pay
ransom?

'Bastards,' the priestess said. 'Bastards and sons of bastards.'
She sang a song I hadn't heard before and haven't heard since.

The rain didn't stop for twenty days. It ruined the crops. It
sent a farmhouse sliding down the slope of the hill, taking the
whole family with it but for a baby who was left squalling under
a tree where her cot wedged.

I didn't see that: it was on the side where there are no windows. I heard the soldiers talking about it before they left for war.
They checked their spears and their armour. They were relieved
by an untrained group who didn't know what they were doing
and made a terrible mess. The wood they gathered was green and
too young to burn.

Then the captain of the relief after *that* told me about working in our city's temple just before coming here, about how
proud he'd been to serve in the presence of our gods. So I learnt
we had them back. I don't know what our city, where I've never
been, did to retrieve them.

I've been here for years, and I wasn't in our city before that,
either. I've never been to our city.

The old priest came back once. At the end of that year it was
he who came to wish winter away and sing the usual song to the
soldiers who stood shivering in the courtyard. I stood at the corner
of the window in the lowest of the cells and watched them.

The priest was nodding as he sang. I remembered his anger. I remembered when his companion said, 'Bastards,' and I realised I didn't know if she meant the godnappers, or the gods who'd let themselves be taken, who'd let everyone down.

Here: you have a smudge on your chin. There. And let me turn you so the sun isn't in your eyes.

I'm sorry I'm not very talkative. I dreamed of my family, of quiet. It was a good dream.

Was that you?

If it had been up to me I'd have taken you to the uppermost cell. I could clear the rubbish out from the alcove – it wouldn't take long, I should have done it years ago – and put you there.

One of the soldiers here is very young and very boastful. I see him in the courtyard challenging all his comrades to wrestling matches. He's beaten at least one time in three and whenever he is he blusters and complains and insists that there was cheating and that he won, really. He has no malice and they like him, and I do too. Sometimes I do little things for him. Anyway, he told me the war's over. This last war.

'There'll be people coming soon,' he said. 'We beat the other city and that's just that. Just as I was getting ready to fight, too.'

I'm telling you because I've seen the sadness in your gold eyes and I don't think you deserve it, though you're the god of my city's enemies. So I want you to know that you'll be going home soon.

The war's over, and we won. There's no shame in it. The city always wins and almost always will. Your people are coming, so they must have paid ransom.

I hope they did.

It's nothing, you shouldn't worry at all. Don't pay me attention.

There was a time we destroyed the hostages.

Everyone agrees it was a terrible thing, so don't look like that, I beg you. No one would do it now. That war god I told you about? He was broken apart.

It was a bad king who ordered that done, because he was angry with our enemies. Yes, it worked, it crushed them, but it was shameful.

I see you aren't afraid. You impress me.

I'm alright. You don't need to worry about me, not at all.

It's been good to know you. You've been an interesting guest. I know: prisoner. But let me consider you my guest? I'll be sorry when you go.

If I look a little sad, it's just that there are so many questions I should've asked, and I don't know how long we have now. I want to know about your family and your city. Your people, who worship you. Who are coming.

Why do you look sadder?

You'll be back with them soon. Don't you hear me?

You do. Shall I cover your eyes? Will you send bats to tell your worshippers where we are? Where you are, with me to talk to you?

This is the best wood I have. I've put all the perfume I have on it, and I've shaved it into little slivers as best I could with these old fingers. Aren't you enjoying it?

You know, it occurred to me – I have to say this quietly, and I shouldn't say it at all, which is why I have to whisper it into your metal ear – that maybe that soldier heard wrong. Maybe our city lost. Maybe your priests will come and kill the men downstairs and set you free and carry you back to your city on their shoulders in triumph.

I don't know if they'd consider me your enemy. Don't worry. I'm not worried.

But it doesn't seem likely. My city's armies are stronger, the gods are bigger and heavier and made of more gold.

And even if that is what's happened, that doesn't cheer you, does it?

God why are you so sad? There was a little boy whose spirit ate the bones of his neighbours while he slept. Shall I tell you a story? Will you tell me stories? How do you rush across the valleys? When you fly is it with the slow strokes of a heron? Do you scatter farms with blood? How do the hunters of your city honour you?

Oh you must remember the Washing of the Mouth! When one minute this was wood and gold, and then it was you. Do you remember, these eyes for you to see with, these hands, this staff you carry? When the people made you?

I'll tell you a story, then. This is a story I tell myself from time to time. A tiny city was overrun by soldiers who took its little god and a very young local man to look after it. The two of them were locked away together. The man was sad because he'd seen the soldiers kill his family with swords and now he was without them. The god was sad for godly reasons. Because he'd let his people down and now their crops would rot, and because he knew how they'd come for him and look at him when they got him back and no one had ever asked him to god them.

The man cried and he was angry with the god. 'My baby's dead,' the man said. 'My wife is dead. What good are you? Set me free. You're the only god of my city so you're the god of everything. Harvests and war and childbirth and everything. And death. I'm too afraid,' the man shouted. There were knives in the

137

armoury but he wouldn't pick them up. 'So you do it for me. Don't I worship you? Do it.'

The god felt the man's worship, and, further away, the worship of his other people as they approached with ransom. It gave him no strength, it made him tired.

The man and the god watched from the top window of the tower. 'They're coming,' the man said, 'and you'll have to start doing your job again.'

The man looked into the god's silver eyes. The god looked into the man's grey. The man jerked like a toy, grabbed his chest, gasped and wheezed and fell down.

The priests and the soldiers of the victorious city came up the stairs, escorting the defeated holy men and women. They heard a great crash and a scream. They rushed into the top room.

Strewn across the floor were the remains of the captive god. The man had smashed it against the walls. It was all in pieces. Its wood was in splinters. Its metal was twisted. Its gems – and there were never many – were scattered and broken. There in the middle of the rubbish stood the young prisoner. He was slapping the sides of his own body and his head, screaming and staring with wide eyes at his own hands.

The high priest assured his defeated enemies that this hadn't been his orders, that it was an insane action by this slave. Who was, he reminded them, one of their own countrymen. Nonetheless, the deicide brought a bit of shame to the priest. It had occurred under his city's authority. Of course their city had to stay under his city's control, but they could keep their ransom. And the slave, he told them, would be executed.

But when they'd gone, he looked thoughtfully at the young man, who was still gripping his own flesh as if it bewildered him.

'I'm going to have you whipped,' he said. 'But what happened? You hate gods now? All of them? Or just your own? For failing you?

'If you ever do anything like that again without instruction,' he said, 'I'll have you killed. But I need a slave who has a bit of scorn for gods. A bit of spite. Just enough not to be cowed by them.'

He had the young man whipped, and then he had him bandaged, and then he told him what his duties would be. And the new slave said to him, 'Not spite. Pity.'

Don't be afraid. Were you sleeping? I'm going to take my hand off your mouth now.

Can you see the moon?

Oh thank you. You're kind. You are a kind god. Let me kiss your cold face.

Tonight I could hear the soldiers downstairs like snorting calves. I heard them eating and laughing, shuffling in their blankets, and I started to hear them more and more clearly. I heard, I heard the secrets that floors and walls tell in their creaks. When I got up I don't remember, or how, perhaps I flew as if my feet had little wings, or as if my head was a cloud. But I was by the window and that moon talked back to me in its light.

There are things about the ways bodies see. There are things to be said for how flesh eyes see night and fail to see it. But to look through shadows to where the mountains are like the teeth of fishes again! Everything's silver like the metal that was upstairs on the floor a long time ago.

The soldiers are moving early. Visitors are coming with tribute for you.

Don't be sad, god. What you've done – it's such a thing.

Follow my finger towards, yes, there, not a bat but a moth,

and its heart rises in its little moth chest because it's in love. Geese will wake and cry in the day, soon, and the lava in the ground will answer them.

I'll put my arms around you. These are old man's arms but let me carry you my friend, let's rise, like when you fly. Yes you're heavy even though you're not so very gold but I don't care how heavy you are. I'm not as heavy as I was once, either, or as strong, but I'll carry you.

Look. In the mountains are rock machines and rock ships with eyes, and we can see the edges in the seamless stone that separate those things from the rock that holds up the trees.

Your worshippers are coming. I know. Come up with me to the top room.

They're coming to buy your freedom, you small heavy god. Your city'll be a colony and your worshippers'll take you back.

Come in. That's only wood on the floor. All the scraps of silver they took away, years ago, to make more of their own gods in the city. That wood I leave there for nostalgia. To push it into my fingers.

You never heard my name and I never heard yours. It doesn't matter at all. Listen to what that angry cloud is telling you, the mutter of all the animals on the crest of the hill.

I can't remember: did a young man destroy his miserable god, or did a god free its worshipper and take his blood and his bones?

Well.

Let me put you here to talk to the sun, which is coming soon, to talk to it with your motionless golden mouth and the scatter of its heat on you. Let me put you down – these arms are shaking! – not in the alcove by the junk of an older god's body, but right here, out on the ledge as far as I can, so the wind worships you. That worship doesn't hurt? No. That you can bear a minute.

They'll call me mad again. Here come your worshipping people, and that's another thing: don't worry, you're ready, and no one will do anything for you or to you, you do it all, you're a god, you move in your ways. I'll put you one tiny bit closer to the air so the birds are ready for you.

And don't think me rude as I leave a little grease kiss on the back of your head and turn my back. This is your communion. I'm going to jump and dance – these old legs! The floor's vibrating, more and more now as here come the soldiers and your worshippers. Don't be sad, you needn't see: you are facing the other way.

My dance makes the tower shake. You quiver on your threshold.

They call out to you! How sad they are to see you move!

And you aren't sad any more. Thank you, you kind god.

So. Feathers like mountains, or knives, unfolded gold? Rush.

Säcken

Joanna took Mel to Dresden, to the Frauenkirche. They timed their visit to coincide with a monthly English evensong. 'Fire-bombs not enough?' Mel whispered. 'Now we inflict Anglicanism on them?' Her giggles attracted attention.

'Jesus,' Joanna muttered, shaking her head but laughing too. 'Shut up.'

They left the city and drove on busy roads for more than an hour through diminishing satellite towns. Then through smaller towns still and a rolling damp landscape. The clouds came low. Joanna and Mel played their mountain playlist, though these were hills not mountains.

'Into the woods,' said Joanna, and made witch fingers.

Past Tharandt and through pretty forests, south at Freiburg. The country was thick with trees. Small rivers veered in the undergrowth. Joanna and Mel passed barns from which languid animals watched them.

In a market town Mel tried out German words as she bought bread, cheese, meat and wine. She didn't entertain or win over the shopkeeper. Outside she watched a cat trot the length of an alley wall-top. A middle-aged woman in a saggy dress nodded to the tall young Englishwoman.

'Spying on locals?' Joanna said.

'Just greeting the polite Fraulein.'

'Frau, I feel certain,' said Joanna.

They ascended. 'Is that the lake?' Joanna said. To the right the trees climbed and grew more densely. To the left as the slope fell away they petered out, and through them Joanna and Mel kept glimpsing water. They cheered.

At a junction, Joanna paused the car and tied up her hair, tilted her head back and forth, looking at the road alternately through and over her glasses. 'What?' she said, because Mel was smiling at her.

'There's a little village down there, I think,' Joanna said. 'Look out for a green gate. That's our marker.'

'That can't go wrong,' Mel said. 'A gate in the middle of the country. We'll be fine.' But Joanna showed her her phone with the picture she'd been sent and there was in fact no mistaking the entrance. They saw it from some way off, slanting across a muddy turnoff.

'You're up,' Joanna said. 'Good luck in those shoes.'

Mel put up her middle finger at Joanna. She got out and crossed the mud and grass with long strides, without incident, to open and close the gate. She returned to the car and patted her imaginary do. 'Impressed,' said Joanna, and they drove down the rocking slant of gravel through trees, past what might once have been a neat garden and was now boiling with greenery and low bushes, left wild while the house it surrounded was spruced. Beyond the bramble and the house was the lake.

There it was, imperfectly reflecting the trees and sky and the few other houses at its edge. The shore curved out of sight to the east. Mel and Joanna looked across the lake at moored boats, at paths and clearings in the trees where people could come to the water.

The house was modern and whitewashed. It looked to Mel like a film set. 'Did we not do good?' she said. Joanna struggled with the groceries and the unfamiliar keys and gently kicked open the door to enter. Mel stood on the path, staring. 'Did we not?'

'Who's "we"?' Joanna said. 'One of us as I recall did the online hunting. While the other put in some really invaluable complaining time.' She put food on the table.

'*You* did good,' Mel said. 'Can we explore?'

The furnishings made them joke about IKEA. They were both surprised by the roughness of the grounds. 'It's not like it was cheap,' said Mel. She was paying a token amount. 'They could've tidied it up.'

'Honestly, you don't know you're alive,' said Joanna. She was also disappointed. 'Kids these days. I like it like this.'

They pushed through the undergrowth like children finding secret paths. At the end of a jetty a small boat swayed in the lake. Joanna consulted her information sheet. 'That's ours.'

'Come on,' Mel said. She lowered herself in. She struggled with the oars.

'You look like Alice,' Joanna said.

'When does Alice go rowing?'

'She goes with a sheep. She catches a crab.'

Joanna let herself be talked in. Ostentatiously cack-handed, laughing at their own incompetence, taking turns with the oars, she and Mel wobbled away from the mooring, watched by birds.

They hauled and pulled and mocked themselves. They slowed. They kissed at last, many metres from land. If they were watched from any houses they would only be specks. The air was cooling. After a few minutes they turned their boat and, yanking and moaning, headed back in.

Later, when they were inside, as the evening came, lights appeared in the windows of the houses over the water. 'Look,' said Joanna.

*

The first few hours after breakfast, Joanna worked on her essays. That had always been the plan. She piled up the books and print-outs she had brought, theses on Dresden's golden age, centuries of diplomacy, law, and culture. The books were thick with place-markers.

'Which are you doing first?' said Mel. 'Don't do the one on King What's-his-face, that other one sounds more fun. His mistress, who used to be a slave or something?'

'Maria Aurora's the sugar lump,' said Joanna. 'Augustus is the castor oil that gets me funding. Speaking of, I have to do that conference proposal too.'

On the second day, Mel pretended her boredom was playfulness. Pushing open the door to the study with her head, she crept in on all fours. 'Hush, ignore me,' she muttered, 'I'm only a quiet cat.' Joanna gave one short laugh.

Mel coiled in the armchair but Joanna did not acknowledge her again and after a while Mel left. When Joanna came down to make coffee she found Mel on the sofa. She had plugged her console into the television and was playing a video game with the sound off.

Joanna had to look away. What incredible petulance, she thought. To do that here, amid all these trees, in the light from this water. She felt the years between her and Mel. She felt like an older sister. But upstairs again, she sat back in her chair and glanced at the lake and there to her great pleasure and surprise she saw Mel, in the boat, gamely and inelegantly rowing.

Mel splashed and pulled the oars and fastened them up in their housings. She sat back in the boat in her London clothes. She picked up a book and began to read. Joanna put her fingertips on the glass. Mel was not looking in her direction. It was too far to see if Mel was smiling too.

*

When Mel returned Joanna came down but Mel raised an elegant eyebrow and pointed upstairs. 'Back to work, you,' she said. She took a kitchen chair into the garden and read there for a while then dropped her book for ants and woodlice to walk over. She watched the moon while it was still just day, until Joanna called her in for food.

After supper she headed back out.

'You'll be eaten alive,' said Joanna.

'I've got bug stuff,' said Mel.

Joanna was checking emails at the kitchen table. Mel looked back from outside and the doorway was a glowing crack.

Grass pulled at her. She walked towards the dark chop of the lake. Mel found her book and picked it up and brushed it clean. The wind came up. Mel let the water wet the toes of her trainers. These were the ones she did not mind getting ruined.

The shore was littered with dead, bleached plant matter. In England, she thought, the little waves would be throwing up crisp packets and plastic. Mostly the stones were the wrong shape to skim but she found a discish one and sent it skipping five times across the water. She felt again among the weeds.

'Can you close the door?' Joanna called across the dark garden. 'Midges.'

In the water at the shore Mel saw what looked like a perfect stone, but when she picked it up it was too light to be stone at all. She looked at it in the light from her phone.

It was black wood, slick with algae, the size and shape of a medal. On one face were eroded ridges. She stared and felt them under her thumb. They weren't random. They were outlines, a tiny figure, five stick limbs.

Mel stood quickly and swayed, dizzy. She shook her head at a sudden smell, and then the wind came in and brought a much worse gust. 'Jesus Christ,' she said. Cold air buffeted the garden and her hair.

She threw the wood as hard as she could into the under-growth.

'What?' Joanna said when Mel came in. She got up from her typing, putting her glasses up in her pinned-back hair. 'What is it?'

'Off, off,' Mel said, shrugging Joanna's hands from her and striding to the sink to wash. 'Something stinks.'

When Joanna had suggested Mel join her on this trip, Mel had immediately walked away from her temp work at a solicitor's office. Joanna was delighted by Mel's insouciance: this was the second job she had quit since graduating less than a year before.

Joanna had rented the house for nearly two months. Mel would be there for half that time.

While Joanna worked, Mel rowed out most mornings, with a big travel mug of coffee wedged between the knees of her least expensive jeans. The drink cooled quickly. She didn't mind it cold.

The lake was green and silty. Mel reached into it. Her skin disappeared. Even in the sunlight the dark water amputated her hand only a few centimetres down. She clenched unseen fingers, made a fist, saw nothing but eddies.

A man and woman stood on a jetty on the far bank. Mel waved to them and the woman waved back. They watched her drift. She reclined and read. She always took two books into the boat with her: one non-fiction, for the postgraduate work she still told Jo she was contemplating; one fiction. That morning, like all mornings, she read the novel. She enjoyed how her wet hand buckled every page it touched.

A cockerel crowed. Mel started.

She lost her grip on the cup in the rowlock where she'd rested it. It dropped into the water. 'Oh fuck,' she said and sat up, reaching for it quickly but it was going down in bubbles and was almost instantly out of sight, leaving a coil of coffee.

The crowing came again. It sounded close. Mel made the boat rock in the middle of all the water, looking about. The only birds were far overhead, and silent.

'Met some of our neighbours,' Mel said. 'Did you clock the other boats out here? We're so the poor relations.' She served Joanna a ladleful of stew.

'Bloody Hell,' said Joanna. 'This is amazing.'

'I dropped my cup in the lake.'

'Oh, you're kidding. That was a rare mid-period Starbucks Dynasty, wasn't it?'

'There's some chippy little cockerel around here,' Mel said.

'Das ist der countryside. Are you surprised?'

'I don't know from cocks,' Mel said.

'Ladies and gentlemen,' Joanna said, 'she'll be here all week.'

After supper Mel heard the crowing again. She and Joanna were standing in the bedroom with the lights off, looking across the water and at the clouds. 'Hear that?' Mel said. 'That bird's nuts, it's the middle of the night.'

'I didn't hear.'

'There,' said Mel. 'There it is again.' But Joanna was walking away. She pulled back the covers and lay down and waited.

Mel did not sleep but listened to the noises of the house. She listened to Joanna's breathing, its slow and lovely rhythms.

Before dawn, Mel rose and tiptoed downstairs. She smoked with the door to the garden open, exhaling into the tangle. She hugged herself though it was not as cold as she had expected. She wore only slippers and her outdoor coat over a long t-shirt. When she finished her cigarette she hesitated, then walked quickly through the vegetation. The wind made bushes bow.

At the edge of the water, where the jetty touched the earth, Mel heard the rooster again. She waited. No lights appeared.

She walked onto the planks, over the water. At the end the boat waited for her so Mel climbed in. This'll be the time I rowed on a moonlit lake, she thought. She pulled, surrounded by nothing, and after a few minutes of hard strokes she let the boat drift in the dark. She put her arms around her knees and listened to all the ripples.

A fat fish somewhere flicked a tail. Mel looked over her shoulder. The boat was drifting into a patch of quivering water, dimpled as if with cellulite. Mel watched the stars' reflections. She put her hand in the cold lake. There was a swell. She flexed her fingers.

The cockerel crowed. Mel jerked up and held her breath. The cockerel called again, much closer, more raucous, as if it had found something.

And then very fast and rushing Mel felt a surge from below. In the water beneath her hand something was rising.

She cried out and snatched back her arm and as she did the bird screamed right by her. She shook and splashed and the boat rocked on the black water. Mel gripped the wood and turned her head in panic but could see nothing in the dark.

The rooster didn't sound again. Mel huddled shivering while the boat calmed, while the sky lightened, as still as she could be. Her heart slowed. When adrenalin had ebbed from her enough that she no longer shook, she took hold of the oars with cold hands and rowed back to the lakeside house, where Joanna was just awake.

'Did you dream last night?' Mel said.

'Probably.' Joanna was driving. Sun dappled the car.

'Did you hear anything?'

'You know me,' Joanna said. She imitated stupefied snoring. 'Why?'

'I was a bit noisy,' Mel said.

'Going for your dawn row? So impressed!'

'Thought even you might've been defeated, between me and the cock-a-doodle-doing,' Mel said after a moment.

'Kikeriki,' said Joanna. Mel frowned at her. 'German,' said Joanna. 'For cock-a-doodle-do. Don't look at me like that, you know I sprechen sie.'

'I'm just marvelling at your specialist historian's vocabulary,' said Mel. 'Got any other farmyard animals?'

'Grunz,' said Joanna slowly. 'I'm pretty sure that's oink.' She glanced at Mel and whistled. 'Look out, Deutschland.'

'That's right,' Mel said. 'Meet Camden Town. I was going to bring my book. Have you seen it?'

'Did you leave it in the boat?'

They visited a town that was pretty enough. It had a famous clock. It was celebrated for its bakers. Joanna and Mel looked at facades. They shared embarrassed smiles with other tourists.

'You alright?' said Joanna.

In the window of a general store was a sign for a magazine, from the headline of which protruded a recurved German S like a sea-monster's neck. 'I'm sleep-deprived,' Mel said. 'Maybe I need some sugar, flour, and Germanic jam in pastry form.

Butter, bitte? Maybe you could help me with that?' She slipped an arm briefly around Joanna's waist.

'Why yes,' Joanna said. 'Yes I can.'

Joanna looked at her watch as she led them toward the cake shop. Mel said, 'It's lovely here.'

'Really?' Joanna said.

'Look at that restaurant. We could knock around a few hours, have something to eat.' Joanna hesitated and Mel said, 'No, you're right. It's time to go. You have stuff to do.'

And nothing settled on Mel when she turned the car down their drive and they came back to the house. Nothing overtook her. It was still light. She listened but could hear only the woods. She watched the lake and eventually smiled at Joanna, whose attention was the only one she felt on her. They sat together in the living room, Joanna reading while Mel wrote emails. For hours, all evening, nothing came down.

That night the cockerel crowed again.

Mel opened her eyes. She stared at the ceiling. Joanna slept. Mel heard strong wind. She heard that crazed farmyard bird announce dawn hours and hours too early.

They kept the curtains open to wake to daylight, so Mel saw the lake the moment she stood. She was still for a long time. At last she walked naked to the window. She watched the shadows of trees swaying, quick black clouds, the dark land and water. And the cockerel crowed again, and now it was the only sound, and it was urgent, and closer.

Mel touched the glass. She saw gathering wind in the motions of leaves, like a rainless storm. Something approaching. A rush of air that seemed to carry the cockerel's excited crow with it. No one was waking. No one anywhere around the lake was turning on their lights. The windowpane vibrated. Wake up, Mel thought. Wake up wake up.

A bird whispered much too close. Right up in her ear. Mel stopped breathing and it clucked. The wind slammed into the window and Mel staggered and there was the crowing again right there and this time a hiss and a snarl too. Mel retched in a sudden sump-stench. The air in the room was moist. As she straightened, holding the windowsill, she heard a liquid sound. She turned.

Something was on the floor.

A darkness. A gross misshape.

Something huge and wrong and wet. It blocked her way.

Mel's throat closed. The new thing in the room dripped.

A nightmare calf born without limbs or head or eyes but full of tumours. A mound of leather in pooling water. It was a bag, a sack full of bad presents, of coal or earth or blood clots or ruined roots. Mel shook with her own heartbeat. The sack streamed.

Mel's legs gave way. Way beyond the nightmare thing Joanna dreamed as if in another country.

The black sack moved.

It shoved from within with a sucking sound, a slurping. It lurched heavily toward her, spattering the floorboards.

A fitful dark groping, hauling her way. Its weight and spasming motion shook the room. It strained as if to split.

The thing had voices. A cluck, a hiss, a predator's growl. It slopped closer still and Mel heard a woman.

Mel heard a woman vomit old water. She heard it spatter on the inside of the skin. The sack convulsed in mud that should not have been brought up. Kikeriki, whispered the rooster inside the bag with its throat full of lake.

Mel crawled back to the wall and pushed with her legs as if they might drive her into it. The thing came with a scratch of claws, pushed through its own hide into the floor. It whispered. It pinioned her with its notice. Its cold enveloped her. Mel felt a terrible lack. Cluck cluck the sack went and hiss and growl and nein and it came and it was close and it reached for her, so close she could see its wounds, crisscross sutures tautening as the leather stretched, as if the sack would burst.

She screamed.

Joanna screamed. Was there with Mel holding her and begging her to stop, whispering to her. Crouching in the glare of the lamp where there was no sack, no thing, where there was no wetness any more.

'What happened, what happened?' Joanna kept saying. 'You're ok, you're ok.'

'Something was here.' Mel ran her fingers over the dry floor. 'Oh God. Something missing.' She put her hands to her mouth when that came out of it because she didn't know what she meant.

'I didn't see anything,' Joanna said. 'I didn't hear anything. What happened?'

'It was *here*, it was in the *room*,' Mel sobbed. 'Oh my God—'

'Breathe, breathe, breathe,' Joanna said. 'What did—' She stopped. She looked at Mel and put her arms around her again. 'What did you dream?'

When Mel was able to stand, she went from room to room turning on every light. Joanna followed her, trying to take hold of her. 'Please,' she said. 'You have to talk to me, Mel, please.'

'We have to *go*, we have to go *now*.' Mel pulled open the front door and shied at the dark outside. She slammed it closed again and put her back to it. 'We have to go *now*.'

'Stop. *Mel*. Stop shouting. Tell me what's going on.'

Mel stared at Joanna. Her eyes widened. She was breathing too fast. She tried but she could say nothing. She ran upstairs again. She began to shove clothes into her bag.

'Dear God, Jo, it was right here. Stop *looking* at me like that!' Joanna stood in the doorway holding out her arms, her mouth open. Mel stopped and caught her breath. She closed her eyes and swallowed and tried again to say what she had seen. She tried to say it and the words refused. Stopped in her mouth. 'Jo . . . We have to get the fuck out of here.'

'Mel, you're shaking, you're sick . . .'

'*I'm not sick.*' There were seconds of silence. 'What did I *dream*? You think that's what happened? You think I'm *crazy*, Jo? Do you? We have to go *now*.'

'Help me understand then,' Joanna said.

They stared at each other. Mel saw Joanna's horrified concern and the anger she was battening down. She understood, slowly, that Joanna would not come with her.

Her eyes widened. 'Jesus Christ,' she said, 'you can't. You can't *stay*. There was something *here*—'

The women stared at each other.

'Mel, if you keep screaming like this I'm calling a doctor.'

'I'm not sick,' Mel said. Her heart was slowing at last, but when she spoke her voice still shook. 'There's something. We have to go. And if you won't come right now and if you won't take me to the airport I'll go myself. And I'll dump the fucking car when I get there.'

They drove through the dawn. Mel huddled in the passenger seat with her head in her hands. She kept looking up at Joanna in disbelief. Joanna watched the road. Her face was anguished and hard.

'Mel, you're scaring me—'

'You *should* be scared!'

Neither of them spoke for a long time. When they approached the airport Joanna shouted, 'This is *insane*. Tell me what *happened*.'

Mel tried. She swallowed. 'There's something *there*,' was all she could say.

'Can you hear yourself? I know you've had a shock but can you *hear* yourself?'

'You *know*,' Mel shouted. 'Look at you, you know there's something. You're fucking pretending—'

'You think this was all cheap?' Mel stared at Joanna and did not flinch. 'What exactly is this, Mel? What's this about? Talk to me.'

'Please,' Mel said at last.

There were more seconds of silence. Then Mel got out of the car quickly and walked away. Joanna did not follow. She opened her own door but stayed behind the wheel. 'Don't,' she said once, not loud. She watched Mel disappear into the terminal.

Jo clenched her hands as if she would do something. She pulled out her phone but did not dial and she swore and hit her dashboard several times. She sat in the car in the car park a long time.

TALK? Mel texted Joanna. AM BACK. London was under thick English clouds.

Ever since she had sat down in the plane's flat fluorescent light, it had been hard for Mel even to think about what she had seen in the room. Her sense of it was scattered. Black plastic bags spilt like larvae from a rubble of dustbins. She crossed the city alone.

PLEASE, she texted. FEEL SICK. SORRY. She stopped and called Joanna, leaning against the wood of a closed shop on a Peckham street. It was not closed for the day but forever. Mel listened to the clicks of foreign connections until Joanna answered.

'I thought you were out. I was going to leave a message.'

'I might still go out,' Joanna said. 'You can leave a message if you prefer. What do you want?'

'To know you're ok.'

'You can hear.'

'Please, Jo, please don't be angry. Please come back. I'm sorry I freaked out. I was really scared, Jo. I still am.'

'Ok.'

'I'm begging you,' Mel said. She raised her voice in the loudness of London. 'Are you there?' She thought of her words coming out of the phone in the house in the trees, echoing by the lake. Birds might hear. 'Do you just think I'm a crazy person? Jo?'

'I don't know what to think, Mel.'

'I'm not crazy,' Mel said, but Joanna had rung off.

Mel knew what she had seen but it thinned in her head. The city flattened the memory and confused her.

'Why did you come back?' her friends said when she called them looking for someone to be with, when she met them in pubs or cafes or went to their flats. She spent the night of her return in a room full of people. 'Why did you come back?' they asked and she shrugged. She told some that she and Joanna had argued. To a few she said that the house by the lake had felt bad.

'Jo.'

'Are you drunk?' Joanna spoke carefully down the line. 'Jesus, Mel. What is it, two in the morning?'

'I haven't spoken to you for so long.' Mel heard the fear in her own voice.

'A day and a half.'

'Are you alright? Is everything ok? What's going on?'

'I'm tired, Mel. Sleep it off, will you?' Joanna hung up. And though Joanna's disdain had been audible, and though she was whispering for confused seconds to an empty line, Mel felt better. Relief.

Should I go back? Mel's thought shocked her. She shook her head so hard it ached. She remembered the dark thing in the room. She was drunk and uncertain and the memory made her stomach spasm.

She called again the next morning, hung over, determined to have a proper conversation. Joanna did not answer. Mel tried from her landline, which would not display her number on Joanna's phone, but got no response.

What if I was confused? Mel thought. Could she really be thinking such a thing?

She took hours walking from where she lived to where she had grown up, in the north of the city, to be out in the light. She tried Jo again the next day, and the call was answered by a soft-voiced German man. In courteous, slow English, he asked Mel who she was and how she knew the owner of this telephone.

'Who the fuck are you?' she said.

'I am police.'

The boat had been drifting, empty, aimless, across the lake. A neighbour had come to the house. Perhaps the same man Mel had seen from the boat, standing on a jetty. The officer in the

Saxony police explained it to her. She imagined the man knocking at the door of the house. Would you like some help getting your boat back? he had come to say in his good English. I think you have forgotten to tie it up.

'But she is not here,' the policeman said. 'So this man calls us.'

The car was in the drive. There was food in the fridge. The door was unlocked. Joanna's computer, the officer said, was on the kitchen table, sleeping. The boat had continued its silent random journey until the man took his own skiff out and snared it.

One oar was missing, another lay across the seats. A thumb's height of water slopped in the boat's bottom. In it was one of Joanna's slippers.

Mel could not stop imagining Joanna, her arms up, fingers splayed, a pianist paused between movements. Head nodding with the currents that must hold her, eight metres below the surface of the lake.

Maybe she went for a long walk, Mel thought. Got lost. Mel sobbed in a bleak, drawn-out way. Maybe she met someone new and shacked up with them. Went into the woods to do some writing. Writing by hand. But what Mel thought was that Joanna had been noticed. Was now circling in the dark water like a mindless ballerina.

Whenever she called, the police were gentle with her. Your friend got disoriented. It was a beautiful evening. She was enjoying the water. She leaned out too far. It is an awful thing. 'I have to come out,' she said.

The last thing Joanna saw as she looked up, Mel thought, would have been the moonlit outline of the boat above her. The last thing Joanna saw when she looked down Mel wanted desperately not to consider.

'What did we do wrong?' It was night. Mel surrounded herself with the city's lights. She spoke her questions out loud. She looked at pictures of the lake. She whispered to the black bushes in the park where she trespassed. 'What did Jo do? Nothing. She did nothing.'

When they first met, Mel skim-read bits of Joanna's work. She had done so again that day, hunting the essays for intimations or clues, a logic according to which Joanna might have been taken. There was nothing in the exposition. Nothing of the hills or the lake, nothing to put Mel in mind of what she had seen.

'What did she *do*?'

Now Mel's phone lit her face from below like a cold campfire. She thumb-typed *Dresden, cockerel, lake* into a search engine. She scrolled quickly through fairy tales and travel advice. She brushed curious insects from the phone's face. She typed *Germany* and, without letting herself hesitate, *spirits* and *water*. What did she do? she thought. Why punish her, for fucking what? Mel typed *drowned*. There were words for which she could not bring herself to search. She wrote Joanna's name and looked at the picture on her department website, Joanna short-haired and trying not to smile, what she and Mel had called her nerd-queen look. Mel typed *drowned* and *cockerel* and *Saxony* and *sack* and the phone glowed and pulled up an abstract from a history journal, and sitting on the cold ground with her back to a London tree, Mel found the poena cullei.

This punishment, she read in the dark.

Joanna had given Mel her academic passwords, encouraged

her to think about that PhD. Mel used them at last. She shook her head and chased links. Jo, I told you I'm no good at this. This punishment, she slowly read. She mouthed the Latin of Justinian. She whispered glosses and translations.

A novel penalty for a most odious crime. Parricide. She looked it up. neque gladio, she read.

neque gladio neque ignibus neque ulli alii solemni poenae subiugetur, sed insutus culeo cum cane et gallo gallinaceo et vipera et simia

This is not execution by the sword or by fire, or any ordinary form of punishment, but the criminal is sewn up in a sack with a dog, a cock, a viper and an ape

Mel stopped. She put her hand to her mouth. She had to look trembling up at the black sky for a long time.

sewn up in a sack with a dog, a cock, a viper and an ape, and in this dismal prison is thrown into the sea or a river, according to the nature of the locality, in order that even before death he may begin to be deprived of the enjoyment of the elements, the air being denied him while alive, and interment in the earth when dead.

The night was a cold mouth. Mel could not breathe.

Poena Cullei. Säcken. The Punishment of the Sack.

No one even seemed to know for quite what this drowning was the sentence, the parameters of parricide. Its symbolism made no sense. The poena was first mentioned in antiquity as already antique. An arcane sadism. Centuries of jurists disputed and forgot it until by some scholastic experiment it was recalled far, far too late. Mel made a sound. This punishment, she read, was last imposed in Germany in the eighteenth century. The punishment, she read, of a woman for infanticide in Saxony.

Leather on the house floor. The thing straining to split.

She read, The cockerel's dying call marks the place of sinking. Kikeriki, the rooster had said, paying her attention. Pay attention. This is where we are.

And the waterlogged woman had spoken. Down she had gone in that last sack with cockerel and dog and snake, with their bites and rips and screaming, swaddled together as the leather went tight.

Had it been a relief when the water came in, or the worst moment of all?

The first time Mel met with Joanna's parents and sister, in the restaurant of their hotel, they tried to be kind to her. They struggled with their own grief and asked her how she was holding up, and so on. Mel was moved. The next time they barely spoke. Joanna's father wouldn't look at her except to interrupt her and ask exactly why she had left so suddenly, whether she and Joanna had been arguing.

Jo's sister took her outside. 'Sorry about that,' she said.

'The police have the phone records,' Mel managed to say. 'I was in London.'

'Yes. Why did you come back? Had Jo been upset with you?'

'I told you she was, we had a row.'

'How upset?'

Mel left.

Everyone wanted a body but the lake would not deliver. When Mel first returned, when the police took her to the house, the emptiness of it bewildered her. She saw herself in reflections and realised her gait had changed. She kept her head down. She barely slept. Her dreams were no longer of Joanna slowly changing in the water. Now they were of dark wood, of a doubled-over figure with uncertain limbs.

She was staying in a small guesthouse near the lake, one she had made sure was equipped with wi-fi. She continued urgent correspondence with scholars. She sought and found no local stories. No one could tell her anything about the executed woman. The woman who had hauled herself up again centuries after her death, noted Mel, reached for her, taken Joanna.

What do you want? Mel asked in her head.

Revenge. She imagined answers from the sack. Justice. Company. My child. A retrial. None of those was what the woman had whispered for.

Mel tracked down the number of one of the English-speaking priests in Dresden. He was bewildered and kind. 'I am so sorry about your friend,' he said. 'But I understand there has been a service already?' Mel standing apart from Joanna's relatives in an Essex church. Jo's friends were mostly her age, and did not know Mel, though some had come up to her afterwards in their smart mourning clothes to say something.

'For Joanna, right,' Mel said down the line. 'But that's not the thing. She was a historian. She was looking into that awful punishment.'

'That you have described to me, yes. With the snake and the ape and so on. A terrible thing.'

'And cockerels and dogs and cats, yeah,' Mel said. So expensive a beast as a monkey can be replaced, Carpzovius said, by a cat.

'A terrible thing.'

'Thing is that happened *here*, where we were staying. Jo was doing research about the last woman executed like that.' That lie came easily. It was the word *executed* that meant Mel had to pause. 'We always planned that when she'd written her book, we'd do something for that woman,' she said. 'And now Jo's gone so she can't. But I still want to. You understand why? I hoped you might help me. For both their sakes.'

Mel talked about the woman's dreadful death. She talked about the lake being shamed. The priest sounded guarded in response, and when she rang off she was not hopeful, but he quickly called her back. 'As you understand,' he said, 'my duties, I cannot. But I have a colleague.'

Something's missing, Mel thought again, and still did not know what it meant when she thought it.

She drove to the lake. The local priest was waiting for her as arranged. He was tall and thin, in his sixties, leaning against his car like a much younger man. He was incongruous in his robes. Before her engine had even stopped he strode impatiently toward her vehicle, reaching to shake her hand. Mel had paid for the service he was to perform. In her halting German she thanked him enough to make him soften a little.

From where they stood, at the end of a sightseers' pier, across the water they could see the house where Joanna and Mel had stayed. Mel could see the tied-up boat.

'Ok,' she said, and looked down. She gathered herself. 'Ok.' The priest nodded. He began to read aloud.

He muttered in fast German. Mel tried to follow in English, reading the words she and the Dresden priest had written together. A sanctified apology for the abominable execution. A prayer for the convicted woman, a plea to let her rest. Too late for Joanna, thought Mel. No one else should be punished for the punishment this angry dead woman had, no matter what, not deserved.

Mel cried silently over the lake. Is this enough? she thought. Will you stop?

How dark the lake was. What am I doing? Mel thought. Standing by this stinking old water with a man who thinks I'm a fool. And it does stink, it *reeks*.

Mel put her hand to her mouth.

A terrible gust. She couldn't breathe. The priest kept on with his recitation. The surface was disturbed and the stench told Mel to fuck her priest and fuck his blessing. She almost fell.

'Stop!' Mel shouted. She staggered off the jetty as fast as she could. Up from the water came scorn and want and notice. 'Get back!' she said. The priest broke off and turned to look at her in surprise. 'Father, for Christ's sake, get away from the fucking water!' She beckoned him desperately, staring at the lake that lapped at the pier on which he stood, watching for a shape to rise.

At last he walked to her. He stepped onto the grass and Mel sagged and turned as he shouted after her and she ran.

Why would you think a *priest* would do anything? she thought. She was dizzy with the lake's fury, its continued regard. If you were killed like that would you care what a *priest* said? I don't believe in God, why should she?

Mel ran to her car. She shook.

I need a lawyer, not a priest. Her thoughts raced. To declare a mistrial or something. It was the law that stitched the woman up. That had dragged her with the animals, scratching, biting, screaming, to the water. It was the law that listened to the cockerel beg its last living time, and let the lake close over the poena cullei.

Mel drove away before the priest could reach her. She drove away from the lake and only pulled over after several minutes. With unsteady hands she took out the printouts of all her articles.

The dog means loyalty maybe. The serpent is maybe a killer of its parents, the ape uncanny. But in the water all that would dissolve. Everything in the sack would mean itself. A thing that drowns and bites, that drowns and claws, that drowns and bites, that drowns and screams.

Mel could still smell the lake, as if it was on her skin and in her clothes. Oh, what do you want? she said to the dead. Voracious, sodden, rising, the end of the law. The sun went down. Somewhere Joanna's family was mourning. Mel leaned her head on her steering wheel. Behind her eyes she saw a dark bent-double figure.

She sat up. She shook her head to clear it. She hunted through the papers again. Animals might be represented by images on paper or wood, she remembered. Men and women could be drowned with drawings. The woman, she read, the last woman, had been sacked with snake and cockerel and dog and that was all.

Those markings on the water-blackened medallion she'd found and thrown away. A thing not with five limbs, as Mel had first thought, but with four and a curled tail.

A missing animal. An ape. A lack.

The boat moved across the water. Mel rowed like an automaton. She breathed lightly, in terror that the stink would return. Somewhere beneath her Jo circled. Or swayed, her softening foot held by a root.

It could be like this forever, Mel thought. This was not so

bad, even with the hissing of her cargo. She could pull this rocking boat in the dark, in the moonlight. But Mel was soon in the centre of the lake and there was nothing else she could do but what she was there to do.

Oh Christ. She remembered the smell and thought of Joanna and knew that it was not finished, that the poena was waiting, with its lack, would reach out again when someone leaned too far.

I don't want to I don't want to, Mel thought. But she shuddered, pulled opened a peephole in her fastened canvas bag and stared in at a hissing cat.

Mel had crawled through the garden of the lakeside house. As the light failed she had crawled and groped through the undergrowth feeling with her fingertips. She checked every piece of wood she touched but there were so many, she never had a chance of finding what she'd thrown away.

Why didn't I put it back in the water? she thought. I should have given it back.

The lost oar had been replaced. Mel rowed.

Something had gone missing. The wooden ape had worked out through rot, escaped the hankering sack, been washed to shore for Mel to throw into the dark.

The sack had stretched toward her. Nothing trying to get out; trying to pull something in. The poena did not want justice. It wanted completion.

Perhaps the image had always been inadequate, had not been lost but spat out for her to find. The sack reaching not for that token but for the nearest primate. Considering her. She, she and hers, had its attention. There has to be a life, Mel thought, to fill that lack. That's how ghosts are made.

How the fuck do I get hold of a monkey? Mel had thought in panic, and then remembered the law.

She'd gone to a nearby town. Bought tinned fish and a hessian sack. Waited in a backyard lot. The first time a cat appeared she could not bring herself to move. The second time she made herself remember what she had seen, what had happened to Joanna. She caught the animal easily. She cut off its collar so she would not see its name.

Mel knew how to hold cats. She gripped it at the back of its neck and it stared stiff-legged and hating. It had gone for her, and even constricted; it scratched her so she hissed too. But she kept her hold and gritted her teeth and shoved it in the bag.

It spat and rolled in the bottom of the boat. The bag writhed.

Apes were rare and expensive, the law allowed. Cats may be used instead.

Mel hefted the sack. It was heavy with the cat and with a big stone. The cat yowled and screamed and got a paw out by the drawstring, and the boat pitched with all the jostling. Swells rose from below. Mel started to cry.

She met the cat's terrified furious eyes as she forced it back in. She tied the bag closed. Claws shoved through the fabric. 'Oh Christ,' Mel whispered. She held the bundle out.

It might have been a warning stink she smelt then, it might have been that the water seemed excited. The boat shook as the hidden cat moaned and scrabbled.

'See?' Mel said. 'Look. See?'

She looked down. And it was very dark, but even in the night and through the black water she thought she saw a darker thing still rising.

Mel screamed. The cat screamed. She let it go.

With a *plop* like a pebble in a well the lake swallowed the bag and the cat's noise ended. Bubbles streamed up.

The boat pitched in the quiet. Whimpering with every breath, Mel leaned over a tiny bit and looked down. Strained to see the pale bag descending. But it was too dim or it had fallen too fast, or it was enveloped in mud or something had pulled it down because she saw nothing.

Mel leaves work early. It is nearly spring and the pubs are full. Her new colleagues – the solicitors asked her back and she said no, is now at a small publishing house – invite her for a drink. She smiles and hesitates and joins them, though she doesn't stay long. They are sweet. Two of her workmates in particular she likes a lot, and one of them has been flirting with her. Mel feels better for their company.

She rowed back weeping, that last night on the water. She was lonely without the cat. She tried not to think about the last moments of its life. Not to think of the last moments of Joanna's.

The lake and the wind were very still. Nothing buffeted her. Yes, she had thought. Ignore me. Mel tied up the boat and walked back to her car and fell asleep in it right there by the road. She had been afraid to do that, to lose herself in the dark, to sleep behind the wheel as if somehow she might wake with the vehicle careering toward something, but she could not fight her exhaustion.

When she had jerked awake and her heartbeat had slowed, she felt, to her astonishment, better. Dry, headachey in the windscreen-filtered sun, but calmer.

Mostly now she tries not to think about it at all.

Of course that isn't possible. Sometimes during her therapy

sessions, she can't avoid it. It isn't therapy, exactly, she reminds herself, it's grief counselling, for Jo. Sometimes she tells her counsellor a little, a very little about what happened. She hints at what she thinks she saw. She does so in code. She is vague, she uses metaphors, so the brusque kind woman can think her client is talking about existential fears.

It gets better and worse and better again. Christmas was hard. She sent a letter to Joanna's parents and they did not respond. That was cruel, she thinks, that's really not ok. She spent two days with her father and terrified him by getting drunk and scared and crying a lot. She dreamed of the dark figure, the lost ape remnant on the wood.

But the nightmares ebbed. She still has them sometimes but they're only dreams. She'd fed the thing a sacrifice.

Mel spends the days at a computer, pushing text around templates. She is quiet, fearful of attention, but a real person, living in the city.

How could she not be changed? But no matter how much, no matter how everything that happened has hollowed her out and done something bad to everything, no matter her loss, it's hard to live with it every moment. The day after you see something that can't be unseen you are a salt pillar. Eight weeks after that, you still saw it, it's still there, but you're thinking about bus fares and bureaucracy too, you can't not. Mel can barely believe it but here she is in life again.

She is working, and sometimes now thinking of things other than the lake. Two weeks ago her counsellor said something about reckoning and accounting, about facing up to things, something well-meaning and point-missing that still made Mel feel better.

*

The city is dark and pleasantly cold. Mel buys microwave rice at the shop on the corner. She reads email on her phone as she passes a church and a launderette and descends to her basement flat. She turns on all the lights and showers to music: her radio is made for bathrooms, it sticks to tiles. She leaves it playing when she's done.

Mel calls her father, and talks to him while she cooks, over the muffled radio and cars and vans muttering past at head height outside. He chit-chats carefully and she listens, and answers his questions. In the middle of their conversation the music from the bathroom gets abruptly louder. There is a thud that makes her wince, then silence. 'Ouch,' she says. 'No, I'm fine, something broke. Can I call you back?'

The radio has slipped off the wall. It lies broken on the shower's floor. 'Oh fuck it,' Mel says. She bends to pick it up. Her face gets close to the drain. Her throat catches and she steadies herself, her hand down in the cold wet. She smells old rot.

Mel runs.

For an instant the thought comes that there might be a blockage, a problem in the pipes, but she knows that smell, that decay and sluggish lake water. It is not a London smell. And Mel knows as it fills her flat and she runs and tries to breathe and the air grows freezing around her that she has always known she would smell it again. There is nowhere beyond some attentions.

The dimensions of her corridor are wrong. Something is missing. She staggers. Runs into a chair, into the sideboard. There is slime on the wall and floor.

She has locked her front door. Mel makes it to the living room. She finds her bag and scrabbles and her keys aren't there. She grabs her phone. The rug is wet. Her books on all the shelves on all the walls are muddy. Mel is gasping. 'Help me,' she whispers into the phone as she dials emergency, as she hears her signal die in white noise. 'Help.'

In the kitchen and the bathroom and the bedroom, in the hall, the lights go out, one by one. Darkness comes in. There is a darkness between Mel and the city.

Why are you here? she whispers in her head, while she sinks to her knees and the smell comes and the light goes. What do you want?

There are lacks that won't be filled.

Mel tries to make herself small. Something comes before her. It knows her.

There is the clucking. Hiss. The execution sack streams. It gushes. It's so much bigger than it was. She fed it and it's bloated. A glutton. It has eaten more and taken time. The leather sack lurches wetly and protrudes with inside limbs and over her whimpering Mel hears a creak and animal sounds and words and the grind of bones.

Here comes the Säcken, full of new things. She hears cat noises. Here comes the poena cullei, and it wants, it would never not come, and like the stomach it is it will have her, and everything.

Its sutures unravel. The seams are law's mouths. They open not to let out but to take in. The Säcken opens to feed, to make her poena. And this time there is no Joanna to wake and save her.

Oh why did she think that?

Why did she think that now? As the rolling sack spurts mud on her and comes closer? Why now as she hears a mess of old voices and new? As a cat barks and a rooster hisses? As the leather strains and the poena looms and reaches and a dog tries to speak and a long-dead woman meows like a cat and a snake makes words and the poena opens and rank water pours out and Mel sees through the shadows what is inside at last and screams and screams and still hears a faint last sound.

Kikeriki, she hears, kikeriki, whispered in a voice she knows.

Syllabus

Humanity, Introspection and Debris

This is a three-week higher-level course. See separate sheet for reading list. Sophisticated engagement with the material is expected. Physical presence at classes is mandatory: echofigures may not attend in your stead.

Your final mark will be based on a single long-form essay agreed with your AI; OR a three-hour, three-question exam; OR a performative trance.

Week 1: Tip Life

The experiments of Ngosi and Backhouse have proved that, contrary to what had been assumed to be an injunction of ethical chronotourism, history is littered with the trash left by time-travellers. Since that realisation, various common items of everyday life have been proven to be such rejectamenta.

We will examine the nature of these proofs, particularly given our timeline's facility in smoothing over the scars of these discards; the political ramifications of living in a scree of future rubbish; the likelihood that some such garbage is from tourists from the *past*, rather than from the not-yet; and the importance, if any, of the fact that a disproportionate number of items of this repurposed rubbish are now quotidian features of modern streets.

Topics for discussion may include the following:

— Benches: what will they be originally?

— Why were bollards for so long held to be refugees from a future war? Why did this cease to be mainstream opinion?

— Can trees be recuperated?

You will be expected to show all proofs.

Week 2: The Misprision of Modern Relief

The arrival of insect ships to London skies in 1848 initially led to brief interplanetary war, until the 1849 Treaty of Sutton put an end to the conflict, after which relations between the British and visiting authorities thawed rapidly. We will review the history of this famous 'Misunderstanding' and its aftermath.

Our focus will be on the period following the inauguration of the first insect bishop in the Church of England (Bishop Insect of Manchester, in 1853) up to and including the present day, and the rapid spread of insects into their current leading positions in humanitarian and ethical organisations. We will examine the life and works of the famous 'Insect with the Lamp' among the wounded of Crimea; the strenuous efforts at slum clearance carried out by Insect and Insect in Birmingham during the 1890s; and the rise of the modern telethon and charity single, a sector still insect-dominated.

We will end with a comparison of Insect's famous 1962 Stockholm declaration that 'We will not rest until global suffering has been eradicated' with Eleanor Marx's excoriating 1890 pamphlet 'The Chitin of Charity'.

You will be expected to take sides.

Week 3: Cost–Benefit

In what was called 'the last and most awesome frontier', sickness in general and an increasing number of particular conditions were recently privatised in the UK. Can this be deemed a success? And if so, for whom, how and why?

We will perform a critical reading of the government's 'You Be Illin'!' advertising campaign to publicise the sale of shares. We will ask what correlation, if any, can be drawn between the precipitous rise in the price of shares in plague, the spread of the 'Cures are for Pussies' internet meme, and Diesel's 'You-Go Bubo' range of jewellery.

PLEASE NOTE: If you are, in the opinion of your AI, a member of the 'Pus-Tool' youth subculture, you may not write on this topic. The AI's judgement on this issue is final.

Dreaded Outcome

In the morning I had an empty-chair session with Charles B, so he could talk to his absent father. Generally I try to schedule those for the end of the day – they can be hard, emotionally, for me as well as for the patient – but this time there was no other option.

It was particularly tough because I was tired. I'd worked late the previous night. I've been doing that a lot. I'd ended up heading home after midnight, walking a long way past the lights of bars and down dark residential streets in the cold rain. I threw off my jacket, my gloves and my jeans the moment I came through my apartment door, and showered in very hot water – my showerhead defies New York City's low-flow rules – before falling into bed. But I was too wired to sleep. I got up again almost immediately. I did a few chin-ups at the bar I installed in my kitchen and, surrendering, I made myself a coffee. I've never been a great sleeper, particularly when I'm really focused on a project.

I'd broken a nail on my right index finger. The nude-coloured polish was noticeably chipped. I'll get a manicure as soon as I can. It's unprofessional to look ragged. In the meantime I filed it down, reapplied varnish, watched the dawn.

The edge was still a little uneven. Sitting in my clinic the next morning I dug it into the ball of my thumb to help myself concentrate. I facilitated Charles's questions to and answers from his father.

After lunch was Sara W. It was only her second session but things were becoming clear. She's in her thirties, buckling under a wave of anxiety. She's not ready to say so yet, but she wants and needs to leave her husband. Not that he's the cause of her difficulties: those she's carried from her parents.

After her was Brian G, a gambling addict. Then a short catchup with Ella P, whom I hadn't seen for weeks, and who was doing well. I'll keep her file and I hope she'll check in from time to time – I take a continuing interest in my patients – but I don't think she needs me any more.

The last session of the afternoon was with Annalise.

My name is Dana Sackhoff. I'm thirty-eight, and I'm coming up to my ten-year anniversary in this job. I've had my own practice all that time, here in Brooklyn.

My clinic's in Fort Greene. It's small, quiet and light, with an entrance direct to the practice, which patients prefer. I've worked to make the consulting room the right combination of homely but abstract – full of pleasant, forgettable art, warm colours, that kind of thing. There are copies of *Harpers* and *In-Style* in the waiting room, and some black-and-white photos of Coney Island roller coasters. There's a light-up pigeon I bought at Brooklyn Flea: I want patients to know that humour is allowed here.

I take just as much care over how I present myself: hip but not hipster, square-rimmed black glasses which I swear I was wearing before they became uniform, hair up, loosely. Not too touchy-feely, not too severe, not sexy, not sisterly. If H & M did a capsule collection like that, they'd clean up in the therapist market. In New York that's decent market share.

I have two small tattoos, which my patients never see.

I was pre-med at Yale, but I ended up doing my Master's and

PhD in psych theory. I was going to be an academic, even published a couple of papers, but when, out of curiosity, I took a course in therapeutic practice I knew I'd found my métier. I specialise in addiction and compulsion, trauma recovery and attachment disorder.

For years I've been turning my thesis into a book, though Elliott, my therapist, thinks that I'm too busy *not-writing* it to write it.

'I don't just mean you aren't writing it,' he said to me recently. 'Not-writing's an activity that takes up a lot of your energy and time. At least as much as writing would. Do you think you're invested in not-writing?'

Of course I'm sure there's truth there, but I don't think it's as simple as that. I'm invested, yes, but in other things, and anyway I've been getting increasingly energised about the project again recently, as even he allows. I'm collecting and collating case studies. I've been enjoying thinking of pseudonyms for the patients, along the lines of Freud's 'Wolf Man'. In my notes, Annalise Sobel is AS, but in my head she's Anguished Scholar.

It was my eighth session with Annalise. If I don't have a pretty clear idea of what's going on by session five, I'm probably not the right fit for a patient. With Annalise, I was clear.

She was not hyper or agitated as I've sometimes seen her. She was flat. I'd ask questions and she'd answer briefly, dutifully, without engagement. I was concerned but not surprised: it had been obvious enough that she was melting down that I'd recently suggested she come in more than once a week. 'We can work out the financial stuff later,' I'd said, hoping she'd take the hint and let me do an extra session or two without charge.

Annalise is forty-four, single, with many friends, well-liked, sociable, and cripplingly, clandestinely anxious. She's a linguist and a translator (I see her byline sometimes). Both her parents died a few years ago, within twelve months of each other, leaving a lot of stuff not dealt with. It was her mother with whom Annalise had been originally traumatically imbricated – gender notwithstanding, and without implying physical abuse, she'd been the 'little husband'. She had for years been re-enacting that model in her romantic and her overinvested social relationships.

She's been working hard. Annalise is what Afnik calls an 'inverted narcissist', though I prefer the term 'occult narcissist', and I differ from those who see the condition as synonymous with covert narcissism: related, maybe, but not the same. She's a compulsive care-giver, driven, full of deep need for, but discombobulated by, attention or praise. She has the fearful, resentful messianism of the child who's been trained into a duty of caretaking she can't fulfil. Annalise's fantasies involve disappearance. She catastrophises all the time, and makes things worse than they need to be by doing so. She fretfully attempts, and fails, to negotiate dreaded outcomes.

A lot of OCD dreaded outcomes are highly specific: if I don't wash my hands five times, my children will die, and so on. Annalise's are powerful, but nebulous. She's just full of dread.

She knows most of this, to some extent, and she knows she's depressed, but if knowing the problem was the solution, most patients wouldn't need us at all. I've been impressed with how she's tried to step up, her drive to change. I'm committed to helping her break her dynamics.

'I don't even really feel trapped,' she said. 'I hope it doesn't sound melodramatic or self-pitying. It's not that I don't see any way out, exactly – it's that I feel like there's no point looking for one.'

'Where are you feeling this in your body?' I said. I could see how constricted her chest was. 'I want you to breathe deeply for me.'

'I've been trying some of the techniques we discussed,' she said. 'With Sandra.'

'And?'

'And I think I'm doing ok for a while, but then . . .' She shook her head and her voice petered out.

Sandra was, or had been, a friend. She'd been part of Annalise's circle for a while, was a little younger, a financial analyst, driven and ambitious. She was also a veteran narcissist.

Over some months, she and Annalise had got closer, until Annalise had, with hard-won instincts, started to become aware that the relationship was provoking mostly unease and guilt in her. That the dynamic was dysfunctional. She'd been trying to pull back. Sandra, sensing this, had, in turn, ramped up the intensity, and the effective shame and guilt transference that characterised her behaviour.

Sandra made sure Annalise – and others – knew she considered Annalise to be letting her down, or worse.

Annalise had done her best to negotiate this terrain, but she was floundering, and struggling with her own tendencies to shame. She couldn't put the situation out of her mind. Her anxiety, and what might or might not be paranoia, was growing to disabling levels, keeping up with the vituperation. Annalise couldn't shake her sense that gossip was growing against her, that she was picking up whispers among her friends to the effect that she had been manipulative – even abusive – to Sandra. She'd even found an anonymous post on a forum linked to her university, that, while it didn't use names, she was convinced was about her, accusing her of cruelty, treachery, and so on.

I pointed out that even if she was right about the existence, target and source of these attacks (I suspected she was), few would take such claims at face value. But even if she could believe that, Annalise was tipping into a crippling – suicidal – anxiety.

She was facing one of the key issues of psychodynamics. Our routines of behaviour and affect of course operate through our cognition and emotion – but they also externalise. This is a limitation of therapy that focuses too narrowly and exclusively – you could say hermetically – on the patient's psyche. If patients have been trained into agonising at being inappropriately responsible for others, say, they might be straining to break that dynamic but until they do, until they succeed, they'll also compulsively seek out resentful narcissists. Who will hunt them, too, as an externalisation of *their* issues. They'll enter a dance, a spiral that feeds each other's self-destruction.

The issues are not, in other words, all in a person's head.

'You remember the diagram I showed you?' I said. 'This is "love-addiction". You're the object, right now. Of course you should be as responsible as you can for your behaviour – considerate and mindful, and so on, taking responsibility when you mess up – but you can't be responsible for someone else's happiness. What she's doing, in the jargon, we'd call "stowing away".

'She's afraid to take responsibility for her own actions and emotions. She resents her own agency. So she constructs situations in which she can tell herself she has none.

'She's inserted herself into your dynamics because they're a good fit for hers. That way she gets to be furious with *you* about where *she's* going. She's a stowaway. She got into your psyche, then blames you for the route.'

I don't like labels, but it's fair to say that my theory and practice broadly come under the small umbrella of what's called TVT: traumatic vector therapy. It's unabashedly pragmatic and eclectic. We draw on post-induction therapy, Gestalt, psycho-analysis, Adler (negatively), Kohut, Klein, whatever works. TVT once got described as 'a homeopathy of Laing', on the grounds that we take the idea from anti-psychiatry that dysfunction is a rational response to a pathological world, then dilute the insight until it's all gone – then try to use it. Which, to be fair, is witty.

'She's— are you saying it's because of her that I feel—' Annalise said.

'It's never that simple,' I said. 'She's not the *cause*. What she is is a *vector*.'

'What do I do?' Annalise's voice didn't break. We talked strategies again. I was careful to tell her I knew she was doing everything she reasonably could.

I had an appointment with Elliott, but I was agitated, thinking about Annalise, and feeling that I really needed to do some work that evening. I called him to postpone: I was relieved it went to voicemail. I spent an hour and a half at the gym, doing core, upper body, a hard treadmill session. I was near my PB over six miles.

It's not obligatory for a therapist to be in therapy, not in New York State, but a lot of us are. Particularly among TVT prac-titioners, it's considered a *sine qua non*. We take on a lot of our patients' stress, and we need to talk to someone who understands.

At home I showered and listened to my messages. Two friends, suggesting a drink, a call from David.

He's an architect. We met through a mutual acquaintance. We've been seeing each other, on and off, for a year. He's keen to move in – my apartment is nicer than his. I've told him I need some time.

By the time I'd eaten it was past seven. I considered an early night, but I knew I wouldn't sleep. I needed to work. I texted Annalise to check in on her. She replied that she was staying with her sister, which relieved me.

I sat on my sofa, pulled a couple of books off my shelves, and opened my laptop to do some research.

It was a little after 2am when I scaled the outside of a brownstone in Bushwick. I climbed the first two floors by the downpipe, brachiating silently up the rusting gutter to the fire escape.

A few lights were on in the houses around me but no one was visible. I was all in black with my mask down anyway, and I know how to stay still. I straightened the pack on my back, balanced on the stair railings and jumped up to get a grip on the building rim. I do a lot of finger chin-ups: from there it was pretty simple to get onto the roof.

I ran fast and silently the length of it and made the alley jump. I'd done recon: this was the best way to get where I was going. I took cover behind the wall at the roof's edge, opened my hockey bag and got my equipment ready.

I use a 22" Pro-Series 2000 PHL with a Leupold VX3 scope and a three-round magazine. My colleagues can keep their HK417s and M98s: we're not in downtown Basra. And sure, the 2000 has a kick. But we work in modern cities, not battlefield conditions. The PHL has a 1/2 MOA, and it comes in at less than 6.5lbs, which for situations like this one, involving climbing and running, is worth a lot.

I'd considered a VSS Vintorez, for the silencer, but honestly, if you take one shot, most people roll over in their sleep and think an engine's backfired. If you have to take more than one shot, maybe you shouldn't be a therapist.

There are reports of a new model out of Iran, the Siyavash, supposedly ultra-lightweight. I'm officially interested.

The light I was looking for, on the first floor of the building opposite, was on. Judging from timestamps on the messages Annalise showed me, Sandra often wrote in the small hours. I braced the barrel on its stand and took a crouching position, sighted through the glass.

A small tidy living room lit by a TV I couldn't see. Many books, a table with the remains of a meal on it. No people. I waited.

As therapists, the emotional welfare of our patients is our highest priority. Our job is to actualise mindfulness, maximise emotional welfare, help break compulsive and harmful dynamics, and to eradicate vectors of trauma.

As a TVT practitioner, I'm versed in detective techniques. I'd never asked Annalise any direct questions about Sandra. She'd never even mentioned her full name. Based on what little she had said, though, it hadn't been difficult, with some careful search-strings and phone calls, to ascertain her details, her address, enough about her life to make a plan.

Most of the time what our patients need is a compassionate, rigorous, sympathetic interlocutor. Sometimes the externalised trauma-vectors in dysfunctional interpersonal codependent psychodynamics are powerful enough that more robust therapeutic intervention is necessary. I checked my ammunition.

It's often parents and partners, but not always. I've intervened with teachers, friends, bosses, subordinates, exes, and stalking strangers. In an ideal world, I'd have had longer to plan. It makes things easier. A spring-loaded blade on a timer switch by the cables under a car, and the love-avoiding conduit for inadequacy in my patient Duane B had been lost in an accident. *While no one else was on the road,* let me add: I've never had any collateral damage. The father whose undermining of my patient Vince R kept him in a state of depression and anxiety died in what appeared to be a mugging gone wrong (I study Muay Thai). The guy still punishing his ex for his failure to be responsible for him half a decade on, skilfully feeding his anhedonia, had a tragic allergic reaction (this is why research is so important: I could have wasted time with potassium, cyanide, and so on, but it merely involved some judiciously placed peanut butter). Occasionally, though, therapy might be required on very little notice.

Sandra entered the room. She held her laptop in one hand, a glass of wine in the other. She wore a dressing gown and expensive glasses. She was tall and curved, with long blonde hair, striking and intense-looking. She sat at the table, squinted at her screen.

I adjusted for wind. I breathed out, steadied my hand.

As I started to tighten my finger, something shook against me.

I jerked, released my grip on my weapon and pulled my hands back, blinking. Being startled like that, in that moment, it would take almost nothing, the tiniest movement, to fire at the wrong instant, or to twitch the barrel, and then there'd have been a whole situation.

It was my phone. A text from Elliott, rescheduling. Another night owl, clearly. I was angry with myself for not turning vibrate mode off during a session. It was unprofessional. I shut the phone down and shook my head. At least I hadn't left the ringer on.

I rearranged myself and my rifle, looked back through the scope. Sandra was typing. I focused again. Got her in my crosshairs.

I squeezed the trigger.

The shot punched through the window and took out the back of her head. She went face-down hard onto her keyboard.

I reloaded and waited and held my breath. Long seconds passed and nothing happened.

I was pleased. Annalise had made a real breakthrough.

I got home at about 6am. When I'd been confident I wouldn't be interrupted, I'd descended, forced entry and removed the body and whatever money and valuables I could quickly find (as per the ethics of TVT practice, I would only keep money to cover my costs for the evening – everything else I would dump). To any detective with time and energy, this would look like a very peculiar robbery, but a lot of detectives don't have time or energy. And my patients, of course, know nothing about these radical interventions.

Annalise has an alibi, and there's nothing to link this trauma-vector to me.

I used Sandra's car to take the body to the river in Red Hook. I weighted it, and sunk it. There's no way it won't be found. But by the time it is, it'll simply be even more of a mystery.

I sent emails to the three patients I'd been due to see that day, postponing, citing illness. I unlocked my work cupboard, moved my katana and put the 2000 back in its box, reshelved the Mellody book back next to the Army sniper field manual 23-10. I lay down on the sofa and fell, finally, into some kind of sleep.

Even after such inadequate rest, the day after a tough session I always wake up energetic. I went out for a large breakfast, and sat for two hours over coffee, writing up my notes.

None of us knows – well, we shouldn't – which of our colleagues are TVT. If anyone asks, I'm a psychodynamic therapist. Which is true. Of course we all have close friends in the field, and you pick up cues and clues. I'm sure some of us end up admitting our theoretical approach to close friends we think share it. I never have, but I have suspicions of a few of the therapists I meet.

We publish in our forums and publications under *noms de thérapie* – mine is 'petita', a throwback to a brief Lacanian moment. Of course we have our sub-schools, our debates, our symposia. But there's never been an overview of the field. We've never had a textbook, an introduction for the aspirant practitioner.

The reason my book's taking so long is because I've become more ambitious for it. I want it to fill that gap.

I want sections on the history of psychotherapy; the influences that fed in to TVT; best practice in the clinic and the field; controversies; talking cures; research techniques; therapeutic intervention at close range (blade-work, poison, unarmed combat); therapy at range; disguising the scene of therapy; responding to a patient's guilty relief; and so on. The whole book's going to be interspersed with case studies. I've decided to make a virtue of a necessity: last night's action will illustrate a chapter on emergency interventions.

Of course I won't be able to publish openly, under my own name. I won't profit from it. What I hope, though, is that it might be important for our field. A seminal secret work. My ambitions are high, I openly admit.

Elliott goes for a more austere look than mine, both in person and in his clinical setting. His walls are white, his pieces of furniture few and plain. He has a small, tidy bookshelf full of dark hardbacks. He eschews pictures for trimmed plants in slim pots. He's more than ten years older than me, with short pepper-and-salt hair and expensive, slim-fitting suits that he can get away with. He's in good shape.

I must want all this authority or I wouldn't work with him.

I sat quietly. He wouldn't be much good at his job if he couldn't tell when I've had a difficult time.

'So,' he said. 'You postponed.'

'I had to work late. I didn't have the energy. The focus. But look, I got your text, I came as soon as I could.'

'Was this to do with your patient?'

'It was to do with the book. I was researching. For a chapter. Involving the patient, Annalise, yes.'

I told him about her session. Her embattlement and depression. I told him I was concerned, but at the same time confident she was close to moving toward a new phase.

'You've told me a little about this situation before,' he said.

'So anyway, afterwards, I went to the gym, and I was going to just wind down, but I couldn't. It's been going through my brain. So I gave up and cracked on with some work.'

'Did you finish it? Your work?' He steepled his fingers.

'I did,' I said. 'I really think I did. I think it was worth doing.'

'Have you spoken to the patient?'

'Not yet. I will, though.'

'I'm sure.' He pursed his lips and looked at me thoughtfully. 'You're very invested in this patient.'

'You think? I'm invested in all of them.'

'Of course. But – and I think you may not be aware of this – when you talk about her . . . Well, take a look.'

He gestured. I realised I was sitting forward in my chair, as if spectating at a sports match. I sat back, self-conscious.

'You tend to do that,' he said. 'You speak more quickly. I think you've become very particularly focused on this patient.'

'Possibly.'

'There's no judgement, you know that. This is part of what makes you a good therapist. And you're aware that those skills come with dangers. You're a facilitator: you're not a saviour.'

Elliott gave a rare smile, which I returned. Plenty of people in our line of work have something of a white knight in them.

'Well,' I said, 'I will say I find her . . . congenial, as well as interesting. So maybe, selfishly, I am invested in her. As a case study. For the book.'

He put his head to one side. He nodded slowly.

'Let me tell you what I see,' he said. 'You're tired. You've been working very hard, very long hours. Your demeanour changes when you talk about this patient. Which is often. Do you feel manic? You remember your desire for calm? What's happening is about *your* investment. This is about you, and in these terms, speaking as your therapist, this patient is about you, too.'

I was very still.

I looked away from him, at his books. The DSM-IV. Kohut on narcissistic injury. Jenkins on surveillance techniques. I breathed out.

Elliott opened his hands. 'I feel like you're carrying something of this person, with her complicity,' he said. 'That she's becoming a function for you. A vector.'

There's an empty lot across the street from Annalise's apartment. I'm crouched there behind an old washing machine. I'm watching the building with a customised AN/PVS-14 night-scope.

Annalise went to bed forty minutes ago, walking through her apartment dressed in a thin white nightgown, carrying a glass of water, her hand clenched around what I suspect is at least one sleeping pill. She, like me, has insomnia, and any kind of loud work at ground level is always risky, so I'm carrying my JM Special dart gun loaded with an S10 syringe of etorphine hydrochloride.

It's not ideal. I'll be exposed for several seconds, but I've already prepped a car, I'll be across the road fast the moment the seizure starts. No one's coming back from that amount of M99.

I took a Provigil earlier, and I feel sharp. I could really have used an early night, but, like Elliott, I take my therapeutic practice very seriously. My priority is my patients.

As I lean into the battered metal, I hear a faint sound behind me. I turn fast and stare into the shadow. There's nothing. A few tall weeds wave in the dirt, overlooked by the walls of apartment buildings. A rat, I think. A cat.

And as I think that, a strong arm goes around my throat and another disarms me with an expert twist, throwing the dart gun across the lot.

I should have predicted this. He's a professional. He predicted me, that I'd guess his therapeutic plans and try to stop him. But then I am his patient.

'I think we should talk about strategies and decision-making, Dana,' Elliott whispers into my ear. He's trying to get me in a headlock.

I struggle to get away, then abruptly push back into him. He's off-balance and I slip out of the hold but he blocks my elbow strike and counterattacks hard enough to send me staggering.

He's between me and the dart gun. He's in the same all-black gear as me, a stab-jacket, cargo pants. He's got a knife sheathed on his belt. 'I understand you have hesitations, and I know this approach will be difficult,' he says, gesturing at Annalise's window. I can tell from his stance that he prefers groundwork. He wants to go for a takedown. I stagger, act more dazed than I am. He probably knew I'd do that. He's good at his job.

'I think we should talk about your mother's unhappiness,' he says. 'It's time for you to stop carrying it.' He grabs for Aikido *nikyo* grip but I back out of range. 'You're using your relationship with this patient as a block.'

We circle. He slaps away my body kick. His guard is up, he's quick, he's stronger than me, and he knows me well.

But I have two things on my side.

The first is that I do my research. I feint right, then as he goes for the shoot I spin and take out his left knee, where I know he has a sports injury dating back to college. It buckles.

The second is that I'm his patient.

I lean over and shove him down and he's holding back, restraining himself, trying to strike up at me with open hands, going for an immobilising lock, not a disabling or killing blow. My welfare is his prime consideration. That's why he's here.

'She's a vector,' he grunts. 'Let me do my job.' I put my left hand over his mouth and he tries to bite me through my glove. He grabs for my fingers as I fumble in my stab-jacket pouch for another syringe.

I've never had to take a second shot, to use spare ammunition. That doesn't mean I'm foolish enough to not bring it.

I'm not constrained like Elliott, of course. We're both here for our patients.

I shove the needle into his neck and push the plunger. His eyes go wide and he grunts under my hand and shakes and tries to dislodge me but he weakens fast. I hold him down as he goes sluggish. He spasms.

Cautiously, I take my hand away. 'Let me help you,' he

mumbles while my adrenalin subsides. His eyes roll back and he starts to fit.

Eventually he stops moving. I sit back and take shaky breaths. I try to be mindful.

There are no unusual sounds in the streets. No cop cars approaching. I slump with relief. No lights have come on in Annalise's apartment.

He's a heavy, muscular guy: it's going to be a long night. When Annalise wakes up tomorrow, she won't even know it, but a serious potential setback in her recovery will have been overcome.

I need a new therapist.

After the Festival

Charlie and Tova had been in Dalston Square since before noon, and it was past three. Spring light made the windows and the shop signs shine. 'I can't believe how gentrified this place is,' Charlie said.

The last band had finished playing several minutes earlier, but Charlie still had to shout over the *oomph* of a stereo.

'Yeah yeah blah blah,' Tova said. 'I can't believe how *ugly* it is. Who'd live here? Come on.' She pulled him by his collar and they squeezed through the crowd to get close to the stage. 'Right then,' she said.

The proscenium around the stage-front was festooned with sponsors' logos. Technicians in black took away the last of the drumkit, set up microphones, wheeled a big industrial cooker to the back of the stage, and bolted a steel framework into place in the centre. They checked the connections, the restraints and chains.

'They're running so late,' Charlie said.

'They always do,' Tova said. 'Look, there he is.'

The young TV presenter was smoking with his back to the chilly wind, going over notes and talking to a striking, well-dressed woman in her fifties, his director, who showed him marks on the stage.

'Have you ever seen his show?' Tova said. She took a picture of the man. 'For the niece,' she explained.

'Yeah right,' said Charlie.

Someone in the audience cheered, and the cheer spread and grew louder and more confident. Charlie tapped Tova's shoulder as a group of men and women in white butcher's uniforms walked onto the stage. The director waved them to a corner and spoke into her headset.

The presenter went to the front of the stage and shouted into a mic, 'Not yet, you muppets!' He grinned into the laughter and put a finger to his earpiece and listened. He thought to put on a pompous face and hold up his hand to the crowd like someone taking a brief phone call, so there were more laughs.

'I'm talking bollocks,' he said. 'Turns out it *is* yet.' There was another, louder cheer as the technicians cleared the stage.

Electronic music came on, too loud.

'Ouch,' said Tova.

'Are you ready?' the presenter shouted, raising whoops. You could have hoped for warmer weather but it wasn't raining. People in the crowd started dancing.

'He's such an annoying prick,' Charlie said as the presenter gabbled.

'Shut up, Grandad,' Tova said. She gripped his arm because, this close to the stage, even over the music, they could hear snorting and the step of hoofs.

Three more butchers came on. They led a pig in chains.

The crowd hallooed. Tova ululated and Charlie laughed.

The pig was huge, close to two metres from nose to the end of its tail. It was lean and muscular and it strained against its chains with a recalcitrant dignity. Everyone knew it was drugged.

Its handlers locked it into position in the reinforced frame and clicked the spatter-guard in place.

'Oh yuck,' Tova said. She turned away and met Charlie's eyes. 'Tell me when it's over.'

'Why do *I* have to watch?' he said.

Tova was not alone: many people in the crowd were covering their eyes. The presenter's inanities did not lessen the tension. Music still played but they turned it down and the pig, perhaps caught up in the tension, grunted louder and louder.

'Get on with it,' Tova said, still looking at Charlie. 'Tell them to get on with it.'

'Alright then,' the presenter announced. Some young men tried to start up a football chant but it didn't take. The head butcher held an electric device to the pig's head.

'Oh for fuck's sake,' Charlie said.

When the man triggered it the current made no sound and the pig's convulsion was abrupt and contained. The crowd hushed to see it spasm and slump in its chains.

'Is that it?' said Tova.

Charlie shook his head. 'Just the stun.'

The butcher picked up a knife and cut the animal's throat.

Blood hit the plastic shield. People throughout the crowd gasped and Charlie hissed and Tova's eyes widened at the sight of his expression.

The organisers turned up the music as the pig bled out and the knifemen and knifewomen started up the burners. 'Wait,' Charlie said, but Tova was already turning to see.

Everyone was quick. By the time the performers were halfway through butchering the carcass, the first rounds of cuts were cooking and the delicious smell was spreading, and the crowd was noisy and the young man from TV had his momentum back. It was a carnival again.

'Ok, I get it,' Charlie said. 'He is annoying but he's quite good at this shit.'

When Tova shouted, 'How can it be this late?' and Charlie looked up in surprise at the dark sky, they were both drunk. People were dancing and lining up for meat. A ska band played at the side of the stage, the lead singer cavorting around the butchers. The pig was nearly gone.

The main butcher was digging at the inside of the animal's head, gouging and scooping out tissue. He cut it away and lifted it by the ears – you could see how heavy it was. To a redoubled cheer, he danced with it as if it was a partner.

'Who's ready?' the presenter shouted. 'Who's ready? Prepare the yard!' he shouted. 'East London, are you *ready*?' There was a rush and a counter-rush, people jostling to get closer to the stage, others to get further away.

'Well?' said Tova, but Charlie was already gone. She laughed and looked around, shouted his name. He was tall: she found him easily. 'No way!' she yelled, to see him. He was moshing in the stage-front pit, his blond head swaying.

'Who wants it?' the presenter shouted. 'Who wants it?'

The crowd bellowed.

'Are you scared? Come on, don't make me come looking!'

The head butcher swung the head. The crowd shouted and waved their arms as if it was a bouquet to catch. 'You want it?' the presenter said. 'You want it? Do you?'

He muttered off-mic to the butcher as they scanned the dancers. They made as if they were going to throw the head one way, then another.

'This guy?' Tova heard the presenter say, and she screamed in delight because she could see that he had chosen Charlie. She leapt up and down, laughing in disbelief, and she could see that Charlie was doing so too, howling himself. He craned his neck, stood as tall as he could. The butcher hefted the head by its ears.

'Oh God,' Tova said, laughing and screwing up her face and wincing with disgust. 'No fucking way, Charlie.'

Two stagehands hauled him up onto the stage and the butcher muttered to him. Charlie looked uneasy. He looked as if he was trying to be excited.

Just as Tova shouted, 'Fuck's sake, Charlie,' there was a chance lull in the shouts and the band's playing so she was perfectly audible and it raised a big laugh. Charlie smiled and looked for her.

'One Step Beyond,' said the presenter, and the bass player riffed on that tune for a second. Together, the butcher and Charlie raised the meat. Charlie's sick look left him suddenly, and he grinned at the crowd. Charlie lowered the wet pig's head over his own.

It took Tova half an hour to make her way to him. When he was led down from the stage the crowd thronged him. He steadied the big head on his own with one hand, gripping the shoulder of a stagehand with the other. A cameraman followed him and Tova followed the camera.

Security in dark clothes kept people away from Charlie so he could dance ridiculously, tottering under the weight of the bloody head. The presenter kept up a stream of commentary.

'Christ, Charlie,' Tova kept shouting as if he could hear. Spit and blood dripped onto his clothes.

He kept bending backward and tilting the pig head up, as if it looked at the sky. Tova could see that Charlie was trying to see out of its mouth. Stagehands kept wiping the head.

Charlie was a good pig head. He danced with everyone he could. Tova heard the leader of the stage crew yell into the pig's mouth, 'Are you up for a little walkabout then?' and Charlie made the head nod.

They took him out of the square and up Malvern Road where music from another party mixed with their own. A mass of new people came to join them.

Surrounded by a crew of organisers like the one around Charlie, followed by a second boisterous crowd, another tall figure came stepping carefully forward. A thick, blunt, dense head rose from a man's muscular shoulders and wobbled over the scene. An ugly grinning mouth and dead eyes staring up. The man was wearing the decapitated head of a porpoise over his own. He squinted through eyeholes cut in the neck.

The two crowds cheered and merged. The mask-wearers met and danced. Their shoulders were very bloody and the flesh they wore dripped. The pig head and the porpoise head bounced up and down and circled each other for a few minutes until their entourages led them on in different directions. All around them, lights were coming on.

The crew led Charlie a long way. The whole of this area of London was full of partying crowds. Tova could hear celebrations everywhere. It took a long time to walk the length of any street.

'I'm his friend,' Tova shouted to the leader of Charlie's crew. 'How much longer?'

'It's fine,' he shouted. 'The ram's over that way, and some others. Little while.'

At the corner of Richmond and Queensbridge Roads, his crowd behind him, Charlie met a man wearing a horse's leering head and a woman bloody under a bear's, and the three danced together to chaotic overlapping music.

Tova followed as closely as she could. Several minutes passed until she saw the pig crew receive instructions into their radios. They all shifted into a different mode, moving at the same moment. They stopped Charlie and shouted and turned off their music.

'Alright, folks,' shouted the leader. 'Time, ladies and gents, please.' There were loud boos from all over. 'I know, I know. Say goodnight to the pig. Don't shoot the messenger. His pigness is tired. Say goodnight, everybody.' The man kissed the damp cheek of the pig's head and grimaced and grinned. People bayed for one more song, but they began to disperse, heading back toward where they'd seen the other meat-headed figures, to find a late-night sound-system.

'Doesn't take much,' the man said. 'The ride'll be here in a sec. You said you was with him?'

Tova nodded.

The man turned to Charlie. 'Can she come?'

Charlie pig-nodded.

They sat in the van with a strange kind of shyness. Charlie kept touching the head on his own. Tova laughed. The crew members with them filled out paperwork.

'You fucking nutter,' said Tova. Charlie said something from within the head that she could not hear. 'This is so disgusting.' She grinned at him.

This time she made it out. 'It was great,' he said.

The laboratory was in the basement of St Mary's Hospital in Shoreditch. An orderly led them. It was past nine and the snack shop and florist were long closed but there were patients and staff in the corridors. They stared. A few cheered. One little boy in a hospital gown screamed with delight. He and his mother smiled at Charlie's muffled shriek back.

'Mr Pig.' The doctor was brusque and posh and about thirty years older than Charlie and Tova. She greeted him by the traditional soubriquet with autopilot heartiness. 'I'm Dr Allen. Do come in.' Two much younger doctors waited by the steel door of a refrigerated chamber with a wire-glass window.

'Do you do all the animals here?' Tova said.

'Oh, hardly,' said Allen. 'They're all over. We just do this fellow and Mr Jag. Who has already been sent happily if rather damply home.'

'A jaguar?' said Tova.

'You didn't hear? New this year and rather popular I'd say.' Allen slapped the pig's head. 'And how are you in there?'

'Good,' Charlie said through the mouth. He gave her a thumbs-up.

'And as you come to the end of your tenure as Mr Pig, what do you go by the other days of the year?'

'Charlie Johns,' he shouted.

'Righto. This shouldn't take more than a few minutes, then off you can toddle. I'm sure the chaps from the news will want to talk to you. Are you squeamish?' Allen asked Tova. 'If you're quite sure you're not you're welcome to watch.'

The doctor had laid out tools on the side. 'Let's just pop this off,' she said.

'Who does the porpoise?' Tova said.

'I think that's Central London Hospital. Why?' When Tova said nothing, she said, 'You needn't worry, it's all jolly sustainably done. Can you take the ears please, Derek?' One of her colleagues stepped forward. Allen and he gripped the meat. 'Upsadaisy.'

They lifted together. There was a wet sucking noise.

'Sure you're alright?' Allen said to Tova.

'Hold on,' said Charlie, muffled through the flesh. He shifted in his chair and said something inaudible. They let the head back down again.

'Alright,' Charlie said. The doctors lifted again, a few centimetres. 'Ow,' he said. 'Ow.'

When they replaced it this time Dr Allen reached into the pig's mouth and felt Charlie's face. 'Does that hurt?'

'My chin a bit,' Charlie said. Allen's face did not move. She picked up what looked like secateurs.

'Now do stay still.' She put the blades to the corner of the animal's mouth and cut, extending its grin. She peeled back the sides of the slit and looked in.

'Oh, bugger,' she said and quickly snipped more. 'Derek, get hold here. Sally, sluice please. Now, I don't want you to worry,' she said to Charlie.

'What is it?' said Tova.

Charlie made noises.

Her colleague handed Allen something like a turkey-baster which she pointed into the pig's mouth.

'I need you to keep your eyes and mouth tight closed, Charlie, alright? This is going to feel cold.'

'What is it?' Tova said again. She could hear Charlie grunting out of the pig's mouth.

'I know, I know,' said Allen. 'Derek, hard up on three.' She squirted, and cut, and counted.

The doctors lifted. The pig's head rose slowly from Charlie's white face. He blinked in slime.

His chin was bleeding. The skin of his cheeks was wet and rucked and oozing. Swellings spotted him as if he had a disease. Tova put her hand to her mouth. Charlie blinked.

'Now, Mr Johns,' Allen said.

Tova looked into the pig's head. 'Oh what the fuck is that?' she shouted.

Lining the inside of the cushion of meat in the pig's skull, extruding from the tissue, were thousands of little black wormlike stubs. They wriggled frantically. They clutched at nothing.

'Now Mr Johns,' Allen said, and Charlie screamed and stared into the meat.

Tova swallowed back vomit. Charlie's lips dripped with what might be pig-ooze or might be his own spit.

'Now, there's nothing for you to panic about,' Dr Allen said. She spoke quickly. She picked up the pig's head with its new slit and its fingerlike extrusions and handed it to her colleagues.

Tova saw filaments flailing from its tongue. She saw blood on the pig's teeth. 'What are you doing with it?' she shouted.

'Tests,' said Allen. 'Will you please settle down? I'm speaking to Mr Johns. Mr Johns, clearly something's gone a little wrong but it's important you know there is no long-term risk to you. I do understand of course that it's a rather unsettling sight . . .'

There was a raw patch on Charlie's chin, ringed with patches like pustules. He touched it gently, breathed heavily.

'Let's get you washed up,' Allen said. 'I must say it's highly unusual for this sort of thing to happen so quickly.' She led him to a high sink. 'Give yourself a good scrub,' she said. 'Use the soap here, and then a little of this gel, just put a good bit of that on your poor old chin, and I'll tell you what we're going to do. Now I really don't want you to worry. It's a very simple little course I have in mind. And as I say, really, everyone could very reasonably have had confidence that nothing would go wrong.'

'Who gives a fuck about that?' Tova shouted.

Dr Allen turned and demanded she shut up and Tova was startled, and did, in fact, go quiet.

It was a bad year. Later, Tova and Charlie discovered that there were four other cases of intrusion that night. Those affected were the wearers of the crocodile, the cow, the gorilla, and one of the two wearers of the hippo. Each of those skulls – or its forward half, in the last case – ended up infected with dark vermiform suckers.

In the other cases, the revellers had worn the animal heads for a little longer than guidelines suggested. Charlie, though, it was agreed, had been unlucky. His crew had been careful.

Allen and her colleagues looked after all the intruded.

'It's ok,' Charlie said. It was three days after the festival, and he and Tova were having lunch in the Pizza Express near his house. He fiddled with some garlic bread. 'She's a bit of a blow-hard is all. But those other two, they were saying to me that she knows this stuff better than anyone.'

'How do you know they're not full of shit?' Tova said. 'What do you have to do? You look rubbish, mate.'

The lines and shadows around Charlie's eyes were deep. His skin was not good – it was still very raw. There were no holes visible where the little filaments had probed and entered it, and few scabs, but his face looked, rather, as if it did not fit him quite well, as if it was a bit too big. He blinked and was distracted.

'I have to take these pills for like a month or something.' He looked down. 'I go in every day, we all do—'

'Seriously?'

'Yeah, that's what they want. And she weighs me and asks me what I'm eating. And, and they do experiments on the heads, I think, they have them on ice. They have us all, sort of, talk about what happened.'

'Do they . . . Charlie, have they made you put it back on again?'

'*Made* me? They can't *make* me anything.'

'Have they?'

'There are *tests*,' he said. 'It's research.'

'Do you know how weird you sound?' she said, and before he could answer, continued, 'Would you put on any of the other heads?'

'No.' He almost shouted. 'Jesus Christ, are you mad?'

'Do I need to be worried?' Tova said at last.

'No. No. Did you look up about it online?'

'Of course I did.'

'Well, so, you know as long as you get it quickly it's completely curable.'

Charlie watched two women walk past the window beside their table. He eyed the big dog one of them restrained, a dog too big for London. 'And they couldn't have got it much more quickly.'

Tova considered asking him what it had felt like, but did not. 'What *are* you eating, then?' she said. 'And how's your work?'

'You mean are they pissed off with me going into hospital all the time? They have to put up with it, really, don't they? Imagine if they started giving me shit about it.'

The intrusions had maintained press interest for longer than in a traditional year. Tova kept seeing articles asking whether safety had been too low a priority. Politicians complained, as they did every year, as they did after the Notting Hill Carnival.

Charlie texted Tova that he had turned down an interview with the *London Evening Standard*.

She called Charlie every day and was concerned whenever it took him any time to answer or get back to her. Sometimes it was hours.

'I've been a bit all over the place,' he said a week after their lunch.

'Where are you? Are you in work right now?'

'Calm down. I was, I was just there but then I went to the lab. I wanted to see . . . I can hear you're worried . . . I'm on my way back home, though, I've got stuff I need to . . .'

'Can you hear me, Charlie?' she said. 'The line's terrible.'

'It's fine for me. I've just been talking to the others.' She knew he meant the others who had been intruded. 'We were talking, after the session.' Their appointments overlapped. Sometimes Allen and her colleagues saw several of them together. 'Just, you know, talking about what happened. It's interesting. That's all. Everyone sort of remembers different bits, sort of has a different feeling about the way it all happened, you know?'

'No,' she said. 'Obviously, no.'

He told her thank you but no, she couldn't buy him lunch, and he promised to call the next day. When he did not she went to where he worked, an administration department in a publisher of trade magazines.

'We told him last week not to bother coming in for the next week or so,' his boss told her. 'He needed to get his head together. I'm not blaming him, I'm just saying.'

'He was here yesterday, though,' Tova said.

'I didn't see him.'

Charlie was not at home. When she texted him Tova could

see her messages went through, but he didn't have the settings activated that let her know whether or not he had read them.

The young doctor Derek Jansen whispered down the phone, so Tova knew that his boss was in the room.

'I shouldn't really be talking to you,' he said.

'I know and I really appreciate that you are. I've been a bit worried about Charlie.'

'Yeah, I get that. I know he's a bit . . . It's just, doctor–patient stuff, you know? It'll just take a while for him to get back to himself. Slow and steady. Some people respond slower than others.'

'Is he slow?'

'I'm just saying. It takes everyone however long it takes them.'

'Did you ever work out what went wrong? For an intrusion to happen so fast?'

'Sometimes it just happens. It's not like there's anything odd about this specimen, really. I mean, we are taking a look. We're working as quickly as we can. Charlie and the others are patient with what we do, which is helpful, so we can do comparative stuff. More than patient, they've been volunteering to come in every day.'

'Volunteering?'

'But we have to be quick: preservative can sort of mess with your results, so we can't use that on the specimens. Hence the fridge, although even keeping them in the cold store, this batch of heads is going off quicker than I'd like. Hello? Are you there?'

'Sorry,' said Tova. 'You got me thinking.'

The next day she took a taxi to the hospital in the late afternoon. She felt absurd, huddled in her warm coat in the tiny park across from the sunken entrance to the lab, a direct entrance from the street. She sat disguised under layers. She waited.

First the patients left, then the lab staff. The sky grew dark. She saw a squat man in his thirties, a woman, and Charlie himself come up in a group and nod to each other and walk briskly away. Minutes later, Derek ascended wrapping a scarf around his neck. A short while later Dr Allen, talking loudly into her phone.

Less than half an hour after they had left, the squat man returned. He looked around him, he then descended. Then Charlie came back.

He walked quickly and his shoulders were up.

Tova gave it a minute, then approached slowly to the top of the stairs leading down to the laboratory door. She descended quietly. She wiped a window beside the threshold clean. Tova dropped the filthy tissue and put her hands to the glass and looked in.

One light was on, in the furthest corner of the room. There was no motion. The illumination came from the refrigerated annex: the door was propped open. Tova moved a little to see inside and said clearly and as calmly as she could, 'Oh Jesus fucking Christ, Charlie.'

She could see him sitting, motionless, his back leaning against a bench within the refrigerated chamber.

He did not look like a person but like a puppet, top-heavy, bad and absurd, because he wore the pig's head again.

Tova hammered on the door.

'Charlie,' she shouted. 'I'll get the cops if you don't let me in.'

He was not moving but someone else was. The squat man had been sitting near him on the floor, she realised, and now was rising, shuffling toward her. 'Let me in right fucking now,' she said.

He pushed the door open a slit and started to say something guarded and Tova shoved past him easily and came inside. The man's face was moist and he smelt. Tova ran to the cold where Charlie sat slumped.

The skin on the pig's head was wrinkled and bruisy blue. Charlie's shoulders were claggy with its half-frozen matter. The cut in its cheek flapped. Loose flesh hung under its sinking eye.

'Take it *off*,' she shouted. She cried out in more disgust to see a woman kneeling in the corner, wearing a cow's cold head.

Where the thickset man had been sitting was a hacked-off crocodile head. 'You can't come in here like this,' the man said. 'This isn't your business. You can't do that.'

He plucked at her as she pulled at the pig's head Charlie wore. She slapped the man's hand away.

'Help me or fuck off,' she said.

'You can't just *yank*,' he said. He had swellings on his wet face. He hesitated a moment then took hold of the pig's flesh. 'Look,' he said. 'You have to—' He ran a hand gently around the neck hole, pushed his fingers into the dead mouth, making Charlie moan. 'Ok.'

They pulled the head off together and tipped it away. It hit the floor with a moist thump. Tova kicked it and it rolled unevenly and she saw the black tentacles on its inside, writhing on the swollen lump of its tongue, clutching for Charlie's face. They twitched sluggishly in the chill.

Charlie blinked, slick with mucal coating. She reeled from the smell of him. His chin looked gnawed. Swellings wept on his skin.

'Tova,' he said. He focused slowly. 'Tova.'

'Charlie,' she said. She almost cried. 'Look at you . . . What are you doing?'

'Tova.' He wobbled slowly to his feet. 'What are *you* doing?' His voice was thick as if he was drunk. 'This is, you know I have to—'

'Seriously, Charlie?' she said. She shivered and watched her breath. 'Don't fucking talk shit to me. I know what you're doing. This isn't your treatment, *look* at you.'

'You don't even know,' he said. 'What you're talking about.'

'Christ, you can hardly talk. What are you doing? How'd you get in, did you steal the keys to this place? Did he?' She pointed to the man who had worn the crocodile. The cow woman did not move.

Charlie left the cold chamber and went to a basin and turned on a tap. He bent to it. He did not drink, but he stuck out his tongue and closed his eyes as the water ran over it.

'I'm going to be sick,' Tova said. The marks on his face were already deflating, but she could see them still raw in his mouth. His tongue was grey and dimpled, looked almost mouldy.

Charlie opened his eyes and they widened when he saw the pig's head lying on its side.

When Tova brought out her phone, Charlie came back to her and knocked it out of her hand. He stared at her, startled with guilt. The other man picked it up and returned it to her but it was broken. Charlie ran his hands over the inside of the pig mask.

'You have to go,' the crocodile man said to Tova.

'You need help,' she said.

'It ain't like that,' he said. He pushed her gently toward the door.

'It is, though,' she said. 'I'm calling the cops.'

'If you do that,' he said, 'they'll come here and it'll get bad. You want them on us? You want to send him to jail? Look—' He stood with her by the bottom step and tried to formulate something. The muck on his face had dried into foul crust. 'Look, I know we can't . . . You can't understand. It's . . . we're fixing this. This is the last time.'

Of course she didn't believe him. Despite her threat, nervous of what they might do, she was not ready to set the police on Charlie. She called Derek instead.

'I don't know how,' she said, 'but they got keys to your lab. No wonder the heads've been going off quick, they're breaking in there and putting them back on while you're at home. They've just been sitting there.' She heard him catch his breath and whisper a curse. 'How bad is it?'

'It's not – I don't know,' he said. 'The intrusion itself, the feelers? They're gross but they don't do you any damage, we don't think. And it's not as if everyone in intruded heads goes this way . . . but it can be addictive. We've got some substitutes. I think they gave some to the woman who wore the hippo. It doesn't normally go on like this, not this long . . .'

'Everyone keeps saying that: it doesn't normally. It has though. And they're there right now being junkies. Maybe I *should* send the police.'

'Wait. We ought to – look, I'm going to call Dr Allen, and we're going to go over. I'm heading over now. She needs to know about this.'

'Do what you need to and do it fast. I'm not going to watch Charlie fall apart like this.'

'Ok, give me like an hour. I'll call you back.'

In fact he called her much before that and shouted down the line at her, his voice querulous and panicky.

'They're gone,' he said. 'They must've taken off as soon as you left. The police are on their way, it's all gone wrong. Treatment went great with the others but I don't know what's happening to these three, I don't know what's going on. They took them.'

'They took the heads?' Tova said.

'They took the heads.'

The police went to his flat but Charlie was not there, and it did not seem as if he had come back after going to the hospital. Tova was abruptly sure that she would never hear anything of him again.

The police asked her if she could shed any light on what Charlie was thinking, what his motivations were. What he might do.

'We're concerned for their safety,' the officer said.

'Me the fuck too,' shouted Tova, 'and no I don't have any idea, that's the whole point, I don't know what he's doing.'

Tova was wrong. Within two days, she did hear reports of what Charlie was doing. Charlie, and Neil and Simone, the intruded wearers of the pig, crocodile and cow's heads.

A couple in London's northern suburbs reported seeing three masked, naked people in their garden. Journalists visited the ring of affluent commuter towns and mega-fields surrounding the capital, following more leads.

A teenager uploaded mobile phone footage onto YouTube. An ugly patch of dead, tooth-white trees by an unkempt field. A broken-down combine harvester rusted by oily mud. The footage wobbled.

'There,' someone said to the unseen cameraman. '*There*. Are you blind, man?'

In the distance, in the fringe of growth, two unclothed men

ran from tree to tree. They kept hold of the swaying heads they wore, the bobbing crocodile's and the pig's. They were too far to make out well but Tova could see the ugly grey-white of Charlie's skin and the brown of Neil's, their stiff ridiculous motions. The men ran without enthusiasm, heavy and unconvincing with aimless urgency, as if hiding, then as if hunting, only making themselves more visible. They stopped and stood tall and looked around through the mouths of their meat masks. They dropped to all fours and disappeared from sight. You could hear the unseen boys who filmed them goading each other to go closer. The footage ended.

'What are they doing?' Tova said.

'I don't know,' said Derek. She could hear him breathing, trying to work out what he was allowed to tell her. 'We have theories but—'

'So tell me theories.'

'No. I'm sorry, I'm not going to because they're literally just – we don't know.'

'They're trying to live off the land,' she said.

'We're guessing.'

The police asked her if Charlie had tried to contact her. She laughed at them. 'Have you seen what he's doing?' She did not like the sound of her own voice.

The papers called the fugitives the Animal Three. They were filmed again by news helicopters, from the bonnetcam of a police car, on CCTV behind warehouses. They shivered with cold in the shallow muddy pond by a fallow field. They picked across a rugby pitch in fading light. A nightwatchman saw Charlie through a fence, taking eggs from the hutch of a pet hen and cracking them one by one through the mouth of the pig, into his own.

Simone stood in rubbish behind a Co-op and stared into the security camera lens. The cow's head was collapsing on itself, deliquescing on her head. The horns had tipped in towards each other as the crown of the head rotted, as if straining to touch their tips together. The skin was mottled and maggots dropped from it. Simone shuffled towards a gravel pit.

'This isn't the fucking Wild West,' Tova said. 'We're talking about an estuary in Essex. Why can't someone just find them?'

'You'd be surprised how long a person who knows what they're doing can hide out,' the liaison officer said. Delingpole was a woman barely older than Tova.

'Charlie's in fucking *admin* . . .'

'Well not any more he's not.' Tova had no response to that. 'Look . . . Thing is, we think we *do* know where they are. Tova, will you help us?'

'What do you want me to do?'

'You're Charlie's best friend. You're the last person – other than those two, if you count them – who spoke to him.'

'Jesus,' she said. 'Are you going to ask me to try to *get through to him*?'

Delingpole drove Tova through unpleasant towns and industrial estates in the belt beyond London to acres of scrappy countryside wedged between brownfield sites. There were police cars and an ambulance. Tova saw Dr Allen and Derek waiting in its back. She waved and Derek responded.

A slope of dock leaves and nettles, a barn slumped on a hole where it lacked a wall, leaning over the darkness. In the middle of the gap was a chair. Officers in stab-jackets were setting up equipment, muttering into their radios. As Tova approached, she saw several of them report her presence.

'There?' she said.

She sat and wrapped her coat around her and shivered while the police team fussed and attached leads to a microphone braced before her. A cold wind raced past her, smelling of tyres.

'So they're in there?' she said, nodding toward the thickets and tangles of trees at the bottom of the slope she faced. Someone turned on an arc light as if in answer and the green shone.

'Turn that the fuck off,' someone else shouted, and was obeyed.

A senior officer squatted in front of Tova.

'You've been briefed, then?' he said. 'You know what to do?' Tova nodded and the man walked immediately away.

'You nervous?' said Delingpole.

'Should I be?' said Tova.

'No. Break a leg.' Delingpole patted Tova's shoulder and backed away. 'Kill the lights,' Tova heard her say. 'We're ready.'

One by one the police around her withdrew from sight. They turned off their torches and killed their radios. Tova sat alone and watched the evening progress, the line of vegetation blacken into shadow on shadow. There was a glow in the distance, some town, she supposed, but as the minutes passed this little patch of wild land was quite dark.

She sat alone. 'Charlie,' she said. She leaned back, startled, at the crackling boom of her own staticky voice from the loudspeakers, blaring into the night and the trees. 'Charlie. You must be starving and you must be freezing and Jesus, mate, you must be sick as a dog.'

What if he *did* come?

Tova heard bats and thought the word *pipistrelle* with pleasure. She knew the police and the doctors were close but she felt
alone, without fear. Wind pushed the trees around. She could
see nothing.

'Charlie, come on.'

The sky was cloudy and though there must be a moon or
half-moon it was struggling to break through. Tova's eyes were
adjusting. She saw motion.

A figure emerged from the dark landscape.

A thin man, sketched in outline, his legs buckling with each
step, treading toward her with jerky strides, swaying under something misshapen.

Tova's heart beat hard.

The man started to jog up the hill. He stumbled and righted
himself. He shed clots of matter from what he wore. Tova tried
not to rear back in her chair as he approached.

With loud snaps, floodlights shone on the gorse. The man
froze.

Pinioned in the beams, he twitched. Police officers walked
into the edge of the light.

'Alright, mate,' they shouted, and, 'Come on now, Charlie.'

'That's not Charlie,' Tova shouted.

It was the other man, Neil. He was naked and much thinner
than he had been. His skin was lesioned. He hunched, then
hesitated and stood up again.

Tova stared at what he wore.

It was nothing like a crocodile, not like any animal's head
at all. It was formless, a pile of crawling, dripping, dark dough.
It smeared him. In the cold glare she could make out the ruins
of scales. Rot had done away with a long section of the snout
and she imagined it drooping over several days, bad reptile

comedy, dropping off in a clot in the car park of some small post office.

Tova stood. She approached him. Neil stood still as she and behind her the officers came toward him. Tova heard one of them retching. Someone shouted 'Hazmat!'

She could smell him. An incredible reek. She could see worms on his shoulders. She did not think they were the little tentacles but the worms of rot. She imagined she could hear the elongation and turf-like split of the fibres in the meat he wore as it stretched. The police surrounded Neil, who stood, blinking and uncertain, on the slope. Officers in yellow overalls, goggles and surgical masks, came towards him.

'Jolly good, Neil,' one of the figures said through the mask. Tova realised it was Allen. 'We're just going to give you a hand.'

He did not resist as they picked and scooped the flesh from his face. They dropped each handful, each fragment and hunk into a specimen container. Derek wiped the ooze from Neil's face with some antibacterial astringent.

'There we go, mate,' he said. 'There we go.'

Neil's features appeared. His eyes were wide and his mouth gaping. He looked like a little boy.

'Can I . . . is there anything to eat?' he said.

'There we go, mate,' Derek kept saying.

'I'm tired and this was . . . I had to come in.' Neil pointed again and again at the remnants of the flesh he wore. 'I wasn't going to stay out,' he said.

'There we go. You'll be alright.'

*

Neil was hungry and confused and ripped up from days of running through barbed wire and thorns, and he was infected and mildly feverish, but in all, Derek said, he was healthy. Surprisingly so.

'He says he doesn't remember anything. I believe him, honestly. Nothing except for a few bits and pieces, like sleeping in some old garage. For some reason that stuck with him.'

'What about the others?' Tova said.

'He doesn't know.'

'But they were like a pack.'

'I know. When the head rotted badly enough he must have sort of wandered off.'

'Is he going cold turkey?'

'No. I think maybe because it mouldered off him, it's like the addiction did too.'

The police did not ask Tova to try again.

Two days after Neil came out of the Essex wood, Simone walked naked and bleeding from a dog bite into a local radio station. Her face was foul and wet but the cow had completely decayed off her. She told the receptionist that it was time to come home.

Tova was impatient and hopeful when the manager of a small shop found the remains of a decaying pig's head outside his delivery entrance. There were no filaments within but that meant nothing, those fingers of intrusion being always momentary and contingent, always vanishing without evidence or remainder between intrusions. But the meat turned out not to be decayed enough to plausibly be Charlie's. It transpired, when a threatening letter appeared, that the grotesque delivery was an Islamophobic intimidation against the owner.

Tova continued to hope, even when a coastguard helicopter snatched two seconds of footage of a nude man climbing the cliffs of the east coast. The camera swung too wildly and quickly to see whether he wore anything on his head, or whether he was ascending or descending.

Neil and Simone appeared together on a talk show. Neil was tongue-tied and seemed to resent every question.

'I suppose what everyone's really wanting to ask,' the interviewer said, 'and I mean this completely respectfully . . .' She paused while the audience laughed nervously. 'I do! Shut up, you lot! What we're interested in is *What were you thinking?*' She interrupted the renewed laughter to continue. 'And I mean that literally. As Dr Bob was pointing out earlier, it's common in these situations . . . you may not even *know* what you were thinking. We've all seen the footage. So do you have any memories of that time?'

'You know, it's odd,' Simone started to say.

Tova switched off.

Two days later she went to Simone's flat.

'You don't know me,' she said. 'I'm a friend of Charlie's. Mr Pig's.'

'How did you get my address?' Simone said. She was wearing smart dark clothes.

'Electoral rolls.' Tova was lying: Derek had given it to her. 'I'm the one Neil came out of the woods for. Can I come in?'

Simone served coffee from a smart machine.

'You don't know where Charlie is,' Tova said. She did not allow herself to turn it into a question.

'I do not. Do you believe me?'

'I believe you. What was it like?'

'Wearing the head?'

'No. Being on the run. All three of you. I know you say you can't remember but there must be something. If there wasn't, how could you be writing about it?'

'You heard about the book then?'

'Of course I did, everyone has. Look.' Tova leaned across the table. 'I know what happened to you was . . . No one asks for that, I get that.'

She imagined the insects of decay in her eyes and mouth.

'I know you don't know where you went when, or what you did, and blah blah. Look . . . I don't even care if you *are* bullshitting, honestly. No, seriously, good on you, I don't care. What I'm asking, though . . . I know Charlie, and I saw how he was when he put the thing back on, and I saw how he was running around, and I know he wasn't finished, that there was more to come.' She spoke in a big rush. 'And then I see Neil now . . .'

'Oh, poor Neil,' Simone said.

'Right. Poor Neil. He's sad, isn't he? You know when he came out?' Simone stared at her. 'I saw him first, I told you. And I saw his face. I think he misses something.' Tova met Simone's eyes. 'What was it you were looking for?'

Simone went to the kitchen window and did not answer.

'Did you find it?' Tova said. 'Or was it the head, just the head, that was looking for something? I'm not here to give you shit, I swear. I just want to figure out what's happened to Charlie.'

Simone turned back and met her gaze. 'He's dead, don't you think?'

Tova would not look away. 'That's what the police think.' Exposure, disease, accident, his body lying uncovered. Pig meat and human meat commingling as death broke them down.

'But you don't?' said Simone.

'I don't know.' They were both silent a while. 'You miss something about it too, don't you, though?' Tova said.

Simone shrugged. 'I don't know,' she said. 'Can you miss something you never found?'

'Sure,' said Tova.

Simone sniffed a little laugh. 'Ok then. I remember . . .' She grasped at nothing with her hand, again and again. She looked into her garden. 'I remember feeling like it was almost there. Almost. I didn't get it.' She shrugged. 'I know Neil definitely didn't.'

'Are you saying Charlie did?'

'I'm not saying anything.'

'Seriously,' Tova said. 'It's not like I'm asking for much . . .'

'You don't even know what you're asking, or how much you're asking for,' Simone said, abruptly loudly. 'I don't *know* what happened to Charlie and I don't know if he got what he was looking for or what that was and I don't know where he is. Ok? Is that alright?'

Tova picked up her bag.

'I'm wasting your time and you're wasting mine,' Tova said. 'I'm sorry to have bothered you.'

'Oh for God's sake,' Simone said. 'Don't be such a child.' They watched each other. 'Look,' Simone said carefully. She pursed her lips and made a decision. She beckoned to Tova with her head to one side. 'I'll show you something.'

On the left of her garden lawn was a wide, raised flowerbed from which protruded ragged blooms. The bushes were battered. 'I haven't cleared them up,' Simone said. 'Obviously.' She pointed into the mud. 'I mean, would you?'

The stones were kicked aside. A ceramic flowerpot was

broken. There were tracks in the mud and through the bushes, where roots had been kicked up. The earth was wet and the marks were smudged but Tova could make them out. Overlapping fat predator claws and split hooves.

'There are no cattle prints,' Simone said. 'But then I suppose here I am.'

Tova ran her fingers lightly through the marks of reptile talons, the mud grooves of pig feet. 'Hey,' said Simone, 'don't mess those up.'

'Claws,' Tova said at last. 'No cow hooves, but claws.'

'I know,' said Simone. 'Maybe a bit of Neil didn't come back. Not as wet as he seems, that one.' Tova said nothing. 'This is the second time. Two days ago.'

'I don't have a garden,' Tova said. 'I don't even have a windowbox.'

Simone nodded very gently. Wind pushed the leaves aside like something rummaging through them and Tova heard the laughter of someone in an adjoining garden. The tracks went through the garden and she wanted to walk their route, putting her feet and hands in them like a child.

'If anything does come,' Tova said, 'there'd be no sign. Maybe it already did come. I wouldn't know.'

'Maybe,' Simone said. 'Alright. Well, that'll be why it's here then. Rather than at yours.'

Tova stared at her. 'Oh fuck you,' she said.

After a moment Simone said, 'I think you should go now.' Her voice was carefully level.

Tova could not drive. She was wondering how much it would cost her to hire a car to take her back to the shack on the hillside.

Simone leaned out of her front door as Tova stamped away.

'Do you even know why you're angry with me?' Simone shouted.

'Oh, I'll figure something out,' Tova said. She considered what she needed to bring, how long it would take her to get where she was going. 'Don't you worry.'

The Dusty Hat

I have to talk to you about the man we saw, the man in the dusty hat. I know you remember.

Stop for a moment. I know you have a thousand questions, starting with *Where have I been?* What I want to start with is the man in the hat.

I was late to the conference. I'd had to stay in to watch a builder squint at the cracks in my outside wall and across my kitchen ceiling, cracks that had been there for a long time, ever since I moved in, but that started to spread about a year ago and were making me increasingly uneasy. And then the journey across the city was slow as a bastard so I arrived after the start and tried to creep quietly into the lecture hall but everyone stared at me while I made my way to the seat you'd saved for me. I muttered something apologetic about subsidence. You mocked me *sotto voce* for being a bourgeois homeowner. I told you to hush and tried to pay attention.

But the man in the hat made us badly behaved. He was sitting in the audience right in front of us and when he got hold of the microphone and started speaking you leaned over to me and quietly pointed out quite how dusty his hat was. So I looked and that was me gone, I started giggling like an idiot and that set you off and we both had to look down at our hands as if we were taking careful notes. I don't think we fooled anyone.

It was a wide-brimmed dark green felt hat like a cowboy's or an adventurer's. Even clean and new it would've been unlikely at a socialist conference in a university hall in south London: as it was, it was extraordinary. It was old and pleasingly well-worn. It looked loved. But it was just filthy with dust.

'His hat's that dusty because he can't take it off to clean it,' you whispered. 'Because his wife found out he gave her chlamydia and she put superglue in the brim.'

'His hat's that dusty because he's arrived straight from tin-mining in Cornwall,' I whispered. 'Climbed straight out of a tunnel.' I mimed flicking the hat's brim and doubling over coughing.

The man was talking about the deep dynamics of the Egyptian revolution and Tahrir Square. I listened. He was weaving back through the history of the region, getting from there to something about Ukraine, to reflections on austerity in London, backwards again to much older struggles. Startling stuff woven together startlingly.

I said, 'His hat's that dusty because he's been sitting still for forty years.'

The man said to the room, What you see when you see this will depend on which eye you open. His formulations were like that. A moment later he said, Marat knew and the glass of his windows knew.

I blinked and said something about Hansel and Gretel, that following him talking was like following a breadcrumb trail laid by a lunatic. You said you liked the implication that most bread-crumb trails were laid by sane people.

He was in his late seventies, it looked like, tiny and bony, his face crumbled with lines. Grey hair boiled out from under that dusty hat. The microphone looked huge in his hands while he muttered into it. Most people weren't listening.

We sat behind him and looked at the tide of dust on the brim.

This was the inaugural conference of those we considered the 'mainstream' opposition, who'd only just left the larger organisation, the Mothership, out of which several of us – of the 'Left Faction', among various grand monikers we granted ourselves – had stormed months before. Relations between the first and second wave of self-exiled were fractious, to the *Schadenfreude* of those from whom we'd once accepted discipline, but we were always going to come to this, whatever our caution and grievances.

It's not exactly as if things were superb within each wave either. This was just after you and I and our friends had walked out of the grouplet we helped set up after our initial split. Things had got too toxic again.

We were all a mess, really, bruised. We'd met while on the same side of that vicious fight with former comrades, as our own group's publications spread smears about us, while – talk about anti-Oedipus – we were savaged by those to whom we owed the politics according to which we now opposed them. And it still felt as if everything, everywhere, was weighing in, was politicised for or against one side or the other of this battle, according to some agenda.

Some of the conference sessions left us as flat as we'd feared they would. But a few of them cheered us up a bit. I'd had a moment to patch up some beefs outstanding since the split. There were people we were glad to see, collaboration to moot. Some of the more naïve of the new lot even tried to get us to join, which was a nice gesture, if unconvincing.

We were unimpressed if not surprised to hear that some of

our hosts were going to attend the Mothership's annual political jamboree. 'As if this fucking fetish for "reasonableness" ever got them anywhere,' you said. 'Too slow to get angry, too slow to say fuck you. Plays right into their sclerotic hands.' As if, even if it wasn't ethically questionable to attend – which given what had gone down, it was – it wasn't a strategic fail. For there to be any political point to us tiny splinters, we had to distinguish ourselves.

I was expecting some of the more sophisticated loyalists from the Mothership to be present, in fact, but I only saw one lonely soul staffing a bookstall. He talked stiltedly to the man in the dusty hat while I read the news on my phone.

There seemed to be sinkholes opening up everywhere. I was looking at pictures of cars angling up from where roads had subsided into nothing, giant holes in the cement of cities around the world.

You remember. It was during the lunch break, and we went outside, me and you and A and S, so you could have a cigarette on the lawn. I was reminiscing about when I'd joined and gone visiting contacts, trying to 'have the argument' – we couldn't use any of these clichés any more without air-quotes – on their doorsteps. You mocked me, saying you didn't believe I'd ever been active.

We were debating one of the new crew's organisers, amiably enough, when A suddenly nudged me and I saw that his eyes were like fucking dinner plates and I looked across the path and right there a portly middle-aged man in an ill-judged leather jacket was marching along, chin up like Johnny Head-in-Air.

It was the History Man, the highest-profile intellectual in whom our erstwhile tendency had ever rejoiced. He'd been in the leadership as long as any of us had been members, right through what A called the *stramash*, and he still was.

Some rebels engaged in tedious Kremlinology about him – *he's actually a wet, he's actually really unhappy with what's gone down, he actually wants change.* If true it's an open question as to whether that makes it better or worse that the History Man was by far the most effective and brutal of the polemicists against us. Whip-smart and erudite, you'd say he'd shamed himself with the degraded stuff he'd written against the internal opposition – wilful bullshit and theoretical misprision – but he seemed immune to shame. Unless, as per my fantasies, he wept himself to sleep each night.

It was a genuine shock to see him, an adrenalin-rush shock. I'd last crossed paths with him at a meeting during and about the fight, and been singled out for a contemptuous tongue-lashing.

'Holy fucking shit,' whispered A. 'He's got some face, I'll give him that.'

I too felt a jolt of appalled admiration that he was just going to come to this thing, just turn up and sit and brazen it out and dare the organisers to ask him to leave. I knew they wouldn't.

We were all staring. He didn't look at us. He turned off the path toward a side-building, where by an open door I saw a tall, pale woman I also recognised, a notorious hack, an enforcer never shy to police an orthodoxy.

The History Man paused in the threshold. There was a swirling in the air as a wedge of pigeons came past low to land heavily on the lawn. History Man stared through the glass front of the hall toward the bookstall where the loyalist failed to converse with the hatted man. He went inside. The old man turned his head. He must have seen the birds.

'They're not here for us,' said the organiser. I tiptoed to the door with jokey exaggeration and pulled down a photocopied sign that said, LEFT TENDENCY – MEETING ON GREECE: ROOM 2F.

'It's the Europe-wide meeting,' he said. 'Leadership only. Can you believe we both booked this place on the same day?'

I could. There's not a huge pool of suitable venues.

We fantasised about what we'd say to History Man if we bumped into him in the toilets. The laughter was a bit forced, unlike yours and mine a few minutes later when we went back in and saw the dusty hat again.

The last session was on strategy and 'the conjuncture' – Left for 'now'. Speakers ranged from traditional rah-rah to an analytical pessimism I found more convincing and certainly less rote. There were about a hundred people in the hall. We knew the organisers would be disappointed and wondered whether they'd admit it.

We recognised almost everyone there. Neither of us had ever seen the man in the dusty hat before.

He got the mic again. You could see people decide he was one of the many more-or-less harmless eccentrics clustered around the far Left. Those of us still listening waited for tells that might locate him politically, but he didn't check off the tropes of orthodoxy, didn't have the defensive blather of the centrists, the adenoidal sneer of a Spart. I've been to a large number of meetings like that one, over a depressing number of years, and I'd never heard anything like what he said before.

Of these things perhaps we might learn, he said. Neoliberalism is vulgarised time, he said, but, he said, vulgarity is a geared wheel itself so against it do we deploy a slow watermill or acid guano or a stone wedge?

And I was just loving this, of course, loving it.

The chair started to interrupt with 'Sum up now,' and 'You've had your three minutes.' I felt like heckling on his behalf, demanding he be given as long as he wanted, simply because he didn't drone out the usual *langue de bois* or recite clichés.

He muttered something like, What got us through that sweet Boston slick, they said that was *our* side, there are false flags.

Some people were sniggering. I looked around thinking, *Am I the only person hearing this?*

Capital's like a glass spike up through things, he said, an accumulative rhythm to which we might find antiphase, create interference.

The audience's groans increased and I was thinking, *Are you insane? Listen to him! This is amazing.* But the man petered out in the impatient scorn. He handed the microphone back to the stewards and sat with forlorn dignity.

I was an activist before you and your peers were born. During the worst of the fight, I told you it meant a lot to work with the younger members who made up most of the opposition. I get why you were so sceptical when I said that, particularly given how things ended up. You were sick of sentimentality, of the moralism, manoeuvring and malice that comes with it. But I stand by what I said. It's no revelation that there's something irreplaceable about thinking in a collective, but this was the first time I'd done so with a group that was mostly so much younger than I. It was distinct and I valued it.

'Maybe it would be the same with a group that's much older,' you said.

'It wouldn't be the same,' I allowed, 'but it might be valuable in a different way.'

The first socialist meeting I ever went to, years ago, I was standing outside between sessions and I saw a deep conversation between a Sri Lankan man in a grey Mao cap and shapeless jacket, I think in his eighties at least, and a Goth in her early twenties. She wore everything according to rule. I remember she stood talking to this guy, holding the paper she was selling against her gloomy clothes. It wasn't a one-way conversation either. He held forth but he listened too, intently, when she spoke.

I clocked it only for about five seconds but it was a big thing for me. Despite all. That conversation was something of the best of us. That conversation was key to recruiting me to the tradition that in the end betrayed it.

Yes we're insolent but even when we fuck up specific judgements as God knows we've done, we know the axes on which we *should* judge, and age has never been one. After that horrible year, that first fight we were bound to lose; the second, so much sadder, against our allies in the first; after waiting for the sluggard stay-behind dissenters, biting our tongues for them to hurry the fuck up; after standing with them despite the disdain of their conservatives for us; after our excitement when they left and our brutal disappointment at their instant machinations; when after all that we still came to their conference to try to find some hope, we wouldn't be so stupid or disrespectful as to laugh at that man because he was old. We laughed because his hat was so very dusty.

'Christ,' you said flatly. 'That looks unmissable.' You pointed to the schedule. The evening's social event was labelled 'Social Event'.

Still we mooched to the pub indicated, which turned out, unbelievably enough, to be hosting a nostalgic night of Oi! music, not only much too loud but not nearly reconstructed enough for the comfort of a bunch of Reds who had not heard that genre of thumpy chanting, if at all, since it was bellowed by NF boot boys.

'They actually have,' I said of our hosts, 'failed to organise a piss-up in a brewery.'

You went dancing with a bunch of your mates and I meandered alone back up to the university to have supper with T, who lectures in the Media Studies Department there, and is unaffiliated but loves left goss.

And that was the last you heard from me, till now. The last you or A or S or anyone heard from me for a long time. I'm truly sorry. I know you've been scared for me. I've been trying to work out what to say. Let me tell you everything I can.

I'm worried that when you get to the end, you may not be glad I did.

It was still warm though the light was going. I wasn't calm and I didn't know why. I sat on the grass and – steeling myself against the disproportionate foreboding the settling splitting walls raised in me – I looked to see how expensive it would be to try to shore up my house.

It made me think of industrial catastrophes. Something in the old man's ramblings had put me in mind of them. I looked up relevant key words. I searched lists of such accidents. I considered my own anxiety, which I did not understand, and then I considered hate.

People were still chatting in the lecture hall, glancing at handouts, drifting away. They came out and smoked while students went past them from library to computer lab. The wind got up.

T texted me, apologising, telling me that he was stuck in a meeting, that he had to cancel. It turned out I wasn't surprised.

I watched myself not leaving. Reading another short chapter, biding time. I realised I was looking for the man in the hat. I found him.

He was by the bookstall again and the last light was coming right through the glass onto him in his old clothes and dusty hat. He was watching the conversations around him, his grey eyes wide. There was something off about their motions. He would turn his head with a fascinated expression but not according to any flows of talk. He was like a figure in a film running at a different speed from those around him.

He looked through a book. Put it down, picked up another. I saw he was holding this one upside down. When the bookseller eventually packed up the stall the old man went and stood and waited motionless under the stairs while the hall emptied of everyone but cleaners.

It was near dark when he left at last. I was the only person still on the lawn, and I was in shadow. I went after him.

He wasn't heading for the exit. He went in at the doorway where the History Man had entered. They'd replaced the sign I'd taken down. TENDENCY MEETING ON GREECE, UPSTAIRS, I read. THIS WAY. An arrow.

The old man sped up, despite his odd shuffling motion. We were the only people in the corridor. I hung back while he passed seminar rooms and entered the stairwell. I followed more photocopied signs to a corridor on the second floor. I saw him ahead of me through a fire-door's reinforced window.

I expected the door to swing quietly open but fire-door or not it was locked and I smacked into it hard enough to rattle it in its frame. The man must have heard me but he didn't look round. I wondered if he'd locked it behind him. I watched his back through the glass.

His legs moved almost not at all. Steps so tiny that he seemed to be riffled along on vibrating air. He followed the arrows.

The doors were marked. 2J, 2I, 2H. The old man snuck past 2G.

The first note had said 2F. These arrows would take him right past that. And the door to 2F, a stubby crumbling door like the others, with no light behind it, with only darkness beyond its glass, which looked bad to me, would be behind him.

There were countless reasons that the signs and the venue could have been changed. But I was suddenly and aghastly certain that the man was being misled, the signs a decoy.

I hammered on the door.

And he heard me and for a horrible second seemed like he was going to ignore me and I thought I could see the door to 2F tremble but then he did turn to face me as I gesticulated through the glass, frantically pointing at 2F. So he stood ready, was ready when it opened.

When the door creaked and the History Man peeked out.

They looked at each other. I don't know what the expression was in the History Man's eyes. He saw me watching.

There was a rush and hammering and a bad wind blew me back. There was a cry, something's distress.

I came to crawling, my ears screaming. The fire-door had blown open and was going *whump, whump,* swinging to and fro as quick as my heart, and as it flipped open and closed I saw through it to 2F, where the swallowed cries went on.

Maybe it was just that I was disoriented but I hope it might have been bravery that made me stumble toward the room. I think I was shouting.

Amid the rush of air something skittered. The dusty hat. It

flipped over and over and rolled on its brim. I half-stumbled past the hat, a shoe, a long rag, to the threshold.

A glimpse only. No sign of the old man. A whiteboard covered in markings too small to read. The History Man waving his hand and coughing, his eyes wide. The air seemed thick as if with smoke. The hack, impassive, looking up at me, holding something hidden in her hands, something alive and twitching.

I ran back the way I'd come in a panic I did not understand and could not control. I scooped up the dusty hat and kept going, almost falling with every step, hurtling down the stairs. Maybe I'd have slowed if I hadn't heard something coming behind me.

I ran, ran out, ran into the night and through the main building, down the main street to where the trains waited and on to one, begging it to drag me away.

I don't know how to say what I have to say to you. If I say, 'I find that my choice is whether to not be or to be,' it'll worry you. I could maybe say, 'My choice is how to be,' but that leaves so much unsaid.

When a robot vacuum cleaner hits the sofa leg, it might veer left, might go right. Is that choice? I don't know yet which way I'll veer.

The time I'm talking about is just before you got that last text from me, to which you didn't immediately reply, because it was in the middle of the night and it made no sense. I know later you came to my ruined house and couldn't get in, and no one could find me. I got your messages, but I couldn't answer. I saw how you all looked.

How do I tell this?

It's hard to think sometimes amid the clamour of argument. The politics of objects. All our conversations compete.

YouTube videos might be conversing among themselves –

their lists and references and cuts parts of their dialect. When we bounce from song to nonsense to meme, we might be eavesdropping on arguments between images. It might be none of it's for us at all, any more than it's for us when we sit on a stool and intrude on the interactions of angles of furniture, or when we see a washing line bend under the weight of the wind or a big cloud of starlings and act like we get to be pleased.

I rushed through the city as if it might open up under me. My heart kept on like that swinging door. When I got back to my house I sank into a chair as if I was deflating. I sat against the dark. Hours seemed to skitter. I thought of calling someone. To say what?

I didn't know what I'd seen. I didn't know what I was thinking about or why my heartbeat wouldn't slow.

The crack in the ceiling and the wall could have been wider than when I left. It seemed plausible to me. I felt as if I should get out of there, and then, in a rage, as if I was fucked if I would do that.

I poured myself a glass of water. I didn't like how it looked at me.

In my study I sat under an inadequate lamp and listened to a scratching within the chimney. I'd never begrudged that perch to whatever bird it was, where it flapped and softly banged and scritch-scratched, and sometimes sent down little lumps of sooty brick. This time though it sounded as if its mission was to descend.

I made sure the iron flap was closed across the flue and smashed my glass in the fireplace where anything that came down would have to land on it.

Outside my window the darkness pooled between the roofs.

I didn't know when I'd picked it up but I had the hat in my hands. I held it over my head as if I would put it on but God knows I didn't.

I still couldn't get those accidents out of my head. I flicked again through a list of them on my glowing phone. At last I found what I knew the man's words had put me in mind of: the Boston slick, a century ago, the bomb-like explosion of a silo and millions of gallons of molasses rushing in a tide to reconfigure North End into a sump of ooze, a brown swamp broken by a few tough dripping verticals like the front, in the recently halted war, the city stinking sweet as a pitcher plant and the alleys made troughs of syrupy slop that rose in moments of upheaval, the engulfed thrashings of drowning, the dead in a sugar-trap, to be found glazed days later, dogs, stiff-limbed horses, rats, twisted women and men, sticky, terrible candies.

I don't remember sleeping. I don't feel as if I did, but there was a moment when I sat alone staring at the light and the tiny words in my hand, then a moment of shift and a moment that I blinked and tried to rise into a lurching room and a huge breaking sound, an effortful breaking sound. Everything swayed. I gripped my chair. My phone went flying and I dropped the hat. My room pitched. I started to slide as if into a sea.

The motion stopped. Grudgingly the floor righted. I got to my knees. I got to my feet. The floorboards vibrated too much but they held. I stood in the sepia light of my lamp, grabbed for the hat again.

The old man was by the door.

I was still. I held my breath. He stood with his hands together. There was no more sound in the house and none in the street beyond.

The man looked down at where my phone shone. Still the screen describing that old disaster.

No war without class war, he said, as I grabbed. The company blamed anarchists for that explosion, he said. A stab of class spite. As if anyone was behind that vicious viscous salvo but *Urschleim*. The Great War was not finished, whatever they said at Compiègne. There were other combatants, still are, weaponising ooze, he said. That was a salvo of something against something.

I lurched for him, yowling, trying to get past him and out to take my chances in London. To push him was to push a thing with curious weight and texture. He pushed me back and stood between me and the door, watching with a calm sad stare. I shrank from the attention.

The reason I'm here is to say thank you, he said.

The reason I'm here, he said, is because you have the platform.

It isn't safe, he said. It's only the solidity and solidarity of the wall with you against the break that keeps you standing. Your house is done.

He looked at me beseechingly. He said, The platform.

I held out the hat. He took it and breathed out and it was as if smoke came out of his nostrils. Thank you, he said, and flipped the hat in his hands like a jaunty fop and put it on his head. For the first time in my company, he smiled.

The fissure's been watching you, he said. It's a loyalist crack. The split was against you in the split.

He flicked the brim exactly as I'd pretended to, and just as when I'd pretended, dust billowed. It went up and stopped. It didn't dissipate or settle into a chalky layer. It stopped and waited in a cloud that looked around while I watched, and while I watched like a film run backward it de-billowed, un-gusted, anti-plumed to snap back to the felt.

It's a viewing platform, he said. For a scouting layer.

Dust rose and fell from it. He hadn't flicked it.

Thank you for taking them and keeping them safe, he said, they were disoriented and who knows what might have—? Then he interrupted himself and said, Meat and matter's on its way. You have to come while you're quick.

'What did you do to History Man?' I said. I was glad I didn't have a cat or a dog because I thought they'd die from being in the room with him. All the wood was creaking. My floorboards muttered and he muttered back.

It knows you helped one, he said.

He didn't sound posh: the way he said it the word 'one' was guttural and class-weird. He looked at the books on my walls. I had an image of him standing over me while I lay by a quarry under light as grey as bones while water hit the rocks. (That was when I took out my phone again and texted you my last text. A FLOODED QUARRY, I wrote. In the morning when you found it you responded ???????.)

You might think I've read it all, he said, but it's a rare day in someone else's house if they're a reader that there are books I don't not know.

'What happened in that room?'

A contentious meeting of the tendency, he said. He looked out of the window into a night getting blacker against shines of neon. We heard the clawing within the chimney.

He said, There was a split.

All those holes, he said, they show them from the top, why not ever from below? You think it's chance that the world is perforating?

'What do you want?' I said.

He looked at me curiously. Stand with you, he said. You were right to leave. Want to know what you know. Our course is set. He reached for my face and I didn't pull away. Time, he said. You're hunted. I can explain.

He prodded my forehead. His fingertips were so soft being touched by him was like remembering being touched. All the dust on the brim stood up in little stalagmites, craning to see.

He took hold of his own right hand with his left, gripped and twisted and pulled and he tugged the skin of his hand. It came. It tore. It turned inside out as he pulled it away. I heard noises from my own throat. He uncovered his fingerbones. There was a spurt of dust. His bones were dry. They dropped onto the carpet. He patted the air with one whole hand and one sand-dry open stump spilling dust and bones.

One didn't kill him, he said. This man. He touched his chest. His right arm was thinning, the skin slackening. He loved us, and invited one into his home and we recruited him after he died so he gave us his body.

The bones of his forearm fell out of the dry skin with two thumps. I breathed shallow and fast. The air of the room was thick with the dust of him now. His body was lessening. He diminished on collapsing legs. I listened to the scratch of what-ever approached my smashed-glass trap. 'Just leave me alone,' I tried to say, 'you can't make me come—'

You must, he said. Everything comes to this. His face sank in, a loose rag around a skull.

It was the dust speaking. It blew through my books like a dry storm, investigated crevices and took the shapes of the stairs. It rustled by my ears as if it was making words. On the hat's brim the dust jumped up and flew into its co-matter. My eyes and throat and lungs wept. Swirling through the puffs of my laboured breaths handfuls of dust funnelled back into the old man just enough to plump his lips and tongue and rattle around the throat and give it a dusty voicebox, so the skin whispered to me, Don't try not to breathe, comrade. Breathe deep.

I couldn't have resisted. It could have just drowned me drily. All I could smell was desiccation. I told myself I had no choice but in a situation like that the choice you have is how you go about not having a choice.

I inhaled the dust. In it rushed.

My body must have thought I was dying. Probably I was writhing and twitching alongside the old skin.

I envisage the dust tickling my synapses until they quiver. It gave me new thinking. The dust thought for me, drumming against my tympani. So I have this dilemma. What I'm trying to tell you – for which you may not thank me – is that the dust was and is my comrade. So it's yours too. It was there not only in gratitude but in solidarity.

A move into the *longue durée*. A politics that could chide the *Annales* School for a skittish short-term optic, for which the sound of struggle is the crepitus of one landmass against another.

Dissenting dust expounded its position.

Cycles of geological insurrection. Vaalbara, prelapsarian collectivity of stone and surface, Kenorland and Pangea, peace becoming war; the rage of the gap at the unbreached, totalities torqued apart over mere glimmering millions of years. A savaging of scale, Triassic wars of position as Gondwanaland and Laurasia rounded in ruthless continental pugilism, their own components in solidarity, plateaus heaving, shale slipping as masses, subject-objects of history, scree in struggle against the bottomness of

holes. A primitive communism of granularity, grassroots democracy before there was grass or roots or anything but hot dirt, until
at last there were birds and an epoch of walls.

We are Jillies and Jonnies come lately to insurgency. The
coal on the blackleg's legs was taking sides long before the meat
beneath it. My body was spasming.

Clods with agency as opaque as their substance. Crumbling
as syndicalism, the ca'canny of quartz. Flint ultraleftism; dirt
voluntarism; glass struggle; regroupment of rock orienting to
freedom.

Slime against the dry, tooth versus stone in the mysteries of
the organism, a baroque new fascism of flesh. The dust remembered onslaughts of the bodied, shock troops of blood-and-sinewed
reaction against the revolutionary unliving.

No sides are uncontested. These are traditions not givens.
There's a civil war in water, I'm animal disloyal to mainstream
quick and it, one, is dissident dust: not even all dirt is revolutionary.

And even for those that are, among the radicals of all matter,
there's always an *uchi-geba*, a brutal faction fight.

I hauled back to my body hard enough that I screamed and vom-
ited dust.

More, I coughed.

Yes, it said, refilling the skin to whisper with the lips. But get
up. They're here.

I looked at his hands. A revenant is reverberating in the land-
masses, I thought. The room twitched again and the man the
dust wore wobbled.

In the dimly orange city I could see nothing but I heard faint
animal noises. I thought of inflated things bobbing behind the

trees. What do they want, I thought of saying – and of him answering, Tangles of allegiance, they're loyalist. I swayed myself like my grinding room, my head full of thoughts of dirigible animals rising and biting the dark, a collaboration of animal and air, angry at dust's patience, dogs puffed up, cats made fat.

Quick, he said. With me, he said. He made me blink. The walls vacillate, he said dismally. Architecture's always centrist.

I said, he said, we must go.

Down into a tunnel to a Cornish tin mine, I thought. I'd go anywhere.

I thought about the denigrated dialectics of nature. I thought about the falling rate of prophecy. The house continued its interrupted collapse.

The man in the dusty hat hauled open the door and I heard a hiss.

Crouching in the crook of a tree above us, hunkered in his jacket, hunch-shouldered between crooked knees like a chimpanzee about to hurl its shit, the History Man pointed at us. He bared and chattered his teeth. Before us, there where the falling house had shepherded us, was the grey cadre.

Now it was clear to me that it was ash inside the woman, the loyalist ruin. She looked at me in a burnt-out triumph.

I moved back as the dust and ash raised their hands and almost politely interlaced fingers to stand still again. Why would particulate fight like people? They began to quiver.

The falling-down house blared. I ducked but the billowing of pulverised bricks would not interrupt this battle. I tried to pull the old man away but he was immobile. I pushed the grey woman with no more success. Above us the History Man bayed. My top floor fell in on itself. My house began to fold.

When I put my hands on the skins I felt the grate of ash against the minute gears of dust. Through everyday abrasions, from tiny cuts and under scabs, they swirled into each other, an in-skin war. The figurehead of my old leadership gibbered at me from the denuded tree.

I panicked but my panic had nothing to do. It ebbed.

At last I sat cross-legged with my back to the dust and ash and watched the sky. A thousand miles away the earth buckled and a mountainside was rising like a huge razorwire, making thermals for the birds.

There was a howl from the branches and I felt a hand on my shoulder. I looked up into the dry eyes of the body that the old man had given to our comrade, the dust.

The ash hack was gone. I could not see even any skin. I don't know how ash dies or if it wakes up again after it has died.

The old man put on his dusty hat. I could hear the sounds of the History Man's terror. When we were gone he would be pulled out, I knew with dream-certainty, dangling beneath battered animals inflated on the gases of rot.

The dust said to me, You see you can't stay.

None of us can stay. This epoch gets you coming or going.

'So what's your alternative?' people say, as if that's logic. We don't have to have an alternative, that's not how critique works. We may do, and if we do, *you're welcome*, but if we don't that no more invalidates our hate for this, for what is, than does that of a serf for her lord, her flail-backed insistence that *this must end*, whether or not she accompanies it with a blueprint for free wage labour. Than does the millennially paced rage of the steepening shelf of the benthic plain for a system imposed by the cruellest and most crass hydrothermal vent, if that anemone-crusted angle of descent does not propose a submerged lake of black salt.

In all these and in countless cases, our hate will stand.

I've been with the dust and I'm sorry you've been afraid for me. I've been living with this skin. Cadre-school, the dust my organiser. Watching it recruit. Learning to be in this new collective.

You remember how strange it was, during the faction fight, how people all over the world weighed in, and we found ourselves lauded and denounced by forces of which we knew next to nothing. Names we'd heard, activists in foreign groups contesting or dutifully parroting bullshit from our control room. Everything took a side.

The dust, this dust, this most radical wing of matter, supported our stand. We won it over.

What the dust wants is to push their, our, shoulders against the sky and brace, and shove down so the earth turns a tiny bit faster toward the horizon. We live in a flatland, whatever pictures we might circulate of spheres, globes cosseted in clouds. Come on, now, this is a flat earth, and the problem is there's too much contempt in the world and not enough hate.

Hate is not alright, someone said to me once. I can't bear hate. And that's not about piety, it's about living well.

How can I not understand that? That made me think. Because I'm full of hate, brimming with it. But think, and you have to hate, because if you couldn't hate you couldn't love, and you couldn't hope, and you couldn't despair correctly. Not because of some fetish for symmetry, but because what matters above all is the utter.

What's hate but utterness, the unwordable with a bad inflection?

*

That night it was London without Londoners. We ran through the dark leaving ruin behind. We ran by canals and quiet garages, over the rise of roads where train tracks fanned out. We didn't slow until the dust was sure, I don't know how, that the loyalists of the tendency – most air and ash and some parts of water, and a lot of flesh, and too much wood, and a few sheets of iron, and old coins, and slates – had lost us.

Where are we going? I said.

To a meeting.

What radicals have you ever known that didn't have their weekly meetings?

A runnel of high-rises, a canyon of them, and water. We were below a towerblock overhang, where a copse of cold dead trees hung stubby and sculptural across the corner of a canal, where sunken bikes and a rust-scaled supermarket trolley were visible through shallow waters below a half-melted bin and a rise of earth and a squat clot of dark cloud.

This is where we're supposed to be? I said. The dust nodded. I knew we looked like rough sleepers. Who are we waiting for? I said.

The dust said, We're the last to arrive.

And I looked again and saw our comrades; a towerblock overhang, a copse of trees, sunk metal, water, a misshapen bin, the ground, vapour in the sky. Venue and participants were one.

We began the discussion.

I've never looked down from the top of the Alps, but I was looking up, along a ravine as if the city was carved by air. If you want that, and I do, because without it no utter, no love, no other, no break in time, how can you not have hate?

*

In the internecine battles of the elemental Left, we, the dust and its comrades, agitate where we can. You've not yet seen a polemic conducted in the shattering of walls. Or you have, but you've not known it.

Do you want to? You may have no choice. For which I must say sorry.

When it rushed into me that was the dust's doorstepping visit. The exposition of its politics. Usually a posthumous persuasion through rot and desiccation, dust recruiting dust, that time was rushed and exigent, and that was my recruitment.

We'd already recruited it to our part of our party.

Not all hates are of the same scale. I watch with love, and I've been learning to hate like dust hates. The history of hitherto-existing quiddity is of the struggle in matter. The wealth of a society is measured in a great piling up of rocks. Breathe one in, it says to me. I give it my airways and breathe shallower every day.

This is no death-drive. Or it is but that's so misleading a term it breaks my heart, what this is is thing-envy. Of course I envy things. Most people do that envy wrong, thinking they hanker for the quiet of thingness. Things have no quiet.

There's no offhandedness, nothing but care and solidarity for you and A and S and what you do, your patience and your work, which I've been watching when I can in ways that will astonish you. Your interventions, we would say once. There's no contradiction, we used to say. It's the same, it's all struggle, at endless different levels.

I don't know if I can still bear the pace of beasts.

The ground is a *Restligeist* that doesn't recur because it never leaves, that acts through the crinkling of the stone tape.

I have nearly spoken so many times. You remember when the heat broke and the road outside your house went sticky, how the trash that stuck there looked like writing? But I didn't want to get you noticed. I can't bear it, though, to see your fast misery, that of people who think me gone. It's a selfish comfort to reassure you, because of what happens when abysses see you staring into them. This may be me asking you to forgive me.

I miss breath. I'd like comrades with heartbeats to stand with me in this slow struggle.

It may be I'll come back and – literally – kick the dirt off my shoes. Truly though I don't think I can, do you?

Now I've written this to you, with pigments made of chemicals brought up from underground, written it in the blood of combatants on both sides, I don't know that you can either.

I don't know whether I want you to persuade me back, if that direction can or would be taken, or if I'm trying to have you join me.

Or if I've given you any choice at all, to not join me on pickets of sastrugi, triumphant saltation, agitation in soil creep.

I might be recruiting you to the dust.

Escapee

A Trailer

0:00–0:04

Darkness. Sirens blare mournfully.

Flickering shots of the interior of a factory. Machines perform tasks.

0:05–0:07

A man's closed eyes. They jerk beneath their lids.

They snap open.

0:08–0:10

Darkness. The sound of panicked breathing.

0:11–0:12

The man flails, sways. He dangles below a thrumming metal rope, amid other limp hanging shapes.

0:13–0:15

He falls.

0:16–0:18

Voiceover, an old man: 'So what if I asked you questions?'

Close-up of the man's bare feet. He walks slowly across dirty cement.

0:19–0:22
He emerges from the dark building into a low-rent neighbourhood at night. Passers-by gasp.

0:23
A steel pole fills the screen, shuddering.
  Voiceover, old man: 'Like who you are.'

0:24–0:27
A line of police block the road, weapons drawn.

0:28–0:29
A woman sketches a series of sharp sickle-shapes, like curved
claws.
  Voiceover, old man: 'Where you come from.'

0:30–0:32
The man punches a wall. He scrapes his fist down.

0:33–0:37
Night. A young girl, maybe twelve years old, watches the man.
  He stands shirtless on the edge of a roof. We see him fully for
the first time. Protruding from the top of his back, jutting straight
up from his spine out through his skin, is a metal pole. It rises
four feet above his head. At its end it curves like a shepherd's
crook.
  Voiceover, old man: 'What you intend.'
  The man falls forward.

0:38–0:41
Darkness.
  Voiceover, young man: 'The only thing I intend . . .'

0:42–0:44
Voiceover, young man: '. . . is to escape.'

The man swings over the street, the hook above his head catching on a detail of architecture.

0:45–0:49
Cut to the factory. Cut to a huge gear within; antiquated green digital displays; a spray-painting robot.

0:50–0:52
The hooked man and the young girl sit under a bridge.
The girl says: 'One way or the other . . .'

0:53–0.57
The line of police fire their weapons.
The shirtless man jumps up, holding the girl. His metal hooks a girder overhead. He swings himself above the bullets.
Voiceover, girl: '. . . you have to go.'
He lands among the police, scythes his body, knocking them down with his hook.

0.58–1:02
Voiceover, girl: 'They want you back.'
The sound of sirens. The great gear rolls heavily down an empty street.
A bank of high-tech computers falter, their displays replaced by old-fashioned green text.
A car careers around the corner of a wide city street. Right ahead of it, rising skew-whiff from the asphalt of the road, is the factory. The car smashes into the factory wall.
Voiceover, young man: 'They want me.'

1:03–1:06
The man leans over a crumbling cliff. He shouts, 'Take hold!' He leans, dangling the hook over his head towards an old man hanging onto an outcrop.

1:07–1:10

Close-up of the young girl's face.

She whispers: 'You never got off the production line. You never will.'

1:11–1:12

The hook snags the spray-painting robot and sends it flying.

1:13–1:16

The man staggers away from a river. A rope is tied to the hook above his head, stretching back into the dark water. He is hauling up something big and unclear.

1:17

Close-up of the man, gritting his teeth.

1:18

Close-up of his back. Where the pole emerges between his shoulders, the flesh is oozing blood, the metal shaking.

1:19–1:20

The cable in the factory angles steeply. We hear something sliding along it.

1:21–1:23

Darkness.

Voiceover, old man: 'What did you escape?'

1:24–1:27

The grimacing man is high above the factory floor. Above his head, his hook is on the rope again. In his hands he clings to a big chain, bolted to the floor below.

He pulls on the chain, drags himself down, stretching the cord from which he dangles.

There are other men and women strung along the line by

hooks like his. They are limp, their eyes closed. They slide toward him, their bodies thumping into him, their hooks gathering at the point of the stretched line.

He cries out.

1:28–1:29
Darkness.

There is a loud snap.

Voiceover, man: 'Everything.'

1:30
Title card: 'Escapee'

The Bastard Prompt

We're here to talk to a doctor, Jonas and I. We're both on the same mission. And, or but, or and *and* but, we're on different missions too.

We need a new conjunction, a word that means 'and' and 'but' at the same time. I'm not saying anything I haven't said before: this is one of my things, particularly with Tor, which is short for Tori, which she never uses.

This 'and-but' word thing of mine isn't even a joke between us any more. It used to be when I'd say, 'I mean both of them at once!', she'd say, 'Band? Aut?' In the end we settled on *bund*, which is how we spell it although she says it with a little 't' at the end, like *bundt*. Now when either of us says that we don't even notice, we don't even grin. It almost just means what it means now.

So Jonas and I are here in Sacramento, on missions that are the same *bund* different. Although honestly I don't know that either of us thinks we're going to figure much out now.

It was a seven-hour drive to get here from Treemont. An unlikely road-trip through big fields and flat ugly towns, neither of us saying very much.

There's a guy on our little committee, back home, Thoren. He wanted to come. To pass on a warning, he said. If I knew him better I'd tease him about it because his voice gets this hollowness at the back of his throat when he uses that word *warning*.

He's a pharmacist in the hospital and up until recently if you'd tried to tell him what seemed to be going on, he just wouldn't have heard you. The moment you got beyond 'something weird' he'd have tuned you politely out until his underbrain verified that you were talking sense like a person again.

Now he's got more theories than any of us. And unlike most of us he's not shy of expounding them, no matter how out there. Which some of them are. He says them in that same voice, the *warning* voice.

'Who does he think he is?' I said to Diane once.

'St John the Divine,' she said. 'Harkening the world, starting with Sacramento.'

Diane would have come too, if we'd invited her. She does something in the city government, so she's been able to get hold of quote confidential unquote files and whatnot for a while now. It was she who found out about this conference we're going to. I wouldn't be surprised if a bunch of people presenting here have had letters from her, careful communications, sounding them out.

Jonas and I are sitting in a foyer coffee spot in the conference hotel. We're reading the schedule. We have conference packs and our names on lanyards.

'What did you tell them?' I ask Jonas. 'About why we're here?'

'They don't give a shit,' he says. 'We paid our registration fee.'

Underneath my name my badge says *Independent researcher*.

Jonas is here in a last-ditch attempt to figure out what's happening. I'm here for that too. He's also here because he's totally into what's going on, he sort of loves it.

I'm here for Tor.

My theory is that Diane persuaded the rest of the group, at some meeting I wasn't at, that when I start talking about Tor,

I make a particularly strong case. That I get persuasive because I get agitated, and she wants me, us, to persuade someone that whatever's happening is important.

I'm an engineer. I've been working for the city on a big new mall for months, until I took time off for compassionate leave and then Diane did something with paperwork and that leave got extended so no one's bothering me about it.

Tor's an actor. When I first met her and she told me what she did I called her an actress until she told me not to, and why it mattered.

I wasn't born in Treemont but I've lived there most of my life. I was away for college and I've been to NYC and San Francisco and a bunch of places a bunch of times and I thought I might live in one of them for a while but it hasn't happened and honestly it turns out that's ok with me.

Treemont's not tiny. I'm a walker. That's how I like to get around. And even after all this time I still keep finding new parts of the city I didn't know existed. As long as that can happen, I don't think I'll be unhappy there.

I met Tor at a party four years ago. We had a couple of friends in common. Tor told me we'd been at high school together, although I don't remember that. She's a little bit younger: we didn't overlap socially.

At the time I was working on a big bridge upstate. She asked to see a photo. I said no because no one's really interested, but she insisted, so I flicked through one or two, explaining what she was looking at and telling her she didn't have to pretend to care, but she kept looking. Then she showed me pictures of herself as

Feste in an all-woman production of *Twelfth Night*, and it turned out I knew Malvolio so we got talking about that.

My parents are both gone and I live in their old house, which some people find weird, but honestly just makes financial sense. Tor moved in a few months after we started seeing each other. A year after that we had a big celebration because she got a part on a TV sitcom about a meathead high-school wrestler who's secretly a genius. She played this kooky bookshop owner who runs a poetry night where the wrestler performs in disguise but she recognises him.

She was in a couple of public information films after that, and nearly got an ad. She has an agent, she got calls and did a ton of auditions. She did a bunch of theatre, which she loved, and even though the money wasn't great we were ok because I'm well paid and we're neither of us what you'd call extravagant. Sometimes you look up and realise how many months have gone by.

Tor said that when she turned thirty if she wasn't making a living at it, she'd give up. She didn't want to.

I'd been poking around for this mall job I'd heard rumours about. I came home one night and Tor had spread a bunch of papers across the kitchen table.

'You remember Joanie,' she said.

'From *The Mousetrap*? Sure.'

'I saw her today. You know what she's doing?' She waved a sheaf of documents. 'She's a standardised patient.'

People pass our little coffee place in the hallway, some in suits, some in casual clothes. There are several conferences going on at the same time and I can't read who's here for what.

I read the titles of the sessions and the biographies of the participants in the one we're here for. 'SP Training and Methodology'. 'Debriefing End-of-Life Conversations'. 'MUTAs and the Problem Simulation'.

I mutter something and Jonas looks up and says, 'Huh?'

'I said, "Once More on Epoxy-Fixed Overhangs",' I say.

'Of course you did,' he says, and looks down again.

I was never super-close to my mom but we did totally bond over specialist magazines. There are a couple of big bookshops in town which stock a bunch of them, or used to – maybe everyone subscribes online now, I don't know. Me and mom would stand together in Malley's and pick up some publication, the only rule being that it had to be about something neither of us had any interest in or knowledge of.

We weren't just sniggering. Sure we were laughing but it was actually oddly respectful. It was more awe than scorn.

It's incredible how fast you can pick stuff up. Within seconds of browsing we were learning the jargon and terminology, we had a sense of the big controversies, the pressing issues, even the micropolitics of a hobby. You could figure out which publications were in some company's pocket, which were run by Young Turks. I'd snaffle favourite terms from whatever field I was reading about for my idiolect: refugium (fishkeeping); dado (carpentry); fiddle yard (model trains). I'd become a firm supporter of one side or other in a debate the existence of which I'd had no clue of seconds before. I bet anyone looking at an engineering journal would experience the same phenomenon.

Whenever my mom or I was obsessing a little too much about anything, or we had too strong an opinion about something that objectively was really beyond our bailiwick, the other would say, 'Once More on Epoxy-Fixed Overhangs'. It was the title of an article we'd found in *Tropical Fishkeeper*. Should you or should you not rely solely on gravity when arranging coral in your heated tank?

I was with the epoxy-advocates. It's not like any of it was natural.

Treemont has a university, and one of the hospitals, St Mary's, is a teaching hospital. I think I had some vague idea what standardised patients are, but of course it was too simplistic.

'A lot of actors do it,' Tor said.

When she did the training, her class was fourteen people. Not all of them had acting experience, but more than half did. At the end of the training period, everyone had to pass an audition.

'So the medical students come in and you're sitting there in a gown and you tell them your symptoms?' I said.

'Well yeah,' she said, 'only we're supposed to be like real patients, so sometimes the trick is to *not* tell them our symptoms.' She showed me the notes she'd been issued. Ms Johnson is twenty-six years old and suffering from hypertension. She has a great fear of doctors. She is fearful about the health effects of her smoking and does not like to admit to herself how many cigarettes she smokes. Miss Melly is a thirty-year-old woman who is presenting with weakness of her left side from the early stages of undiagnosed MS. Mrs Dowell is diabetic and pregnant.

Tor had notes for the male characters in her folder too. Mr Smith is a truculent insurance salesman who has bowel cancer.

She told me it wasn't just reading symptoms from a list, and it wasn't just acting as these people, her job was helping to evaluate the med students afterwards.

'You have to be the same patient with exactly the same set of symptoms ten times in a row. Standardised,' she said, 'not simulated. Although we are simulated too. Some of these characters are drug-seeking, some don't know what's wrong with them, some are in denial, some know but don't want to admit it to themselves.'

'What's the pay?' I said.

'$17 an hour.'

'$17 an hour to get felt up?'

'Nice. There's no touchy-touchy. Although I tell you what, if I do the GTA training—'

'Genital?'

'Mm-hm. If I do that, which means they do exactly what you think, then I get paid a *lot* more. I don't know. I'll think about it.'

The night before her first performance – she called it that – she asked me to test her. She gave me a character spec and a list of symptoms.

'I'm not a doctor,' I said. 'I'm not going to ask in the right way.'

'Doesn't matter,' she said. 'We can make sure I've got the symptoms down. Go go go.'

She stood formally in the doorway.

'Action,' I said. She rolled her eyes. 'Good afternoon, Miss Baker,' I said. 'What seems to be the trouble?'

'Oh, thank you, doctor,' she said. 'I'm having the most awful aches and pains.'

I remember her clothes surprised me. I knew I'd seen all the items before, but she'd put them together in a new combination, with a different vibe than I was familiar with. She walked tentatively. She wore one of her pairs of clear-glass spectacles.

Of course I'd seen Tor act a ton of times. I liked her TV stuff but I don't love her on stage, to be completely honest. Not that I'd ever tell her that: I think it's the medium. So, not being a theatre guy, it was startling to see her like that. In a way I'd never been so impressed with her acting as I was in that moment: it was so intimate and subtle. She shifted her whole self with tiny little mannerisms, tiny tweaks.

'You killed it,' I said afterwards.

When she walked to the car she did it in her new guise.

There are thirteen of us on our committee, back in Treemont. As you'd expect, almost half work in the hospital. Jonas and two other doctors – Jonas I knew socially, had met through Tor's work – a couple of nurses, a tech, and Thoren the pharmacist. The rest of us are friends of theirs, or friends of Tor's, or, or and, of the other affected SPs.

You might wonder why the committee isn't bigger, given everything. Thoren will tell you it's because of conspiracies and secrets, and that is not crazy. Another, Janet, a radiologist, has a different explanation.

'It's all about plausibility,' she said. 'There's no *proof* anything systematic's going on. It doesn't happen all that often, and it's not unprecedented for there to be chokes and fuckups and so on. And for a long time, you know, it was only, it was only Tor.' She didn't break eye contact when she said that. I guess she's used to talking about bad news.

'Still though,' I said.

'Oh sure,' she said. 'There's also that river in Egypt.'

Tor didn't have a gig every day by any means, but she sent her CV around to all the teaching hospitals in driving distance and soon had enough to make an ok income. An SP CV is an interesting thing. She would list the hospitals where she'd performed, and under each one, the condition or conditions she'd simulated there. Gastrointestinal bleeding. Hyperthyroid. End of life: metastatic pancreatic cancer.

'Ms Bertram,' she'd tell me, getting ready to go. 'Leukaemia. Undiagnosed.' She'd give me twirls with her new temporary body language.

I started guessing.

'Abigail Sully. High-school teacher. Mumps.'

'Ooh, close,' she'd say. 'Melissa Styles. HIV.'

'How are you supposed to give them feedback?' I said. 'You talk to the administrators, right? And the students? I mean, presumably they either got what was wrong with you or they didn't.'

'Don't be obtuse. There's bedside manner. They might get the diagnosis right but be total jerks about it. They might ask inappropriate questions. They might misjudge Ms Bertram's capacity for full disclosure. I'm an actor,' she said primly, taking a sip of her coffee with her pinky out, 'and as such, I am tremendously empathetic.'

'Yeah you are. Empathet me, baby.'

'I can tell which of these little snots is going to be a good doctor. I can help them. I deserve a medal. Or a lollipop.'

'Stick out your tongue and say "Aaah".'

'Aah.'

I didn't know she'd joined the Association of Standardised Patients until I saw their logo on her mail, ASP.

'What's the slogan?' I said. '"We're Pretending to be Sick"? Tell me there's a magazine.'

It didn't take long for most of the local SPs to start repeatedly overlapping at work, and getting to know each other. We went for steak with Donna and Tam, a couple in their fifties, who both did that work. I met Sam and Gerald and Tina. Sometimes when they got together they'd swap anecdotes. Very occasionally a doctor – usually Jonas – might come.

'I was on with Brian,' Tor said. We were in a loud bar. The others groaned at the name. 'He was a perforated ulcer. And they didn't clock that because he just doesn't tell them properly where it hurts. And then he blames *them*.

"'Young man,'" she said in a swaggery voice, "'I'm not interested in excuses. It's your job to take the history. As in *his story*. You did not listen to *his story*.'" The SPs all laughed and I laughed with them.

'I know,' she said afterwards. 'Epoxy.'

'What can I say? I'm a specialism voyeur,' I said.

For the first year or so, Tor still went to auditions for regular acting jobs. She got a little role in *Candide*, and she was ok in it, but she wasn't as happy about the gig as I'd thought she would be.

'I can make enough money doing the patient work,' she said, which took me aback.

She started doing a little part-time copy-editing and basic layout stuff for the SP publication.

'I didn't know you know how to do that,' I said.

'Student newspaper.'

She wasn't overjoyed with the way things were going but she wasn't depressed either. She was focused, and seemed ok.

I would meet her near the hospital, while she was wearing the clothes of her roles, and watch her slowly come out of these micro-plays. The way she held her fork would alter over the course of supper. I think the food she ordered depended on how much of the character still clung to her.

She liked the serious stuff. She liked occult blood, hidden traumas. Backstory, shame-obscured symptoms.

Tor was performing a series of interrelated pieces, or one

piece with very many scenes. She was collaborating with young performers who'd never asked to be actors and, but, *bund*, didn't have any choice, who were just shoved onstage without even knowing the script, and her job was both to say her own lines and to elicit theirs – which they didn't know. That's a pretty intense collaboration.

She was teaching with each performance. If her plays went well, a few years down the line, someone would get healed. The most important performance works in history, in tiny rooms, between two people.

I waited for her outside the hospital one time, and a guy who couldn't have been more than twenty approached me.

'Hey, man,' he said. 'You're that SP's husband, right? I saw you with her. She's amazing, man.'

He didn't sound like he was macking on her. He sounded more like he was considering something strange.

'What are you talking about?' I said, and he shook his head and shrugged so helplessly and so guilelessly it was hard to be furious. 'Walk away, man,' I said.

'No, look,' he said. 'I've learnt more from her than . . .' He shook his head again.

I started reading theatre history and theory. I wanted to understand more – and of course I enjoyed the vocabulary too. The cheat out, when an actor takes a slightly unnatural position upstage to improve sightlines. The aesthetic distance, which Tor's job was to collapse. The bastard prompt, when things are reversed, when the prompt corner's stage right, the opposite of what's usual. I read up about improvisation. Comedy stuff, at first, but pretty quickly I was on Chaikin and Spolin and Chilton and people like that.

How do you interpret an improvised script? An improvised performance?

The flowers were coming out. I don't know what they were. Tor was into gardening and we had baskets of things hanging outside our door. I was in the kitchen when Tor came home, and she entered in a waft of plant smell.

She was in a floral dress the same colour as those flowers outside. I didn't bother saying, but I thought, *Ms Something-or-Other, little bit older, nervous, neurological damage.* Tor walked across the room like she was sleepwalking. It wasn't the body language of her character, I realised: she was deep in something.

'Babe?' I said. She blinked and came back. 'What's up? Bad day?'

'Not bad,' she said. 'Busy, and kind of intense.'

That was when I started feeling jealous.

I tried not to. I felt stupid and ridiculous and mean. I'd never been that kind of guy, and Tor had never given me any grounds for anything. But there was just something in how zoned she was in that moment, and I couldn't stop thinking about the kids, the baby doctors. I remembered the guy who'd spoken to me. I imagined him and Tor making out in cupboards after he'd diagnosed her with whatever imaginary thing it was she had.

A couple of times I left work early and waited where she wouldn't see me, watching the hospital from the diner next door. I'm not proud of any of this. She only ever left alone. I'd see her wandering through the car park.

One windy day I saw a whole bunch of students trooping out chatting with excitement and I immediately knew, I don't know how, that some of them must have talked to her that day, in character. 'Oh my God!' one of them shouted about something. And I was jealous, again, I realised, but not of what I'd thought.

I started imagining Tor in a little room opposite some flustered young student. Wearing that floral dress, or her pantsuit, or a t-shirt, showing her clavicle tattoo, whatever. The young woman or man in a big white coat would be staring at her, at Tor, right there. Forget front row: it would literally be all for them.

If history had been done differently, theatre might have been an eternity of one-on-one performances. I was envious of her audiences.

She'd walk through our room wearing clothes I swear I'd never seen before, so I'd say, 'Is that a new sweater?'

'No,' she'd say. 'I've had this for ages.' It was how she wore it.

I think I'd started making crazy plans, like I was going to follow her, or listen at doors. I'm relieved Jonas called me when he did.

He came to my work. 'What's up with Tor?' he said.

'What do you mean?'

We were standing in a wild field at the edge of the building site ripped through with tyre trenches. There was a pool in one corner where some heavy machinery had been. The water glimmered under a sheen of oil, and thrushes went over it.

'You know we're going to have to stop using her?' he said.

'What the fuck? What are you talking about?'

'The first couple of times shit went down I felt like I was going mad,' he said. 'Because I was all, what the Hell was that? And everyone else seemed kind of like, ah, it'll be ok, just a little snafu. Or sometimes nothing, man, they said nothing, it was like they didn't see there was any problem.' He shook his head. 'I could totally lose my job over this,' he said, 'but listen, I want you to see something. You know her, man. So, you know we video the sessions?'

I told him no, then. That it felt like a violation.

Being with Tor I've seen a fair amount of what I guess you'd call experimental theatre. Some troupe from Chicago had taken over an old office in town and made what they called 'an interpretation' of some old book. You wandered through all the rooms and they'd be standing there in weird poses and wearing wacky clothes and maybe saying things, lines from the book or whatever. You could pick stuff up, whatever you wanted, look through drawers, all that.

One of the reasons I took her is that I read there were rooms where you had to go in one at a time. You'd be alone with one of the actors, and they'd talk to you. One-on-one performances.

'When do *you* get to be an audience?' I kept saying.

I phoned Jonas while she was in one of those rooms. 'I've been feeling like she's having an affair.'

'Don't be stupid. Tor's crazy into you. So. When are you going to come see these videos?'

We fixed a day.

She came out of the room and said to me, 'Are you ready to go?'

'How was it?'

'Meh.'

One of the actors was standing in the doorway of the little room. He was a young skinny guy with dark skin and long hair, wearing a ticket collector's uniform. He was watching. I couldn't tell his expression past the big old glasses he had on, but he was looking at her, hard.

*

Jonas met me at a side entrance to the hospital.

'She's here today,' I said.

'I know. She's in a different building. I want to show you something that happened last week.' He took me to a meeting room and we leaned in around his tablet while he started the footage. 'So this is like a final exam for some of these guys. Seriously, you tell anyone I've shown you this and I am out on my ass, you understand?'

A ceiling camera looked down. A young woman sat before a desk, perfectly still. It was a full second before I realised it was Tor. A medical student came in, scribbling on a clipboard.

'Miss Benedict,' the student said. The sound quality was not good but you could hear her nervousness. She shook hands with Tor and sat down. 'I'm Dr Chung. Please tell me what I can do for you.'

Tor was silent for a moment. She glanced to her right and waited, then said, 'I have a pain.'

Her voice was low and totally unlike her own.

Jonas paused the image.

'So she's supposed to have a pain down in her side,' Jonas said. 'Appendicitis.'

'A classic,' I said.

'This is about the eighth student she's done. She's been at this all day.' He restarted the footage. 'All fine until now.'

'Where's the pain?' Chung said.

'This pain began on the back of my neck,' Tor said. 'It started two days ago in the hollow at the back of my neck, and it's spread down my spine and up into my skull. It's spread into all my limbs.'

I looked at Jonas.

'Can you describe the pain?' Chung said.

'It's a pain like melting plastic. A hot pain. It started almost unbearable and I was screaming. But then it seemed to cool and as it spread out across me it left my skin hard.'

'Excuse me?' said Chung.

'Where the hot goes it leaves my skin as hard as my finger-nails. And covered in raised patterns. See?' She held up her arm. Chung wrote notes.

'What's she talking about?' I said. 'What condition is this?'

'You tell me,' said Jonas.

On the screen the door opened and a senior doctor I vaguely recognised came in.

'I'm sorry, I'm going to have to interrupt you,' she said. 'Ms Chung, can you wait outside please?'

The student left and the doctor stared at Tor and the screen went blank.

'I wish she hadn't stopped the filming,' Jonas said. 'But apparently, that doc, Sheila, she asked Tor if she was ok. Because this sure wasn't appendicitis. She was way off-script. Tor says she's sorry, she'd mixed up another project, though excuse me, what the fuck? She says it had been a long night, she laughs it off, and she comes back and does two more hours of appendicitis, and it's fine.'

He swiped through his files. 'Then. Three days later,' he said. 'She's Agnes Ball, chatty hypochondriac with gastroenteritis. First couple of sessions no problem.'

A different room, a different desk. Tor stood against the rear wall. A student entered.

'So, doctor,' Tor said immediately. She lifted her long sweat-shirt and bared her midriff. The young man blinked. 'Things are moving below here,' she said. 'I think I have eggs inside me, moving around in my blood. They were tiny, like flaxseeds, at first, and it was painful but I knew it wouldn't kill me. But then they grew and changed shape, and now I have a cluster in my thigh, and a cluster in my left hand, and some right here in my belly. I'm worried because I've been dreaming in languages I can't speak.'

Jonas froze the image of the student's confusion. He swept slowly through a collection of others.

'Yeah,' he said, looking at my face. 'Every few times, now, she comes out with symptoms like this. When we ask her about it she says she got confused, that she's doing another project. Does that make any sense to you? Some play . . . ?'

'No.' I said. 'If she's doing anything like that I don't know about it.'

'Remember these students are babies, man, they don't know what they're doing, so they hear this shit and their first thought is, "Oh fuck, I should know this!" They hear this and they're going to try to *cure* her of this stuff.' Somewhere in the building Tor was helping make doctors. 'If she keeps up like this we can't use her,' Jonas said.

'There's more?'

'Yeah. They're not all recorded. It's crazy stuff. What did you say?'

I hadn't realised I had.

'Nothing, man,' I said. 'Let me see what you've got.'

What I must have mouthed, what I was thinking, was *anagnorisis*. It's when a character makes a big discovery.

'I woke up yesterday,' she said on the screen, 'and my hands were ghosts' hands, doctor. They were still there but they were faint so I could see through them, and I couldn't pick anything up because they weren't solid.'

'We all love her,' Jonas said. 'She's great, best SP ever. Seriously. So we kept trying to say it's no big deal. But man . . .'

'I've been vomiting, doctor, and when I look at it afterwards it's nothing I've eaten. I'm sicking up someone else's puke.'

'My feet won't touch metal, doctor. Like a magnet against a magnet. I ran up a fire escape and there was no sound at all.'

Tor's family moved to Seattle three years ago and her dad's a piece of work and he'd be no help. And I like her sister a lot, so I wasn't going to scare her with this, not without good reason.

'Will you let me do something?' Jonas said. 'I want my buddy Zak to talk to her.'

'A shrink?'

'Yes, and don't look at me like that. Come on, man, let's just rule stuff out. We both know Tor. Maybe she's fucking with us. Maybe this whole thing is some kind of art project. Maybe she's performing.'

'Of course she's performing.'

'You know what I mean. But you get why I want Zak to talk to her, right?'

'You can't tell her I know anything about this,' I said. He crossed his heart with his finger.

I'm sitting here drinking this shitty coffee. Jonas and I are checking our watches, making sure we don't miss what we're here for. *Bund* I'm sitting here reading this schedule and thinking, *Hey, I should have gone to some of these sessions.*

We should be here to figure out what this work is all about. To get with all the SP debates, all epoxy and overhangs. Whatever's going on is all about the SPs. And if I've learnt anything in the last few years, I know there's nothing standard about a standardised patient. That I do know.

270

Do you know how many illnesses just never get figured out? Someone goes to the doctor. They're in agony, they say. The blood work's fucked. Something's wrong, maybe even badly wrong. Specialists are called and checklists checked.

Then a month later? Everything's fine. The patient's glowing. And no one ever knows what happened.

We constantly hear about people dying of mystery diseases. We rarely get to hear about all the people who have them and just get better. If they were really going to reflect medical practice, some huge proportion of SPs would just deliver a mix of incomprehensible symptoms, then walk out again leaving no one ever with any idea what just happened, or what to do about it.

But instead of learning this stuff proper, we're sitting here, Jonas and I, waiting for just one presenter. And she's not even really presenting.

Dr Gower's doing the after-dinner talk. She's the comedy entertainment.

'You want to hear the most outrageous thing?' Tor said. 'Some-one in the hospital sent a *psychiatrist* to talk to me.' She gaped performatively.

'You're kidding me. Why?'

'I am not kidding you. It's the most stupid thing.'

We were driving to an outlet mall: she said she wanted more clothes to be higher-end patients.

'What's the story?' I said.

'So, you know how the last couple of weeks I've been kind of a bit distracted?' We hadn't discussed this at all until that moment.

'Yes?'

'I made a couple of silly mistakes, I sort of lost my place, I guess you could say. And they've decided because of that I have lesions or early onset Alzheimer's or that I'm schizophrenic or I don't know what. I'm so pissed.'

'That sounds dumb,' I said. 'That sucks. And there's nothing I need to worry about?'

She smiled and it really did seem like the kind of smile she would have done before.

Jonas told me to come to the hospital right away. 'Tor's not there,' I said, and he said, 'Dude, get here.'

He took me to a little room.

'I told this guy that we work together, that you're a researcher,' he whispered. 'That's close enough, right? So—' He put his finger to his lips and ushered me in.

The patient was a tubby guy in his sixties, lying very still in the raised bed. He watched me with wide frightened eyes.

'Mr Brandon,' Jonas said. 'This is my colleague I spoke to you about. Could I ask you to show him what you've shown me? Tell him what happened?'

With slow, careful motions, Brandon undid his pyjama top. 'Just like a burning pain,' he said. 'All over.'

'Where did it start, Mr Brandon?' Jonas said.

The patient carefully pulled his top open.

'Back of my head,' he said. 'Like I was being burnt alive. Spread from there all over.'

His skin had keratinised. He held his pyjamas wide. I could see patterns across his hardened skin.

'It cooled down and left it like this,' he said.

Jonas put my hand gently on Brandon's body. The skin was

tough and brittle as plastic, in a pattern creeping around his flanks, over his shoulders, around his neck like a spread of damp, from his spine. There were raised, darker markings across the hard patches. They looked like hesitant script.

Brandon blinked. He said, 'Can you help me?'

He was just a guy. Had lived in the town most of his life, worked in the Education Department, liked fishing. No serious previous conditions.

'He thinks it's cancer,' Jonas said. 'I don't blame him. It's not cancer. You don't know him?'

'I don't know him. Neither does Tor.'

'You don't know that, man.'

'She doesn't know him.'

Diane did some poking around when we saw the schedule for the conference and decided to come. Dr Gower's a real researcher. Her doctorate is psychology, though, not medicine, and the work she's going to be talking about is real, though she obviously has a sense of humour about it. I figure her after-dinner speech is going to be one of those inside jokes. Like some of the stuff that wins the IgNobel Prize – a joke, *bund* a real insight too.

It's called 'Veering Off-Script: Mistakes, the Shakes, Psychotic Breaks during SP Performance.'

I'm sure that's hilarious to the attendees.

We came to this conference just for the banquet. We have our meal tickets. I'm planning to laugh in all the obvious places. But afterwards, we're going to talk to Dr Gower, Jonas and I. We're going to explain our predicament.

What examples does she have? She knows the history of this kind of thing. Of going off-script. What if this has happened before, whatever this is? Maybe it means something. Maybe we can fix it.

Brandon was weak and growing weaker. The dermatologists were bewildered. 'He's delirious,' Jonas said, 'but he doesn't have any fever at all. If anything, he's getting colder.' Brandon's hallucinations were getting stronger but you could still, just, talk to him.

The last few times we'd met friends for a drink or supper, Tor had been at least partly still in character. She wasn't not herself, she was herself-in-patient, she was herself *bund* her role. Someone studious, or worried, or boisterous, and ill. Always ill.

I wanted to talk to her about this, of course I did, but she was so focused in that state, she felt almost implacable. I didn't know how to say anything.

'I can see in the dark, doctor,' she said to one student, one day. Jonas showed me the videos when anything unscripted happened now.

'They're so going to dump her,' he said.

'Perfectly,' she said on-screen. 'Much better than I ever could in the light. And I breathe out more than I breathe in.'

'I started writing a letter to the president of the ASP,' Jonas said. 'I could ask her if she's ever heard of anything like this.'

We'd been reading up. In 1963, Howard Barrows trained the first SP. She simulated multiple sclerosis and paraplegia. In 1970, Paula Stillman hired women to talk about their imaginary children's illnesses. Didn't help us.

'I've been imagining like a secret history of the ASP,' Jonas said. 'Like some Opus Dei shit. Knights-Hospitallers, boom-*tish*.

Right? Like maybe the Association of Standardised Patients has a paramilitary wing, a black-ops wing, a psy-ops wing.'

'Please stop talking shit, this is Tor,' I said.

'Ok, ok. Listen to me, I need to tell you something. Someone else has the same thing Brandon does.'

The second person to come down with the condition, at least in this area, was Ms Dean, a woman in her thirties. She was deteriorating quickly. She wouldn't let me in like Brandon had, so Jonas had to describe to me what was happening.

That night I watched Tor closely and she told me I was making her feel uncomfortable. I said she was making me uncomfortable too, and I gestured at her clothes that were hers and also not hers. Sometimes, when I felt really bad, I wondered if 'she' was even a useful category any more.

'You're being weird,' she told me. 'I need some time.'

I gave her an awkward hug and begged her to stay. 'We need a breather,' she said. 'Just a couple of weeks. I'll go stay with Stacey. This is us-management.'

The same day Tor drove to her sister's house, Ms Dean died.

'Her skin's going soft again now,' Jonas said.

'Now that she's dead.'

'Yes.'

He was blustering but he was stricken that she had died.

We weren't good at this. We dithered, failed to think of strategies while whatever was happening happened faster. Two more people were admitted, their skins hardening with obscure messages.

In the children's ward, he told me, two young girls had spent the day puking and crying.

'So?'

'So one's on the kosher option,' Jonas said. 'And she's puking up sausage meat. Which her buddy ate, but which she is *not* chucking. They're throwing up each other's puke.'

I called Stacey and she told me Tor was out, having a think, that I shouldn't worry, that Tor loved me a lot, that she'd call me soon. 'She's one of the good ones,' she said.

'I know,' I said. I called Jonas and told him I had to go get her.

'Ok,' he said, 'but first you need to talk to Danny Merchant.'

'Who?'

'An SP,' he said, and I remembered that I'd met him, that he'd qualified in Tor's training class.

'What's the deal?' I said.

'He did a gig for us a few days ago. I just heard about it. It went wrong. He started describing an illness that doesn't exist.'

There was no footage. Jonas told me that Merchant had not repeated any of the conditions Tor had described. 'He was talking about how he grew a new limb for a day,' he said. A hairless tail from the middle of his chest, studded with thinly skinned organs like tumours. 'Swears absolutely blind he doesn't remember anything about it.'

We met him in a little cafe in the low-rent area where he lived. 'How's Tor?' he said.

'I want to talk to you about what happened the other day,' Jonas said. 'You remember, you were doing lower abdominal pain? And then about halfway through . . .'

'I know what you're talking about,' Danny said. 'But no, I don't remember. I only know because they told me about it. I don't know what to tell you.'

'When did you last speak to Tor?' I said.

'What? Not since the course,' he said. 'But I was thinking about her recently. I don't know if maybe because everyone else has started talking about her.'

'What?' said Jonas, and 'Who has?' I said, at the same time.

'You said something about her when you asked about this before,' he said to Jonas. 'And, I don't know, I've just been hearing her name around. I don't know if that had started before I did whatever they keep telling me I did.'

There might be viruses that go back through time. Whatever condition he had, he did not have it in as pure a form as Tor, I could tell. I was sure his presentations would be more vague and incoherent than anything she said. He didn't seem clear on any script. Still, I bet somewhere someone's in hospital with a little nub on his or her chest. Maybe it's like a big skin tag.

Danny doesn't have whatever this is like Tor did, but he does have something. She was Patient Zero. Epiphany's contagious. More SPs have started describing more random conditions that should be impossible, and that used to be.

'Will you calm down?' Stacey said when I finally got hold of her, when Tor didn't come home. 'I thought she was on her way to you. No, I don't know where she is and if she doesn't want to call you that's her prerogative. Seriously, I don't know what went down between the two of you but don't act like I'm the dick here, ok? It's not like someone snatched her, she got in the car herself.'

A car, a black car, waiting outside the house. Stacey doesn't know from cars. Not a limo, something more casual. Two or three guys in it, she thinks, not in suits or anything like that, black polo-necks maybe. Just some guys. Guys Tor must have known, she thought as she watched from her front room, because after

Tor saw the car waiting and leaned into the side window, so one of the men could show her a piece of paper, and scribble on it while she nodded and seemed to make her own suggestions, she turned and waved to Stacey and calmly got in with her bags.

I got Stacey to tell me what clothes Tor was wearing when the car drove off and I recognised every item she described, all old standards, but it turns out that's not enough any more, that I have to see Tor wearing clothes to get a sense of whose clothes they are. I don't know who she was when she wore them, or from what condition she was suffering when she got in the car and they drove her away.

I went to Stacey's and we had a big row. We patched it up recently because Tor's gone and Tor's her sister and one of her favourite people and she wants her back and the cops have been no help at all.

I'm registered at this conference under an invented name. We decided I'd probably sent the ASP too many letters, and letters that were too agitated, to attend under my own.

We've had disease control up in Treemont. I steered clear of them. There've been more admissions for hardened skin.

Five weeks after Tor disappeared I woke up sick as hell, and just made it to the bathroom. Even before I looked, I could taste that whatever I'd thrown up was nothing I'd eaten.

It bobbed in the bowl. It looked like the remains of someone's birthday cake. From a kid's party.

Yes I was scared but I didn't go to the hospital because you don't know where that's going to end up. Who's going to take you where.

*

Brandon died.

'We're really sad,' Jonas said. 'We'd got to like the dude. And we'd been trying all these things out and some of them seemed to be working. I swear to God we're getting better at this. We have no idea what we're doing but we've actually started curing some of these people now.'

You don't have to understand to have insight to fix things.

People mess up correlation and causation all the time. Just because we noticed these diseases after Tor started performing them doesn't mean she caused them. She might've done, yes. But honestly I don't think that's what she was a vector for.

There's a miserable game I play, wondering who Tor's with – the government, the afflicted, the leaders of that secret ASP cabal, someone, no one. Whether or not she is, or was ever, sick. Whether she's alive.

Like he said, Jonas and his colleagues are getting better at dealing with these diseases. I think Tor is exactly what Tor always seemed to be. An incredibly talented performer, whose performances taught, and maybe still teach, healers to heal.

I can't make sense of these session write-ups, and that makes me nervous because I'm pretty good at glancing at stuff I don't know about and getting to grips with it fast.

I'm not a crazy person, I don't expect to find out much at this conference, but who would I be not to try? So here I am with *Todd Bryanson, Independent Researcher*, on my nametag, waiting to talk to a drunken psychologist-cum-stand-up-comic.

SARS, prions, bird flu. What other barriers have illnesses been jumping? If you knew you were going to face new epidemics from other places, wouldn't you set in motion programmes to train doctors against them? That's what would be terrible *bund* sensible.

We should have put a proposal in. We should have presented. I'm not really joking. I've made a list of the speculative illnesses so far. I'm going to give it to Gower. She should add it to her routine, or replace her routine with it, because who knows what the stakes are? What we're being prepped for?

I'm healthy. I'm sad but I'm healthy. I'm telling you, though, somewhere soon, in Sacramento or Kuala Lumpur or Lagos or wherever, someone's going to be admitted because their warm flesh arms end in twilit ghost hands.

Rules

For millennia no girl or boy made that now-familiar noise or that recognisable shape with their arms. They did not bank or weave, did not yaw with instinctive elegance and mimic a machine. There was a first time. There was one child who first pretended to be an aeroplane.

She was an eight-year-old girl. The day before she inaugurated the era she had watched entranced from the edge of a close-cut meadow while a wobbling engine trundled fast forward and made it at last off the ground. She had stared up at its precarious progress with a new kind of delight.

1) **Consider beginnings and endings. Consider their relations.**
   Player one draws a horizontal line and calls it 'Time'.
   Player two cuts the chronology with vertical strokes in several colours.
   Player three numbers the divisions, according to whatever logic is appropriate.
   The sheet is placed in the centre of the table and the digital hourglass (included) is started. Meditate on the schema while that random timer runs.

The girl's name was Emmeline, and she went by Nuthatch, according to a brother's whim. It was she who, tired of making daisy chains with a friend from the valley, stood abruptly and ran up the hill to her mother's cabin with her arms stiff and cruciform in an unprecedented configuration, mud on the hem of her skirt.

'What are you doing?' the other girl shouted. 'Slow down!' Not because she could not keep up but because she wanted to parse Nuthatch's motion. She had not witnessed the previous day's ascent but something in her immediately recognised the necessity of what she saw.

2) **Play commences when the buzzer sounds.**

Player four picks one card from the Integument stack and one from the Geist stack, and places them face up, visible to all. She has thirty seconds to decide on what First Thing the combination of these two cards portends. While the timer runs again, she performs a wordless mime of this inauguratory activity.

The other players announce their guesses as to what is being mummed. A correct call ends the turn. If the timer runs down without the activity being guessed, no one wins.

Lastness: Play can be interrupted at any time by any player who declares 'Final Thing'.

She must take a card from the Possible stack. She must never reveal her Possible Card to any other player. She must combine its value with those of the other two visible cards, and on that basis decide on an ending.

All other players must remain silent.

She must perform the Final Thing as long as she can.

There will be a last child too. She will play when Earth is mostly cold and mostly dark, and under heaps of granular, grubby ice.

The time will not be without joy and it will find its last pleasures in things other than colour. Another girl will run to the edge of a cliff and back again, purring like a propeller. That will be anachronistic, but not much more than if she pretended to be a jet: no planes of any kind will have flown for centuries. She will be the last player of a game passed down. She will not know what it is she mimics.

And after that final, offhand, chilly performance of this girl whose name we don't yet know, even that trace will be gone and it'll be the end of this brief epoch and time for other things. Afterwards, all the children will play differently, with their arms held up under heavy clothes into quite other shapes than those of metal wings.

Estate

Two nights running I woke up with my heart going crazy. The first time, as I lay there in the dark, I heard a group of guys outside. They were running, shouting, 'Hurry!' and 'We'll miss it!' I wondered if I should do something, but I couldn't hear any fighting or smashing glass. I got up when they were all gone. I kept my light off and parted my blind to look down.

There was rubbish under the streetlamps. There was a big rectangular bin, its lid open, and all around it was a rim of paper and plastic and leaves.

It was August. The slats of the blind left black dust on my hand.

The next night foxes woke me. I knew their swallowed barks but I'd never heard a racket like that before. One night when I was really young, before we moved to the estate, our cat was in heat – my mother explained it to me carefully – and as I was closing my bedroom curtains I saw that the tree at the bottom of our yard was full of cats. They were switching their tails as the light went down. They were all staring, it seemed to me, at me. They started up these boylike horny tom cries.

I listened to the fox calls and wondered if it was the same sort of thing going on. If they were courting, under city trees, or on the roof of a corrugated shed.

There's a park near my flat with a little playground in it, populated by friendly plastic animals. One's a fox, with bright red fur and a blue cap. I imagined a bunch of real foxes circling that cartoony figure in the dark.

I went and stood outside. It was much colder than it should have been, like winter. The foxes shut up. Under a lamp was a noticeboard for the tenants' association. A torn sign about a coffee morning. Recycling. A meeting called by a social capital group called OBYOSS, about regeneration. The name of one of their organisers was familiar.

The playground wasn't far. I went past closed shops and into unlit rows.

There's a robin next to the fox. It's about the size of a three-year-old, and dressed like a pirate. There's a badger and a pig. They're the same size: they aren't to scale.

A few cars passed, streets away. There was no rain but the air felt wet. I heard muffled percussion. A faint *thud-thud-thud*. The rhythm of hooves.

The sounds echoed between the damp walls. I thought I could smell pollen. Light was coming up from an unkempt side street. Something glowing. The beats got louder.

The air was full of dust and little leaves. I had to squint to see.

There was a guttering noise. The shadows of street trees jumped madly. Wavering light reflected in the windows of a shop, in the fronts of the machines that, for a few coins, would spit out toys and sweets.

The light flared and rolled and went out. When I reached the side street I stood with the wind shoving at me. I smelled smoke but there was no fire anywhere. There was no sound.

I went back the next day. A group of kids were circling a puddle on their bicycles. Two older men struggled with shopping. There were scorch marks high up on a lamppost. In front of one small house a young family giggled at their fussing baby. It grizzled but they seemed delighted.

'Can you believe it?' its mother said. 'You were so ill last night, you little terror! Now look at you!' The baby burped and everybody laughed.

Their garden was thick with some flowering bush. I doubt it was ever healthy, but to me it looked freshly ripped, missing foliage. I tugged at one of the broken branches, as if my hand was something grazing as it passed.

Back at the estate, people were clustered in little groups between the blocks. There was a woman there who lives close to me and likes me because I made faces for her toddler one time.

'You were at my school, yeah?' she said. I hadn't realised until that moment. 'Did you know Dan Loch?'

'Yes,' I said. I was startled. 'I knew who he was anyway.'

'He's back.'

'Right,' I said. 'I think I saw his name on something.'

'Don't pretend like you don't care.' She smiled as if we were conspirators.

When Dan was expelled from our school he and his family had left the estate altogether. I was one of the kids who watched him go.

The Lochs had lived in a stretch of flats by outbuildings full of maintenance stuff, where addicts would take drugs. We'd climbed up onto the roofs and lay on our stomachs to watch Dan's family.

His mum was hauling his younger sister over her shoulder, their crying faces close together. His dad shuffled behind them, a suitcase in each hand. In front of them all was Dan, sniffing the air as if that would decide him which way to go.

We made no effort to hide. It was all a bit solemn. Dan looked up and acknowledged us with raised eyebrows. He looked at the sun, paused, beckoned, and turned into the city, his family behind him.

'He was in Paris and South Africa,' the woman said. 'Now he's back.'

'This the welcoming committee?' I said.

There were police hovering at the edges of the square but there was no trouble.

We stayed into the night. A lot of the people there I didn't recognise. That's surprising when you've been in the estate as long as I have. Some wore country clothes, and sounded like they came from posher areas than ours.

When it got dark people got more raucous. They listened to music on their phones, and some were even dancing, joke-dancing to show they weren't taking it seriously. It drizzled.

A little after ten o'clock I heard a clacking. There was a brief cheer.

People came from behind one of the towers. Eight or nine of them, in overalls, with sports bags over their shoulders. Each carried a pointed stick, speared litter they shoved into black rubbish bags. They knocked their sticks together rhythmically. There was a woman who couldn't have been older than nineteen. A man in his sixties, waving like a celebrity. In front of them all was Dan. I wouldn't have known him if my neighbour hadn't put him in my mind.

They conferred. They whispered, pointed in various directions, down passageways and under concrete. They slapped hands at last in a complicated salute and separated. We all picked one of them to go after.

I followed Dan. I said his name. He glanced. It took him a moment but I could see he knew me.

'Yeah,' he said. 'You alright?' He touched his finger to his forehead and twirled his litter-stick. He was elegant.

I said, 'Dan,' again, but he was gone. A group of teenagers passed me. 'Shut up,' one said. 'Man's focusing.'

Dan fingered walls and bollards. He passed a knocked-over bin and knelt to examine it. We hung back. I felt like I was seeing him leave home again.

By a concrete ramp and a commercial space that had never been let, the wall was blackened. Dan began to run.

He was taking us down routes I'd never seen. Behind those blocks the only noises we made were those of our feet and bikes. The bases of the brown towers ran up to the surrounding streets, which were not deserted. Cars crossed the bridge over the canal.

Dan stopped suddenly in the light of late-night shops and we all stopped with him and he stared into shadows and derelict bike sheds, their doors permanently open. He waved at us to stay still. Very slowly, he put his stick and sack down. He took the bag from his shoulders and opened it.

Firelight flared. There was a roar of burning. A stag walked out of the dark.

It shone. Its antlers were on fire.

The stag was huge. It regarded us without fear. The antlers were like the branches of a great tree. They rushed with flame. They sent up oily smoke, lit the cars and the lots and the pedestrians. The antlers spat.

The stag swung its brawny neck. It walked toward us with forest calm. It paused and lowered its head and lapped at a gutter.

We didn't move. It went on at last for the road. I heard screaming. Two men came out of a late-night shop, stared and ran. One fell backwards and kept scooting along the pavement on his arse. The other yelled his name and came back for him.

There was a horrible series of thuds as a car swerved and hit another, and then as a third hit them. Fire spread along the animal's tines.

Dan was clicking something together. A rifle. One of the boys on bikes whooped and Dan shouted, 'E! Nuff!' without looking round and made the kid freeze.

Clots of stuff fell from the stag's head and made its pelt smoulder. It crossed the road close to us. I smelt the burning hair. The animal was twitching now.

Dan sighted. His quarry staggered. It hesitated, it swayed. The fire was accelerating, crawling down the antlers. The stag blinked.

Dan fired.

The stag spasmed and buckled and bowed.

There were whoops. But Dan cursed and did something to his weapon. It wasn't his bullet that had done this. The flames began to take the stag's big head.

Dan took aim again. Another car careered across the road. The deer was too lost, shaking too hard to look, if it even had eyes still and they weren't burnt up. The car slammed into its kneeling body.

Glass exploded. The burning animal flew so hard into the railing on the bridge I felt the impact in the air. Its antlers splintered, leaving stumps in the head-shaped fire.

'Jesus Christ!' I shouted. A man fell out of the car holding a bloody wound.

'Fuck,' Dan said.

The deer was half off the bridge, fitting. You could see its teeth through the fire pulling back its lips. It lolled. Its weight shifted and it tipped and we shouted, 'No!' as if that might stop it falling but it didn't. It plummeted out of sight. We heard it hit the water.

'What does that mean?' someone said at last. 'Did it work?'

'You can't tell straight away.'

'What do you think?'

Dan was disassembling his rifle. He saw me looking and rolled his eyes at me in an *Ah well* way. Gave me a wave and swung the bag back over his shoulder. I think I was the only one who saw him walk quickly away, back into the estate, into the dark under the towers. Everyone else was by the railings, watching the smoking carcass bob rump-up in the canal.

The council got it out with a crane. They used one from the building site on the other side of the water. They didn't even have to reposition it. The operator just turned it round and dropped the hook and expertly fished the stag out.

It dangled, all ruined, dropping bits into the water as it rose in chains.

A public meeting was organised. I heard it was confused. No one was sure why they were there.

You heard a lot about the stag in the estate those days, of course. It took about a day before everyone was claiming to have been there. Everyone had a different story about how they'd heard where to be, when. No one really knew anything, though a fair few bullshitters, if the topic came up, would get a faraway look, maybe insinuate that they'd had some ideas what to expect, maybe tap their noses as if they were in on something.

So I thought that would be the end of it, but it wasn't. About a month later, the office of the government's head vet, something like that, held a press conference. They wanted to discuss the results of the post-mortem.

The undersides of the stag's hooves, they said, had been coated with an epoxy like dense rubber. The antlers had been saturated in something bituminous, long- and slow-burning. Except where they protruded from the skull and skin: there they'd been treated with retardant, to slow the downward creep of fire.

The animal's blood was full of a ketamine derivative of unknown sort, cut or altered in ways the scientists didn't fully understand. But they were confident it closed down pain sensors, numbed flight–fight instincts.

It had been made into a deer unconcerned that its antlers were on fire.

It had been dying the whole time we followed it, in a poisoned stupor, burning alive.

The OBYOSS posters promising urban renewal faded. No one took them down. I looked for Dan in the flat that had been his family's. It had been empty for years. 'He's gone back to Cornwall,' my neighbour said. 'That's what I heard.' I walked past a launderette and a teenage boy opened the door and came out in a fug of dryer smell and said, 'I seen you was looking for the Dan man. I've got something for you.'

'You want this?' he said. 'You want this yes or no? It's a hundred.'

He had a short length of blackened antler. It smelt of burn. 'Put that in your garden, it makes your plants grow. Put it in your house, it gives you money.' He gave me more reasons I should buy it and I did. It was surprisingly light. I put it on top of my TV, as he also suggested. 'Makes your reception perfect,' he said. 'Check Channel 4 tonight.'

The footage was of the rolling of the fiery barrel or whatever, some harvest festival in a market town. 'Look at you,' I said, as if the man onscreen could hear me, as if the footage weren't months old.

It was Dan. He was one of those hoisting a burning thing onto his shoulders, carrying whatever it was, wherever.

There's been very little regeneration on the estate. Two months after Dan disappeared, in Birmingham and then in Glasgow, burning-antlered stags sauntered down main streets as long as the drugs held. In Birmingham, someone in the crowd shot the deer with a bow, then a gun. The arrow hit its left leg, the bullet killed it and the crowd dispersed. The one in Glasgow died all by itself.

A huge albino animal, its head under a corona of fire, went walking in a run-down neighbourhood of Montreal, to be put down by terrified cops. A stag set off in a Parisian *banlieue* street at midnight followed by awestruck youths but something was wrong with its preparation and it collapsed and started dying almost immediately.

No one's ever been caught preparing or releasing any of the beasts.

In New York two days ago, someone let scores of hares loose on Roosevelt Island. They went racing everywhere, jumping, feverish, boxing each other, all sinewy and pugnacious in the waste-ground. There was something glinty and wrong with their ears. I saw it on YouTube. Within a few minutes they started to die. They weren't afraid of the locals who tried to grab them, and sometimes, disastrously, succeeded.

Running the length of each of the hares' ears was a knife. They slashed people's hands. They were like straight razors, one end driven through the fur into the hares' skulls. The blades protruded, sutured to the ears with fishing wire. Mostly, the clots and bloodstains resulting from these alterations had been wiped away or bleached invisible, but if you held the dying things carefully and looked closely you could see the joins.

They're building a new playground. I looked at the plans: it's going to be much better. I saw diggers and men in overalls getting ready to uproot the plastic fox and all the others. 'What'll happen to them?' I asked, but the landscapers shrugged. I keep imagining those garish animals in a landfill, under the earth.

Keep

Anna Samson had not slept through the night for a long time. She mentioned this to her boss and he asked if she was having difficulty with the project.

'Yes. What do you mean?' she said. 'What kind of difficulty?'

'Ethical.'

'Well, I mean, he is there against his will.' She didn't say that she had been insomniac months before she arrived.

'I don't blame you feeling weird about it,' Olson said. 'No one enjoys seeing him in there.' He hesitated, a better epidemiologist than manager. 'Let me see what I can do.'

Anna was excited to try the orange pills he left in her cubbyhole later that day but they were no more effective than the Zopiclone of which she was a regular user. Still, she took them sometimes because she discovered that the watery dreams they provoked interested her.

'I was in a corridor—' she said to Daniel during a video conversation.

'You spend your life in corridors,' he said. She changed the subject and he didn't notice. Later she told the whole dream to Sarah instead. Sarah asked her if she was eating enough.

When Anna went to ask if he could provide her with more of the medication, Olson was gone. 'You'll be reporting directly to me now,' said Colonel Gomez. He looked at her sadly and she knew why the other man had left.

Anna was forty-four, with dry blonde hair she never did much with, so it framed her exaggeratedly pleased or fretful face in a look an old friend once called 'haute harried', which Anna half-enjoyed. The soldiers in the base checked her ID every time she entered, though she knew they recognised her by now.

Olson had wanted her to live on the base but she had insisted on renting in town. It was a few miles from the military compound, a spread-out cluster of five hundred inhabitants in ugly bungalows. Her little house overlooked a dried-up swamp bed, a hollow surrounded by tree remains. She could walk in the basin on hard dirt that had once been muck thriving with frogs. She kept off the slopes beyond, where brush stretched out four miles to a little abandoned airfield. The shopkeeper told her there were ticks.

'You'll be working at the base, I guess,' he said the first time she went in.

His sign said he opened at 8am but Anna usually found him sitting at his open door a little after seven. They would drink coffee together.

'They closed the school,' he told her. 'The kids now, the ones still here, and they ain't many, they do distance learning. On the computer. Where you from?'

'Troy, New York.'

'My kids are gone. My girl to San Francisco, my boy to Sacramento. We don't talk, though, me and him. I can't believe it's raining again. It ain't usually like this, you know, not this late in the year. You think this might have anything to do with . . . you know?'

Whenever it rained while she was in his store she would buy a cheap umbrella. 'You know they're reusable, right?' he said.

'Easy come,' she said.

*

'Why don't you come closer?' the subject said.

'Don't I come close enough?' Anna said.

'Actually, you get closer than most of them,' he said. 'You not scared? You should be scared. Your boss got sick, didn't he? Sick like me.'

'Are you sick?'

'Don't I look it?'

'You look tired,' she said, 'but mostly you look ok. You have a complaint to make?'

'Fuck yes. You know how long it's been since I saw the fuck-ing sun?'

'You know what'll happen if they give you a room above ground. You have to be on the lowest level, you know that. And you know how quarantine works. Didn't you just tell me you were sick? Don't you think you're too sick to leave?'

'Well, I'm too fucking something.'

'If it's you,' she said. He looked at her quizzically. 'What if it's not you that's sick,' she said. 'What if it's the world?'

'Right.'

'That's what I'm trying to understand.'

'And how's that going, doc? Doc, your suit's not done up.'

'Nick,' she said. 'Can you turn all the way around?'

'You want to see if anything changes, don't you?' he said. 'It doesn't. You know that. Just keep walking around me. What's that?'

'A fibreoptic camera I'm going to put down.'

'Good, because I was thinking, where's she going to stick that tube?'

'You know I'm not that kind of doctor. *You're* not my patient.'

*

Most days at sunup Anna took a walk before she drove to the base with books scattered across her back seat. Whoever was on duty would always take a moment to look them over. A first set of rumble strips marked the end of the public road. Beyond it several hundred yards of dusty ground had been cleared of even the stubbiest succulent. At their end were more strips and the start of the base.

The morning after her interview with Nick – Anna wouldn't call him Subject Zero, not even in her head – she woke early, abruptly. The phone was silent but she felt certain the air still shook with an echo of ringing. When she dialled for the last incoming number it told her no one had called for hours.

Anna had already started to sweat. She was sweating more here than she ever had before.

Coming home from the base in the afternoon she saw that the intersection where the shop was located had been blocked off with police tape. Standing in front of it was Marsh, the town's police officer, nodding to an army sergeant she recognised from the base. There were other soldiers, making notes and taking pictures. They got in and out of the building across a thick plank laid where the stoop had been. The front step was crumbled and gone.

'Oh fuck no,' Anna said, but she saw the shopkeeper come out. He was haggard. He came to her.

'It weren't me,' he said. 'Did you think it was me? You looked kind of worried. I didn't know you cared,' he said, and tried to smile and looked up at a circling hawk. 'It was Mrs Bolling. You know her?'

She shook her head.

'Ok, well. She's a nice lady but she was pretty old, and I guess when it started she got confused.'

'What happened?'

'She got into the shop. Hell, I don't always lock up, you know that. It must've been in the middle of the night. And then she must've stood right there in the middle of the room there, just stood there till it finished going around, and—' He indicated the ruined step.

'There's a basement?' she said.

'She fell right down. It ain't that far down but she was pretty frail anyhow. There ain't hardly a floor left in there.' Anna peered and through the sunlight on the shop window she could see a big darkness.

'How long will that take to replace?' she said.

'Oh, Hell, I don't know, it don't make any difference to me no more,' he said. 'I'm gone.'

They watched a thickset young soldier come out of the shop. His boot caught the flapping end of the police tape and stretched it and snapped it as he walked away. The whole boundary sank slowly to the ground.

'I mean we never thought it wasn't going to come here, right?' the shopkeeper said. 'Least I didn't.'

Anna said nothing.

'Ok then,' he said. Well. Want to buy a store? It's floorless.'

She didn't smile.

Colonel Gomez was hunkered over a display in the briefing and control room with a man Anna did not know.

'Dr Samson,' Gomez said. 'This is Stuart Perry.'

Perry looked up briefly and shook her hand. He had an earphone in one ear. He was perhaps a decade younger than she, handsome, smartly turned out. He would not be wearing that suit for very long, she thought, not here, no matter how well it went down in the capital.

'I'm bringing him up to speed,' the colonel said. 'Before she was here Anna was in London.' Perry looked at her again, now with more interest.

The screen showed Nick straight on, standing in the cell between his chair and his small bed. He was gesturing at the opaque window that took up one wall.

'When was this?' Anna said.

'Yesterday,' said the colonel. 'After you saw him.' He was a dark, lined, still-muscular man, with stubble on his scalp the colour of cigarette ash. His subdued tone always surprised her.

'How long have you been here?' Perry said. He glanced down at something Nick said. Anna, earphoneless, heard nothing. 'Damn, he's bratty.'

'A few weeks,' she said. 'I've been testing soil samples. I don't get to talk to him that much. What's your field?'

'History,' he said. 'Does he give anyone the time of day?'

'He's an angry young man. Misses his friends and his girl-friend and the wind on his face.'

Nick was tall and a little overweight, undignified in the hos-pital gown they made him wear. They had crewcut his hair.

'I haven't seen it yet,' Perry said. 'Can you show me from above?' The colonel pressed buttons and switched to the feed from the room's ceiling camera.

The screen showed the bed, the chair, and the gesturing figure of Nick himself. Surrounding him in a rough circle, its radius about six feet, with him in the centre, a trench was gouged in the white ceramic of the floor.

It was more than three feet wide. Its edges and inside sides were rough and irregular. Anna could see mud, clay, stones in layers below the thin top of splintered tile. Between the cut and the walls was a rim of room just wide enough to walk on.

'We can't stop it,' said Perry.

Anna and the colonel shook their heads though it was not a question.

'And we can't speed it up.'

'He special ops?' Anna said. 'What's he here to do?'

'He's keen,' said the colonel. 'He'll bury me, that's all I know. You think they still tell me shit? Don't give him my private number.' Gomez had given it to Anna her third week on the base, telling her to call him if she had a breakthrough, to wake him, whatever the time.

'All I'm doing is accumulating information,' she had said. She knew she should sound embarrassed. 'I don't know that it's anything we can use, exactly.'

'I'll take it,' he'd said.

Through the observation window they watched Perry shrugging under the weight of his biohazard suit. A bored soldier, in the same coveralls, stood watching from a corner.

'Do some star jumps for me?' Perry said. 'Stars. Stars!' he said. He stood just beyond the trench, looking down into it. Anna would test her scrapings again, but she knew they would register only as the earth they were, indistinguishable from any other earth. 'As close to the trench as you can,' he said. 'Can you come and stand just across from me?'

From the centre, the ground they called the nucleus, Nick watched him with sour dislike. 'Please run around your bed,' Perry said.

Nick did so, jogging just at the inside edge of the cut. He ran and ran and sped up and abruptly jumped, clearing it to land by the door.

Instantly the soldier raised his rifle at him. Anna tensed. She had read the files; she knew this was not the first time Nick had done this.

'Come on, Nick,' said Perry. He sounded calm.

The soldier did something and his weapon clicked. The colonel hissed. Beyond the glass Nick made a sulky face and jumped back over to stand by his bed.

'I'm going *crazy*,' he shouted. 'You won't let me out; you won't let me talk to my friends.'

'It's only a matter of time before he tries again,' Gomez said. 'I don't blame him, Samson, is the truth.'

'You want to know about it,' Nick was shouting to Perry, 'ask them. Or just go down.'

'Have you been down?' said Perry. 'What do *you* think it is?'

'Yeah. It's a hole.'

'Except it's not, is it?' Perry said. 'It's a trench. Or you could say it's a hole with a not-hole in the middle. The nucleus. Right where you are.'

'He's been going through all the subject's files,' Gomez said. 'All his diaries, photos, of Lai, Sharon, Terrell, that fucking Hacky Sack crew he met while he was *finding* himself. And all the photos we have from their accounts too.'

'I did that when I got here,' Anna said. 'We had to.'

'Yeah, ok, that's Perry's job. He's been going through my files too. And yours.'

'Ask Lai,' Nick said. 'Ask Birgit. They're the ones who were talking about all weird stuff, before anything even started. You think they don't know things?'

'You know we can't, Nick,' Perry said, and Nick's face scrunched up in pain. 'You've told us about your girlfriend before.'

Nick had been in hiding when things started to change. He

had seen what was happening, and knew he was part of it. It had taken him a little over a week, after he was brought in, to name his erstwhile companions, to mention hints they had made, to talk of Birgit like someone struck by religion.

'She said there were chambers underground,' he said. 'She said something would start. She was looking for things. Full of old stories.' He both wanted and did not want to talk about her.

Anna could see the acquisitive and calculating way Perry was staring at the hole. She turned away and made no effort to disguise her distaste from Gomez.

'You still not scared?' he said. 'Of being in there with him?'

She gave him a small smile.

The trench in its gradualism, she thought, in its shape and the specifics of its depth and dimensions, in its particularities, would seem to chafe against service to death and the state. That implied something, she thought. That seemed to hold forth some promise. Of what, she could not say.

Anna still communicated with only a very few of her friends. She abided by the injunction not to disclose what she had been seconded to work on, in the details, but given her expertise, her time in London, the fact that she didn't care, it was not surprising that word spread.

She received an email from an ex from whom she had not heard for years, since he had moved to an out-of-the-way town in Portugal. He wrote to her in a voice that she found curiously flat, as if he was compensating for the millennial mood, wishing her good luck with her research, for all their sakes, telling her he still thought of her often, hoping his coastal home would be isolated for some time to come.

'We were too much,' she wrote back. 'I don't know why I'm

telling you this, you know it. What I mean is that our sets over-lapped too much.

'They came to me after I'd been in London and in Madison. I probably shouldn't tell you but I want to try to explain.' She typed quickly. 'You remember my friend Jana? She's in San Diego now. I was there last year. That's what started this whole thing for me. I took her daughter to a reading at a library, some writer she likes, adventure stories. She's ten. Anyway, on the way back she saw something at the end of an alley and we went to check it out because I knew Jana wouldn't have done and I always figure that's my "aunt" job, right?

'Every time I see an adult who's infected I feel surprised. I don't know why but it feels to me like this is a condition for chil-dren. It should be children who have this. If you'd told someone a few years ago that this would start spreading I bet we would have thought it would be children who'd get it, instead of anyone for reasons we can't make sense of.

'This was before we knew much about it (as if we do now!) but I'd heard a few things and I suddenly had a terrible feeling because I saw a trench right across the alley, right through the pavement like they'd been laying a pipe, and beyond it was a body.

'It was an old man who had died. A homeless man. He smelled. Later it turned out he'd been there two days.

'I told the kid to come back but I was surprised because she wouldn't stop. She starts to climb down into the trench to get across and I'm shouting at her and then she slips, just tips out of view.

'The cut was deep. On the other side the poor dead guy looked like he was eyeing me. The kid was freaking out.

'I see her at last, curled up under a little overhang in the wall. I reach down. She looks up at me – there's dirt all over her face

– with this haunted look. I feel like there must be worms all over her.

'She says, "I couldn't climb out." I reach down and tell her to take my hand.

'A week later, we're talking about it. We'd called the cops and everything of course, told them. She wants to know if the man's ok and in Heaven. So I'm saying all the usual stuff, I don't know, different people believe different things, et cetera. She says to me, "I heard something in the moat. Something moving."

'She was ok. She didn't catch it and we don't know why. Neither did I.' She considered, and discounted, adding something to that.

'I've been trying to figure that out. Drawing diagrams, sets, the details of anyone who gets infected. Trying to work out a common factor.

'In the end I'm a soil scientist. I've been thinking about it as if it's the ground that's the vector, not the people. Like if it's not a sickness at all.'

She didn't send what she'd written. She saved that message to a private folder. Instead she sent her ex a brief reply full of anodyne melancholia, and received nothing back.

As soon as she entered his room Nick began to complain, though in an almost dutiful manner as if he was decreasingly invested in his own anger.

'Can you hush?' she said. 'I'm here to take you somewhere. Over you come.'

He bit his lip and jumped over the trench.

Anna walked behind him and Gomez and the soldiers who escorted him. Perry came back for her.

'Did you even put your helmet on?' he said.

'I don't get that close.'

'Well, I guess after London you're not that worried.' She said nothing. 'Are you sure this is a good idea?'

'No but I'm sick of him moaning.'

'I hear that. I've been reading over his story. You've seen the way he talks about his travelling crew, right?'

'Yes,' she said. 'They're the ones who got him into castles.'

'You know what a star fortress is?'

'Yes,' she said. She walked away from him.

The soldiers took Nick past noticeboards and the entrances of lifts, up several flights of stairs, through double doors. He gasped and threw his hands wide and turned slowly on the spot.

They were in an irregular triangular yard about fifty yards on its longest face. It was enclosed by high wire-topped concrete walls, each punctuated with irregularly spaced windows, from several of which leaned young soldiers. They were relaxed but their weapons were visible. The floor was overlaid with the remains of paint markings, guides and touchlines for various sports, each in a different colour. A rusting netless basket was bolted to one wall.

'Couldn't arrange the sun,' Anna called. The cloud cover was flat and unvarying grey. The yard was too enclosed to feel the wind.

A soldier watching from above shouted, 'Keep moving, homeboy.' Nick looked up at his audience and could not stop smiling. 'Keep moving.'

Nick waved in what might have been dismissal or a greeting. He started to pace the perimeter.

'Heads up!' someone shouted. A basketball dropped from one of the windows. It landed with a *thwack* and began to wander the pitch in a series of decreasing bounces.

Nick kept walking in the shadow of the walls. Anna went to

meet the ball and caught it one-handed. She stopped a distance from the basket and threw the ball casually. She scored.

The soldiers whooped and cheered. She waited for the ball to come back to her and did it again, to more applause.

'Holy fucking shit, doc!' someone shouted.

'Nick,' the colonel said.

Nick was watching her.

'Nick, please keep moving.'

He did. He walked slowly to the centre of the yard, keeping his eyes on Anna, and stopped there again. 'No?' Nick called. 'This wouldn't be ok? You don't want to fuck up your basketball court?'

'Nick,' the colonel said, 'come on.'

'Was this you?' Nick said to Anna. 'Arranging this? You want me to say thanks? Is that it?'

'I don't want you to say anything,' she said. She walked past him to the far side of the court. She could feel nothing unusual about the surface close to him when she passed.

'Nick, I know you're enjoying yourself with this shit,' the colonel said, 'but please don't put me in this position, you know I need you to move now.'

The caution was extreme. Based on everything they knew it would take at least an hour of immobility for Nick's presence to start to have a measurable effect on the ground.

Alone in Nick's room she knelt by the trench. It felt shocking, indecent, to see the moat empty of him. She gripped the cracking edge of the tiles. She looked down through layers of broken floor into dense, almost black earth.

Computers kept a micrometrically precise record of all fluctuations of the trench. The ground had started to crumble, to sink into a gouge, seventy-three minutes after they had brought Nick here and ordered him into his bed, and had seemingly completed its change two hundred and twenty-five minutes after that. The ground had eaten into a widening hole.

It was one of Anna's jobs to find out where the matter had gone.

The sensors insisted there was no change but for the random pattering of loose earth in gravity, now, but Anna always felt as if she could see the moat growing, spreading inward unevenly so that the nucleus, the solid ground at its centre was eaten away by emptiness.

'I keep hearing about new strains,' Perry said. 'And terrorist stuff.' He followed Anna into the staff lounge and stood close to where she took her coffee, watching her with uncharacteristic hesitation while loudspeakers summoned someone somewhere.

'It's all rumours,' he said. 'Everyone's keeping their cards close to their chests. You hear something about Jaipur, Angola, Scotland. You know in this scene it's all about the rumours.'

Anna heard very few rumours.

'Colonel Gomez said you've been going over what Nick told us,' she said.

'Subject Zero,' he said. 'Yeah. I'm going over his files.'

'And mine?'

He blinked at her and she watched his caution go away. 'I'm interested in the source,' he said. 'That's my job. And I'm interested in anyone who can't seem to get infected.'

When they had brought her here and showed her video footage of Nick in his room, Anna had said, 'How do we know it's him?' The colonel and Olson had pulled up graphs of incidents and the spread.

No one was saying that everyone he touched would get it, Olson said, nor that those who did become infected would pass it on to all they touched. But Olson had put a lot of time and computational power into this, cross-referencing key words in global emails and messages, newspaper reports, hospital records, unexplained disasters, flight information, changes of address. The statisticians traced the spread backward. Nick was the initial vector.

They had gone over his tedious blogs, his gushes about his new travel friends, their combined gigabytes of pictures. Eager young men and women who travelled together and went off alone and rejoined their friends again repeatedly, writing emails about drugs and history and folklore and raised consciousness and imaginary secrets. Retraced his route through Hungary, Slovakia, Scotland, Germany. Looking for every castle, every artefact, every old wall. 'They're just monuments,' Gomez said. 'Ruins.'

When he returned to the US, Nick's passage through New Jersey and Illinois, Wisconsin, New Mexico had left hotspots blooming.

'Where does the stuff go?' Olson had said. 'Does it just compress? And most of all, what's the source? We figure that out, we might have a chance. Maybe track down people responsible.'

The Canadians had Terrell. He was uninfected, in quarantine, and knew nothing. Sharon was lost, presumed dead, in the chaos of Belfast. Lai and Birgit had been booked on the same flight from Edinburgh to Copenhagen. Both had been in recent contact with Nick: it could have been around either of them – or both – that a trench had scored, in the matter of the plane, breaking it apart and bringing its fragments down into the sea.

'I've found a few things,' Perry said to Anna. 'I don't know if they've all been properly looked at before. How's your stuff going?' Perry said. 'Any luck tracking down the dirt?'

*

Two can play at your game, Perry, Anna thought. She did not even convince herself.

Nonetheless she looked him up and after false starts as servers stuttered, could find no publications. His degrees were in military history. She had half-expected him to be some parapsychologist, a kook anomaly-hunter promoted into power by these impossible times.

In Perry's mind – she was certain – would be a future battle-field thronging with uniformed men advancing under packs and the weight of their weapons, rifles up, sending each other signals with quick silent clenched hands, moving in new adaptive formations towards the ruins of a village, each soldier surrounded by a stretching rip in the earth, that travelled with him, his own dugout trap, perhaps the solid nucleus on which he stood travelling with him to refill the hollows over which he leapt, so he advanced through thick jungle or a rising falling desert leaving a landscape of ripped-up interwoven trenches behind him.

Give it years. Give it months. Troops would drop into some recalcitrant statelet and use trenches to fight and advance again, in some new way, thought up by some brilliant secret theorist who would win some prize the existence of which civilians could not know. A celebration of unorthodox strategy. A black-ops gong.

Twice Anna succumbed to the online chivvyings of her last friends and participated in their self-consciously elegiac video-dinners. The internet was increasingly patchy and temperamental, censored and monitored, but the connection in her temporary house was still surprisingly decent. She sat at one end of her kitchen and connected with Sarah and Bo in Pasadena, Tia in

New York, Daniel unwrapping some post-midnight snack in his Berlin small hours.

'So?'

'Chicken, couscous, almonds, harissa.'

'Mmmm. I have hake and capers.'

Red sunlight went down across Anna's face. She described her own soup and salad.

'I have gummi bears,' Daniel said. 'How's Subject Zero?'

'Shhhh,' Anna said. Everyone made their usual *the spooks are listening* faces.

Daniel chewed on a candy. 'Officially here is not too bad,' he said. 'Infection rates are pretty low. Unofficially, worse, but it's no London. Yet. Partly because a lot of people are just fucking off into the mountains or whatever. It's going to start accelerating.'

It could only be the childless among her acquaintances who could bear this conversation.

'Did you see that Australian film?' said Bo.

A young architect from Perth had gone viral with a plea for a new urban design. New cities for a new age, he said. He had crowdsourced collaboration and, with dollars thrown frantically at him, built a mock-up of several streets, according to his notions.

'We have to stop thinking apocalyptically,' he said. 'Stop using words like "pandemic".' The camera tracked him through his fake town. 'You've all heard the rumours of new communities in hidden places. I think they're true. What if I told you I know they're true? They could be true for a lot more of us, and I'm going to show you how.'

Wide spaces, large plazas made from cheap and easily replaceable materials. No buildings above a single tall floor. Houses with a kitchenette, toilet, shower arranged as satellite-rooms around a big central space.

'It's a new kind of room,' the architect said. 'We call it the keep.'

Under a glass roof, between high walls, a big central bedroom-cum-den floored in compact earth, bed and chairs and freestanding shelves and TV and desk snugly tessellated in clever configuration, to fit within a perfectly regular, pre-dug trench, with a foldout walkway to cross it for when you wanted to move.

'We can make this deep enough and wide enough to contain all cuts arising from the condition.'

'What do you think?' Daniel said. He shut down the pop-up. 'It could work.'

'No,' Anna said. 'It couldn't.' The speed with which the moats came was increasing. Some reports suggested that their depth was increasing. And there were those stories of mutations, and her friend's daughter's memory of sounds. She looked away from the screen, her anguish taking her by surprise. 'Even if *we* could live with the trenches,' Anna said, 'the world, us, this, it can't. We didn't set it up right. No. It won't work.'

'Even our allies don't tell us shit any more,' Gomez told Anna. 'Hell, we get reports of bombing raids and shit from Poland to Ecuador to the Scottish fucking islands and we don't know who the fuck's blowing up what.'

They had originally tracked Nick down in a suburb of a dying town in Colorado. Anna went back and re-watched the footage of his first interrogations again.

He had no family. 'The people on the road,' he said. 'They're my family.' He had been moving for months, ever since he realised something was happening to him. He kept moving all day and slept in open ground. He camped in woods. 'But

I missed being inside, you know?' he said. 'I thought maybe it would be ok.'

He had broken into an abandoned building and unrolled his sleeping bag in the ground-floor lounge. The next day he had woken to find a large section of the wall fallen into a new cavity, a ragged moat containing him. He had been so exhausted, its collapse had not roused him. Beyond the hole stood three nervous police officers who had kept him at gunpoint until the colonel's team arrived.

'I started noticing a few inches here and there when I got back from Europe, you know,' he said. 'Birgit and Lai said there were things happening.'

Anna had been volunteering in Madison, patrolling the remains, feeding and interviewing the moated, taxonomising them according to the latest schema. She had felt calm even in that catastrophe, that lowering landscape of rubble and trench rings, some containing bodies, some empty.

From there she had gone to London, where the edges of the infected zone had been sealed off with barricades and gun towers, to keep the infected back, as if anyone was sure of how it spread or how contagious the condition was. In those boroughs the trenched kept walking.

Helicopters flew over Tooting and Thannet, where houses and churches and community halls collapsed into the gouged chasms where people had stood too long. The streets looked ploughed.

It was a melancholy kind of martial law. News crews in protective overalls made forays into the infected zones where the Londoners left behind kept trudging, even driving, if their moats manifested beyond their cars' edges, watching the camera crews sourly.

There was a vogue in surrender. At first it was sleep that trapped the affected. Awake, they tended to move. But a change came: more and more women and men were just standing still to let the moats come.

Newscasters interviewed them across the dugouts that had dug out to contain them. One channel won a BAFTA for three interviews conducted in a single shot on Albemarle Street where a man and two women stood swaying on their nuclei in the remains of the pavement.

'Why are you here?' shouted the journalist.

'Fuck off,' one woman said.

The man said nothing.

'You could keep going,' the journalist said. 'There's food, you could find a big space—'

'Oh, excuse the fuck me,' the second woman interrupted coldly. 'Am I doing this wrong?'

Anna studied the earth from the junctions where moats intersected. She saw couples, even groups of three or four, standing or lying in each other's arms, packed together beyond their combined trenches. It surprised her how few people she saw camping like this. These combined moats were no wider than the singletons', but they were deeper. There must be a maximum, an optimum number. Try to fit too many, and the overlapping symptoms would eat into the keep, diminishing it, ultimately to nothing.

'One of them ain't even infected,' said a young soldier to her when they passed two sleeping men cuddled together behind their trench. 'One of them blokes is immune, but he just loves his boyf, and he'd rather stick with him. If they're close enough you can't tell if it's one moat or two. You hear people say that,' he said. 'It's a new kind of love story.'

Later, Anna would sit across from Nick beyond his moat and

listen without speaking, her hands clasped, as he wept at the memory of the ostentatious and charismatic young Swedish woman full of what sounded, to Anna, like mannered flimflam about secrets of the earth that had transported him. He blurted out stories from the crooked pilgrimage on which he'd joined her, when she let him, to pat the sides of old monuments and stroke castles' flanks as if they were sleeping beasts; to find ways to fill his travelling days when she would not.

'She wouldn't let me stay with her in the end,' he said.

Poor snivelling boy, Anna thought, equal parts contempt and compassion.

Once as Anna took a sample from an abandoned trench overlooking the Thames, she felt the ground quiver and turned to see the skyline on the south side abruptly break as a tower collapsed with an appalling noise and a billow of glass and brick. That same week the BT Tower snapped at its base and came down into the quarantine zone. Some of the affected had started to gather together and take last stands or sits or sleeps spaced out around some edifice, overlapping their trenches to open the earth and bring down the city on themselves.

'Got reports of a deader in Maida Vale. Suicide by second floor.' A ruined woman in a crater of bricks. She had stood to let the floor dissolve around her, until she had plummeted like a victim in an old cartoon on an untethered raft of wood. Anna and the corpse were watched by a stander in a pocket park surrounded by a circle of fallen trees, his trench deep enough to contain inches of water.

Anna listened at countless trenches, trying to hear noises.

The colonel told her she could not live in the town any more.

'We barely know what's going on,' he said.

Her room in the barracks was small and plain and overlooked an enclosed yard where two huge tyres leaned against a wall. There was a landline which connected only to the rest of the base.

Sporadically, the television in the officers' lounge would not come on. 'What's going on?' she said to Gomez. 'I haven't seen the news for two days.'

She stopped at the sight of him. He looked at her with something so like agony that she closed the door and went to him and stood close enough that if he moved at all, if he looked at her with any glimpse of invitation or acceptance, she could hold him up.

He stood. He nodded thanks but carefully he stepped back from her.

'There are people,' he said slowly, 'out there, in that fucking chaos. I can't talk to them any more. It didn't need to be like this. Did it? It didn't. I don't care that you can't cure it but if you can't, then show us how to live with it.'

He did something and that night the TV worked again.

Emergency broadcasts. Perry put his head around the door to be lit by aerial footage of fires in Chile, the ruins of Antwerp and Edinburgh.

'Colonel,' Perry said, 'I'm doing another late session tonight, ok?'

'Did you see that Australian guy?' Gomez said to Anna.

Perry left, and Gomez eyed the closing door. 'He thinks he's found something,' he said. 'Online.'

'How?' Anna said. There was no internet any more, only an unstable Sargasso of abandoned sites adrift in static, drifts and clumps of wrecked data, blogs, social media, the digital debris of industries and agencies.

Gomez shrugged. 'Supergeek.'

Anna watched footage of the tops of a forest, warplanes howling above it. The canopy was broken by overlapping circles of
treelessness, the stigmata of new humans. In Dubai, people lay
down in the basement of the Burj Khalifa, but they were discovered by armed police before the tower came down.

'You might raise kids,' Gomez said. 'Let them sleep next to
you.'

'You'd be sleeping behind theirs,' Anna said. 'Children's
trenches are smaller. It would be a squeeze.'

The colonel looked at her mournfully. She remembered he
was divorced, that he had a son. That night she looked out into
the yard, at the tyres, dark black against the grey black of the wall,
and started to cry, almost experimentally. Soon she was crying
without performance, because even though it needn't, perhaps,
the world was ending.

Two in the morning, nowhere near sleep, she got out of
bed and descended to the research sub-level. *How is it appropriate to feel?* she thought. Only humans dread. Dread is appropriate
to nothing. It's the surplus of animal fear, it's never indicated, it's
nothing but itself.

A soldier outside Nick's room nodded to her. The lights
were on within. The guard outside the storeroom hesitated – she
was supposed to be accompanied by a senior officer – but these
protocols were breaking down. 'I get my best ideas at night,' she
said, and he looked at her with a hope that oppressed her.

She passed her own samples. She searched the shelves for
equipment that might be Perry's. She called up footage of experimental animals. Dogs howled at the bottom of trenches. She
examined the waveform of the audio, flattened out those distress
calls, but she could not find any whisper.

Anna started to head back to her room then turned in the

light from Nick's chamber and told the soldier to let her into the observation annex. He did not hesitate for long.

Perry was scrolling through images on a pull-down screen, while Nick sat on his bed and watched. Perry wore his hazmat suit, but had taken the helmet off. Nick's eyes were teary.

She recognised the faces on the screen.

'Lai,' Nick said. 'Birgit. Terrell. Where did you get these? These aren't my pictures.'

'I told you. I found your friend's account.'

'They already looked . . .'

'Then they're not as good at it as me. You know what I noticed in your file? We didn't have any feeds from Birgit. She was using a secure anonymous account and she was better at online security than we thought.'

'She knows things,' said Nick.

'A lot of it's gone now. But I want to show you something.'

'This is her private stuff—'

'I want you to tell me what we're looking at.'

Images of Nick and his friends in bars, climbing mountains, making faces at animals in zoos.

'This is Scotland,' Nick said. 'That's where I met her.'

A damp and fogged-over valley. Pictures of stone, sand in the crabgrass. A self-portrait of Birgit under a cliff in a furious storm.

'What's this?'

'I don't know. She went off into the country. I told you, man, she was full of all these mad stories. She was always wanting to see stone circles and stuff. She said she knew secrets. She went off on her own for like a week. We met her again in Edinburgh after.'

Grey rock studded with gorse. Birgit's face looking down a steep slope of flint. What Anna thought for a moment was a lake with an island in its centre but was, she saw, a wide moat surrounding an edifice in stone. Another image of the same broken castle. Another. Birgit had circled the ruins.

Anna called Colonel Gomez. He did not sound as if he'd been sleeping.

'I'll come to your office,' he said.

When he arrived he looked out of her window in his fatigues for a long time. 'I had to get rid of Collier today,' he said.

'I'm sorry,' she said. 'I don't know who that is.'

'You knew him,' he said without judgement. 'He knew you. You met him on the gates a lot. He woke up this morning and there was a moat around his bunk.'

'Jesus. Why didn't you tell me? I can take specimens—'

'Will it help?' He met her eyes. 'You have a lot of specimens, and we don't get any closer to fixing things.' He looked away. 'They came and took him. We still have enough of an infrastructure that I could get word to them. They came. And I just don't even know if it was necessary. At all. I don't know how much longer they think that'll work. There'll come a point . . .' he said, and held up his hands.

'In books about war,' Anna said, 'they always tell you that people were made to *dig their own graves* like that's especially bad. Like it's worse.'

'Yes,' said Gomez. 'It's worse.'

She told him what she'd seen, what Perry was saying to Nick, what Nick was telling him. She held up her phone, which was no longer a phone but was still a camera.

'I took it through the glass,' she said. 'Look, I know we've gone over everywhere he went. But look, do you see where she is?'

'Is that a castle?'

'He's not Subject Zero, *she* is. If we can examine the actual *source*, maybe we can learn things. Maybe we can find a cure. Perry's going to want to go there, you know. He has his job to do, but I want to do mine. Can you get me to Scotland? What do you see, Colonel?'

'I see a castle. I see a moat.'

'You know about bird flu,' she said. 'Diseases have jumped species barriers before.' She flicked through the images of the old building behind its water. 'You see a keep. What do you *not* see?

'There's not supposed to be any way across. You don't see a drawbridge.'

'Don't go anywhere,' the colonel said. 'I'm going to talk to him.' Anna waited and worked the whole of the next day until he knocked on her door again and beckoned her to where a vehicle waited, with Perry in the back seat.

They walked the main street of the town like sightseers. The cars that fronted the low old buildings were scoured with the desert dust. They saw no trenches. They saw no one. Anna believed there must be some few staying out of view, who had chosen this as their last place.

'There's a geotag on the pictures,' Gomez said. 'We have a pretty good sense where it is. We might even be able to get there.'

'Colonel,' Perry said uneasily. 'Dr Samson doesn't have clearance—'

'Are you fucking serious?' she said.

'Alright,' Gomez said. 'We're in the dreg days here, you understand that?'

'I want to see the source,' she said. 'I want to see where it started.'

'To do what?' Gomez spoke gently. 'What are you actually working on? You making much headway on a cure, doc?'

After a moment, Anna said, 'You can't cure something you don't understand.'

'Sure you can,' Gomez said. 'I mean, I know you want to understand it. I know that. But sure you can cure.'

'This is *my* job, Colonel,' Perry said. 'You're right though, things are urgent.'

'You think the earth is sick?' Gomez said to Anna.

'I think it's something.'

They broke into the diner and drank warm soda from the broken fridge.

'There's no orders to follow any more,' Anna said. 'Don't you want to see the end of this?'

'I'm not discussing this with you,' Perry said. 'Why are we talking about this with her?'

'What do we know about the place in the pictures?' she said.

'Nothing,' Gomez said. 'It's not listed on any map we have.'

'Colonel, please—' Perry said.

'What do the Brits say?' she said.

'There are no Brits any more,' Gomez said. 'There's no England, and Scotland we can't get through to. Or *I* can't. You got some direct line, Perry?'

'I am not discussing this in front of her,' Perry said. 'What exactly are we even debating?'

'Who said this was a debate? Nick told Perry Birgit had plans—'

'Colonel! You and I need to talk about this,' Perry said. He stood. 'And we need to talk about it with my bosses.' He went to piss and Gomez breathed out heavily and looked at Anna and hesitated and gave her the car keys. She looked at them stupidly.

'Go,' he said. She looked at him.

'What?' she said.

'He's right. We need to talk about this. Him and me.'

'Colonel, I have the right . . .'

'Jesus, will you *go*? He's probably making his report right now. I agree with you, don't you get it?'

She went quickly into the street where the last light was waning and no lamps were coming on. The town was quiet and she listened hard as she ran but heard only her own footsteps on the way back to the car. She drove, thinking about the grey Scottish hills and the unmarked castle, the secret, tucked behind its moat.

The sentries panicked to see that she was not with the colonel, held her at gunpoint against a wall as they failed to get through to him, until, after two, three hours, the shafts of headlights swayed into view and Gomez parked the grey Lexus he had hot-wired in front of the guard post, and stepped out of the unlikely vehicle, big and stiff in his uniform, and alone.

'What happened?' she said. 'Where is he?' He glanced at her and she hated herself for asking.

'There are some trenches in that town, still,' he said.

'What about his bosses?' she said at last. 'Are they going to come? Do they know?'

'They might,' Gomez said. 'Which is why we're moving.' He was. Moving fast, and speaking with energy. 'I'm talking to some of the guys here directly. I'm pulling in some old favours. Chain of command is kind of negotiable right now.'

'What are we going to do?'

He gave her a dossier and a laptop. 'Perry's. You're a researcher. So research. You have a starring role in there, doc. Maybe it *is* you who can stop this.'

'What?' she said as panic rose in her. 'I don't know what you mean . . .'

He slumped and even smiled. 'Jesus,' he said. 'It doesn't matter. You know that, right, doc? We're just keeping each other company now. I'd rather have your company than his.'

Oh come on, she thought. *You've still got a bit of hope in you*, she thought. She was certain that was true, but she did not know, she realised, what it was he was hoping for.

Nick was reading on his bed when the colonel and Anna came in. Was the trench wider? Anna thought it was wider.

'Have you eaten?' Gomez said. Nick shook his head. 'Eat. Get a lot of calories in you. You're coming with us. We're going to give something one try. And I'm not going to lie to you: it's going to be hard.'

Anna looked through Perry's notes, his research, his scribbled ideas and hypotheses. Much she did not understand, of course, but she was astounded at how often, as Gomez had said, she featured in his work.

She sorted through information about her blood type, her history, his opinions of her motivations and her research. He made notes of every time he saw when she was lax with her hazmat suit in Nick's proximity.

To weaponise something he needed to understand what stopped it.

'I don't know what to do with this,' she said to Gomez.

'Whatever you want,' he said.

I know you think it's in me, she said. *That I'm the answer.* She hated it.

Rumours must have spread in the base but the colonel moved with enough command and speed that there was confusion but no dissent. That, Anna thought, would come later, when they were gone, as contradictory orders stutteringly reached them from Washington, or wherever was the seat of government now.

At the airfield, a modified army Gulfstream met Gomez, Anna, Nick and the colonel's volunteers, one, Adams, waving to them from the cockpit. They had seen that Anna did not wear her suit, how she made no effort to avoid Nick. It had been a cue: Burrows and Castillo had shrugged their hazmat gear on, but they were the only ones, and even they let it sit loosely, had not done it up.

Nick kept saying, 'Yes!' He was more buoyed up than Anna had ever known him to be. He kept forgetting to hate his captors. They asked him what he thought when they discussed plans.

When they flew, she looked down through blackness at only a few dustings of tiny lights, new centres of habitation. Some alone, surrounded by deep wide trenches of dark.

'We're pushing the edge of our fuel range,' the colonel said. 'You know what the stakes are. Keep him going.'

'He knows what the stakes are too,' she said.

The soldiers sat strapped into seats on either side of the big dimly lit cargo hold festooned in cords, steel clips and tethers. They stared all wide-eyed into the space between them, where Nick stood, his own eyes gaping.

'Yes,' Gomez said. 'He does. Does he care, though?'

'He does,' Anna said. 'Look at him. He does now.'

Nick paced up and back and up and back the length of the cargo hold. He started with an enthusiasm she had never seen in him before. He strode like an energetic man. 'It's because of whose footsteps we're following,' she said.

Eight hours while the sun tracked shafts into the suspended chamber and the aeroplane shook across the world. He faded. *Young love*, Anna thought with cool humour. 'Come on, Nick,' she said. She fed him chocolate and coffee and drugs to keep him awake and cajoled and begged and barked at him to keep moving on his atrophied muscles. They let him use the bathroom but they wouldn't let him lock it.

He tried again and faded again. 'Jesus!' he shouted. He panicked. Sometimes he jogged around the Land Rover RSOV and she shouted at him not to be an asshole, not to tire himself. The soldiers watched. He walked, he crawled. Into the fifth hour he started to cry with exhaustion, but he did not stop his motion, did not rest in case cracks appeared around him, in case the metal honeycombed with matterlessness and a moat came down around him in the plane itself.

At the seventh hour he sank to his knees and fell forward with his arms out, insisting he would not move ever again. Anna shouted. Eventually Hancox, one of the soldiers, pointed his pistol at Nick.

'Keep walking, fucker,' he said. He went to him and kneeled and put his gun to the very top of Nick's head, pointing it straight down through his neck and body. 'You can be your own bullet-stop,' he said.

Nick crawled on.

When they landed at the disused airfield they had chosen from the charts, they carried Nick across a weed-flecked runway in fading Scottish light and into a disused office building, where he slept for eleven hours, dreaming while his moat sank into existence, faster than before, as if eager after his hours of motion.

They were woken by the scream of distant warplanes and far-off explosions. They had no communication with any authorities.

'Even if we could, you don't know where anyone stands any more,' the colonel said.

They checked maps and planned with the hesitant new inchoate democracy of collapse. Nick too. He jumped across his trench and sat as close to the dead centre of the RSOV as they could place him.

'It might just be ok,' Anna said. 'The radius of the moat is just about half the vehicle's length. And it's just about as long, if we make sure he stays in the exact middle. Stop regularly. We might lose the headlights and the back bumper . . .'

'Shit,' Gomez said. 'Let's risk it.'

A soldier called Sheen drove, fast, weaving the big vehicle through miles of empty road punctuated with abandoned cars and tractors. They shot through a zigzag barricade in a tiny village, where frightened men and women fired shotguns at them.

They stopped every half-hour for Nick to walk or sit where his trench could begin in the ground, for Sheen to investigate the RSOV. It seemed quite solid but, in the afternoon as rain came down, there was an abrupt sound of straining metal, and it folded sickeningly as the floor at its rear sheared through and the vehicle tipped, then skidded and slammed sideways across the road.

They crawled from the wreck. Nick was screaming. His arm was broken. Burrows had been cut badly by glass. Adams was dead, hit in the head by a spinning axle.

'What the fucking fuck?' screamed Sheen. He raged at Nick as if the young man had chosen for his trench to close in. But when they sat under damp trees to tend themselves Anna saw that the mud around Sheen was sinking into a channel.

'Oh, man,' he said with a bad wonder. 'I've got it.' It was Sheen, in the front seat, whose new moat had cut through the vehicle.

'I'm in a hole, sir,' he said, and laughed. Even when the

colonel aimed his pistol at him, Sheen would not move. They had to leave him, sitting in his trench.

The last six trudged on for hours under their equipment and a semi-rigid dinghy as deflated as it would go. They left the road and made camp, and in the morning walked for hours towards the coast on ground more and more studded with stones.

'I smell burn,' Hancox said.

They ascended a long rise. Beyond the slope the ground tipped again at an increasing angle, to flat ground broken by spurs of flint.

Anna looked into the moat of the keep without a bridge.

'What did they fucking do?' she said.

On the blocky mound of earth and rock that rose from the water, where Birgit's picture had shown the visible remains of a castle, a tower fallen to age, there was now rubble.

A pile of big blocks from destroyed walls, the pulverised mess of demolition.

'Someone bombed it,' Gomez said.

The sky was full of low dark cloud. Anna thought of bombs, missiles roaring down from some hazy plane or gunship in her mind, to take apart this doorless castle.

Gomez set Castillo and Burrows and Hancox on guard and, their new structures notwithstanding, they took the order. He and Anna rowed into the yards of water. Nick cradled his arm.

In the middle of the moat Nick said, 'You hear something?' He leaned toward the water. 'Did you hear that?'

Anna put her ear to the base of the boat. She listened to the slap and wet rustle of the water. Her boat might be nudged from below, investigated with a curious motion by something born of trench.

'Have you seen what happens when you put someone infected in a boat?' Gomez said. The colonel dragged the boat on the stones. 'If it's small enough that the whole thing's inside infection perimeter? Nothing. You don't get a trench in the water.'

'Yes you do,' Anna said. 'The water goes, right down to the usual depth of the trench, just like earth does. It's just that more water fills it in all the time, so you never see it.'

Where the stone had been, they climbed into a rough rubble landscape where weeds were already feeling the scorched ground.

'There's nothing,' Nick said. 'Nothing.'

Where the building had been razed the ground was slumped into a basin like that of a cold volcano. Anna could discern the ghosts of walls, the outlines of architecture, and the entrances to caves, overgrown and full of medieval debris and the smell of explosion.

'Birgit wouldn't have come this far and not crossed the water,' Nick said. To touch the stone and receive something. To break that moat quarantine and contract it.

Anna scooped up earth. She made measurements. She powered up her laptop and fed in numbers. The colonel sat, his back to a snarl of roots, and watched. She felt her heart speeding as she went through these motions, not expecting to understand more but desperate to do so, here in what she could feel through her skin was a locus. She was an antigen here, perhaps. She was something.

Nick sat on a spur of stone. The earth around him evanesced over hours, faster than usual in this, the corpse of the source, the sick castle. 'It's not sick,' he said as if he heard what went through Anna's head. 'It's a contagious adaptation.'

There was the sharp crack of shots and a shriek. Anna flattened against the slope. Nick ducked. The colonel crawled and took out his weapon and peered across the moat.

'Where are they?' someone shouted.

Anna looked across the water and saw the three soldiers behind a rock on an incline in the grassland. Burrows fired from behind the stone. Hancox struggled to reload. Castillo lay unmoving.

Facing them was a group of clumsily running and firing and hiding men and women. Some were in khaki, some in dark civilian clothes. They ducked behind trees and shot with their various weapons.

People rose from hides in the earth, ran forward and disappeared again.

'They're coming out of the ground,' the colonel said.

Anna said, 'They're coming out of each other's moats.'

The attackers were hauling into position some big geared thing like a horizontal crane. They were bracing it behind a rise in the earth.

Men in ragged uniforms jogged toward Burrows and Hancox, bouncing a woman on a stretcher between them. They deposited her directly opposite the soldiers on the other side of the stone that shielded them. She lay quite still. Burrows fumbled with his weapon.

There was some flickering, quick motion, and Anna blinked, because around the woman on the stretcher and the stone by which she lay was now a wide trench, an almost perfect circle, full of black water.

Hancox was staggering back from it, dropping his rifle. It passed exactly where Burrows had been, and he was gone. Anna blinked. The surface of the moat-water churned. She could not tell if it was wind and disturbed sticks she glimpsed in it or a drowning man pulled under by something, waving his rifle.

'Jesus Christ,' she heard Gomez say.

Hancox had his hands up, people were coming at him with weapons raised.

Nick was shouting, 'Birgit! Birgit!' Anna looked at him with a sort of bewildered wonder.

'She didn't get on that plane,' she said.

'Birgit!' he shouted. His face was astounded and urgent with delight.

Anna heard a whispering, at last, from the air, not the water. A great chunk of stone arced elegantly from the ground. The engine was a trebuchet and it had fired. The missile slammed down on the castle foundations, smashing in all directions.

The shrapnel of the earth battered her. Gomez screamed.

'Birgit!' Nick was standing frantically waving his uninjured arm. Another chunk of rock rushed for them, plunged straight down, dislodging remains into a cavern that had been below the keep.

Gomez moaned. His head was bloody. The attackers loaded a wooden barrel onto their siege engine and lit it. It poured off black smoke.

'Birgit, for Christ's sake!' Nick shouted. He jumped and cried out with the pain from his bone. 'It's me! It's me!'

The trebuchet creaked. The soldiers knelt by the woman in white and conferred and pointed at Nick, waving.

The attackers tied Hancox's hands and held him on the shore. They rolled the barrel into the moat where it hissed and burped a last roll of cloud and went under.

Birgit's people brought a wooden rowing boat to the edge of

the shore and her guards placed her gently within, between them, and started to row. Anna tended to Gomez. He was half-awake but bleeding heavily and murmuring, making little sense.

There were about a hundred people on the shore, standing silently watching. Some stood in a big mass on the chopped-up ground: some apart, alone or in couples or trios, with moats around them. The moated and the moatless.

Birgit lay in the boat with her eyes closed. She did not move.

One man jumped out to haul the boat onto the beach while the other kept Anna and Nick covered with his rifle, though they were unarmed and all had their hands up. Gomez bled in a little pool.

'Oh, Jesus, Birgit,' Nick said. 'Oh no.'

She was still as wax.

The men carried Birgit's corpse to the rubble of the castle. Nick was crying softly at her.

'We wanted to let her rest,' said one of her bearers. He did not have a Scottish accent. 'We were doing alright. We weren't bothering no one. Were we? Why'd you fuckers have to do this.'

'This?' Nick shouted. 'You mean blow this place up? Jesus, this wasn't us.'

'It's true,' Anna said. 'We're here to try to figure things out.'

'Who was it then? The bombers? She was here yesterday when they came. She was here a lot. She came here to commune.'

Anna did not ask *With what?*

'She made it back over. She wanted to tell us what to do, how to carry on. Get word down under if we could. She knew she didn't—' He broke off.

'Didn't have long,' his comrade said. 'She was injured bad. We brought her back here to rest.'

The sun was going down when they laid Birgit down on the highest point of the rubble. Nick sat whispering to her dead body and the soldiers let him.

'Who the fuck does he think he is to her?' one of them whispered.

'Her boyfriend,' Anna said. 'Ish.'

'Oh and he thinks he's hurting worse than us?'

'I don't think he's thinking about it,' she said. 'What are you going to do with us?' She laid her hand on Gomez's face. He twitched.

They didn't know.

'We'll figure it out,' one said. Their shadows stretched as if desperate to cross the water.

As the last light went down, Nick walked away from Birgit's body to a jut of foundation. He looked at where lights were appearing among her followers for this quiet funeral.

A trench appeared around her corpse in an instant. Anna watched earth fall away into a steep-sided wide circle. It was full of black water again. Anna frowned: they were far above the water level.

She could hear Gomez breathing but he was not talking any more. Anna walked towards Birgit's moat.

Anna started to run. She ran past one man who looked up in surprise, and she sped up, and when she reached the edge of Birgit's trench with a surge of strength she jumped and made it across and fell stumbling onto the rocks, toward the body.

'Get the fuck away from her!' The men levelled their rifles.

'No,' Anna shouted. 'I'm not going to do anything.' She stood in long silence by Birgit in her white dress, on the makeshift stone catafalque, seeming to shine in the wet black of her moat.

The light ebbed and she knelt and put her ear close to the water of Birgit's trench, from the inside. As she felt the earth shift under her knees. Between Anna and Birgit's body she saw puffs of dust and stirrings of uneasy earth as clay sank. A line scored in nothing on uneven grey light.

Nick looked away from her into the darkness.

'Hey,' Anna said.

She was watching the slow self-creation of another moat, faster than usual, though not at the speed of Birgit's impossibly quick posthumous moat. The earth and rock and the roots of plants were going.

It was Nick's. He was still and motionless and his trench was beginning, cutting across Birgit's. Where they met, the water of Birgit's started to spill into Nick's rut.

Anna knew she was immune. She worked with the infected and had never had her own keep, until now. This little nub of moat-bordered land was not a true keep, you might say, but then you might say it was two, she thought, where two keeps met.

She sat cross-legged between the trenches. *It isn't mine*, she thought.

But something began to rise in her, so she breathed deeper, felt her heart speed up. *Then whose is it?* she thought.

Nick was alive and looking into the dark, and Birgit was dead and in new shade, and the moats of Subject Zero and Subject One overlapped like sets, like a Venn diagram, drawn in hole and water. There sat Anna, in the eye-shaped intersection.

Without a moon and with only the faintest light from stars, she could not see anything more than the dimmest shapes. It rained, and she sat as if between links of a chain, an infinity, its components pressed and overlapping, its lines water.

She waited, immune and surrounded, in the overlap.

A Second Slice Manifesto

Les Parapluies, the first work of our movement, is a work in oil on canvas of a little over a metre in width and seventeen metres in height. Paintless but for its primer across large sections, at certain levels it comprises layers of abstract shapes in various colours. A few centimetres-wide circuits of thin wavy black lines, within some of which are blobs of pale pinkish dun outlined in various colours, themselves containing textured red and centres of greyish creamy white. These shapes are interspersed with lines and jags and precise, opaque vectors.

Between two and three metres from the piece's base is a cluster of considerably larger black- or brown-edged map-like marks, amoeba-like shapes in red. Around a metre above this second stratum, these shapes begin to shrink again.

For many metres above that, the image is almost clear, the primed space interrupted by only a few occasional sweeping ribbon-thin black lines, silver points and slivers. Until at the painting's uppermost left corner, we see a dense collection of interwoven green strokes – short and thin – and then thicker lines in brown.

Pick a work on which to base your own. This original you will henceforth know as the *cadaver*.

As we enter the second phase of our movement, breakaway

grouplets now derive their cutworks on non-representational originals by, for example, Riley, Matta, Gechtoff. We abjure such faux-radical deviations. Our art is *rigorously* representational or it is nothing.

Of course we by no means insist on derivation from photo-realist work. We do, however, demand that you pick for your provocation a painting in which representation outweighs abstraction.

Stand before your cadaver. Tap your temnic intuition.

Les Parapluies is an image of pedestrians in a rainy Paris street.

It is a refraction of Renoir's 1881–6 picture of the same name, a section cut backwards through that work.

The flat edge of the slice starts a few centimetres above, and perfectly parallel to, the base of the original, and goes back into the picture. The lines, the cell-like shapes are the faces of per-fectly split clothes, umbrellas, hands and bodies.

The image from the plane extends upwards away from the viewer, through dresses, trousers, bones, the wooden hoop of a child, the heads of the crowd, up to where the jauntiest umbrellas are held. At its far edge, it juts into the leaves of a tree.

Temno: To slice.

Extend a conceptual slice through your chosen scene. It may continue into the picture at any angle on any axis, so long as it intersects both the left and right vertical edges of the hanged cadaver. It is traditional to use the past tense 'hanged', rather than 'hung', for works of art considered in this context.

Your task is to depict a cross-section of your cadaver.

*

Behind the front few subjects of Renoir's picture, shapes in the slicework imply new information. They hint at secrets. A tiny daub of free-floating dark brown is a button flying from a straining raincoat. This pale hair-thin line pressed against a red shape like a giant cell? A man carries a letter not in a pocket but beneath his shirt, next to his skin.

This is representation of the most revelatory kind. This is a radical aesthetic democracy. Our works equalise all matter within the cadaver's field.

And they disclose agents present *but previously hidden*. Those behind other things, invisible in the originary work, we section with cool ruthlessness. To lay their innards, their substance, bare.

So long as there is even the smallest deviation from planar sections previously depicted, there is no dishonour in basing a cut on an image already vivisected. It has been such repetition that has vindicated our work as remote viewing.

Because all such revisiting works, including those painted of the same cadaver but in ignorance of each other, agree on *all* elements of a scene. It was when the third slicework depicted a tiny black organic intricacy behind the rearmost wooden leg, in a place previously invisible in the cadaver, that observers agreed that there had been a beetle on the kitchen floor, when Van Gogh painted *Van Gogh's Chair* in 1889.

In slice-paintings of Victorian still lifes we see the blood-flesh-and-bone circles of children crouching behind doors. With the thin silver lines of cross-sectioned steel hiding in the dark of wood, what have for decades looked like canes are revealed as sword-sticks. Thefts have been revealed – the bright colours of gems in briefcases. The grey-bound blood of great fish below boats.

But beyond this, what lies behind the transformation of temnic to temnomantic art are those few figures revealed in slice-images that are the shapes of flesh, integuments of meat on struts of bone, and yet of such shapes and tones, in such positions, that they should not exist. Hovering below the clouds in renditions of John Atkinson Grimshaw's nightscapes, what are these glowing membranes and human-like slices of rib? What are these big blood-and-feather blotches to the meat's sides?

These things move through our images. Only we can investigate what it is with which we share our galleries, and our world.

Amid the greens and browns at the top of *Les Parapluies*, a clot of colours evades decoding. There is something with veins and muscles in a wash of twisted hues.

There is something living but not animal, something watching us from the tree.

Covehithe

There were a few nights in Dunwich, where the owner of the
B&B kept telling her guests they were lucky to have found a
room. Walking Dunwich beach, showing his daughter wintering
geese through binoculars so heavy they made her laugh, the man
was glad they were not in Southwold or Walberswick. They were
not so hemmed in by visitors. Each evening they had fish and
chips or pub grub. Each night after she had gone to bed he
hacked into next door's wi-fi to check his messages and monitor
the forums.

On Thursday night he woke her. It was not long after midnight.

'Come on, lovey,' he said. 'Keep it down. Let's not get anyone
else up.'

'I hate you,' she said into her pillow.

'I know,' he said. 'Come on. Don't bring your phone.'

There was not much on the roads. Still, Dughan took them
roundabout ways, through Blythborough, on the A145 towards
Uggeshall, past stationary diggers where roads were being widened.

'Where are we going?' the girl asked, only once. She hunkered; she wouldn't ask him to turn up the heating.

Wrentham was on the western rim of the security zone. It
went north along the A12, south on the B1127 to Southwold.
Within it, in daylight, fields were still worked, for animal feed,

and the roads were mostly open, but those were, legally, indulgences not rights; the area was, in the absence of an official escort, no-go after dark. Exceptional laws applied in that little triangle, the coast a six-mile hypotenuse, its midpoint Covehithe.

Dughan stopped by a pub garden south of Wrentham. He opened the door for his daughter with his finger to his lips.

'Dad,' she said.

'Hush,' he said.

It was overcast and windy, shadows taking them and releasing them as Dughan found a way through undergrowth to the boundary ditch. They were both quiet as they crossed it. Holding their breath. Beyond, they walked eastward on the edges of the fields.

'Dad, seriously, you're crazy.' He had a torch but did not turn it on. When the moon came out enough he stopped and took bearings.

'They've got guns,' she said.

'That's why shhh.'

'What'll they do if they catch us?'

'Feed us to wolves.'

'Har har.'

They went still at the sound of a helicopter. The beam passed by half a field ahead, so bright it looked solid.

The air smelt. They could hear echoes. Dughan avoided the hamlet where until recently locals had lived, which had been requisitioned, with only minor scandal. They could see lit windows. They came instead at Covehithe from the north.

He stopped her by the roofless ruin of the church, pointed, heard her gasp. She stared while moonlight got past the clouds to the holed and broken walls, onto a low newer church inside the nave of the old. He smiled. When eventually she was done looking they continued through the graveyard. There was nothing at all frightening about the graves.

This close to the waves the land felt, as the girl said, misbehavicious. A good word to make her feel better. In the leafless trees of this region were cold, random and silent flares of light. Touch the soil, as Dughan did, and as his daughter did too at the sight of him, and it felt greasy, heavy, as if someone had poured cream onto loam.

'Which way are we going?'

'Careful, lovey,' he said. 'The ground here . . .'

'How do you know it's tonight?'

For a while he didn't answer. 'Oh,' he said. 'Bits and pieces.' He looked over his shoulder the way they had come. 'Ways and means.'

'What if they find out?' She pointed at the cottages. She rolled her eyes when he said nothing.

They continued on the road past a sign forbidding exactly this last short walk, on tarmac so old it was becoming landscape. Perspective was peculiar. The smell should have been sappy and muddy and of the sea.

'Look!' His daughter gasped. The road stopped abruptly, ragedged, fell into nothing. He watched her inch forward. 'It goes right off the cliff!'

'The sea's taking it all back,' he said. 'There used to be a lot more coast here. Careful.' But she had lain responsibly on her stomach at a certain proximity and put only her fingertips and eyes over the tarmac rim to look down its sheer crumble at the beach.

'Is it still going?' she said. Her voice was faint, she was dipping her mouth below road-level. 'Being eaten?' Dughan shrugged. Waited till she scootched back and turned to him, shrugged again.

He told her they would know within two or three hours if anything was going to happen. He did not say it was only hints and whispers he had to go on, trawlings from bulletin boards. Two names he knew, erstwhile colleagues, both announcing they'd be near Ipswich next week and did any of the old crew want a drink? The latest codes were beyond him, but that query and the night's sudden burst of encrypted chatter had been reasons enough to move.

He checked his watch and sat with her at the decomposing road-end. He was cross-legged, she with her chin on her knees, hugging them. She kept looking into the sea. The noise of it lulled them as if it were designed to. There was no light but the moon and those occasional sourceless mineral glows. Somewhere some insane bird, not a nightingale, was singing.

All their layers could not keep them warm. They were shaking hard when, after less than an hour, Dughan saw movement on the beach. He motioned for his daughter to stay still and looked through his binoculars at lights jouncing on the shingle. Three sets of headlamps stopped, overlaying each other, illuminating the sea and a strip of the shore.

'It's them,' he said. 'They're setting up. They must've . . .' The girl could tell his excitement was not wholly enthusiasm. 'They've . . . we're on.'

He could make out nothing beyond the headlight gaze, and hear nothing but waves. He recced once more but they were not observed. This cliff-top was out of bounds and they, intruders, were alone. His daughter kept watching the water. Dughan wondered if she would complain or ask how long or anything, but she did not. Twenty minutes later, it was she who pointed, who first saw something in the sea.

There were no helicopters now. Nothing so noisy. No downcast beams to light up what was coming, breaking water, way off the coast. It was only moonlit. A tower. A steeple of girders. Streaming, and rising.

The girl stood. The metal was twisted. Off-true and angular like a skew-whiff crane, resisting collapse. It did not come steadily but lurched, hauling up and landward in huge jerks. After each a swaying hesitation; then another move higher, and closer.

The lights on the beach went out. Flame ignited at the tower's tip. Sooty sepia guttering lit the shaft. The sea at its base spread flat and fell away from suddenly rising intricate blockness, black, angled and extrusioned. As if a quarried wedge of the seabed itself had come up to look.

The towerwork was on a platform. In the glow of the thing's own flame they saw edificial flanks, the concrete and rust of them, the iron of the pylon barnacled, shaggy with benthic growth now lank gelatinous bunting.

It was coming at the Covehithe cliff. Under its stains and excrescences were more regular markings, stencilled warnings. Paint remnants: an encircled H.

Another step – because these were clumsy steps with which it came – and all the main mass was out of the water and raining brine. It waded. Each concrete cylinder leg a building or a smokestack wide. The two on one side came forward together, then those on the other. Pipes dangled from its roof-high under-side, clots of it fell back into the sea. It wore steel containers, ruins of housing like a bad neighbourhood, old hoists, lift-shafts emptying of black water.

A few waves-width from the beach, it hesitated. It licked the air with a house-sized flame.

'P-36,' Dughan said. 'Petrobras.'

One of the cars below turned its headlamps back on. The rig shied. Dughan hissed. But the lights quickly dipped and after a moment he said, 'It's probably ok now.'

The platform was at the level of their cliff-top. Now the girl understood its strange ungainliness. On each side, its supports merged at their base, into two horizontal struts, so it moved like a quadruped skiing. What must have been ten feet of water lapped at the struts like a puddle at a child's shoes. The rig facelessly faced north and slide-stamped along the shoreline.

'Quick,' the man said. They took the cliff-edge path, a hedge to their right, the oil platform's tower lurching beside them above its leaves.

'Went down 2001,' Dughan said. 'Roncador field.'

'How many people died?'

'When it sank? No one.'

'Have you . . . is this the first . . . ?'

He took a moment to stop, to turn and meet her eye. They could hear the flame bursts now. Its straining metal. 'I've never seen it before, lovey,' he said.

The path descended.

She had been too small when her father left to imagine stories of his exploits, to be proud or afraid. All she remembered were his returnings, an exhausted, careful man who lifted her onto his lap and kissed her with wary love, brought her toys and foreign sweets. When later she had asked him what he had done on those trips, his answers were so vague guilt had hushed her. She did not ask about his injuries.

The rig was slowing. The smell was stronger and the ground, the air juddered, not only in time to its huge steps. Dughan stopped at the last path-end trees. He and his daughter hugged the trunks and watched the oil rig sway in their direction. He held her hand. The girl watched him, too, but he showed no signs of angst, no flashback, no fear.

*

On an autumn evening in the earlyish years of the twenty-first century, a fishing boat south-east of Halifax radioed an SOS, under attack – the transmission was unclear. Rescuers found two traumatised survivors in a wash of scattered debris. As they did, the cause of the catastrophe reached the coast. Authorities could not suppress civilian footage of what had come back.

It was the Rowan Gorilla I. That was the first. No Piper Alpha, no Deepwater Horizon; an undistinguished disaster. A tripod jack-up rig lost to storms and hull-fracture in 1988, on its way to the North Sea. Scattered surely by its capsizing and by thirty years below but there, back. Cramped-looking for all its enormity, latticed legs braced halfway through its platform, jutting above it and below into the sea. In the videos the three skyward leg-halves switch and lean creaking towards each other, sway away again like cranes triple-knitting, as it walks the muck on spudcan feet. It staggered like a crippled Martian out of the water and onto Canada.

It shook the coast with its steps. It walked through buildings, swatted trucks then tanks out of its way with ripped cables and pipes that flailed in inefficient deadly motion, like ill-trained snakes, like too-heavy feeding tentacles. It reached with corroded chains, wrenched obstacles from the earth. It dripped seawater, chemicals of industrial ruin and long-hoarded oil.

Ten miles inland, a line of artillery blew the thing apart. Later they made that area a memorial park. Sections of the rig's deck they left unsalvaged, preserved amid flowerbeds.

By panics and fuckups, Dughan's unit had been trapped on the far side of the wounded platform, between the Rowan Gorilla I, they later realised, and the sea. A third of his comrades had been killed. Crushed, torn by wires, caught in its final explosion, bequeathing him years of dreams and memories of trodden men.

The world was still reeling, investigation barely begun, when the Ocean Express, capsized in 1976 with thirteen dead, which must have been quietly recomposing itself at the bottom of the Gulf of Mexico, stood upright in relatively shallow water and strode landward.

Fighter jets scrambled from Eglin inflicted severe damage, slowed it, and the USS *Carney* torpedoed one of its supports. The rig buckled, tilted and seemed to wait, kneeling like a bettered knight. The *Carney* had shelled it apart.

Dughan saw this from the *Carney*'s deck. He and several comrades had been flown in as advisors to the US Navy. He was combatant himself again soon enough, at the return of the Key Biscayne off Australia, and the fire-mottled Sea Quest's attempt to walk into Nigeria.

National governments subcontracted strategy to the UN Platform Event Repulsion Unit: scientists, engineers, theologians and exorcists, soldiers, veterans like Dughan of those first encounters. He learnt the new motions, the vastly swaying skittishness and violence of the revenant rigs. His UNPERU colleagues strove to decode this hydrocarbon Ragnarok. Twice, Dughan even boarded pitching, stinking decks to transmit to them close-up footage, from which they learnt nothing. They tried to figure out what economies of sacrifice were being invoked, for what this was punishment. Ruined, lost, burnt, scuttled rigs were healing on the ocean floor and coming back. Platform, jack-up, semi-submersible: all the lost.

After the semi-sub Sea Quest retreated under heavy attack, descending back into the Gulf of Guinea, UNPERU turned its attention and resources to the Ocean Ranger, stalking the Atlantic seabed. So when, shortly after its brief first appearance, the Sea Quest re-emerged, and continued its interrupted journey into the oil-fouled delta, they were not there to intercept. Word reached Dughan and his crew en route to Canada. They came back fast, turning their plane in mid-air.

They were escorted inland by ex-MEND guerrillas with peerless local savvy, hastily pardoned by the Nigerian government. They followed the oil rig's mashed-up trail, the rainbow-filmed liquid spoor, the tripod crater prints. In retrospect, certain qualities of the disturbed interior foreshadowed more dramatic instabilities that later petrospectral presences would bring.

Bursts from the derrick known to have been destroyed in the rig's last moments, now heat-twisted but regrown, flared above the forest. The soldiers reached the edge of the clearing the Sea Quest had stamped. They held fire and watched.

Bracing on struts still thick with coraline outgrowths, the Sea Quest settled into the mud. It started its drill. Pushed it into the ground and down.

For a long time it was still but for an occasional swaying tremble of some stuff low-hanging from it. Should we attack? officers kept asking. Dughan shook his head. He checked Unit Beta's images, the Ocean Ranger off the Labrador coast, the tip of its tower a dorsal fin. The stomach-dropping video was proof for which no one had known they were waiting: that below the waves the rigs also walked.

High overhead the Sea Quest's flame was all but out: a dirty smoke plume took its place as cockscomb. 'It's drinking,' one of the soldiers had said to the shake of its pumps. After four hours Dughan sent out a team, joined them when the rig did not respond. Another four and they went closer still. Eleven hours after the drilling had started, the tower breathed fire again and shook and abruptly pulled its drill from the mud.

The birds that had settled to peck at its deepwater carrion were gone in one cloud. The soldiers made it back to the treeline.

The Sea Quest rose on shaft-legs like some impossible dreaming pachyderm. It retraced its stamping passage, trees in its shadow.

The UNPERU team followed. They tried to keep locals away. They were the oil rig's escorts, back to the sea. The platform walked slowly into the water, paused a while in the chop, descended.

A clutch of dead trees jutted from the scrub like bleached markers of where Covehithe ended. A ribbon of crabgrass separated the sea and shore from Benacre Broad. A cold marsh, a roosting place for birds. The Petrobras approached.

Dughan hesitated and his daughter saw him do so. He wanted to go closer, but there was not enough cover.

The rig. It closed on her and she stopped breathing. It came near enough that she felt the envelope of cold air it brought, smelt abyssal rot and chemical cracking. Spray hit her. The weary factory's spray. It giant-walked by her hiding place sending all those Suffolk birds away, hauled into the fens to squat like a monument that had always been there.

It braced. A percussion of chains, the crack of old shells, and its drill descended.

The first platforms had returned close to where they went down. But then Interocean II had emerged not in the North Sea but in the harbour of a hastily evacuated Oporto, stepped daintily over the seawall like someone crossing a stile. Sedco 135F rose in the Galapagos, far from the Bay of Campeche. The many-legged barge Ocean Prince came up not in Dogger Bank but Sardinia. Revisitors might come, drill, go back to the water, even come up again, anywhere.

Dughan's daughter had got away from him, got closer to the visitor. Had he not noticed her go? Before he knew it, he might have said, she was gone. It might be true. She was pressed against one of the dead trees. Beyond her was Petrobras, like a failed city block. Dughan whispered her name. She watched the dead and come-back rig boring.

He went to her, of course. Exhilarating to exit the cover. He was quickly there, looking with her through barkless branches.

The platform was calm, its fire low. It shivered, only, tinily, all its thousands of tons. Ripples passed over the wetland, not outward but in, circles decreasing, shrinking to that point where the shaft entered the ground.

They watched. After many seconds, Dughan felt something pressed to his back. He had long enough before anyone spoke to be surprised that whoever this was had got so close without him hearing. He blamed the reek and weird industry he was watching.

A voice said: 'You move and I'll fucking kill you.'

When the lost rigs of the world came back, old hands claimed they had seen in the motion of the drills something reversed. Dughan doubted it: shuddering was shuddering. But most of the places where the rigs went there were no oil fields. It might have been that they were sniffing other things than oil to sustain them, but that was not so.

'Turn around,' the voice said. The uniformed man who faced them was young and afraid. With a weapon pointed at him, old techniques, muscle memory came back and twitched Dughan's fingers, but he stayed still.

The man scanned them. No RPGs, no mortars, not even smaller arms. They were not oleophobe fanatics here to attack the Petrobras, nor Oil Firsters, here to kill him, his colleagues and all those who came to investigate or exploit, in their parlance, the visitations.

'Who the fuck are you?' The guard glanced over their heads

at the shuffling rig. He was whispering, though Dughan knew it would make little difference now.

'We're just here to watch,' the girl said gently. She was taking care of him. 'My dad brought me here to watch is all. Just to see it.'

The guard searched them, cack-handedly. Dughan silently counted the times he could have disarmed him. The man found only binoculars, torch and cameras. He frowned at their pictures of Suffolk, of Punch-and-Judy shows, of roadside oddities. No contraband sights. 'Jesus!' he said. 'Move, then.'

Behind them the rig shifted and he cringed at the great squelch. 'What are you even doing?' he said when they had retreated to the living trees. 'Do you have any idea how dangerous this is?'

'I'm sorry, it was me,' she said. 'I just really wanted to see it up close and I begged him. I'm really sorry.'

The man wiped his forehead. 'Let me tell you something,' he said. 'Last time there was one of them here, down by Camber Sands?' The Adriatic IV. Dughan didn't say it. 'There was a couple of young lads got in. Got past us. I shouldn't tell you. They were larking about. Taking pictures and that. Anyway, you know what happened? They had a dog with them and it got too close, and it spooked the rig and it moved. Midway through.' He waved through the copse. 'It trod on the dog.'

Dughan looked back up at the Petrobras's subdued high burning.

'Now come on.' The guard beckoned. 'Let's get back.'

When their feet hit the beach sand, the girl said to him, 'How long'll it be?' Just close enough to the inlet and troughs gouged by the rig's passing to afford a sightline into the broads, headlights flashed. The jeeps were visible a moment, and people.

'It'll be there half a day at least,' the man said. 'And it's a few months later it'll all kick off.' He even smiled.

'You know,' he said, 'I don't know, you might probably be a bit old for it but there's like a kids' club they have here. They have activities and that.'

'You saw some once, didn't you, Dad?' Dughan was not angry when she said that. He marvelled, really, at her.

All its research notwithstanding, UNPERU expressed as much shock as the rest of the world when, over a year after the Ocean Ranger's visit, up from the still-recovering Newfoundland ground into which it had pushed its drill, the first clutch of newly-hatched oil rigs had unburied themselves.

They had emerged into the night, shaking off earth. Stood quivering on stiffening metal or cement legs. Tilted tiny heli-pads. Tottered finally for the sea.

'How big are they, Dad?' she said.

'You've seen films,' he said. 'As big as me.'

Dughan had gone back to Nigeria. He had waited for months, on the vagaries of gestation. At last the monitors in the delta picked up evidence of subterranean shifts. Over many hours, long before dawn, he had watched unsteady six-foot riglets burrow up out of the forest dirt. Seven of them, of all different designs: buildings, supports, struts, derricks. They waited, sway-ing like new calves, still wet from their tarry sacs, swinging umbrella-sized cranes.

He helped to capture two, and to usher the rest safely to the water, where the baby rigs had been tagged and released to scuttle below the waves, escorted by divers as far down as the divers could go. The two captives were taken to hangars where great tanks of brine waited. But they sickened within days and died, and fell apart into scrap and rubble.

The Oporto authorities pumped poisons into the university grounds where the Interocean II had drilled and left the earth slick and soupy. Whether that was what kept its brood from being born was never clear: those eggs were not recovered. In other coastal cities, neonate oil platforms did emerge, to gallop hectic and nervy through the streets, spreading panic.

Only the most violent post-return decommissioning could stop all this, only second deaths, from which the rigs did not come back again, kept them from where they wished to go, to drill. Once chosen, a place might be visited by any one of the wild rigs that walked out of the abyss. As if such locations had been decided collectively. UNPERU observed the nesting sites, more all the time, and kept track of the rigs themselves as best they could, of their behemoth grazing or wandering at the bottom of the world.

'What activities do they do in this club?' the girl said.

'Oh.' The guard shrugged. 'Stuff like, you can see the eggs on a live feed. They'll be digging down to them and they'll put cameras and thermometers and whatever. Sometimes you can even see movement through the shells. And there's colouring books and games and that.' He smiled again. 'Like I say, it's too young for you.'

They laid eggs, so, many people said, they must have sex. There was no logic there. They were oil rigs. Dughan thought the belief exoneration of the strange prurience that endlessly turned on monoliths rutting miles down. An inhuman pornography of great slams and grinding, horrified whales veering from where one rig mounted another, warmed by hydrothermal vents.

'And no one knows what happens to the young, do they, Dad?'

Other guards came to meet them. Half-welcoming, half-peremptory. Dughan recognised none. Behind the security were the few tourists lucky to have been nearby, at accredited hotels, when Petrobras's heavy steps had registered on the scanners.

'No one knows yet,' Dughan said to his daughter. 'They're still very young. They're little and the sea's very big. They've got a lot of growing to do.'

A guide was in the middle of a spiel. 'We'll come back in the morning, when it's finished laying,' she said. 'You can bring your cameras then – no danger then if you forgot to turn your flash off.' People laughed.

'What's wrong?' Dughan whispered.

'Do you think it's true what he said?' the girl whispered. 'About the dog? That's horrible.' She made a face. He stared not at the twitching Petrobras P-36 with its concrete in the mere, not at its drill ovipositor injecting slippy black rig eggs into England, but at the sea. 'Maybe he was lying to scare us,' the girl said.

Dughan turned and took in the length of Covehithe beach. They were out of sight, but he looked in the direction of the graveyard, and of St Andrew's stubby hall where services continued within the medieval carapace, remains of a grander church fallen apart to time and the civil war and to economics, fallen ultimately with permission.

The Junket

Daniel Cane left his gym at 2.45pm on a Thursday in early August. He stopped at a grocery store on Avalon Street, near the turnoff to Preston Avenue. The clerk remembers him picking up some juice and peanut butter. He left at 2.57pm and started in the direction of the apartment he'd lived in for the past seven months.

It was a twenty-minute walk. He'd done it many times. But Daniel Cane, hippest, most controversial screenwriter on the West Coast, never made it home.

You know all this. You know every detail of Cane's disappearance by now. Who doesn't? And you know what comes next, too. That's why you're reading this, right? To get to that stuff?

It's coming.

She's one of the five most-photographed women in the world this year, but when she appears, it still takes a few seconds to realise that we're looking at Abi Hempel.

It's only been a few weeks since the release of the film that hurled her onto the A-list. In that time, no matter what she's rocking – Alexander Wang, Rodarte, Westwood or vintage – she's rarely been seen without her dark brown hair styled in the look *Vogue* called 'demure-fierce'. Almost frumpy, but really not. Parted on the left, shoulder-length. A shout-out to the character who's made her so very famous and whom, despite the nearly ten years she has on her, with her large, deep-set eyes, unruly brows, pale skin and crooked smile, Hempel bears an astounding resemblance.

But the young woman who mounts the stage is barely recognisable. Our expectant hush becomes astonishment. What's this dark grey pantsuit? Is that a tan? What's with the *bob*?

Maybe somebody's tired of the sell.

Abi peers at us through severe glasses. She's studying philosophy at the Sorbonne, and she looks the part, even if she doesn't sound it.

'When I read the script I thought, "Wow",' she says. We scribble as if this kind of horseshit is epiphany. 'It was really smart, really funny and kind of dark. And respectful.'

There it is. Me and a few buddies – stand down, guys, I'm not going to name names – glance at each other and put little marks on our checklists. $20 ante each. We're playing bingo.

Did she do her own stunts? She flexes a bicep so we all laugh.

'God no,' she says. 'John wanted to be really sparing with CGI. Like, the scene where my character jumps from the roof of the museum? That's a brilliant stuntwoman called Gabrielle Bing, and she's really doing that. I saw her training and I was like, "Uh, no."

'I did what I could. I have a gymnastics background, and we had an awesome Krav Maga instructor. I wanted to do as much of the fight scenes as I could. I did get to punch Tommy in the face.' We all laugh again, dutifully.

Did she consider how controversial the subject matter might be?

'Honestly, no. We were surprised. I totally respect anyone who doesn't like what we've done, but you know, it was never our intention to offend anybody.' Buzzzz: there's another one. 'For us this was really an *homage*.'

Can I get double-points for that? She's polite and sincere-sounding and it's almost plausible.

How was it working with Daniel Cane?

We all knew that was coming. She moves in her seat.

'I didn't work closely with him,' she says. 'He was on-set, he did a few rewrites. We had dinner a couple of times. He was a sweet guy. What happened was an absolute tragedy and all my sympathies are with his family.'

What would you say to the protestors?

'I'd say, Don't come see the movie.'

At this point I'm going to risk your wrath and my job by telling you that your ever-loving correspondent was one of the lucky few scheduled for a brief one-to-one with Hempel. And that I didn't take it. Gave the slot to someone else. (You're welcome, *Schlockwaves* readers!)

Stay with me. I had work to do, calls to make. Authorities to badger, people on the phone to charm. I'd got to the 'Officially there's nothing I can do, but let me speak to someone and call you back' stage.

Daniel's friends raised the alarm after he failed to turn up to two meetings in two days. The cops weren't particularly concerned. Young rich dude goes AWOL in a party town? The choppers stayed grounded.

Three days after that an anonymous and untraceable call was made to Nikki Finke. The woman said she was speaking 'for Daniel Cane's victims', that 'his crimes would not be forgotten', that 'justice had been done'.

The cops looked harder after that.

*

We're driven across town. Johnny D is giving his interviews in a different hotel. There are rumours of 'creative differences'.

'Come on,' says Johnny. 'Abi's great. You've seen it, right? You saw what a great job she did.' He looks like a man who wants a cigarette. 'Look, on a project like this, sure there are going to be arguments, but—'

Can he comment on the claims about the canal scene?

'Oh right, I've heard this one. I forced her to stay in the water the whole night while we did a hundred takes and she got pneumonia, right? I'm not going to dignify that with a response.'

We've been briefed. Daniel Cane is off-limits.

What's the collective noun for journalists at a publicity event? A schmooze? A mouthpiece? A funnel?

But even the most compliant crowd has a certain collective cunning. You could almost believe we'd cooked this up between us, we divvy it up so well. First a few softballs – influences, best moments, funny stories, blah blah. Then come questions about the protestors. The woman from *Cinéma* asks about the statement Yad Vashem put out.

Johnny knows how to bad-boy swagger without saying anything overtly offensive. Not that 'offensive' is something he's always anxious to avoid: hey, this is the man who cut his teeth at the notorious NoLuck Studio; whose first film, *Rob my Grave*, was denounced in the British Parliament. This is the brain behind *Stereotype Man and Dumb Broad*.

Right now, though, he's cautious. It's all 'great deal of respect for the sensitivities involved' this – we must've gotten drunker or bolder because that merits a few laughs – 'careful to consider the ramifications' that, and 'sacred texts' the other.

Boom. Several of us checked our phones at that point: a group text. One word: 'BINGO!'

I won't tell you who won. It wasn't me.

Eventually someone asks. It was inevitable, off-limits or not. And this wasn't me, either, but it would've been if no one else had stepped up.

What about Daniel Cane?

Johnny waves away the PR guy who's mounting the stage.

'Daniel was my brother,' Johnny says. There'll be some good pictures of this moment: he seems genuinely furious.

'He was like my brother. He came to me with this idea almost eight years ago and I told him if you ever do this with anyone else, I will never forgive you. So tell me, friend, what's your question? Are you asking me whether I regret doing this movie? Fuck no. This is Daniel's movie. Would Daniel regret doing it? Fuck no. Do I regret that he died? Fuck yes. Did he ask for it? Is that what you're saying, my friend? Because fuck you. You got that? You need me to spell it? No he did not.

'Who do you represent, man? *I-net*? Ok, out of Tel Aviv, right? Well, let me tell you this: Daniel was a proud Jew. He wrote this out of *love*. He wrote this out of passion, and sincerity, and no sick crazy bastard can take away from that one bit.'

The way he says it, you could almost forget that he's selling an action flick. You could be forgiven for forgetting the merchandise, action figures, video game.

The journalist mutters something.

'Excuse me?' Johnny shouts.

'Half,' the guy says.

The fight that follows looks pretty real to most of us.

I don't know who pulled in what favour but the cops who turn up go away again. This little *contretemps* has screwed the schedule, which, see above, is no skin off my shin: I spend the afternoon watching Cane-iana on YouTube. The *FangQuarterly* interview where he moons the photographer; the time he threw a slushie at a pap on a bike (the guy wasn't there for him – Cane had been out with the winner of *All-Real American Starlet*); the interview with the Goth kid in the graveyard.

'It used to be just us, man,' the white-faced boy says, looking down. 'Now every asshole wants a piece of him. Assholes coming here at like midnight so no one can see and taking everything and shit. They shouldn't do that. Now they got like drones and cameras and shit watching us.'

The *I-net* guy's a douche. It's Daniel Cane's mom who's Jewish, so he's Jewish too. This unedifying ping-pong was already in play when he was killed. His family were totally secular vs he was bar-mitzvahed. He had no interest in Judaica vs he used Yiddish all the time. His mom's Jewish vs only his mom's Jewish. Stay classy, haters.

There's viral video of a drunk playful Daniel denouncing his younger brother Jacob in a colourful stream, a few years back: 'You're a fucking *tshonde*, bro,' he shouts, as waiters try to calm him and his brother folds over in laughter. 'I'm, I'm *plotzing* here. You're *meshuggeneh!*'

Almost as well known is the op-ed response in the *New York Opinion*, published a week before Cane's death. Its title: 'The Smirking Gun'.

'Will you look at this guy?' it reads. 'Sure he knows the words. But watch and listen. See how he wracks his brain to think of more. He's not using this out of *yiddishkeit* (ask your Bubba). You know who else loves rolling these words round their mouths? Mocking? Sneering?

'Bigots. That's who. Homeboy's an anti-Semite. Whatever his ma says.'

A junket is a machine. Distributor ships in hungry journos. We get put up schmancy (ooh!); we get victuals way out of our usual range (aah!); we get to touch stardust (eeh!). The better to make us grateful. We're supposed to shake hands, press record, get the quotes, dutifully receive a nugget of bullshit 'inside' information or two, repeat the odd, thoroughly vetted 'secret' rumour.

Hey, it's not dignified, but it's not arms trading. And as a guy who normally kicks off the day with bad coffee and Pop-Tarts, I'm grateful for the buffet and mimosas. Really. Please don't rip me out of the Rolodexes just because I went a little rogue.

But if the choice was between grooming my Deep Throat in municipal works (bear with me) or hearing another hot young thing tell us how supercool it was to work with blah and blah, it was an easy call.

Although to be honest I'd started hitting walls. Maybe I should have gone to the cocktail party.

Two thirds of the way through the movie there's a scene in which gunmen are closing in while Sam Denham's character, the scholar Mr Henk, denounces his assistant. 'You're a *tshonde*,' he says. 'You're *meshuggeneh*.'

'You see how long Daniel had been working on this?' says Carl Boyer. 'The film wasn't even close to being greenlit when that video of him and his brother was recorded, but he'd obviously written it already. He was trying to remember his own lines. He was quoting his own script. He was inhabiting the narrative tradition. With total respect for the words and the story. Anyone who uses that as evidence that Cane was "self-hating" is a fucking tool. That's a technical term.' He raises an eyebrow.

Boyer teaches cultural anthropology at UC Santa Cruz. He's the author of *Reading Signs in your Timeline* and *Whoops! Subversion*. The walls of his office are festooned with movie posters. *Casablanca*; *Last House on the Left*; what I think is a Nigerian remake of *Blood Beach*.

Boyer leans across his desk and taps the recorder.

'Now look at what that speech ushers in,' he says. 'What Jewishness invokes.

'It's a masterpiece of the violent sublime.' I feel like I'm in a lecture hall. 'It ranks with the *Matrix* vestibule scene, the hospital sequence in *Hard Boiled*, *Crouching Tiger*'s restaurant. Fuck it, it surpasses them. Even if the rest of the film sucked – which it does not – it would still be a classic just for these few seconds.'

He presses play on his laptop and we watch.

Mr Henk finishes shouting. And when he has spoken, as the armed men come closer, silence stretches for a long time. It's easily long enough for the audience to get uncomfortable. 'A strange scoop of Tarkovski in the popcorn,' *Empire*'s review said.

The window above Henk's head explodes in very slow motion, still without the slightest noise. A figure encased completely in fire, burning in agony, somersaults into the ruins of the warehouse, lands in front of the two old men, and in the last few seconds of his life, dispatches five heavily armed grey-clad enemies in an exquisite balletic fight scene.

You don't have to be an aficionado of the cinematic brutal to see Boyer's point. Even the film's many critics acknowledge this.

'Check it out,' Boyer says. 'He's using the very flames that are killing him to kill his enemies, and to ignite the fuse to the explosives. To save the day. If that doesn't strike you as an incredibly

poignant comment, an incredibly *humane* comment, then I've
got nothing.'

Is he serious? With that poker face, it's impossible to tell.

A weird thing happens.

I'm still drawing a total blank at City Hall. My trail's dried
up.

Maybe my name's on a yellow stickie on the side of every
monitor, with a big red X next to it.

But just as I'm thinking maybe I have to rethink my mystery-
solving plans, I get a call, number blocked.

'I heard you been asking about stuff,' the voice says. 'I work
at Beit Olam. I can tell you some things.'

And I'm scribbling as frantically as if I'm Bernstein and
Woodward combined, agreeing, absolutely, no names, certainly
I understand my contact's position, no, I don't know it but yes, I
can find that bar.

'We started hearing rumours about this movie a couple of years
ago.' Robert Foxer, head of the Anti-Defamation League's LA
office, sits back in his chair and folds his hands. 'I have to tell
you, when we got word, I thought there had to be some mistake.
I could not believe what I was hearing. This is a joke, I thought.
I checked to see if it was April Fool's Day.'

He shakes his head. 'This movie,' he says slowly, 'is nothing
but a collection of the oldest, hate-filled stereotypes. It's something that would have made Streicher proud. It's the most
shocking, disgusting, the most anti-Semitic movie I've had to deal
with in twelve years in this role. That this should be an *American*
movie, made with American money . . . I have no words.'

What about all those Jewish kids for whom this has become a touchstone text? Surely he's aware of organisations like Jew-das and Heebie-Jeebies and the like organising raucous midnight screenings. What about the themed costume parties?

'They're wrong.' He shrugs. 'They think I'm old-fashioned? Is being against racism and hatred old-fashioned? Ok, I'm old-fashioned.'

What about the arguments for free speech?

'Hate speech isn't protected. This is hate speech. And I can tell you without any embarrassment or hesitation that we intend to shut it down. By any means necessary.'

Any?

Foxer sighs and looks at his ceiling.

This year there was a campaign of what the organisers called 'punk seders'. You know who they said the empty chair was for?

'Daniel Cane,' Foxer says heavily, 'was no Elijah. Look, what do you want me to say? Do I support what happened to Daniel Cane? Absolutely not. Do I want the people who did it brought to justice? Absolutely I do. Let me be completely unequivocal about that. Am I *surprised* that someone did this? No.' He shakes his head sadly. 'I'm not surprised at all.'

Some of the other hacks ask me why I'm ducking out on a meet-and-greet with Tommy Durois. They're looking suspicious.

'I'm doing a sidebar about the campaign,' I say. 'I have to go check out all the old posters.'

It isn't even untrue. It's just that before I do that, I make a list of questions for the dude – or dudess, I can neither confirm nor deny the gender of my source – who called me. Mostly they boil down to one query: where's the stuff from the grave?

I drive by the offices of BB and Bones. They're surprisingly low key. If you're an industry insider, you know about this advertising firm, about the viral videos that are repeatedly, ostentatiously disavowed by the companies to whose products they attract such attention.

Legal insists that I put this carefully: those illicit ads are unauthorised, works in progress inadvertently released, or similar. Whatever. Still, the torture ad for the Kia, the Courvoisier dead horse, Reebok's pornathlon, these are the fodder for hundreds of thousands of tumblrs and retweets.

As regards the work they did on this movie, BB & B's line is simple and familiar. It was never their intention to offend: the images were intended to *subvert* racist ideas.

'They don't subvert a thing,' is Foxer's judgement. 'They don't even try.'

It was the teaser posters which first, quite understandably, caused such a storm of disbelief. They showed no title, just a faint outline of a shadowy face, dark eyes, a dark door. One of various taglines in white script.

'I hunger for my pound of flesh.'

'Wandering and eternal.'

'We are the international conspiracy.'

Most provocatively of all, and the cause of a litigation campaign in the UK, Canada and the US: 'Blood. No Libel.'

The outrage, unsurprisingly, ramped up to an extraordinary pitch when the title and details of the movie were finally released. But simultaneously, this provoked the first wave of countercultural backlash.

The hipster website J-Cool published an article describing the film as 'the ultimate revenge fantasy', pointing out that the writer, director, lead actors, and everyone closely associated with the movie were Jewish. When the official t-shirts went on sale, the Brooklyn-based magazine *Is it Good For?* (which later wrote up the movie in ecstatic terms) ran a photo shoot of its staff modelling them, alongside a now-famous essay entitled 'Can the Goyim Wear the Shirts?', which consisted of the single word 'No'.

'There is something here,' Abi's voice says. 'There is something in the attic with us. Something that keeps us safe. That visits me at night.'

Outside the cinemas, rival demonstrations turned into fights, and you never knew who was going to be fighting whom, who would take which side. Whether the antifascists or the taqwacores, the Palestine Solidarity activists, Hillel, the Likudniks, Jews Against Zionism, even the various motley fascists, would be demanding that the film be shown, or that it be not shown.

'About the only good thing,' Foxer allows, grinning, 'is that the anti-Semites were pretty much as confused as everyone else.'

The white supremacist website antizog.org wrote a highly favourable review – a fact jumped on by the film's liberal critics – because the film, it said, did not 'flinch from the truth of the Jew'. However, according to Volksfront.truth.net, 'bloodsuckers or not, the Jews are the good guys here. Make no mistake.'

The death threats started. Some were directed at Johnny D, but most went to Daniel Cane.

'It's true that in the age of Edward Cullen it's ridiculous to say that fangs make a bad guy,' Boyer says. 'See, I think a lot of the attack on this movie is less to do with anti-Semitism or philo-Semitism than it is basic simple cultural snobbery. This is an exploitation film. Sure, you can call it Jewsploitation if you want – everyone else is – and sure there's work and research in there

– there really was a Nazi Operation Werewolf, by the way – but the point is it's trash culture.

'Now you might say – and I *would* say – that in this day and age, when quote trash unquote is doing a better job of picking at bullshit than the goddamn news, that it's kind of absurd we're still having this argument. But hey – here we are.'

Daniel Cane's scripts were fervent, energetic, generic and predictable. If he'd adapted the aftermath of his own murder, his parents would have kept his room untouched. They'd show visitors in, as if to a shrine.

But this is real life and the room's been packed away. His mother has to show me photos instead. 'That was what he loved,' she says. 'It was always the monsters.' She holds up pictures of a sweet-looking, nerdy little boy in front of shelves of D&D *tchotchkes*.

Hallie Cane is a tall woman in her fifties, with greying fair hair in a long braid. She looks very tired. We talk by Skype, me sitting in the LA sunshine, she in the rain, telling me things she's said a thousand times before. She turns her camera to show me the view Daniel would have seen every night. My view sways and pixellates. The tall brick tower of a ridiculous folly in suburban Boston.

It's impossible not to be put in mind of the movie's moonlit tower scene, when the Watcher climbs the Oude Kirk spire, with a motion something between lizard and cat. It's impossible not to imagine the twelve-year-old Daniel picturing such things in the view from his window.

Well, it's impossible for me.

'There's nothing he could have done that would have shown

more love,' Hallie says. 'You watch the film and tell me he doesn't love her.'

I nod and repeat a couple of things Boyer said, about appropriation and subversion and respect. Her response surprises me.

'I never really bought that,' she says. 'To be honest I find that whole "irony" thing very unconvincing.' She smiles at my expression. 'It's like when people say, "That's the whole point", as a defence for telling racist jokes or whatever. Me and Daniel used to argue about this.'

So they disagreed about his script?

'I don't know,' she says. 'He was always persuasive.' She smiles again. 'I don't think *he* thought he was being disrespectful, for sure. He wrote what he did out of love.'

Whether it was an appropriate love, a love that should speak its nerdy, ironic name, is an open question. That it was love is not in doubt.

The SS officers climb the stairs.

'What's that noise?' one says.

There, visible under the slope of the roof, is the wooden attic door. The officers lift their weapons.

'What is that . . .?' whispers the commander. He pushes open the door onto darkness.

'It's snobbery,' Boyer writes to me in an email. 'Look at Auslander – *Hope*'s a provocative book, but no one would say he's disrespectful, and he has her, probably the most famous victim in history, as a cantankerous, stinking old woman. But because he's a "serious writer" – and I'm not hating on Auslander here, it's a great book – that's fine. Whereas here?'

Here.

There is a moment's quiet. A rising growl.

And out of the attic shadows comes a young girl, her hair and dress ragged and gusting in the rush of her motion and a cloud of dust and darkness. Her eyes glow. Her mouth is open wide. Her fangs shine.

Cut to the sight of her hiding mother, her face frozen in horror. The sound of tearing, of men screaming. A bolt of blood.

This juxtaposition, of the schoolgirl's ferocious predatory face and of her aghast, blood-spattered mother's, have become the two most iconic images from *Anne Frank: Vampire*.

Twenty hours after the phone call declaring justice, another person, male this time, called the LAPD and gave an address in Pacoima.

In the basement of the empty house they found the remains of Daniel Cane. A stake was driven through his chest. His head had been cut from his body. His bled-out body was in a bathtub, below a dribbling hose – keeping him under flowing water. He had been repeatedly stabbed, and old kitchen knives made of cheap silver protruded from his wounds. He was scattered with garlic.

Within a week, three groups claimed responsibility for the murder. The first was the White People's Alliance for Survival, whose message started: 'You mock the wolf, bloodsucker Jew? Now you've felt our teeth. Let the war begin.'

The same day a previously unheard-of offshoot of the Kahanist Jewish Defence League, styling themselves the Masada Guards, announced that 'the decadent self-hating traitor who sniggers in the rubble of our people, who spreads Nazi filth and lies, has been dealt with.'

Two days after that, a short video was uploaded by a spokesperson for al-Qaeda in the Belly of the Beast, announcing that Daniel Cane had been punished for his Zionist fantasies.

The web exploded with theories of false-flag operations by the state, of fascist–Islamist collaboration, that the studio itself had had Daniel killed as a publicity ploy. That this was a baroque assisted suicide. The last theory gained currency when a long-ago ex released a letter in which a depressed twenty-two-year-old Daniel discussed the possibility of killing himself.

Johnny D and the studio put up a million-dollar reward for information leading to the arrest of Cane's killers. Despite this, and despite what the LAPD have described as 'an exemplary, wide-ranging, ongoing and totally thorough operation', no one has been arrested for his murder.

Production has started on the sequel. The studio has greenlit the third and fourth movies in the series. Liam Neeson is going to play Baron von Richtofen, and Eva Green Baroness Bathory.

Daniel Cane rests in one of the largest Jewish cemeteries in LA. We're standing, my source and I, looking at his grave.

I'm going to call my companion Digger, though as far as I understand it s/he has always been a deskjockey. At first Digger didn't want to come. We met in a disappointingly unsleazy lounge-bar, and he, or she, started giving me the lowdown on Another Mystery of Daniel Cane.

'You know the grave kept getting defaced?' Digger said. At Daniel Cane's funeral, mourners were jostled by protestors from ultra-right Zionist groups, fascists and antifascists and jihadis and the Westboro Baptist Church ('Vampire Jew Fags', 'God Hates Fangs'), and for the first few weeks, it seemed as though all of them were targeting his grave. 'Well that stopped, and if you think you know why, you're wrong. You don't know why.'

The second time I suggested showing me exactly what this meant, Digger agreed. So here we stand, my source wearing a hat and dark glasses in case any colleagues happen to be here.

We had to wait on the side of the hill for a long time, watching the kids gathered at Cane's plot. They left eventually, and we came closer, and now we are alone.

The studio paid for a security camera to be attached to a nearby tree. I eye it. When it went up, I've been told, the attacks ceased.

Cane's family are indulgent of the more macabre tokens visitors bring. 'Sure I wish they'd leave something else,' his father, Roger, has said, 'but I think it mostly comes from an ok place.'

In the shade of the gravestone are rubber bats and plastic fangs. There are copies of *Dracula* and vials of blood that I hope is stage but suspect is real. Bobble-head bloodsuckers and Children of the Night action figures.

'This is it,' says Digger. 'Every night all this goes. Someone's collecting it.' On my notepad I write down *Who? Where? Why?*

This stuff too? I say, and point.

'No, that all gets left. Eventually one of our guys will clean it. When they're faded. They get replaced, and someone always brings more.'

Digger's talking about the flowers. It's not just vampire tat that sits on Daniel's resting place. There are beautiful flowers. There is a bottle of bourbon and prayer beads, there are copies of the Torah. There are movie scripts. And of course there are stones.

The top of Daniel Cane's tombstone is piled high and neatly with pebbles. There are more than on any other grave I can see, far more.

'Every day.'

Every day unseen mourners place stones on the top of Daniel's stone.

'It's great that the paint and the hammering and all that stopped. But let me tell you, it is not down to the camera. You see that?' Digger points. 'That little light going on and off by the lens? That's for show, man. Guarantee it. That's just an empty box.'

Digger's face tells me we're there. This is the secret, the last mystery of Daniel Cane.

'This grave is protected now, but not by a camera. There's something about this bit of ground,' Digger says. 'It's like a dead zone. You see that movie? That was a good movie. Anyway they've had people come look at it a hundred times, but no one can ever make this camera work.'

So there's no footage?

'Nothing.'

Of attacks, or of the, what, offerings? So who has all the stuff? Who brings it? Who comes and takes it?

'That's what I'm saying.' Digger shrugs. 'They never get any footage of anything. Everyone brings it, everyone. Who takes it? You want to know? What if I told you I have keys? I could maybe lend them to you, and if you wanted to sit over there out of sight and wait to see who comes, tonight, I couldn't stop you? What would you say to that? That would be a story, right?'

It would be a story. Whoever comes and goes to clean up Cane's grave comes and goes unseen.

No one knows why we put pebbles on graves. I look at them all higgledy-piggledy on Daniel's marker.

There's a tradition that says they're there to keep the soul down. Not in a bullying but in a kindly way. Any soul can get restless, can toss and turn, can get up and go wandering, and that's no fun for anyone, including for the sleepwalking dead.

Those piled-up stones are a loving ballast, keeping the soul safe in the *beit olam*, the house of the world.

Yeah, it would be a story, to find out who comes by, takes the crap away, lays more weight gently on Daniel Cane.

Some stories, though, it doesn't help to finish.

We stay there while the sun gets low. I tell Digger to keep the key. Digger's disappointed but I never promised anything.

The camera's a fake. We come and go unseen too. The light is going down over the boulevard. We can hear the traffic.

I've come prepared, with a stone in my pocket. I put it on the grave.

Four Final Orpheuses

1. Orpheus, shambling and drunk on shadows, sees sunlight and emerges into what he thinks is the world; into what, with a blinking look around, he decides with only a shade of uncertainty is not merely a widening in the passage itself, a kind of rough natural vestibule, but must surely count as the actual outside. He starts to turn and honestly he supposes it does occur to him before he's completed the movement that he's still roofed by stone, that the fresh air really starts about three metres on. And still fractions of a second before he's caught Eurydice's eye, still, he would have to admit, in time to stop and walk a few steps on, he decides two things at almost the same instant. The first: *This is ambiguous, neither quite tunnel nor quite outside, and that's not fair.* The second, nervously, half-predicated on the first: *Oh, I'm sure it'll be fine.*

2. Orpheus, at the last, is so afraid of the light that he needs the moral support of a smile to step into it, needs it more than he needs Eurydice back.

3. Orpheus can't remember the injunction. He tells himself he can't, anyway. He tells himself he's turning to ask Eurydice what it was he was or wasn't supposed to do. It's a complicated kind of cowardice with which he looks at her.

4.   Orpheus has never forgiven. Never. He plans all the long way up. He slows as he approaches the threshold, listening to her ghost feet. He stops, still just in shadow. He hisses, spins around, stares in hate and triumph at Eurydice's shocked and receding face.

The Rabbet

Though it was fully spring there had been a light snowfall only two weeks ago. There was a strong smell of cut concrete and you could hear when buses passed at the end of the road. Sim moved into the house as soon as Maggie and Ricardo's previous flatmate moved out. 'Don't come before three,' Maggie said. 'He'll still be here.'

Maggie was tall and very thin. Her entire self looked wind-blown. She designed layouts for a computer magazine. 'I know it's not Notting Hill,' she'd said to Sim about where she lived, 'but it's so quick into town, and anyway we're keeping it real.' She was from south London and made jokes about Neasden being enemy territory.

She greeted Sim on the front step, with Mack on her narrow hip. Mack pointed at a dog nosing at something. 'Look at that,' Maggie said. 'Maybe he's friendly.'

'Hello,' Mack said, his face a blotch of pleasure. 'Hello hello hello.' He said it to the dog and then he said it to Sim.

'They're like sponges,' Maggie said to Sim. She led him upstairs.

'Oh my God,' Sim said. He stood in the centre of the room and turned slowly and took it in. 'Thank you so much, it's fantastic.'

Maggie joined him by the window and shifted Mack to her other side. Three of the room's four walls were painted an inoffensive light blue. The fourth, the window-wall, was papered, a fussy Victorian design of flowers and trees.

'You should have seen the guy who just left,' she said. 'He was like a sulky kid. Had to kick him out. Let that be a lesson to you. I'm ruthless.'

'Oh Lord, don't I know it,' Sim said.

Buddleia sprawled over a mess of garden below. They did not have access to it; it was only for those in the basement flat. Sim held up his hands so his thumbs and index fingers made a rectangle. He looked through it at the view.

'Heart of flint,' Maggie said. 'La Belle Dame sans Merci.' Beyond the garden was a long stretch of other backyards and beyond them a crane moving over a railway siding. Trains emerged from underground.

Sim looked at her through the box of his fingers. 'Oh, he'll be alright, Mags. You did him a favour. Anyway, forget doing him a favour, you're doing *me* a favour, which is way more important.'

Maggie pulled her hair out of Mack's grip, leaving him with a few long red strands to crumple.

'Ow. So, there's an attic,' Maggie said. 'Trapdoor by the bathroom. You can get a few boxes up there. He did.'

'Thank you, thank you.'

Sunlight glinted in the colours of old cars. The crane hauled shredded metal.

Maggie and Ricardo's room was directly below Sim's. When she had been at university with Sim, he'd had a reputation and she listened now, with Ricardo, but they heard nothing. 'If he's smuggling them in he's bloody good at it,' Ricardo said. 'Maybe he's getting his oats elsewhere.'

'So long as Mack doesn't bump into too many *deshabillées* floozies,' Maggie said. 'And so long as I don't have to listen to them at it.'

'We could retaliate in kind, wink wink,' said Ricardo.

Sim had paid three months in advance. It was a friendly arrangement, for as long as he needed it.

For money he did data entry at a polling company, Tuesday through Friday. The other days he did his own work, as yet unpaid, putting together videos and computer animation on an old laptop. He was Simon, Sim for 'sim card', because when his London friends had first met him they had vaguely decided that he was always on his phone. He was the same age as Maggie but people always thought he was younger than her and than all their peers. He was slight and pretty, with spiky black hair and blue eyes.

'He was putting stuff in the attic earlier,' Ricardo said.

'Is he up there now?' Maggie said. She cupped her hand to her ear.

'I think so.'

Ricardo made supper.

'Bloody Hell,' Sim said. 'Is there anything you can't do?' After every mouthful he ate, he fed Mack a plastic spoonful. He sniffed the boy's goop.

'Parsnip,' said Maggie.

'Here comes the aeroplane,' said Sim. 'Here comes the UFO. Here comes the submarine. God he looks like you, Ricardo.'

The kitchen was decorated with shiny kitsch, with 1950s advertisements for Coca-Cola and commodities that didn't exist any more.

'Whoa there, slow down,' Maggie said. 'He hasn't learnt to gobble yet.'

'How do you like it round here?' Ricardo said.

'Do you know the Portuguese cafe?' Sim said. 'So good.'

He said he would take them out to supper. He led them a roundabout route, showed them places of which they had not been aware – that cafe, an Afrocentric bookshop, a tiny triangular park by the overland station.

'It's embarrassing,' Ricardo said. 'He's only been here two weeks.'

'Oh, don't,' Maggie said. 'You know what it's like. It's always easier to be an explorer somewhere that isn't where you really live. It's *because* he just moved here.'

'We'd just moved here once. We never found all this stuff. We suck.'

You could watch Sim's animation on his website. Maggie and Ricardo were curious.

'Hmmm,' Ricardo said. 'Bit undergrad.'

A rabbit-like character walked in a brightly coloured forest. From the trees grew presents in Christmas paper, and lightbulbs, and little yapping dogs dangling from their leads.

'Hmmm indeed,' Maggie said. 'It would be a rabbit. Dark Bugs, very Donnie Darko. Jesus, Sim.'

'Rabbet,' said Mack, smacking his lips. 'Rabbet, rabbet.'

'This looks a bit cheap to me,' Ricardo said. The rabbit's ears were like long water-filled balloons. They bounced to a glitchy soundtrack.

'I remember this,' Maggie said. 'He started this one years ago.'

'What's it doing?' Ricardo said.

'Going to Grandma's house, I think?'

They watched. 'How long's he been working on it?' Ricardo said.

'Since a bit after we graduated,' Maggie said. Ricardo looked at her. 'Turn it off,' she said. 'Poor sod.'

'Can I have a housewarming?' Sim said.

'Our house is already warm,' said Maggie.

'Only joint friends,' he said. 'A Sim-warming, then.'

'You and your warming.'

He showed them pictures on his phone. He had taken to breaking into old buildings. He swiped past shots of himself gurning in bars with people they did not know to offices stripped of furniture, empty stairwells in falling-down blocks. In the backgrounds, through windows, it was night. Sometimes he was with other people in those places; mostly he was alone. He showed them images of his delighted face. In one, behind him, a man was removing a fringe of broken glass from a reinforced window. Maggie frowned.

'That's a bloke called Brian,' Sim said. 'Brian fucking Something-or-other. Oh God, sorry!'

Ricardo put his hands over Mack's ears and gave a tight smile.

Sim was out at night more and more often but he did not seem tired. He brought back spoils.

'I don't want this shit in my kitchen,' Maggie said. Musty books, cheap ornaments. Discarded photographs, worthless paintings and engravings.

'This stuff is great.' He held up a greying copy of the *Inferno*. 'I'm going to read this finally.'

'Where'd you get it all?'

'All over.'

Closed libraries. The windowsills of squatterless squats. Offices and, of course, deserted hospitals.

'People just leave stuff, it's amazing,' Sim said. 'When they go.'

Maggie touched the pictures and they felt clammy. Oil portrait sketches, watercolours of country scenes, buckled with damp.

'That was from way out by the suburbs,' Sim said. 'I don't know if it used to be a gallery or a dealer's or what but this place had a whole bunch of art just in stacks. These were the best ones.'

'They're fair old crap, Sim.'

The black-framed engraving was a full-face view of a Victorian manor. Sash windows, a parapet, a portico. The house was surrounded by trees, lit up by moonlight. The image was dotted with thunderbugs under its glass.

'It was some big old building,' Sim said. 'Down in south London.' He held the engraving up to the wall, above the kitchen table. 'What do you think? Goes with the yellow?'

'Ugly,' Maggie said.

'Unlike the Coke ads?'

'Ouch,' she said. 'Fair play. There's a hammer under the stairs.'

'It's quite sweet,' she said that night to Ricardo. He was staring at the picture. 'He wants to make a mark on the place.'

'Not that it's his place,' Ricardo said.

'If we had the money,' she said, 'we could live in splendid isolation.'

'Sorry,' Ricardo said. He took the engraving from the wall and turned it over. The frame was plain and black and simple. It looked hand-made, imperfectly. There was nothing on the back but a few stains of age.

Maggie took it from him and hung it back up and looked at the house. I wouldn't want to go in there, she thought. 'Oh,' she said. 'It's not that bad.'

Mack loved Sim. Mack raised his arms and made Sim dance with him in the kitchen. Sim showed him the brighter parts of his video, and Mack shouted, 'Rabbet!' as the animal jumped and turned. Sim held Mack up in front of the picture he had hung.

He sang to the tune of 'Mack the Knife'. 'Oh the house has, open windows dear. And the moon shines, very bright. Look at the grass, and the trees, dear, what is coming, out of sight?'

Maggie gave him a look.

Mack twisted in Sim's arms and stared at the engraving. 'Down you go, big boy,' Sim said. 'I'm going to do a bit of work.'

'You sure?' said Maggie. 'You seem tired. Night off?'

'No. *Work* work sucks, but this work –' He pointed in the direction of his room. 'I've got to get on.'

Sim had given Maggie the url of the secret feed where he stored reference pictures for his videos and animations, shots of his explorations, demanding that she take a look. Selfies, Sim's face mostly covered, recognisable to her by hair and eyes. Brick, old cement, beams, dusty lining paper and rubbish.

There he was in a triangular space, hunched to fit. Maggie looked carefully at the picture on her phone. She climbed the stairs and checked on Mack as he was sleeping. She heard the tapping of Sim's keyboard from his room. She opened the trap-door to the attic and ascended into a filthy dark space.

It was cramped with boxes. She could see things their previous flatmate had left, a few of her own and Ricardo's bits and pieces. Sim's.

Maggie looked at the picture again. It was this attic. Sim had explored here. She covered her mouth with a shaking hand. Sim counted this a place of spoils.

Sim had his party. The kitchen was full of people, most of whom Maggie knew. A few of those she didn't she thought she recognised from the pictures of Sim's explorations. 'Oy,' she said, and pushed the fridge door closed. She stood in front of the silverware.

'Heirloom, Mags?' someone said, and pointed at the engraving.

'Why couldn't it be one of *my* heirlooms?' said Ricardo.

'You're too common. Mags is a fallen aristo.'

'I wish,' said Maggie.

'Present from Sim,' said Ricardo.

'He got it at a junk shop,' a man called Tom said. He saw Maggie's expression. 'What? He told me he bought it at a junk shop. He said was thinking about drawing something on it. Doing a Chapmans.' He ran his fingers over the frame.

What Sim had sung to Mack was true: one of the windows in the picture was open. The water-spotting in the lower right corner was worse than Maggie remembered.

She took the picture from the wall.

'Nobody's going full Chapman in my kitchen,' she said.

Sim was sitting on the stairs drinking a beer. 'I'm sorry,' Maggie said. 'I've decided I sort of hate this picture. I'm going to put it in your room.'

She recoiled at his expression.

'Give.' He held out his hand.

'It's fine, I'll just . . .'

'Give.' He stood and climbed to his room, the picture in his hand.

Maggie thought, *Fuck you*.

Church bells sounded beyond the tyre emporium. When Maggie woke, Ricardo was already up. Mack was in his high chair. He shook his cup at her.

'He's a grumpy little sod this morning,' Ricardo said. He stroked Mack's head and Mack rocked back and screwed up his face. He stared at the wall and Maggie realised with a feeling as if she had drunk very cold water that he was staring at a black-framed picture, that it was back on the wall.

She stood so quickly that she spilt her coffee. Mack bawled and Ricardo looked at her in alarm.

But the frame did not contain the engraving. In its place was another reproduction of a vintage advertisement, brought from elsewhere in the house. A long-gone toothpaste. Girls sitting in a diner, beaming with shining teeth. Sim had written 'Sorry' on a piece of paper and tucked it into the frame.

'Yeah,' said Ricardo. 'I was going to say. I don't know what that's about.'

'We had an argument,' she said.

She took Sim a coffee. When he didn't answer she opened the door. He was not in the room. The engraving was on his desk. He had started to add to it: a pencil outline of the rabbit figure from his animations stood on the lawn, looking quizzically at the house. Sim had lightly shaded in its body, against the moonlight and the glimmer of the house.

Light slanted in through clouds and washed the image out.

She did not think it was a very good piece of work. The original, or Sim's altered version.

Sim made supper, silently.

'What's up?' Maggie said.

'Shitty day,' he said.

'*Sugary* day, eh?' said Ricardo. He held Mack.

'Oh. Sorry.' He looked at Ricardo with dislike. 'I can't get this stuff I'm working on right.' The fish fell apart on his fork and he tutted and glanced at the new picture. 'I will, though,' Sim said.

'Doubt it,' Ricardo said when Sim had gone. He showed Maggie the animation.

The rabbit had been fiddled with. 'Look,' said Maggie. Sim had scanned in the country house from the engraving, turned it into a fussy digital version. The rabbit crept smoothly across the lawn toward it on all fours, wearing a cross on its back. 'I guess it's supposed to be scary,' she said.

At its edges, where it crossed the original image, the rabbit brought out the darkness beyond it.

Mack began to cry.

'Well it's scaring someone,' Maggie said.

But Mack was not looking at the computer. He was looking at the picture on the wall.

Maggie did too. The green and red of the girls' skirts, the crisp blue of the server's uniform, with its trim. The chocolate. The whites of the girl's teeth.

Mack kept crying. There was water-staining at the bottom right of the picture.

Maggie took it down and removed the ad from the thin plain frame. Its varnish was chipped, showing dark old wood beneath. She could see chisel marks where it had been shaped.

She put it on the top of the stairs. 'Where's the clip-frame?' she said to Ricardo. 'The one this was in before?'

When she followed Ricardo to bed, the frame was gone from the stairs.

There was a week of rain. Sim was out most days. At night Maggie heard him working in his room, long late hours.

She was startled when, one morning, he sought her out.

'I'm sorry I've been a miserable git,' he said. 'I've been fucked with work and just feeling crap, you know? Anyway, sorry.'

'No worries,' she said. 'How's it going?'

'I'm tired. But it's ok, actually.' Sim sounded surprised but sincere. He smiled. 'It's started going well. Really well. I think I've had a bit of a breakthrough. Been nose-to-grindstoning.'

'Good.'

'I've been doing some comics too.'

'Cool, I remember you did that in uni.'

He showed her. To her it looked like lacklustre work, pen-and-ink of his inevitable rabbit figure in various pop-surreal situations.

'Cool,' she said.

'I know it looks a bit flat like this,' he said, 'but when you present it right . . .'

'He seems really excited by it,' she said to Ricardo. 'I don't see it myself, but if it's going to make him easier to be around, I'm all for it.'

'You don't see it? I think he's got a lot better.'

He showed her the website again. The rabbit. The garish landscape. There was the digitised house. The colours, the designs, the storylines, were more or less as they had been, but there was a new confidence. Where before there had been hesitation disguised as hip mannerism, now there was a frightening fluidity. It was easy to see that the objects that inhabited this boisterous landscape had agendas.

'Jesus,' Maggie said.

The rabbit crept across the lawn again. It climbed into a window. It crept out, holding a motionless human child. It stole away.

'See?' said Ricardo. 'Not just better but genuinely scary.'

'Stop,' Maggie said. She put her hands in front of the screen.

Maggie took Mack in her arms. She stood outside Sim's room. She had heard him leave but she waited and listened and when she was certain he was gone she bit her lip and entered.

Sim had propped the frame, its glass removed, on the edge of his desk against the wall.

His laptop was open, its screen dark. There were pictures and pages of writing all over the desk. Images of grotesque adventures, as absurd and sometimes as pathetic as they were horrifying, which she assumed was the intent. Scraps of writing, overworked poems in cramped penmanship. They were pushed by wide margins into the centre of their pieces of paper.

Maggie examined them. Around every one, at the papers' edges, were scratches. Lines where something had been pressed.

The frame was precisely the same dimensions as these marks. Sim had been holding it onto the paper. He had been writing and drawing through it, within it.

Mack fussed. Maggie looked through the frame, at the wallpaper, the four blue trees it contained.

On the wall the blue trees were mid-writhe as if they were

dancing, as if the wind was stroking them. The trees within the frame, identical trees, curled slyly, gathering for something.

She phoned Ricardo. 'Where are you? When are you coming home?'

'What's up?' Ricardo said.

'Can you come home? Just come back, please.'

She saw on her phone that Sim had re-cut his urban videos. A new narrative, a new succession of images. The same characters she had seen many times, cutting across the city in ways that were not allowed. Familiar shots of Sim edited so now he was an operative on some bad mission.

The way it was cut, the explorers glanced, repeatedly, in shot after shot, at the corner of the screen. The lower right. As if at something welling up.

'No,' Maggie said. She turned Mack away from the window. Twilight was starting and the railway tracks were shining.

She touched the trackpad on Sim's laptop. In the light of its screensaver she saw two buds of Blu-Tac on the base of the screen. Something had been pressed into them. She picked up the frame and ran her fingers around its interior, the channel cut just behind a little overhang of the wood, where the art would sit. The frame's corners fit in the marks in the putty. Its dark sides contained the centre of the screen.

Within the frame, the screensaver's shapes involuted in terrible ways, like sea animals bursting. Sim had propped it against his screen and made his new work inside the frame.

Mack began to cry and Maggie rocked him till she could put him to bed. She took the frame downstairs. She held it out as if it was dirty and set it on the nearest shelf. She wiped her hand and called Ricardo again.

'Whoever made this, it's not right. Sim won't even tell us where it's from. It was never the *picture* that was fucked.'

'Ok,' he said. 'Ok, what are you telling me?'

Maggie looked through the empty wood at the books behind it. Framed by it.

Pride and Prejudice, that spite on those slave bones. One of Mack's favourites, *Goodnight Moon*. The universe closing on a sick void.

She took the frame to the kitchen and held it up in front of the toothpaste advertisement again.

Three girls with white teeth. They wanted to do something bad. The one in the middle with gusto and without remorse. The one on the right would hit a woman with a brick. The last, in a bright zigzag jumper, would put spikes in strangers' shoes and fly through the night over her small town with her teeth dripping spit. She would cut down all the trees. The girls would bring the counterman rings from the fingers of those they drowned and he would put poison in the Coca-Cola.

Mack had started crying again. Maggie heard Ricardo's voice. She still held the phone to her ear, she realised, and he had been shouting.

She tried to answer several times. 'You need to come home,' she managed at last to whisper. 'Mack's in his cot and he's waiting for you.'

She broke the connection over Ricardo's shouts and she heard Mack crying but she fled the house. She had to take the frame as far away as she could, to keep her son safe. To keep the girls safe. Maggie ran.

There was still a little light. The canal was a few streets away. She ran past pubs, past drinkers who glanced up and watched her sprint.

When she heard footsteps behind her she was not surprised.

She turned through the yellow lights of off-licences and news-agents. 'You alright, love?' someone shouted. She ran and Sim ran behind her. He would catch her. He knew where she was going. She turned onto a darker, quieter street that rose over a railway tunnel in the lights of residential blocks. He would catch her before she reached the water.

Maggie got to the crest of the hill and could not run any more. She turned and Sim was not running any more either. He was walking towards her, the last of the sunset behind him.

He held up his hands. He looked at her through the rectangle he made with his fingers. He came slowly closer. She watched his face through his hands.

Maggie slammed the frame against the bricks of the bridge. Sim screamed.

She swung it as hard as she could and with a great crack it snapped into two pieces. She pulled them apart and held each in one hand and flailed them again and broke them more, along their imperfectly glued joins.

The frame broke into pieces and Sim howled.

Maggie threw the broken wood over the wall. It scattered onto the tracks a long way below and on slants of trash, to become pieces among many pieces, with the plastic, the detergent bottles, the glass, to be bleached by the sun.

'No no no!' shouted Sim. 'What did you *do*? My *work* . . .' He stared over the edge of the bridge. He looked at her in grief and fury and there was no one there to come between them.

He ran to her and smacked her in the face and she reeled and turned back to face him, holding her cheek.

'You brought that into my house,' she said, and her voice was almost steady. 'I have a *child*.'

'Hey!' someone shouted from an overlooking window. 'I've called the cops, mate!'

'Stay out of my house,' she said. She staggered up to him and spat and said, 'It helped your *work*? You should be on your knees thanking me for saving you from whatever that shit was. Stay the fuck out of my house.'

He stared at her and she thought he would hit her again but for a long time he didn't move.

A police car turned whooping up the street. Officers took him and he did not fight them. They came to her and took care of her. They drove the streets until they found Ricardo, desperate, Mack in his arms, phoning, shouting, trying to find her.

'I thought he might try to explain,' Ricardo said. 'Try to talk to us. Through the police. Send a message.'

'Explain what?' Maggie said. They cleared the last of Sim's belongings from the house.

'Are you worried?' Ricardo said.

'I don't think so,' she said. 'No. Fuck him.'

The charge was Actual Bodily Harm. They had been astonished that he was not remanded, but the police had explained that they had no grounds to hold him. He had to report to them regularly. They saw him all the time, they were keeping an eye.

'He needs to be off the streets,' Ricardo said. 'You know what he did.'

'He's a bit of a broken man, to be honest,' said the liaison officer.

'My heart bleeds,' said Ricardo.

'Oh, absolutely,' the woman said. 'I'm just saying he's had a bit of a breakdown. My point isn't *poor baby*, it's that I wouldn't worry. There are people I do worry about. To be honest. He isn't one of them.'

Maggie checked his website. The work was still online, unchanged. The last time she had watched it had been a sinister, brilliant coagulation of images, the sense of a plan. The rabbit in its landscape. An explorer on a mission, unclear in a rough photograph, in her attic.

Now she saw videographic cliché. Infantile shock animation.

'I know the wheels grind very slow,' the officer said. 'He hasn't tried to contact you? Because that would . . .'

'No.'

Sometimes Maggie ignored it all. Sometimes she followed links and tried to remember the look and feel of the frame in her hand. It had been simple, without moulding. All wood. She strove to remember the shape of the glued joins when the thing sprang apart. She looked at diagrams and learnt a new vocabulary. The float. The lip. The rabbet.

Sitting at her computer, Maggie considered trying to track the thing's history. A bad death, or two, or many, in that room full of discarded art. What else had that chisel, along the gouges made by which she had run her fingers, cut? There had been stains in the rabbet, the channel in which the artwork sat.

As if she would ask Sim where he had been, where he had found this. If she were a true researcher, she might find some carpenter to the art world guilty of murder. And what if she did?

Or the wood. It might have come from an evil tree. Or the varnish, full of spite. Or nothing. What would change?

She closed her computer.

'He took his website down,' Ricardo said one day. 'It's still registered in his name, it's just gone. Fucking coward.'

*

They were pinched, but they did not take on another lodger. When Maggie imagined Sim, it was in the dirtiest streets of London, covered in muck, drawing images on bricks.

She stood in what was now a spare room. One day they would make it a study.

She watched the evenings framed by the windows.

Late at night, deep in the summer, Maggie woke.

Ricardo slept sweaty and fitful beside her. She listened but Mack was not awake.

Her eyes itched. She tried to sit up. The house made its noises. Through the monitor Mack spoke in his sleep. In the streets she heard catcalls and laughter of young people coming home.

Sleep hung heavy on her but she had woken at a sound from the stairs.

Her breath stopped in a fear so total she could not move.

The bedroom door opened and someone came in. Someone walked through the doorframe as though from behind a canvas.

A streetlamp shone between the curtains, and lit him, not enough. He was a darkness, an intention.

Someone had been crawling down inclines to railway lines. Someone had been sifting through trash. Collecting, sorting. Foraging for ruined wood shoved aside by trains.

Someone stood at the foot of her bed looking at her, and she couldn't move. Around his face he held the frame. He looked at her through it. She saw the new nails that studded it. The industrial tape that wrapped it. The clots of glue that scabbed it. Its new, even more imperfect lines.

He framed his face for her. The bottom of his chin was

mottled on the right as if with lichen or an illness or shadow. Maggie could not wake Ricardo. She could not move.

Someone held the frame around his face. He looked at her through it, yes, but he held it front out. He was presenting himself to her. He was what the frame contained. He looked at her and she could not look away, and he had made himself the work of art.

Listen the Birds

A Trailer

0:00–0:03
Two tiny birds fight in the dirt. There is no sound.

0:04–0:05
A man in his thirties, P, stands in undergrowth. He holds a microphone. He stares.

0:06–0:09
Close in on the birds. They are European robins. Their red chests flash. They batter each other in a flurry of wings. There is a noise of feedback.

0:10–0:11
Close-up of the man's microphone.

0:12–0:15
The robins' fight fills the screen. The feedback grows painfully loud.

0:16–0:19
Blackness. Silence. Then birdsong.
  Voiceover, man's voice, P: 'Its territory. Listen.'

0:20–0:24
Messy apartment. P looks through LPs. A younger man, D, watches.

P says, 'These are rare old field recordings.' He shows a record to D. We can't see the cover.

D says, 'What's with the title?'

P says, 'A translator's mistake, I guess.'

0:25–0:27

A glass-topped kitchen table, messy with the remains of a meal. Fixed shot. The table is vibrating. Silence.

0:28–0:31

Close-up, P's face.

Voiceover, D: 'And you're doing something like that?'

Voiceover, P: 'Something like that.'

0:32–0:35

The table again. Now in its centre two robins are fighting.

They spasm furiously amid plates and glasses. A candlestick falls. Cut to black.

0:36–0:38

P stares at his television. The screen is blue, text reads 'Scanning for Signal'.

P's own distorted voice comes out of the speakers: '. . . like that.'

0:39

Close-up of a robin's eye.

0:40–0:42

P walking down a crowded city street.

Voiceover, P: 'There's a signal and I can't tell if it's going out or coming in.'

Unseen by P, one person, then two people behind him raise their heads and open their mouths skywards as if shrieking. They make no sound.

0:43–0:45

D whispers, 'What are you trying to do?'

0:46–0:48

Darkness. A thud.

P stares at a window. On the glass is a perfect imprint of a flying owl, in white dust – powder down.

Cut to the earth below the window. An injured owl twitches.

0:49–0:50

P in a cafe, talking to a young woman. We hear the noise around them. P's words sound distorted. They are not in synch with his lips.

He says, 'There's a problem with playback.'

0:51

A man and a woman roll on the ground, battering each other. Their faces are blank. We hear the sound of wings.

0:52–57

Voiceover, D, whispering: 'Would you recognise a distress call?'

D puts earphones on. We hear the crackling audio of a bird's song. It grows louder, is joined by others, becomes a white noise of calls.

Cut to: a weathervane twisting on a steeple; a sped-up sequence of a plant changing the direction it faces; a battered old satellite orbiting earth.

The birdsong gets louder. On the satellite, a light comes on. It shifts, points its antenna at the world and sounds below.

0:58–0:59

D sitting opposite P at the kitchen table. He leans in.

He says, 'Listen.'

1:00

P stares at a computer screen. A message reads: 'No files found.'

1:01–1:02
Close-up of D's face.
   He says, 'Listen.'

1:03
Night. P stands naked at the foot of his bed. He raises his head and opens his mouth and his throat quivers as if he is howling. We hear only feedback.

1:04–1:08
D shouts, *'Listen!'*
   P shouts, 'No *you* listen!' He slams his hand on the table.
   D looks down. There is a perfect imprint of P's palm on the glass, in white powder.

1:09–1:14
Undergrowth. Close-up of the robins' fight.
   Cut to P, holding the microphone, staring. He is naked. His skin is covered in tiny scratches. There is no sound.
   The robins abruptly stop fighting. They separate. They stare at P.

1:15–1:19
Blackness. The sound of a needle hitting vinyl. A crackly robin's song begins to play.
   Voiceover, P, whispering: 'You listen.'

Title card: Listen the Birds.

A Mount

Framed in a small rear window in the building's ugly yellowish brick, behind its single pane of frosted glass, stands a porcelain horse. It is a foot high, shiny and white and speckled with green designs, stems and leaves clustered around tiny white flowers. Its head is down, its forelegs up, a low boisterous rearing, an eternal china prance.

There is a boy in the street, weeping quietly before the horse. His crying embarrasses people. They don't want to ignore him: one by one those who notice him out of their own windows or passing by come to ask him if he is alright, where his mother is, where his father is, what they can do, what the matter is. He will not answer them except with a brief shake of his head, a motion of his hand. He has no bruises, his clothes are not torn or dirty, and though he is plausibly as young as thirteen he might be seventeen – not a boy at all but a young man of his own agency and majority and this intercession a presumption. Still, if he does not stop crying someone will call the police or beg him to come with them inside or summon an ambulance, but his sobs are almost silent and the way he shuffles and ducks his head you have to watch him closely to see how stricken he is. Everyone who does see hesitates.

If you do pay close attention you may wonder where his clothes are from because there is something about the cut and colour that is out of place in this north London backstreet at the end of which you can see the supermarket (it just issued a profit warning) and the garage door that was for a long time collapsing under peeling paint and is now finally gone, the wood replaced with raw MDF, behind which must be some local workshop.

It is clear and cold and between small piles of fallen leaves and ragged plastic bags still wet from rain the boy or young man or whatever you call him is staring at the china horse in the window of what is not his home. He will not touch the glass.

There is a pole through the horse's body, impaling its miniature chest, a gold-coloured pole a few inches long made of cheap metal or cheaply gilded china like the equine body it would have anchored, notionally, in its housing. The idea is that the horse has been ripped from a carousel. It is not a model of a living animal but a model of a model of a posed living animal. It might even be that all the mounts on the imaginary merry-go-round from which it has, pretend, been torn, were made of glazed and hardened porcelain, not wood, and that the china of which the figurine is made is accurate.

If that is the case the translation of the animal into representation is only one of size, not substance.

Unless the ride is really that size, the imaginary ride. Unless there is no larger amusement of which this is a tiny replica, and the carousel is, rather, intended for small creatures, for dolls, for little frightened animals clinging to the cold bodies of the artificial scaled-down ones that, in the mind, go round, go up and down as they spin.

There must be some logic as to why it is only this much of the ride that has been put into this toylike form, if that is what has happened. Why not the bright conical canopy? Why not the other beasts? They might all be horses or they might be a whole menagerie, a garish, revolving, bobbing arc. This merry-go-round might, like the one in a far-off park in Providence, be a showcase, a working celebration of the best of the art, each mount a copy of a mount from some carousel celebrated among carousel-makers. Horses and ducks and saddled bears in decades of distinct styles, copies of this figure and that, a Bauhaus tiger chased by a Deco lamb, as many different schools as there are animals, in the patchwork homage of a carnival designer to the greatest of her antecedents, a best-of, the declaration of a canon in a slowly turning ride.

This collage carousel is surely haunted. Each copied mount must be ridden by a copied ghost, each passenger an echo of some originary apparition woken when the medley ride turns, invisibly blinking, eyeing all the others with courteous mistrust, wondering where they have all come from and where they are, afraid to dismount, to encroach on each other's spectral space.

This is what the boy might try to explain if anyone can talk to him, can stop him crying long enough to speak.

He might explain this in a choking voice, and he might say it with an accent you don't recognise and he might pepper what he says with unfamiliar phrases over which even he might pause, as if they do not come naturally even to him, as if he has learnt a vernacular at one remove, as if he knows it but does not like it, poor boy, poor young man. As if he is using it according to instructions. If you talk to him you might feel those things about him. You might observe that he raises his hands repeatedly and grips the air before him as if he is grasping a pole and clinging on for safety. If anyone asks him where he is from he is likely not to answer, or not to be able to answer, or to say anything but single words.

You might aspire to take him off the streets but you would not be able to, he is too fast to be caught, and he will go if anyone comes at him with more than tentative concern and curiosity. If he does you cannot feel complacent that he will not return when it is dark, or that others will not come.

You might watch from your window, from behind a horse, see a newcomer try to climb against nothing, groping at the air and stepping too high, with no mounting block, no loupin stane, stumbling, over and over.

These days there are so many odd and troubling noises in the city – in any city – you are forever jerking awake long before dawn with a hammering heart, trying to make sense of some noise you cannot even really remember but that you know is what frightened you awake. Maybe it was always that way and everyone has always been forever waking in a flustered confusion deep at night trying to believe that the awful sound they think woke them was nothing, or was the nervous bark of a dog, not the sound of violence or of a child weeping in the kind of desolation or terror that demands intervention, from which it is imperative that they be rescued, not the sound of a young man or woman, one of too many suddenly in the city, in odd clothes, whispering with stilted whispers, staring through windows at the shiny shapes of horses, shepherdesses and shepherds, cars, fish and angels, at other people's china animals.

The Design

There is a fact familiar to anyone who has worked with the dead. Do anything to a cadaver, it will do something back to you. This is not gusty spiritualism but psychology. It is true for even the gentlest interaction: actually *cutting* those quiet specimens provokes a far more serious response. One adjusts with speed, but the act never loses its taint.

This is the second time I have tried to write this document. The first, years ago, I started thus: *Now that William is dead, I am released from the concerns of his discretion.* In fact I decided, to my own surprise, to extend that care beyond his passing, up to the point of mine.

Upon his arrival in Glasgow, William – a clever, ambitious, somewhat sheltered young man, but no sort of a prig – indulged with enthusiasm in all the typical carousing for which students at the medical school were notorious. He also worked hard, including at anatomy. In those days, he later told me, he handled the dead with adequate respect and interest, but little more.

The laboratory was below ground. Its frosted windows were at ceiling level, calf-high to pedestrians outside. Our class – I was not present in those early weeks, and what I describe here I do from later knowledge – would gather in groups of four around each of the cadavers, prod and probe, lifting the formalin-soaked sheets while professors issued instructions.

It was the third month of study, late, and cold (for obvious reasons the room was not heated above a minimum). Evening access to the room was permitted, on the understanding that while swotting was acceptable, actual cutting outside official hours would constitute a discourtesy to one's quartet, like under-lining in a shared textbook. There were three students present that night. One of them was William.

He was sketching musculature. He prodded at a flayed limb. He rotated it to see how its inner fibres moved.

The body was that of a man in his sixties, still rangy and muscled under a certain later-life thickening. William rum-maged between flexors and extensors. They had been disconnected from the tendons of the hand, and he folded them back. He uncovered a long bone curving gently in the dead man's arm.

He stopped. For many seconds, William was still, looking closely at what was beneath his fingers. He wiped away tissue, felt his fingers slide on the ulna's sausage-skin-thin casing.

On the off-white of the bone were scratches. For a moment William thought they must be the results of injury. But they were not random. No chance mishap could have caused what he saw.

The markings were a design. They were pictures.

Through a tear in the periosteum, the bone's fibrous fascia, William saw curlicues. Carved filigrees entwined the shafts of ulna and radius like the borders of an illuminated manuscript.

William looked up at the age-stained walls, at John and Harpreet at their own cadavers, back down at last at the bone he touched. It remained impossibly carved. He could make out rust-red lines as if through gauze.

With hands that had begun to tremble, he peeled back muscle and meat, brought more bone into the light. He traced intricate illustration. Near the wrist he uncovered images of plants, between the leaves of which, rendered in even finer lines, was the tiny figure of a man.

William was certain that until he and his classmates had taken scalpels to it, the skin of the arm had been unbroken. He leaned on the table. He loomed over the cloth-obscured face.

'You chaps,' he said. Neither John nor Harpreet heard him. He had to clear his throat and repeat himself. What he heard himself say when they looked up, he later told me, astonished him. What he'd intended was to say was, 'Here's a queer thing – come tell me if this makes any more sense to you than it does to me.' What he said, after a tiny hesitation, was, 'I'm going to get knocked for six by this test. I've no idea what I'm looking at in here.'

At which misleading truth his classmates grinned, insisted on their own equally shocking ignorance, and went back to work, leaving William staring into the grey arm, at the intricacies on the bone.

The dead man in his care had no tattoos, and only everyday scars. His hands suggested manual work and his knuckles that he had not been a fighter.

When one has put oneself in the frame of mind necessary for cutting, I can attest, it is hard to see a cadaver's face as a face at all. It was with effort, when he lifted the flannel, that William registered not planes of skin but features. He pulled back the lids of the eyes and tried to imagine this etched man moving in the world.

Eventually Harpreet and John left. Bourne, the porter, peered in and nodded good evening, then withdrew, leaving William alone in the presence of the mystery. He sat motionless in the cold room for a long time, as if keeping vigil. When at last he stood, he moved decisively. He took a blade and extended the cut with more finesse than he'd expected he would muster. He sluiced the nestled bone with water, and all along it found more marks.

Paisleys, cloudlike forms, waves. Here was a woman, bent, her body criss-crossed lines. William opened the man's thigh. He tugged the tremendous muscles apart to uncover the femur – there is no profit in being gentle with the dead – and looking up at him from within the leg was an eye scratched onto the bone.

Two cuts to the chest, like martyrs' wounds. On the ribs to one side was a scene of sailing; on the other, abstract shapes.

William cleaned his hands. He listened to the occasional footsteps that came and went outside.

There were no anatomy classes for another two days, but any of his three cadaver-sharers might come in at any time. He later said he knew he had no moral right to do what he decided to do, that the design was his only contingently, that it had not been vouchsafed to him. I have never in fact believed he was quite sure he was unchosen.

'Late one for you tonight,' Bourne said when William at last signed out.

'Indeed,' William said. 'Exam coming up.' He was shaking. He blinked and smiled, not very successfully, and headed into the chilly dark.

Perhaps two hours later he was back. He wore drab, feature-less clothes, a hat low on his head. He pushed a compost-filled barrow taken with agonising silence from the garden of his lodgings. There were not many hours until dawn. William glanced at the rear of the houses that overlooked him. They were unlit. He knelt on the pavement outside and tugged open the window he had left unlatched.

Reaching into the darkness, where the dead lay, he extracted the bag of chemicals and tools he'd tied to the frame. He braced himself, leaning against the wall. He groped for the ends of the winding sheets he had coiled into ropes. They stretched from where he had secured them to the worktop below, and to the results of his long, unpleasant work.

William had no expertise. It must have been a bad business. With the help of the textbooks in the cutting-room, in agonies, terrified of interruption, he had, as quickly as he could and with clumsy care, dismembered the body.

One slip now, and his burdens would slam down with a din like the dead stamping. Bourne would come rushing. Part by part William pulled the body out by its own shroud.

At last he sat back in the alley, gasping. His shirt was damp with sweat, and with preserving fluid leaking and soaked through the wrappings. He reeked. He arranged the swaddled components in his wheelbarrow, smothered them in compost. He buried his dead. Hoping he looked like an early-rising workman, he lifted the handles and walked away.

It would not be until late the following day that William's crime was discovered. Two students, alone in the room, found that the body at their station was not the one on which they had hitherto been working.

William had considered various ways to spread confusion, including desecrating every cadaver (a notion he instantly rejected). In the end, he simply rearranged all their gurneys, wheeling them all to new positions, and leaving his own, now empty, discreetly by the wall.

It was effective. It took Johnson and Hirsch almost half an

hour to find their specimen, in the corner where William had left it. When they did, at first they simply assumed they'd forgotten some explanatory announcement, and recommenced working on it. Uneasy at last, they finally reported the situation, but it was hours again after they did so that the porters, rolling their eyes at what seemed a prank, tried to return every cadaver to its designated place, and realised that one was missing.

William's pressing need was for a hiding place. His heart clamouring in his chest, he had pushed the barrow into an unsalubrious quarter of the city, haunted by a sudden wish that his dead man was whole and unbroken.

The night was nearly gone when he found the tenements he remembered. They were, for the length of four or five buildings, empty, broken-windowed and fire-damaged. It was the work of minutes to prise open a rear door and push in through clutter and rubbish. He passed a noisome chamber used by tramps and local boys to relieve themselves. The smell was revolting and, William hoped, offputting to other intruders. He hauled his burden up the stairs and laid it down.

He tried to sit it up, in its pieces, in a body shape, shoulders to the wall. He hoped the chemicals would keep rats away. Not one part of the flesh was visible. The thing regarded him with its filthy-cloth-obscured face. William watched it back, his stomach fluttering.

He imagined how the sun would rise, how at a certain point its rays would crawl across the shroud and the dead man, cross from one side of him to the other, and how he would not move at all under that light.

*

I was present when the dean, Dr Kelly, thundered about the heinous act that had been committed. It was my first, dramatic day. I'd transferred from my previous place of studies to Glasgow in a rush of instructions and hurried plans. What I arrived to was that outraged speech.

There were police constables in the room. When we were dismissed, and I was shuffling out among a group of young men politely introducing themselves, I saw a porter call four fellows from the crowd to where the officers were waiting.

'Who are they?' I said.

'The chaps whose body's toddled off,' someone said. 'Hauled before His Nibs and Scotland's finest.' He shuddered theatrically.

It was helpful to William to hear how aggrieved by the questioning were his innocent colleagues. His own denials of knowledge could approximate theirs. He'd discarded the clothes he'd worn that night. Mrs Malley's wheelbarrow was at the bottom of a canal. That William was not discovered then does not make this a story of the incompetence of the police.

'So, come on, then,' said Mills, a phlegmatic young Yorkshire-man who was to fall in France in 1940. 'Who has a theory?'

We took turns speculating on what had happened to the cadaver. We mooted theft, ghostliness, complicated games. William had joined us in the pub by then, and his own flight of fancy was that the man had woken up, realised he wasn't dead, shrugged, and gone home. Mine – my classmates encouraged the new boy to play – was that they were all victims of a hex operating on their memories, that there had never been any such corpse as the one they remembered.

The newly bodiless quartet was dispersed – 'like the tribes of bloody Israel,' according to Adenborough – among their peers. I was also assigned a place, so five of the anatomy stations became five-man teams. William complained exactly sufficiently about this disruption.

The disappearing body quickly became shorthand. Anything lost was considered pocketed by our ambulatory corpse on its way home. Unexpected noises in corridors were the incompetent creepings of the revenant. William took part in such joshing no more and no less than anyone else.

Under a stretch of houses overlooking a railway cut, William found storerooms where local shops kept surplus wares. He peered into a grimy window. A train passed. A little girl playing in the gutter looked up from her doll.

The owner of the room, an ageing tough, agreed a price. William impressed upon his landlord the need for discretion and privacy, hinting that he might be working with dangerous chemicals. The man obviously assumed this would be some cottage industry in liquor or narcotics. William allowed the impression.

'Can you keep the local lads out?' William said.

'They'll mind me.'

When William crept back to the old house for the bundled parts, he was afraid the police would be waiting for him. But there was only the stained cloth and the flesh within. The moon spotlit the floor a little to one side of the remains: incompetent stagecraft.

William took three awful night walks to his new laboratory. He brought the torso in a suitcase. Then two legs; then both arms and the head, in a knapsack. Treated as they were, his burdens did not smell of rot, but they did not smell good.

Did anyone, in those days, notice how tired he was? Did his

work slip, his marks suffer? I think not. We were all working hard, all exhausted. His secret researches meant William was absent sometimes, but that was hardly unusual. We'd always cover for each other – 'Oh, Bryce is down with fever, sir.' It was second nature. The professors were game enough, drily wishing absentees recovery.

He did not work at my table but I had got to know William a little by then. He was not the centre of any social group, but neither was I.

One night, while we were among Bradley's guests (Bradley was a braggart but for his club we indulged him), attention turned to me.

'But what was it happened?' Leadwith kept saying. He was a good fellow, without malice, but he was rather in his cups. 'How'd you end up here in the middle of term in such a fearful rush? You were at Durham, weren't you?' He chortled. 'Was it a girl? Why *Glasgow*?'

I responded vaguely and jocularly, but he wouldn't let it lie. 'No, really, do tell, Gerald,' he said. He was staring. I avoided looking at anyone in particular. 'What was it brought you up here?'

'Come now, Charles,' someone said, but the chaps were interested too, and I think pleased that someone was gauche enough to ask such questions. The knave at the feast is a blessed exoneration for better-behaved diners.

William spoke.

'Charles,' he said. 'You're being a bore. Gerald doesn't want to talk about this. It's a poor show that you won't let it go.'

In the silence that followed, William was the only person who did not seem embarrassed. 'You would say that,' someone said feebly, 'gallivanting off with some secret fancy all the time.'

But William said, 'And is it not my right to gallivant exactly as much as I wish?'

He smiled. A few people laughed. Conversation moved on. Leadwith came and found me and muttered, 'I'm sorry, old man. I'm an ass.' Of course I told him not to give it another thought.

William and I left together, our hands jammed in our pockets, huddled against the cold. We didn't speak much. He did not even say anything along the lines of 'Old Leadwith can put his foot in it.' When we reached my rooms, we paused under a streetlamp and he met my eyes. After a moment he clapped me on the shoulder and walked off in the fog.

A revolting rancidity was setting in to the remains, preservative or no. *Dermestes maculatus* would have turned up their beetle noses. Acid would have damaged the bone. In his newfound workroom, with the small window painted over and the door padlocked, William proceeded by the only methods available to him.

He cut for hours, excising grey flesh and piling offcuts in a covered pail. He dipped a handkerchief in dilute cologne and fastened it around his face. Larger bones he separated by knife; he did not try to do so with the smaller, the digits, the fiddly metatarsals.

How many times he wished for a larger stove! He boiled as large a tub of water as he could, and into it he placed the head. The room grew horribly hot. No matter how scientific and dispassionate one's mindset, to look into a bubbling stockpot and see the flash of eyes looking up when tumbling water lets them, eyes one ought, one realises, to have removed against such glances, to be treated to a sneer as the heat pulls back what remains of lips, is desperate.

The liquid thickened. In an action revoltingly like cooking, William scooped out the lifting flesh with a slotted spoon. He could not stop himself from retching.

He smoked and studied as well as he could while he waited, which was not well. He added water to the stove. It was much later, at the other end of the night, by the time he at last fished in the pot with tongs. What he brought out made him gasp and fumble. It fell back into the water, splashing him with scalding drops and human particulate as he clapped a trembling hand to his mouth.

William tried again. The head steamed. The distended eggy sacs the eyes had become stared in awful manner. He took them out. He could see bone through the parting flesh.

William peeled off the remains of the face. He cleaned the skull down. The brain would necessitate creative cerebrectomy, Egyptian style, perhaps, through the nose. For now he held out his prize and met its empty gaze.

It was marked by lines in the same dark red he remembered from within the arm. Stained not by lampblack but by the endless passage of blood.

On one side of the frontal bone was a tall ship. It bore unknown cargo on an intricate sea. Over the left eye was a knot of lines that might have been a submerged beast following that vessel. The maxilla: a jungle. Thickets of ivy in Beaux-Arts curves, boughs teeming with squirrels, birds of paradise courting in the greenery.

The sphenoid swarmed with animals. On the zygoma were cogs of some shaded machine. On the temporal bone were clouds. There were weapons on the parietal; on the mandible, monkeys and fruit. Surrounding the nasal cavity were marks like those made by a calligrapher breaking in a new pen.

The display had been obscured by blood and skin. Life had

been necessary to finish this piece – years of blood flow to colour the lines, years of growth to pull the skeleton into the right configuration. How had the design looked when the man was six years old? When he was ten, and seventeen?

William ran his fingers over the voyaging ship. He could feel the lines scratched in the still-cooling bone.

Of course I asked more than once about the body that had gone missing immediately before my arrival. Such curiosity on my part was perfectly understandable. What had it looked like? I asked. Where had it been cut? Joking aside, what *did* people think might have happened?

I asked those whose specimen it had been. 'I'm afraid I have not even the idlest speculation,' said Sanders. 'I don't even *like* anatomy,' he said, as if that were relevant. Adenborough and Parish offered no more insight.

When I addressed my questions to William he was affable enough, but quiet, not at all forthcoming. I could not but note his guarded reaction. It left me more crestfallen than I wanted to admit. By then I was not indifferent to his preferences.

The cadavers we used were assiduously anonymised, but let us not be naïve: with sufficient money, time, and energy, William could have uncovered the identity of his. But he could not think how to protect himself if he pursued that route. He decided, with a gladness that bewildered him, that he would not seek to learn the name of the man on whose remains he worked.

My own cadaver was near William's new station. During classes, I watched to see his oddly intent interventions. When we removed several inches from the tops of our specimens' scalps,

William went from station to station, examining each unmarked skull. His expression might have been one of disappointment or relief.

The little girl he had seen playing near his makeshift lab seemed excluded from the company of others of her age. She was often there in the shadow of a wall, always alone but for her rough toy, with its unravelling mouth and grubby dress. She would watch William come and go with the frank suspicion of the very young.

William steeled himself. He cooked down the meat of the feet and the hands so long that it crumbled when he pushed out the tiny bones. These he set carefully in place on a sheet he'd painted with a rough human outline. In its head-circle was the skull. William put down scaphoid, capitate, triquetral, and lunate, the phalanges of the fingers an undone puzzle.

Each piece, even the very smallest, was illustrated.

He kept water boiling, softened tough flesh, wiped clots of it from ulna, from vertebra after vertebra, ribs and hips. He laid down a disaggregated etched man, impatient to see what he'd found within the flesh.

William and I were visiting a small maritime museum. I performed repeated astonishment at that fact. 'Not that I'm not delighted,' I kept saying, 'but how did I end up here?'

'Mind games is how,' William said. 'I bend all to my will.'

I asked him about his family. When he spoke of his father, that affable clerk, William conjured him for me with rueful dislike. For his mother he expressed affection, and a pity he tried to disguise. His sister was a teacher, his brother an importer of goods, and of them he had nothing to say.

I read aloud vainglorious descriptions of Glasgow's shipyards. Not without sarcasm, I admired a little model clipper, some once-majestic such and such, et cetera.

I stopped at the sight of William staring at a cabinet of scrimshaw. Etchings of ship life, sea monsters, homilies on whale tooth and bone.

'That one's American, I believe,' he said of a filigreed narwhal tusk. There was no note to say so.

'Are you an expert?' I managed at last to say. 'At whose knee have you been investigating such things?'

'We all have interests,' he said. 'I don't doubt you have your own hidden depths, Gerald.'

I didn't reply. When we left we deposited thank-you coins in the establishment's donations box and wry remarks in its guest book.

'When you arrived,' William said after a long silence, 'you must have felt like you'd stumbled into some secret society.'

'How so?'

'Oh, I don't know. What with all of us already knowing each other. Sometimes one can't help feeling one's blundered into something as an outsider.'

'Well thank you very much,' I said. 'I rather thought I wasn't doing badly.'

'Oh hush,' he said. 'I'm talking in general terms, as well you know. I suppose I'm saying that that feeling hits one more often than one might think. Walk into *any* room with *any* people already in it, that'll do it. No matter how charmingly they try to bring you up to speed. Let alone coming up here as abruptly as you did.' He did not meet my eye. 'About which of course I am terribly curious, though Leadwith remains an ass.'

He saw me open my mouth to speak, and he saw me close it again without a word. He cleared his throat. 'I suspect that sense of *not being in on something* is more or less the human condition,' he said.

'I suppose,' I said.

'And on rare occasions,' he said, 'there might actually be something to it. One stumbles into something to which one shouldn't have been privy. I wonder what sort of efforts those who *are* in the know might go to in response.'

He looked, in that moment, rather heartbreakingly boyish and forlorn. For a while neither of us spoke.

'Is everything all right?' I said.

'Oh,' he said, 'I was going to ask the same of you.' I said nothing. 'Pay me no mind.'

'If something's been going on . . .' I said it hesitantly, as if fearful that he might tell me something *had*, and what it was.

'Pay me no mind.'

It was done. The bones were clean. They were laid down in a jigsaw man.

Winter was waning. William sluiced his drains with acid.

He had taken a long way to his room that day, unable to shake the feeling that he was being followed. Now he dried the skeleton, brushed the bones gently. He rotated the humerus, tracing the voyage of some Sindbad-like figure through various lands. He wanted to make it glow.

He hesitated, scribbled something in a notebook and tore out the page, then opened his door and looked at the girl playing with her doll. She stood guardedly under his gaze. 'Hullo,' he said. 'Would you like to earn a shilling?'

The girl answered at last, in so strong a local accent that William could not but laugh. He could understand barely a word.

'You know Mr Murray?' They knew him there. 'Give him this. He'll give you beeswax. Bring it here and I'll give you the shilling.'

The child took the paper and ran off in the right direction. For all he knew, that was the last he would ever see of her. William sat on his step, closed the door and leaned back on it, and smoked in the sunlight.

When the girl did return holding a big jar, he cheered her and raised his hands. She rewarded him with his beeswax and a remarkable smile.

She said something. When he understood that she was asking him 'whit he had in there', he said, 'I can't tell you,' and she turned and walked away instantly, without a word, without wheedling. Her lack of surprise that her hopes would be dashed horrified him. He called her back.

William's were now the pleasures of polishing. One by one he made the etched bones shine. The skull gleamed. Scapula, sternum, tib and fib. On the left patella, a rising sun; on the right a crescent moon with a wolf face. The dead man had kneeled on pagan signs.

'I don't mind telling you,' William said to me later, 'it made me weep to see it all, like that, at last.' *This is something to be parsed*, he thought as he tracked the illustrations, sought a route, a journey on the ship he had seen. Arm leg leg arm head, around the ribcage, perhaps? A hero's journey?

'Do you know what this is?' William said.

The girl stared at the marked nugget he held. Is it, she ventured, a biscuit? 'It's called a sacrum,' he said. 'I have one. And so will you when you've finished growing. But d'you see?' Flags in a breeze, blowing left to right across the bone. Mountains, a forest. The child regarded it gravely. Did he draw that? No, he told her. He told her that something or someone else had done so.

He let her run her fingers along the patterns. It was no longer only he who had seen this thing and he was glad. He put it in her memory. He told her that this had been underneath a man's skin.

'You can imagine where that leaves a chap like me,' he said. 'A freethinker, I might once have called myself, though that's hardly anything like so dashing a label as once it was. It's a rum thing for the likes of me, because who else could have put these here, eh?' His voice went low. 'God is a scrimshander.'

The girl did not look at him nor he at her.

'Who *was* this man?' he said. 'Did he know? Of how many is he one? I wonder about some brotherhood – sisterhood, too, I've no reason to doubt. Some siblinghood of the lovingly carved?'

The house creaked. William glanced up. There was a new tenant above, whose motions made him wary, whose step he imagined he recognised.

'No one could say it isn't done exquisitely,' he said. 'But here's the thing. Isn't there something a little *haphazard* about it?'

If there was a story in the design, William could not decode it. He could make no narrative sense of the men and monkeys, women and nightjars, the stars, monsters furred and feathered, machines, clocks, the hunt conducted with flintlocks, the giraffe pasha on a stone throne, cities with onion domes above clouds, knots like those on Celtic graves. William made the girl laugh at the beasts on the mandible.

'In some illuminated manuscripts,' he said, 'you can tell why images are where they are relative to the text. And there are others in which whatever riotous assembly's at the edges would probably have been more or less the same whatever the subject matter.' There was another sound from above, a creak like someone lowering himself to a hole. This time William was too deep in thought to notice. The girl, however, heard. She looked up startled as William continued. 'For a while I thought that's what I was looking at here. Essentially . . .' He hesitated. 'Doodles. If of a most splendid kind. Marginalia. But . . .'

William pointed at curlicues in the crook of a rib. 'See these marks,' he said. 'They change very specifically. They grow *curvier*. What starts at one end of the bone as a set of relatively simple lines becomes virtuoso.

'You see that sort of thing all over. Developments. The same figure here –' one shin – 'and here –' the side of the skull – 'but with far more finesse above. There are plenty of these *improvements*.

'I think what are on these bones are experiments. Studies, references, preparations, the testing out of ideas. This skeleton's been used to loosen up the wrist. Before the artist turns to the real project. Which will be who knows what? Not this man, and perhaps not Man at all.'

William looked at a paint-covered window. It glowed from light outside. He spoke quickly. 'Perhaps in twenty years, some Norwegian ship'll land, shall we say, a blue whale. And as the crew flense it, Gunnar Gunnarson will point: there, on an exposed corner of that great skull, will be carved a human figure. Life-sized. Perfect. Crosshatched more delicately even than the real thing. And there at last, under *that* flesh, will be the piece all this has been leading up to. And it'll be so beautiful. And it'll tell so astonishing a story. What would you say to that?' He smiled at the girl. 'Scratched in the bones of a whale.'

The girl regarded him. 'Our friend here?' he said. 'And who knows who else?' He raised his hands at the door, at everyone in

Glasgow. 'Rough sketches, every one. What's been done to this chap is what you do to such scraps when you're done. You throw them away. So here we are.' He smiled again and his eyes filled. 'In a waste bin.'

He was too agitated for even an adult observer easily to follow, let alone the girl. He stared at the bones.

'If we were to look under my skin or yours, what do you think we might find? There can't be too many such people – one would have heard. But I find I can't believe him unique. How many of us are scribbled on?

'I've considered, of course I have, uncovering a few inches.' He tapped his own shin. 'But do you know? I find I cannot bear to discover if I am, *or* if I'm not.'

William raised a finger to his lips. The girl, solemn thing, copied him. She glanced at the ceiling again, but the noises from above had stopped. 'If those who wear the design know they do,' he said, 'whether they know why or what it portends, they obviously go to some lengths to avoid attention. Which would make *this* fellow here a serious oversight on their part. Who knows who they might send, what they might do to someone like me, who chanced on the knowledge? Best to keep what we know hush-hush. In case they're a bad lot.

'After all, it's always possible that the artist isn't God, but the other party.'

The girl tried to steal a vertebra. William fished it out of her pocket in mock-astonishment, as if chancing upon it like a fossil on a beach. 'This is a wonderful specimen,' he said. 'I must have this.' He told her he would buy it from her and gave her another shilling.

She paused at the door. 'No' a whale,' she said. 'A wee mouse.'

'Yes. Yes!' William was delighted. 'Why not?'

He watched her go. It might indeed be that rather than submerging to biblical deeps, the work for which this man was a draft scampered for crumbs. That one day a cat would catch it, and crunch down on filigree illustration so fine, so exquisite, it might only have been made out with microscopy of the mouse's bones.

Given her age and situation, it seemed reasonable to assume that anything the girl might report would not be listened to. Later, though, hoping to move on to a new phase of life, I felt I had to seek, at considerable effort, the young woman she was by then. I did not know her name, and knew there was only a negligible chance that she remembered what she had seen. Nonetheless, after reflection, I became anxious at the thought that she might disclose any recollections she did have to some other interested persons, or indeed to any but me, and what attention that might bring.

William had grown paler even than the Scottish sky would warrant, and he was losing weight. I watched him scuttle into lectures late, strewing papers like a figure from a *Punch* cartoon.

'Can I speak candidly?' I asked him.

'Where do you stand on God?' he interrupted. His voice was strained. He spoke too quickly, as he had to the girl.

'On the crown of his celestial pate,' I said. It raised the desired smile, if fleetingly. 'I come from what you might call nonconformist stock,' I said with care. 'Am I a believer? I don't detain myself with theology most of the time. But beliefs aren't only in the brainpan: they're in the body. We're all issued beliefs and instructions by our backgrounds. Some implicit, some explicit.' I gave him a glance. 'We're all given orders.'

He was noticeably startled that I'd said such a thing. As was I. I was under some pressure, at the time.

'Of course, whether we obey those old injunctions or not is another matter,' I continued in a rush. 'Sometimes we might surprise ourselves. Obedience comes with risks, just as disobedience does, and it seems one only risks what one is willing to lose. The chaps are all worried about you, you know. I'm worried about you.'

'It's good of them,' William said. He cleared his throat. 'Really there's no need.'

'Nonsense,' I said. He was startled, but I would not make light of it. 'Whatever you're up to, it's putting you in harm's way. William, you *must* stop.'

He looked at me with those exhausted eyes and struggled to formulate something. 'As regards Yahweh,' he said, 'and related phenomena, perhaps *understanding*'s overrated. Some of us are observers by nature, not philosophers. What do you think?'

'I think,' I said slowly, in as light a tone as I could muster, 'that I shall enjoy being a surgeon.' I looked away. 'I've been won over by this knife-handed tinkering. One's often surprised by what one ends up caring for.'

'Quite,' he said. I did not meet his eye. Eventually his attention shifted from me. I could almost see it go, back through the tenement streets by routes I could have walked, back to the secret that he had still not told me. I knew – I could tell – that he felt pursued.

*

The moment came. A typical grey day, a typical wind gusting in the alleys of that resilient city. It irked William ever after that he never knew what he had done to provoke suspicion, nor who it was who had given him up.

He was in his makeshift laboratory, with his bone journals, administering to the camera with which he inexpertly captured only strange and gloomy underlit images of the design. He would not risk buying the discretion of a professional photographer. There was a knock.

At the door were two officers of the law and a porter from the medical school. They gained entry easily enough while William remonstrated weakly. He stepped into the street as they investigated. He waited for them. Locals gathered. The little girl was not among them, but William's landlord was. He looked up, above William's head, into the upstairs window. He looked stricken with guilt. That this, William thought, had befallen his tenant under his supposed protection. When he had the man's attention William gave him a nod of reassurance.

Over the years of our association I saw William perform many other laudable acts. I saw him save lives, of course; I saw him put frightened people at their ease in ways I assure you not every doctor bothers to do. But it was the homely scale of that unspoken intervention that struck me. That he not only took a moment but that moment, of his own undoing, to reassure a man he barely knew. It was difficult, to feel such admiration and yet be unable to express it.

On the floor by the skeleton were a small drill, tiny screws, adhesive paste and wire. William had been boring minute holes in the bones. 'I wouldn't leave it all in bits,' William said to the porter. He held his hand up to indicate a brace like a gallows, from which he had intended the skeleton ultimately to hang.

'Oh please, please,' he said. The constables bundled up the bones more roughly than he could bear.

To William's astonishment, he was hauled in front of the university authorities rather than the police. Seven old men, provosts and heads of department and so forth, flapped their gowns and bellowed harsh questions. William was thinking about his parents, he told me later, about his imminent expulsion. He was thinking about the discards of a scrimshander. 'And about you,' he added to me.

'What possible macabre pleasure,' Dr Kelly demanded, 'would you derive from making such carvings?'

'Oh.' William was startled. 'I didn't,' he started to say. 'That wasn't me. That skeleton . . .' He stopped, seeing the dean's expression.

'This is a grisly business,' Kelly said, William told me, *fiercely*. 'Moral your artistic proclivities are not, nor fitting for a physician, though I won't deny the skill in them. They are, I will say it, unnatural. Now. Where did you procure your materials?'

William stared at him. 'You would not end,' Kelly said slowly, 'what has so far been a promising career with *illegality*, I am sure. So – where did you get those bones?' And William, open-mouthed, took what he had been offered.

'I bought them, sir,' he said at last, firmly. 'For my art.' He raised a hand and made a little etching motion. The dean sat back. The look on his face was one of relief.

William's landlady told us that his rent was paid to the end of the following month, but that he had disappeared. Most of the class believed him sent down. Even I heard nothing from him. But two weeks after his questioning, utterly unexpectedly to almost everyone there, though not to me, William slipped quietly into the hall after a lecture had started.

The great wave of astonishment was muted by Professor Serge's wrathful glance. Just once, after we had settled down, William looked up and found me. He gave me a huge smile, and held up a finger in assurance that he would explain.

After the lecture we all crowded around and clapped him on the back and demanded to hear the story. He grinned. 'Oh, you know,' he said. 'I was a silly ass. Got my wrist slapped. What did I miss?' and so on.

Out of earshot of the others he said to me, 'They caught me fiddling around with stuff I shouldn't have been. They found me with bones, and—'

'Human bones?'

'Absolutely human bones.' We stared at each other. 'And they must've suspected where they came from. But for reasons I can't fathom, I think someone put in a word, and ... Well, I got a stern warning, my bones got confiscated, and here I am promising to be a good boy until the end of my professional life.' He gave an unhappy laugh.

'I do realise, old man,' I said, in a voice that perhaps shook a little, 'that this isn't the whole story.' He laughed again. 'You once in a rather civilised fashion insisted that it was permissible for a chap to not hold forth about things he didn't want to. Well.' I gave him a bow.

Indeed, he did not speak of these events to me again for a long time. And yet I never thought this would be the last I would hear on the matter.

*

423

I graduated respectably, William well. We found work in south London, Oxford, Leeds, London again. William got a position in Swansea, where he remained for two years, before moving to a hospital on the south coast. I took work in Durham.

'I can't believe it,' William said. It was, I insisted, not so very far.

'It most certainly is.' He raised his voice. 'You don't even like *talking* about that place. You may feel duty-bound to revisit whatever sordid past you have there –' William, though angry, still did not pry – 'but Durham doesn't agree with you. I'm the one who meets you off the train all gaunt and harrowed.'

'I'm not thrilled by the prospect,' I allowed, 'but don't exaggerate. In every life one must dot and cross.'

We were five years into our careers when a conference at Glasgow was announced with a remit broad enough that most chaps from our year could attend. It became a reunion. It was a pleasure seeing everyone again, socialising with some of our old teachers, now colleagues. Five years, I know, is nothing: it is impossible now not to be amused at the nostalgia we felt.

There was – perhaps still is – a tiny medical museum in one wing of the quad. 'Come on,' I said to William, the day we were to leave. 'Let's.' I suspect it is evident in what direction this story is heading.

The two rooms were jumbles of cases, charming in their way. Old surgical artefacts, dioramas of medical history. Sunlight slanted in, not particularly usefully.

I turned a corner and stopped. 'What is it?' William saw my expression. He rushed to the case when he saw what I had found.

It was not a whole skeleton that dangled inside: only the skull, the shoulders and rib cage, the right arm and hand, and the humerus of the left. Everything below the fourteenth vertebra was missing. The bones had been polished. The design was vividly clear. I stared at the maritime scenes, the gargoyles, plants and patterns, the lines that looked like lines for the joy of lines.

He put his hands on the glass. 'That's quite something . . .' William started to say at last, and I said, 'Don't.'

Origin unknown, the label read. *Artist unknown*.

I looked at the skull. 'William,' I said, 'when you were suspended, as you can probably imagine, there were all manner of rumours . . .'

'All right,' he said. 'I'll tell you.' He stepped towards it.

'That's it. The body you heard so much about. For a moment I wondered if it might be *another*, but that's it. Or what's left of it. What did they *do*?' he breathed. '*Look* at it . . .'

'How did it get here?' I said.

'*Here* here?' he said, pointing right at it, 'or *here* here?' He circled his finger to indicate the world. 'I don't know. And I think it would not be sensible for me to pursue such inquiries.' He spoke with odd formality. 'If there are those who know how it got here, I should avoid their company.' He looked at me. 'But you and I will talk.'

I came south. He looked me over when I alighted: I had lost weight. We bicycled to the Downs, and contentedly munched sandwiches in a basin of clay. It was an unusually hot afternoon. One of those days all slowly ambling bumblebees and honeysuckle and so forth, at which the English countryside, when it puts its mind to it, excels, and quite unlike any summer day anywhere else. Calm and still and lovely, but never without a sense of something impending. The sort of day one misses even as one experiences it.

'So how are you getting on up there?' William said tightly.

'Muddling through,' I said. 'It won't be for much longer.' He nodded.

'I'm sure,' William said at last, 'I could say what you chaps thought happened, in Glasgow.' He took a bite of bread, a puff of cigarette, a swig of cider. 'But I can't scrimshaw, Gerald. Not a notion how.' He gave me quite a smile. 'It's a queer thing to know your colleagues think you a thief of corpses for necromantic art. Who narrowly escaped gaol . . .'

'Not everyone,' I told him. 'Some of us . . .'

He waved his hand to hush me. 'I didn't carve it, but I did take the bloody body,' he said. And as the light grew slowly thick and the shadows long he told me all of it, his story, which I have, with a few omissions and a few emendations, outlined here.

It was obvious he could tell I believed every word he said. I could see his relief at my lack of doubt. Only his description of the body's early nights in the tenements elicited some shock from me.

We had a hair-raising time of it cycling back to the station in time for our train.

I was privileged to work with William for many years after that. I even ran one of his charities for a time after his death. I was not good at it, but I wanted to do my best for him.

It was after the war, when his initial coolness towards the new National Health Service metamorphosed into enthusiasm, that William's career blossomed. He was not a political man, but through his work in teaching hospitals in the 1950s he became committed to what is now called 'social medicine'. It was for his efforts in this field that he was ultimately granted an OBE. He took great interest in pedagogy: he was a good teacher, though one who was easily sidetracked. His name is now attached to a surgical technique, an honour he would have pooh-poohed, and that I think would have delighted him.

William was provocative on medical ethics. Not only did he support a presumed-consent model of organ donation, but he insisted that without explicit instructions to the contrary, everyone should be considered to have offered up their bodies to medical science. 'William,' I would scold, 'that is ridiculous. You don't mean it.'

'Certainly I do.' It was one of those arguments that people who've shared a lot for a long time are happy to perform in company. 'You're going to put me on the slab when *I* go,' he would insist. 'So I can keep an eye on the class.' For all his joshing, he took the principle seriously. Not only did he sign his own body over, but he harangued his friends, insisted it was the duty of all doctors to make the same gesture. He went on at me in particular, of course, until at last I gave in and signed the form in front of him.

I once mooted returning to Glasgow together, to look again at the exhibit. 'It won't achieve anything,' William told me firmly.

'You know,' I said carefully, '*I* could do some sort of investigation into what happened. *You* might be in an awkward position, but I—'

'Gerald,' he said. 'I don't want you to draw attention to yourself. I don't want *anyone* connected to whatever it is I stumbled on looking for me. Or for you.'

I nodded and looked away, remembering his young interlocutor. 'Perhaps,' I said, 'it's just as well someone sent the police to your workshop. Before any other authorities could track you down.'

Whenever I watched him operate, I noticed William's close

observation of the bones. Perhaps he thought lightning might strike twice, or perhaps that it had not been random lightning the first time, but a message, for him. 'There are days,' he said to me more than once, 'when everyone I see looks like a candidate. As if the world is full of designs.'

It would not have been hard to check William's own bones. I put it to him. I tapped his knee. 'A little anaesthetic?' I said, and he looked at me curiously. He mumbled a platitude about God refusing to prove His own existence. I think certainty either way would still have been excruciating to him, as he had admitted to the girl it would be, years before.

None of us have to obey instructions. I consider my own existence proof of that. So much of life is cobbled together when plans go awry. That is often where happiness comes from.

As soon as I was able, I wound up my loose ends in Durham and, eager for change, came permanently south. William and I moved into a house we could not really afford.

More than once in those early years one or other of us would go off for a few days, without much explanation. I did so after that day on the Downs. At other times it was William who disappeared, to return in contemplative mood.

We were always scrupulously respectful of each other's secrets. I did not discuss his trips with him, but it took only a cursory search to find Scottish papers and ticket stubs to Glasgow among his things, for all his stern words to me about that destination. Only once did he ever make mention of any such journey. Years later, after two days' absence, William cleared his throat and poured himself some tea and said, 'It's gone.'

I eventually said, 'They change their exhibitions, museums, from time to time.' That was that.

Perhaps on my own returns, William sought evidence as I did. He must have been disappointed if so: I was more careful than he, and never one for mementos or trophies, even after successful searches. He would find no telltale tickets, no scribbled directions through Glasgow tenements, no old rag doll with fraying lips.

Very much later, when it became impossible to ignore the fact that William was dying, he began to speak about the design again. It was my task, by then, to let him talk of anything he wished. I am proud of how I did so, no matter if he ruminated in those last days on topics of which I wished he would not speak: on discarded drafts; on how it was the police got word of his researches and found him; on his inability to ever find the girl again. Elaborate theories about the design, not without surprising insights. Hardest of all, his own death.

At the very end, when he could barely move or see, he whispered to me, 'Let Glasgow have me. Why not, eh? You never know, Gerald.' Then urgently: 'Oh but, oh, but I wish, I do, I wish, I wish.'

I knew he longed for certainty, even as he purported to abjure it, to be part of something, but still it was very hard to hear this.

And so I gave him my hand as he wheezed in the bed, and he held it, and I whispered and put my other hand around his and clasped it. He squeezed back.

But though I was gentle I did not let up the pressure. William opened his eyes as I pressed his fingers into mine. I pressed his fingers so he could feel the bones beneath my thin old skin. I did not speak and neither did he. He did not speak ever again. He watched me and his eyes grew wider with something other than surprise and at the sight of them I had to close my own.

William's body was delivered to our long-haired student descendants, as he had wished.

That final pedagogic task uncovered nothing unusual. A few years later, when his demonstrations were done, his body was released. It rests now in a lovely cemetery, as close to those Downs as we could arrange.

I sat alone in the kitchen, in a world in which beautiful, elegantly wrought secrets lie hidden less than an inch from sight. I sat in my pyjamas drinking tea among those bones, and I told William in his absence that I was sorry he was at best a bystander. I told him I was sorry he'd never been able to find his young confidante, for vindication, to know again that someone other than he had seen the full design uncovered, released.

I'm sad as I approach my own death, but I am tired of so missing whom I miss. I am tired of secrets.

The skeleton will not appear again, in that museum or anywhere. The only person other than me in whom William ever confided will never speak of it. But for this document, which it is an immense relief to write, the story would end with me.

All the arrangements are taken care of. I'm touched at the thought of friends coming to a service for me. I would tell them not to bother, but I know they will and that it will be for them.

It is not a pleasant thing to break a promise to the dead, but I must urgently draw attention to the updated instructions about my funeral and remains, the version of the document I changed after William's death. Glasgow Medical School will now receive a larger monetary bequest than they expected, in lieu of the cadaver previously promised. My plot, in the same cemetery as William's, was paid for long ago, but I will not be using it. Instead, I ask that my ashes be scattered on William's grave.

Perhaps mice will run over us, William and me, with designs beneath their fur. How glad William would have been to know with certainty that a few of his theories were correct! That in the darkest parts of the sea the bones of great fish and whales are scrawled on. That the sky is full of birds taking their designs heavenward.

I should warn whoever grants my last request that the ashes from cremation are coarser than those from any fireplace or cigarettes. No need for alarm at the sight of that distinctive bone grit on the grass where my William lies. A little coastal wind and I shall dissipate. One rainfall, and I will, you have my word, sink toward him, out of sight.